Volume 16

Secrets

Satisfy your desire for more.

Never Enough by Cynthia Eden

For the last three weeks, Abby McGill has been playing with fire. She has become Jake Steele's lover, and bad-boy Jake has taught her the true meaning of desire. Abby knows she has to end her relationship with him—Jake is her father's worst enemy, the man who almost destroyed McGill Properties. But Jake isn't about to let the woman he wants walk away from him, and, even if he has to use a bit of sensuous blackmail, he will keep his lady, because he just can't get enough of Abby.

༅ॐ

Bunko by Sheri Gilmoore

Life is but a roll of the dice. A story about the masks people use to obtain their darkest, most basic, desires—love and sex. Tu Tran has a dilemma: which man will she go home with tonight? Forced to decide between Jack, a man, who promises to share every aspect of his life with her, or Dev, the man, who hides behind a mask and only offers night after night of erotic sex. Tu is torn between what everyone tells her she wants and what she knows she truly needs. Will she take the gamble of the dice and choose the man, who can see behind her own mask and expose her true desires?

༅ॐ

Hide and Seek by Chevon Gael

Millionaire's son Kyle DeLaurier ditches his trophy-fiance in favor of a tropical paradise full of tall, tanned, topless females. Private eye, Darcy McLeod, is on the trail of this runaway groom. Together they sizzle while playing Hide and Seek with their true identities. But will destiny send Kyle back to the altar, or into Darcy's arms for good?

༅ॐ

Seduction of the Muse by Charlotte Featherstone

He is the Dark Lord, the mysterious author who pens the erotic tales of an innocent woman's seduction. She is his muse, the woman he watches from the dark shadows, the woman whose dreams he invades at night—the only woman who can reach through his darkness and love him, scarred body and soul.

Reviews from Secrets Volume 1

"Four very romantic, very sexy novellas in very different styles and settings. ... The settings are quite diverse taking the reader from Regency England to a remote and mysterious fantasy land, to an Arabian nights type setting, and finally to a contemporary urban setting. All stories are explicit, and Hamre and Landon stories sizzle. ... If you like erotic romance you will love *Secrets*."

— *Romantic Readers* review

"Overall, for a fan of erotica, these are unlike anything you've encountered before. For those romance fans who turn down the pages of the "good parts" for later repeat consumption (and you know who you are) these books are a wonderful way to explore the better side of the erotica market. ... *Secrets* is a worthy exploration for the adventurous reader with the promise for better things yet to come."

— Liz Montgomery

Reviews from Secrets Volume 2

Winner of the Fallot Literary Award for Fiction

"*Secrets, Volume 2*, a new anthology published by Red Sage Publishing, is hot! I mean *red hot!* ... The sensuality in each story will make you blush—from head to toe and everywhere else in-between. ... The true success behind *Secrets, Volume 2* is the combination of different tastes—both in subgenres of romance and levels of sensuality. *I highly recommend this book*."

— Dawn A. Long, *America Online* review

"I think it is a fine anthology and Red Sage should be applauded for providing an outlet for women who want to write sensual romance."

— Adrienne Benedicks,
Erotic Readers Association review

Reviews from Secrets Volume 3

Winner of the 1997 Under the Cover Readers Favorite Award

"An unabashed celebration of sex. Highly arousing! Highly recommended!"
— Virginia Henley, *New York Times* Best Selling Author

"*Secrets, Volume 3* leaves the reader breathless. Each of these tributes to exotic and erotic fiction offers a world of sensual pleasure and moral rewards. A delicious confection of sensuous treats awaits the reader on each turn of the page. Sexy, funny, thrilling, and luscious, Secrets entertains, enlightens, and fuels the fires of fantasy."

— Kathee Card, *Romancing the Web*

Reviews from Secrets Volume 4

"*Secrets, Volume 4*, has something to satisfy every erotic fantasy... simply sexsational!"
— Virginia Henley, *New York Times* Best Selling Author

"Provocative... seductive... a must read!" **4 Stars**
— *Romantic Times*

"These are the kind of stories that romance readers that 'want a little more' have been looking for all their lives without crossing over into the adult genre. Keep these stories coming, Red Sage, the world needs them!"
— Lani Roberts, *Affaire de Coeur*

"If you're interested in exploring erotica, or reading farther than the sexual passages of your favorite steamy reads, the *Secret* series is well worth checking out."
— *Writers Club Romance Group* on AOL

Reviews from Secrets Volume 5

"*Secrets, Volume 5*, is a collage of lucious sensuality. Any woman who reads *Secrets* is in for an awakening!"
— **Virginia Henley,** *New York Times* Best Selling Author

"Hot, hot, hot! Not for the faint-hearted!"
— *Romantic Times*

"As you make your way through the stories, you will find yourself becoming hotter and hotter. *Secrets* just keeps getting better and better."
— *Affaire de Coeur*

Reviews from Secrets Volume 6

"*Secrets, Volume 6* satisfies every female fantasy: the Bodyguard, the Tutor, the Werewolf, and the Vampire. I give it Six Stars!"
— Virginia Henley, *New York Times* Best Selling Author

"*Secrets, Volume 6* is the best of *Secrets* yet. ...four of the most erotic stories in one volume than this reader has yet to see anywhere else. ... These stories are full of erotica at its best and you'll definitely want to keep it handy for lots of re-reading!"
— *Affaire de Coeur*

Reviews from Secrets Volume 7

Winner of the Venus Book Club
Best Book of the Year

"...sensual, sexy, steamy fun. A perfect read!"
— Virginia Henley, *New York Times* Best Selling Author

"Intensely provocative and disarmingly romantic, Secrets Volume 7 is a romance reader's paradise that will take you beyond your wildest dreams!"
— *Ballston Book House* Review

"Erotic romance is at the sensual core of Red Sage's latest collection of short, red hot novels, *Secrets, Volume 7.*"
— *Writers Club Romance Group* on AOL

Reviews from Secrets Volume 8

Winner of the Venus Book Club
Best Book of the Year

"*Secrets Volume 8* is simply sensational!"
— Virginia Henley, *New York Times* Best Selling Author

"*Secrets Volume 8* is an amazing compilation of sexy stories discovering a wide range of subjects, all designed to titillate the senses."
— Lani Roberts, *Affaire de Coeur*

"All four tales are well written and fun to read because even the sexiest scenes are not written for shock value, but interwoven smoothly and realistically into the plots. This quartet contains strong storylines and solid lead characters, but then again what else would one expect from the no longer *Secrets* anthologies."
— Harriet Klausner

"Once again, Red Sage Publishing takes you on a journey of sexual delight, teasing and pleasing the reader with a bit of something to appeal to everyone."
— Michelle Houston, *Courtesy Sensual Romance*

"In this sizzling volume, four authors offer short stories in four different subgenres: contemporary, paranormal, historical, and futuristic. These ladies' assignments are to dazzle, tantalize, amaze, and entice. Your assignment, as the reader, is to sit back and enjoy. Just have a fan and some ice water at your side."
— Amy Cunningham

Reviews from Secrets Volume 9

"Everyone should expect only the most erotic stories in a *Secrets* book. ...if you like your stories full of hot sexual scenes, then this is for you!"
— Donna Doyle, *Romance Reviews*

"*Secrets 9*...is sinfully delicious, highly arousing, and hotter than hot as the pages practically burn up as you turn them."
— Suzanne Coleburn, *Reader To Reader Reviews/ Belles & Beaux of Romance*

"Treat yourself to well-written fiction that's hot, hotter, and hottest!"
— Virginia Henley, *New York Times* Best Selling Author

Reviews from Secrets Volume 10

"*Secrets Volume 10*, an erotic dance through medieval castles, sultan's palaces, the English countryside and expensive hotel suites, explodes with passion-filled pages."
— *Romantic Times BOOKclub*

"Having read the previous nine volumes, this one fulfills the expectations of what is expected in a *Secrets* book: romance and eroticism at its best!!"
— *Fallen Angel Reviews*

"All are hot steamy romances so if you enjoy erotica romance, you are sure to enjoy *Secrets, Volume 10*. All this reviewer can say is WOW!!"
— *The Best Reviews*

Reviews from Secrets Volume 11

"*Secrets Volume 11* delivers once again with storylines that include erotic masquerades, ancient curses, modern-day betrayal and a prince charming looking for a kiss. Scorching tales filled with humor, passion and love." **4 Stars**
— *Romantic Times BOOKclub*

"The *Secrets* books published by Red Sage Publishing are well known for their excellent writing and highly erotic stories and *Secrets, Volume 11* will not disappoint. "
— *The Road to Romance*

"*Secrets 11* quite honestly is my favorite anthology from Red Sage so far. All four novellas had me glued to their stories until the very end. I was just disappointed that these talented ladies novellas weren't longer."

— *The Best Reviews*

"Indulge yourself with this erotic treat and join the thousands of readers who just can't get enough. Be forewarned that *Secrets 11* will whet your appetite for more, but will offer you the ultimate in pleasurable erotic literature."

— *Ballston Book House Review*

Reviews from Secrets Volume 12

"*Secrets Volume 12*, turns on the heat with a seductive encounter inside a bookstore, a temple of naughty and sensual delight, a galactic inferno that thaws ice, and a lightening storm that lights up the English shoreline. Tales of looking for love in all the right places with a heat rating out the charts." **4½ Stars**

— *Romantic Times BOOKclub*

"I really liked these stories. You want great escapism? Read *Secrets, Volume 12*."

— *Romance Reviews*

Reviews from Secrets Volume 13

"In *Secrets Volume 13*, the temperature gets turned up a few notches with a mistaken personal ad, shape-shifters destined to love, a hot Regency lord and his lady, as well as a bodyguard protecting his woman. Emotions and flames blaze high in Red Sage's latest foray into the sensual and delightful art of love." **4½ Stars**

— *Romantic Times BOOKclub*

"The sex is still so hot the pages nearly ignite! Read *Secrets, Volume 13*!"

— *Romance Reviews*

Reviews from Secrets Volume 14

"*Secrets Volume 14* will excite readers with its diverse selection of delectable sexy tales ranging from a fourteenth century love story to a sci-fi rebel who falls for a irresistible research scientist to a trio of determined vampires who battle for the same woman to a virgin sacrifice who falls in love with a beast. A cornucopia of pure delight!" **4½ Stars**

— *Romantic Times BOOKclub*

"This book contains four erotic tales sure to keep readers up long into the night."
— *Romance Junkies*

Reviews from Secrets Volume 15

"*Secrets Volume 15* blends humor, tension and steamy romance in its newest collection that sizzles with passion between unlikely pairs—a male chauvinist columnist and a librarian turned erotica author; a handsome werewolf and his resisting mate; an unfulfilled woman and a sexy police officer and a Victorian wife who learns discipline can be fun. Readers will revel in this delicious assortment of thrilling tales." **4 Stars**
—*Romantic Times BOOKclub*

"This book contains four tales by some of today's hottest authors that will tease your senses and intrigue your mind."
—*Romance Junkies*

Satisfy Your Desire for More... with Secrets!

Did you miss any of the other volumes of the sexy **Secrets** *series? At the back of this book is an order form for all the available volumes. Order your Secrets today! See our order form at the back of this book or visit Waldenbooks or Borders.*

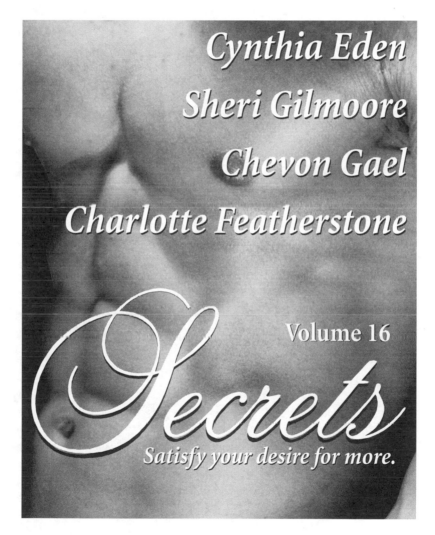

Cynthia Eden

Sheri Gilmoore

Chevon Gael

Charlotte Featherstone

Volume 16

Secrets

Satisfy your desire for more.

SECRETS Volume 16
This is an original publication of Red Sage Publishing and each individual story herein has never before appeared in print. These stories are a collection of fiction and any similarity to actual persons or events is purely coincidental.

Red Sage Publishing, Inc.
P.O. Box 4844
Seminole, FL 33775
727-391-3847
www.redsagepub.com

SECRETS Volume 16
A Red Sage Publishing book
All Rights Reserved/December 2006
Copyright © 2006 by Red Sage Publishing, Inc.

ISBN 0-9754516-6-9 / 978-0-9754516-6-3

Published by arrangement with the authors and copyright holders of the individual works as follows:

NEVER ENOUGH
Copyright © 2006 by Cynthia Eden

BUNKO
Copyright © 2006 by Sheri Gilmoore

HIDE AND SEEK
Copyright © 2006 by Chevon Gael

SEDUCTION OF THE MUSE
Copyright © 2006 by Charlotte Featherstone

Photographs:
Cover © 2006 by Tara Kearney; www.tarakearney.com
Cover Model: Chayne Jones
Setback cover © 2000 by Greg P. Willis; email: GgnYbr@aol.com

Printed in the U.S.A.

Book typesetting by:
Quill & Mouse Studios, Inc.
www.quillandmouse.com

Contents

Never Enough

by Cynthia Eden

To My Reader:

I've always had a soft spot for *Romeo and Juliet*. To me, star-crossed lovers are just so utterly compelling. You know the lovers want to be together—forever—but something, or someone, is always standing in the way.

When I wrote *Never Enough*, I knew that I would have to create a hero strong enough to overcome the obstacles standing between him and the one woman in the world that he has to have. My hero, Jake Steele, may not play by the "good" rules of Romeo, but he's a man who gets the job done... even if he has to resort to a bit of sensuous blackmail in order to claim his lady love...

I hope you enjoy reading Jake and Abby's story. Please feel free to visit my website at www.cynthiaeden.com or send an email to me at info@ cynthiaeden.com to let me know what you think of my tale. Happy reading!

Chapter One

"We don't have much time," Abby McGill whispered, her fingers moving quickly to the zipper in the back of her dress.

"Then we'll just have to hurry, won't we, Abby?" Jake Steele's voice was a sensual growl in the dark room.

Heat pooled heavily in her stomach. She slid the zipper down and let her black cocktail dress fall to her feet. She wasn't wearing any underwear. She'd dressed, or rather, not dressed, knowing Jake would be at the party. She'd known they would be together. She'd known he'd touch her. Hold her.

And she'd also known that it would be for the last time.

His hands were on her now. Warm, strong hands. God, how she loved to feel his touch! A soft moan rumbled in her throat, only to be instantly swallowed by his hot mouth and swirling tongue.

"Careful, Abby," he whispered against her lips. "You don't want the others to hear."

Her heart pounded. His hands slid down, and his nimble fingers toyed with her nipples. The tight peaks ached for him, yearned for him. Jake plucked her nipples, teasing them lightly with his fingers.

Her sex grew moist.

Her hand slid down to the front of his pants. She rubbed against the soft material, easily feeling his thick length.

She wanted to feel that length inside of her. Just once more. "Hurry," she whispered. "We don't have much time."

Jake's hand slid down her stomach, slid down to the heated juncture of her thighs. And he touched her, his broad fingers sliding into her moist heat.

"You're wet for me, aren't you?" He didn't wait for an answer, but then her body had already answered for her. Jake shifted, lowering his zipper with a faint hiss of sound. Then he lifted her, pushing her back against the wall. "Take me. Take all of me," he growled the words against her throat. And then he thrust deep.

Abby gasped at the thick feel of his cock in her. So heavy. So full. It was too much. Not enough. She pressed down, rubbing like a cat against him.

His hands were locked around her waist. He lifted her easily. Once, twice. The thick head of his penis pushed deeper, deeper into her.

Abby bit her lip, struggling to hold back a moan. God, he was so big! So hard. It was too—

Jake thrust harder. Deeper. Abby began to moan.

Her climax built, spiraling closer with every movement of his body.

He kissed her, his tongue thrusting in time with the strong thrusts of his hips. She could taste champagne on his lips. Champagne from the toast her father had given just minutes earlier...

His hand slid down, rubbed between her moist folds.

His cock slammed into her again.

Abby climaxed on a choked scream.

Jake groaned against her, shuddering heavily, sending a long, hot splash deep inside of her body.

He held her captive against the wall, his dinner jacket rubbing against the sensitive skin of her breasts. His breath panted out. Harsh, ragged. And she could smell him. A clean, masculine scent that always clung to him.

She leaned forward and kissed him once more. A quick, gentle kiss.

A kiss good-bye.

"I'll come by after the party," Jake was saying as he slowly pulled away from her. "I'll come by and—"

"No." Abby grabbed her dress and pulled it on with hands that trembled. This was going to be hard. Harder than she'd thought. She jerked her zipper back into place. And she clenched her thighs. She would need to clean up before going back to the party. She should have thought of that, thought that—

He pressed his handkerchief between her thighs. Abby jerked, startled by the contact. The cloth was soft, cool to the touch. He rubbed her lightly, smoothing over her delicate flesh. Rubbing her clit.

Abby jumped away from him. "I don't think we should do this anymore."

He froze.

Abby took a deep breath. "I— I... it's over."

Jake's hands locked around her shoulders. "*What?*"

She took a deep breath. She was grateful for the darkness of the room, she was glad she didn't have to see him, didn't have to look him in the eye.

She was glad he couldn't see her. She didn't want him to know how much this hurt. "We can't do this anymore, Jake, we can't—"

"So you're going to fuck me and walk away, is that it, Abby?" His voice was a growl, hard and deep.

And his words were a blow, battering her.

Abby lifted her chin. She wouldn't cry. She *wouldn't*. She pressed her lips together, refusing to answer him.

His fingers tightened around her, digging into the tender flesh of her arms.

"You're hurting me," she gritted, pulling away from him.

His hands dropped. "Why?" The word was stark.

Her hands trembled. She had to get away from him. Had to leave, before she broke down. "I—it was a mistake. I— if the family found out—"

"Screw the family!" Jake snapped, his voice a near-shout.

Abby took a step back. The doorknob pressed against her lower back.

"So what was it?" He pressed. "You wanted a screw for the road? One more time for kicks?"

Abby swallowed. "No, I—I just wanted to be with you... one last time." She exhaled on a sad sigh. "I'm tired of hiding. Tired of the secrets. I can't do it anymore." She couldn't live with the fear that her family would find out, that they would discover her relationship. Because if they found out about Jake, they would be devastated.

Her lover was her father's worst enemy. He was the man who'd almost destroyed her family's business.

"So now that I backed off the take over, you're breaking up with me? Is that it?"

"I can't be with you anymore." Her voice was soft, final. "I just can't do it." She turned, fumbling with the lock. She wrenched open the door, stumbling into the hall.

And she fell into her brother's arms.

"Whoa! Abby! Abby, what's going on?" Trent's face was bright with surprise. "What were you doing in there—" Trent froze, catching sight of Jake.

Jake stepped out of the darkened bedroom, his blond hair mussed, his face a stone mask.

"What the hell were you doing with my sister?"

Jake's lips twisted into a taunting smile. "Why don't you ask her?"

Her cheeks burned. No, this was the last thing she'd wanted. She couldn't let Trent know, couldn't—

"Abby?"

She looked back at Jake, back at his beloved face. His eyes, bright blue, glared at her. His sensual lips were set in a hard, uncompromising line.

He wasn't a handsome man. His face was too harsh. Too rugged. His cheekbones were high slashes, his nose a sharp blade. His jaw was strong, with a faint scar running on its left side.

He was tall, easily over six feet, with a tough, muscled body. He worked out three times a week, ruthlessly keeping his body in prime shape at a local gym.

"What have you done?" Her brother's voice was a whisper.

Abby closed her eyes, shutting out the sight of Jake. "It's over," she said and turned, walking carefully away from them. Squaring her shoulders, she held her back ruthlessly straight. She wouldn't break, wouldn't give in to the pain ripping through her. Not yet. *Not yet.*

She didn't look back, didn't let herself glance back for one last look at Jake.

It was over. It had to be.

᠄᠋ᢀᡧᢗᢗᠫᢣᢥᢞ

Jake watched silently as Abby walked away from him. He wanted to grab her, to force her to turn around and face him.

Abby. Beautiful Abby. From the moment he'd seen her, he'd been obsessed with her. He'd had to touch her. To kiss her. To claim her.

He'd had her naked beneath him within three hours of their first meeting. Of course, he hadn't known who she was. He hadn't known that he was days away from buying out her father's company.

And she hadn't known.

They had just been a man and a woman. And they had wanted each other. Badly.

Abby was a small woman, built like a delicate ballerina. Her body was supple, slender. She had a mass of long, flowing black hair and pale, porcelain skin. Her face was a gentle oval, with wide, deep green eyes. Her nose was small and perfect, and her lips, God, the woman had lips made for sin.

Her breasts were small, but perfect for his hands. He loved to touch them. To suck them.

He loved to hold her slender hips and thrust deep, deep into the hot depths of her body.

Now she was walking away from him. Ending things. Telling him to fuck off.

Hell, *no.*

It wasn't over, not by a long shot. He hadn't gotten his fill of Abigail McGill. He doubted if he ever would.

He'd be damned if he'd just stand by and let her throw their relationship away because she was afraid of her family.

"Stay away from my sister," Trent ordered, his boyish face tight with anger.

Jake grunted and shouldered by the younger man. He had to find Abby.

Trent grabbed him. "Did you hear me? I said stay away from my sis—"

Jake's voice was hard. "She might be your sister, but she's my woman." And there was no way in hell he was going to stay away from her. "Get used to it."

He'd had a taste of Abby, and he wanted more. He wouldn't stop until he had all of her.

᠄᠋ᢀᡧᢗᢗᠫᢣᢥᢞ

Abby had just stepped out of the shower when the doorbell rang. She froze, her heart pounding a frantic rhythm.

It was almost two in the morning. It was far, far too late for a neighborly visit from any of her friends.

She jerked on her black silk robe and padded down the hall. Who could be at her house at this hour? Who could—

"Dammit, Abby, open this door!" Jake's voice was fierce.

Her mouth dropped open in shock.

The pealing bell echoed through her house once again. "I'm not going away! I'll stay here all damn night if I have to!"

She knew he wasn't lying. Jake would indeed stay out on her doorstep, ringing her bell and yelling her name all night. So what if her neighbors saw him? Jake wasn't the type of guy to give a damn about what people thought of him.

But she didn't have the luxury of not giving a damn. Because of her family, because of her father, she had to care.

She took a deep breath and marched slowly toward the door. She could handle Jake. She *would* handle him.

Her hand shook as she reached for the lock. She closed her eyes a moment, and then opened the door.

Jake stood there, glaring down at her, his jaw clenched, his hands tight fists.

Abby moved forward, putting her body solidly in the doorway. "I told you not to come here." And she had. Those words had been so hard to utter. But she'd done it. She'd ended things with Jake.

His eyes, his brilliant blue eyes, shone like chips of ice. They were locked on her, their intensity sending a shiver through her.

He took a quick breath and gritted, "What you told me was to fuck off, but I'm not going to do that." He took a step forward, bringing his body inches from hers. The heat of his skin seemed to burn her, and the light scent of his cologne filled her nostrils.

"You have to do it," she said, forcing the words out and lifting her chin. "It's over, Jake. I don't want to see you anymore, I *can't* see you—"

He grabbed her, pulling her into his arms and capturing her mouth in a heated kiss. His tongue plunged past her lips, igniting a wave of desire that Abby was helpless to fight.

"You want me," he whispered, pulling back slightly. "And God knows I want you."

Her nipples pressed against her robe, and she knew that he could see them, knew that he could feel her need for him.

His fingers moved, slipping under her chin and forcing her to look up, forcing her to meet his penetrating gaze. "Why would you throw away what we have? *Why?*"

Abby pressed her lips together. She could still taste him. She looked into his eyes, drawing in a deep breath. Could he see her fear? Because she was terrified, of him, of her own feelings.

His breath caught as he read the expression in her eyes. "You're afraid." His voice was full of sudden understanding. "You're scared to death... of me... of us."

Chapter Two

Abby jerked away from him as if she'd been burned. "Get out of my house."

He shook his head and his eyes glinted. "I'm not going anywhere."

Damn him. Didn't he know how hard this was? Why did he have to keep pushing her? "I don't want you here. I don't want—"

"I know what you want," he purred, his voice a sensual rumble. His gaze dropped to rest on her thrusting nipples. "I know exactly what you want."

She read the sexual intent in his eyes and stiffened. No. No, he couldn't touch her. She couldn't bear it if he touched her. Not now. She was too raw. Too… hungry. For him. Always, for him. "Get out," she gritted, hunching her shoulders and crossing her arms beneath her breasts.

He kicked the door closed and took a step toward her. He shrugged out of his jacket, carelessly dropping it to the wooden floor. His hungry gaze locked on her. "Do you remember what it was like that first time, Abby? God, you were so tight and so damn wet. I thought I was going to come the moment I pushed inside you."

She remembered that night. She couldn't forget that night, would *never* forget it.

She'd attended the opening of the new art museum in downtown Atlanta. She'd seen him across the room. He'd been watching her. All night, she'd felt his stare. Deep. Burning. When he'd approached her, she'd been breathless.

With just one touch, he'd ignited her need. Just one touch. A light caress of his hand against the side of her breast as they danced. Then a whisper of breath against her neck as he bent to whisper to her.

I want you. Come with me. She could still hear his voice, hear the need echoing in his words.

She'd responded to that need, to that hunger.

And she'd left the museum, leaving without a backward glance. For the first time in her life, Abby had lived for the moment. She'd left with the tall, sexy stranger. She'd gone back to his apartment and she'd let him—

Touch her.

Hold her.

Kiss her.

Make love to her.

For hours. For an endless night.

Her friends would have been shocked, if they'd known. But no one had known. Jake had been her secret. Her fantasy lover...

"At first, I thought you were a virgin," his deep voice was a sudden, startling growl of sound. "I had to force my cock in you. Deep and slow."

Abby swallowed and took another step back. He was too close. Her living room was too small.

"Do you remember, Abby? I had to hold your hips while I thrust. You were scared. I could see it in your eyes. But then, I felt your heat, felt your cream, and I could see your pleasure."

Yeah, she'd been scared that night. She'd only been with one other man, and her college boyfriend Sean hadn't been built anywhere close to Jake's proportions. And Sean had always been fast. *Too fast.* With Sean, sex had been a brief, almost humiliating experience. She'd just wanted it to end. But with Jake... with Jake...

She'd screamed with pleasure.

She stepped back. Her back rapped against the wall. Her eyes widened.

He smiled, a smile full of teeth, a tiger's humorless smile. "Looks like there's nowhere else to go." He reached for her, pulling her against him, crushing her breasts against the front of his shirt.

His hand slipped down, sliding under the edge of her robe. He touched her, his warm fingers curving over her thigh.

His head lowered toward hers, his lips stopping just inches away. Hunger blazed in his gaze. A deep, consuming hunger. Her hands started to shake, her thighs trembled.

"There's something you should know." His voice was hard, rough. "It's not fucking over." His mouth slammed down on hers.

His hand slid up, his fingers cupping her mound. Stroking, plucking. He parted her folds and pressed one big finger into the mouth of her opening.

His tongue thrust into her mouth and he pushed another finger into her. His fingers rubbed, sliding in and out in a fast, hot rhythm.

Abby moaned, arching her hips against him. *It's not fucking over.* His words echoed in her mind.

His right hand brushed aside her silk robe, baring her breasts. The nipples were flushed a dark pink, and they were pointing, proudly begging for his attention.

Jake tore his mouth from hers. His fingers thrust deep, making her body shudder. "I can't give this up," he said, the words little more than a snarl. "I can't give *you* up. I won't." His head lowered and his lips, those incredible lips, closed around the aching tip of her breast. He licked. Sucked.

And his fingers thrust.

Abby bit down on her lower lip, choking back a scream. Dear God, she couldn't stand it. All he had to do was touch her—

"No!" Abby shoved against him, her heart racing. She couldn't do this. She couldn't! "I don't want this!" *Liar*, a soft voice whispered. She did want him. Wanted him in her, deep and hard. But she couldn't, *wouldn't*, give in to her need. She had to stay strong, had to stay in control. Too much was at stake.

Her heart was at stake.

Jake stepped back. Slowly. A muscle flexed along the hard line of his jaw, but he didn't speak. Didn't say a word. He just stared down at her, his gaze narrow and intent.

She took a deep breath, trying to calm her frantic heartbeat. Her sex was already wet, creamy, and inside, deep inside, she felt an emptiness. An emptiness that she knew he could fill. But she couldn't let him. *She couldn't*. "I—I want you to leave now."

He didn't move.

Abby fumbled with her robe, pulling the soft silk over the sensitive skin of her breasts.

His gaze flickered, dropping momentarily to her chest. His lips tightened. Then his gaze locked on hers, swirling with anger. With need. "Do you know," he asked softly, "how much money I lost tonight?"

Abby blinked. What was he talking about? Why was he

Jake cocked his head to the side, studying her in the faint light. "I let your father keep his company. I backed off. You know why I did that?"

No, she didn't know. She'd been stunned when she'd learned the news. Jake Steele didn't back away from anything or anyone. Her father had thought for certain that he'd lost the business. And then Jake had eased off the takeover. He'd let McGill Properties stand.

"I did it for you."

What? Her eyes widened.

"So, the way I figure it, you owe me." He licked his lips and his gaze once again fell to the mounds of her breasts. "And you can damn well believe that I'm going to collect."

Abby stiffened, the implication of his words stabbing her in the heart. "You can't buy me. I'm not a whore."

"No." He shook his head. "But you're *mine*. You're mine, and I'm not ready to let you go yet."

⁂

No, Jake thought, he wasn't ready to let Abby go. Hell, he didn't know if he'd ever be able to let her go. Abby was a fire in his gut, a need he couldn't ever seem to fill, no matter how many times he had her.

Just looking at her made him ache. His cock was hot and hard for her now. He wanted to rip the robe off her slender body. He wanted to lift her up, to thrust deep into her tight core.

He wanted to hear her moan. To hear her beg.

He wanted to feel her, wet and creamy, around his dick.

He just wanted her.

And he was going to have her.

"One call, Abby, just one call."

Her brow furrowed.

He smiled, the gesture deliberately threatening. "One call and I can have your father's company. I can destroy his house of cards with one word."

"Bastard!"

His smile disappeared. "True." He'd never claimed to be anything else. Abby knew that. And she'd taken him into her beautiful, tight body anyway. She'd taken him in, shown him warmth and tenderness, and now, when he was addicted to her, she was trying to shut him out.

No fucking way.

"I'm the bastard who can destroy your family's business. And I'll do it..." He let the words trail off, shrugging.

Her face drained of color.

He took a frantic step forward, grabbing her when she trembled. "Abby..."

"What? You'd do that? Wh—"

He stepped back, dropping his hands. He kept his face carefully expressionless. He couldn't let her see past his mask. Too much was riding on this moment. "I'll do whatever I have to do."

"What do you want?" Was that fear in her voice? Was Abby actually *afraid* of him?

Jake clenched his fists. He didn't want to do this. He didn't want it to be this way between them. But he had to make her see, he had to show her how good it could be between them.

He couldn't let her end things, not yet.

What did he want? There was only one thing that he wanted. Only one thing that he craved. "You. I want you."

"You've had me." She shook her head, sending her dark locks flying. "There are probably dozens of women lined up, waiting for you. Go to one of them."

Yeah, there were other women who were interested in him. Interested in his money. But he didn't care about them.

He only cared about her. *Abby.*

None of those other women had a shy, sexy smile. None of them smelled like lilacs. None of them drove him crazy with just one look.

Abby. There was only one Abby.

"Give me a week. One more week. Let me prove to you how good it can be between us."

"My family, my father—"

He held up his right hand. "I promise. I won't touch the business. You give me my time, and they're safe."

"Wh—what if they found out, what if—"

Jake didn't care if they found out. Hell, he *wanted* them to find out. "Then they find out. I don't really give a fuck." He wasn't going to try and hide their relationship anymore. They weren't kids. If her family didn't like it, too bad.

"My father," she paused, taking a deep breath, "he hates you, Jake. If he knew..."

"Your old man needs to be damn grateful he still has a business. And I don't give a shit what he knows. This isn't about him. It's about us, Abby. *Us.*"

She bit her lip, that sexy, full lower lip he loved to suck. "Just a week?" She queried softly.

Elation rushed through him. "A week." A week would be a good start. And he could always negotiate for more time. He was a great negotiator. Hell, his negotiation skills had helped him to build a multi-million dollar business.

"And you promise you won't ever go after McGill Properties again? You'll leave the company alone?"

He had no plans to go after the company. The only acquisition he wanted was staring straight at him. "I won't touch the company."

Her lashes swept down, hiding her dark green stare. She took a deep breath. "What would I—what would I have to do?"

He smiled. "Everything that I want you to do." Everything that he could imagine. And he could imagine a hell of a lot.

She swallowed. Her lashes lifted. A trace of fear lingered in her eyes.

But behind the fear, he saw desire. *Just like the first night.*

She wanted him. Good. Because he was dying to have her.

Jake glanced at her robe. "And you can start by stripping."

Chapter Three

"W—what?"

"You heard me." Jake's voice was cool, but his blue gaze blazed. "Strip."

Her hands clenched around the belt of her robe.

"Drop the robe, Abby. Now."

Her hands shook as she untied the soft, silky belt.

She lifted her chin, and her robe dropped to the floor. Abby stood in front of Jake, completely naked. Her nipples pebbled from the sudden cold that swept over her, and from the hunger that filled her.

One week. To do anything, *everything* Jake wanted.

Abby knew she could have refused his bargain. She could have told him to go to hell. And for a moment, she'd thought about doing just that.

But the temptation that he offered was too strong. *One week*. One more week with Jake. She couldn't resist.

His gaze swept over her body, caressing her like hands. Her breasts, her hips. His pupils dilated as he stared at the soft, black triangle of hair at the juncture of her thighs. "Come here, Abby." His voice wasn't so cool anymore. His speech sounded rough, almost ragged.

She took a step forward, lifting her chin. Jake was still fully clothed and she felt vulnerable, so very vulnerable, standing in front of him without so much as a stitch of clothing on her body.

His hand reached out and touched her hair. She'd left the shower only moments before he'd arrived, and her dark locks were still damp. His fingers tightened around her hair. He took a deep breath, then stepped back, dropping his hand. "Get on the table," he gritted.

Her eyes widened. She glanced toward the dining room table. Its mahogany surface gleamed faintly in the soft light. She looked back at Jake, back at the hard, tense lines of his face, and her gaze dropped, falling to stare at the unmistakable bulge in his pants.

Heat flooded through her body. Her heart pounded. As she took a step toward the table, her legs trembled. She walked forward slowly, feeling Jake's eyes following her movement. She stopped at the table, her hands lifting to brace herself against the cool, hard surface.

Jake's arms wrapped around her waist, lifting her up and spinning her around in one quick move. He lowered her onto the top of the table, his hands hard on her waist. Abby had a moment to be grateful that the table top was empty. Otherwise, she had a feeling Jake would have thrown the contents to the floor.

His blue eyes were dark, turbulent, and his cheeks were flushed. He licked his lips and ordered, "Lie down."

She swallowed and slowly obeyed, leaning her body back against the wood. Her legs dangled over the table's edge. She tried to close them, because it was too much, she was too exposed.

But Jake grabbed her thighs and pushed them apart. His burning stare locked on her exposed sex and he licked his lips.

Her sex creamed, and a low moan rumbled in the back of her throat.

His head lifted and he smiled at her. His hand, his strong, skillful hand, slipped down and parted her sensitive folds. He pressed against her, rubbing, stroking. And he slid one big finger inside of her.

Abby shuddered.

"Is this what you want, Abby?" His hand thrust again, harder this time.

Pleasure snapped through her. She arched her back, thrusting her breasts up, their hard peaks seeming to beg for him. For his touch, his mouth.

His hand kept thrusting, stroking her nether lips, then plunging into her. He leaned over her, and licked her breast. One long, delicious lick.

OhGodOhGodOhGod. Abby's entire body felt too tight, too hot. She needed more, she needed him—

"Is this what you want, Abby?" He asked again, before bending to lightly stroke her aching breast with his tongue. "Is it?"

No. No. She wanted *more*. She needed more. "Jake—"

Jake smiled, lifting his head from her breast. He pulled his hand away.

Abby ached, the loss of his touch almost a physical pain. She opened her mouth to call him back, to beg him to touch her—

Then his hands were on her thighs, warm, strong. And he pushed her legs apart, farther, another inch, two. He moved her legs until she was spread wide.

Abby used her elbows to push herself up. "What are you—"

His gaze was locked on her creamy core. "I'm going to taste you. *All* of you." He dropped down to his knees and then he put his mouth—*Oh God, his mouth*—on her.

At the first stroke of his tongue against her clit, Abby shuddered. Pleasure whipped through her, fast and hard. Her hips bucked as he continued to stroke her. His tongue slipped over her nether lips, plunging into her body.

His tongue was wet, rough. He licked her. He sucked. And he stabbed his tongue into her body.

Abby heard herself moaning, heard herself begging mindlessly. But she didn't care. In that moment, she didn't care about anything or anyone. Just Jake.

Her body clenched, and the promising spiral of a climax shot toward her. She lifted her hips. His tongue swirled against her, *right there*—

And he pulled away. He slid away from her, and stood, breathing heavily, between her spread thighs. He licked his lips, as if to taste her one more time.

Abby wanted to scream. Her body was on fire. She needed him, needed him to thrust into her, to give her the orgasm that was so close, so close...

His fingers tightened around her breast. "What do you need? *Who* do you need?"

Abby shuddered. "You. I need you! Please, Jake—"

He moved against her, coating the tip of his cock in her cream. Then he thrust his cock into her, slamming into her body. And pleasure exploded through her. Abby's body bucked and shuddered beneath him, and, vaguely, she heard herself scream.

Jake kept thrusting. Hard, deep thrusts that shook her body, that sent aftershocks of pleasure ripping through her.

His face was a mask of hard intent. His pupils were huge, his eyes almost black as they locked on her. Deeper, harder, he thrust.

The table squeaked a protest beneath them, but she didn't care.

"You're mine, Abby! *Mine!*" His hand slid down, rubbing against her sensitive clit.

Another wave of pure pleasure slammed into her. For just a moment, she could have sworn the room went dark as molten heat pounded through her.

Jake shuddered against her, groaning heavily.

His cock pumped into her, and a heated rush filled her as he came deep inside of her body.

His arms clenched around her, and Jake whispered her name.

❦

Jake didn't want to move. He wanted to spend the rest of his life with his cock in Abby's snug warmth, and with his arms wrapped around her soft, slender little body.

She moved against him then, pushing against his chest, bracing her small hands against his shoulders. He sighed, and lifted his upper body away from hers. He didn't withdraw from her body, though. He didn't want to leave her. Not yet.

She blinked, staring up at him. Her eyes, those beautiful cat eyes, were huge. "Y—you didn't—" She broke off, swallowed, then said, "You didn't use anything."

Jake froze. *Shit.* She was right. He hadn't stopped to put on a condom. He'd been too far gone. He'd been locked in her silky depths, feeling her tight little muscles clench around him. And he hadn't even thought about stopping to put on a rubber.

And, with a pounding heart, he realized he hadn't used protection at the party, either.

Abby could be pregnant. With his child.

A swift, hot elation roared through him.

If Abby were pregnant, then she couldn't, *wouldn't* leave him. She wouldn't leave the father of her baby.

Then he noticed her lips, those sensual lips that played havoc with his mind, were trembling. And he realized that while he might be thrilled by the idea of a pregnancy, Abby obviously wasn't. Dammit. Could he do nothing right with this woman?

He pulled away from her, hating to give up the touch of that sweet flesh against his. "I'm sorry—" No, he wasn't. He wasn't sorry that he'd spilled his seed deep into her body. He tried again, "I don't want you to be upset—" Now, that was the truth. He didn't want her angry.

He just wanted her.

"Upset? Upset doesn't begin to describe the way I feel," she snapped.

He stepped back, quickly righting his clothes. Abby sprawled on the table, her beautiful body spread before him.

His cock hardened. Damn. Just one look, and he was ready to go again. Only with Abby. Only with her had he ever felt this insatiable need.

But Abby obviously didn't feel the same way. She pushed off the table. Her face was flushed. She grabbed her robe and wrapped it around herself, shielding her body from his hungry gaze.

"If you're pregnant, I'll take care of you," he said solemnly, and he meant it. He would see to it that Abby and her baby never wanted for anything.

"I don't need you to take care of me." Her chin lifted and her green gaze flashed. "I can take care of myself. I've been doing it for years now."

At twenty-eight, Abby was the successful owner of a small boutique on Charles Street. It was a high-end retail shop. Jake had never been to the shop, but he'd had his team of investigators check it out shortly after he met Abby.

He knew Abby had opened the business after she'd graduated from college. "Southern Charms" was a nice, upscale shop that featured an assortment of collectibles and those fragile holiday gifts people seemed to love.

Yeah, Jake knew Abby was more than capable of taking care of herself. She was a strong, independent woman. Hell, her independence and strength were what drew him. But, he wanted to take care of her. He *needed* to take care of her.

"If you're pregnant with my child, *I'll* take care of you." Jake had never slipped up and forgotten to use protection with a woman. Usually, he was almost obsessive about using a condom. But with Abby, it was different.

Abby was different.

Her lips tightened. Then she sighed. "Look, it's probably the wrong time anyway."

He sincerely hoped it wasn't.

"Don't worry about me," Abby continued, oblivious to his thoughts.

Don't worry about her? Like that would be possible.

"I'll know in a week, two at the most. But it's not the right time," she repeated, a hint of stubbornness in her voice. "So there's no problem, okay?" She straightened her shoulders and walked toward the door. "Now, I think it's time you left." Her hands were clenched around the belt of her robe.

Jake blinked. Abby was trying to kick him out. Again. Not five minutes ago, the woman had been screaming his name. Now she was showing him the door.

He shook his head.

Abby frowned.

Jake paced across the room, his steps deliberate, measured. Abby stood her ground, not moving an inch. He stopped a foot away from her and stared down at her upturned face.

"I'll be careful from now on," he promised her softly. "I lost my head. I won't do it again." He hoped.

She didn't speak. Her hands went to the doorknob and she unbolted the door. "Good night, Jake."

Jake shook his head. Abby swallowed.

"I told you that I wanted a week. One week, with you."

He reached around her and locked the door. The snap of the lock seemed to echo in the quiet room. "There's only one place I'm going, and that's to bed. With you."

She opened her mouth, probably to protest, but he placed a finger against her lips, stilling her.

"One week, remember? You're mine for the week, and you said you'd do whatever I wanted." And there were so many things that he wanted to do with the delicious Abigail.

His gaze drifted slowly over her, and he ordered, "Leave the robe here. You won't be needing it tonight." No, she wouldn't need a damn bit of clothing for the night.

His cock was hard, ready for her. It was as if he hadn't just spent himself in the heated depths of her body. He needed her again. He had to have her.

"Right now, I want you. Naked." Moaning, screaming his name. "Get in bed, Abby. It's going to be a long night."

Chapter Four

Abby awoke to the warm weight of a man's hand on her breast. His fingers teased her nipple, plucking lightly.

A moan was on her lips as she opened her eyes.

Jake smiled down at her. His thigh was between her legs, his hand posses-sively covering her breast. "Morning, baby."

Heat rose in her cheeks. She wasn't used to waking with someone beside her. When they'd made love in the past, Jake had always left before dawn.

In the morning light, she wasn't quite certain how she was supposed to act, or what she was supposed to say.

She wasn't one of those sophisticated women who knew all the right words to say to a lover. Jake was only the second man she'd ever been with. She stared up at him, completely lost.

If possible, his smile seemed to spread. "God, you're beautiful in the morn-ing." He leaned down and kissed her, a hard, fast kiss. "And, just so you know, you sleep like the dead."

An unwilling smile tugged at her lips. "I do not."

He nodded. "Oh, yeah. You do. I've spent the last hour staring at you, wait-ing for you to wake up."

He'd spent the last hour, just watching her sleep? A tingle of pleasure zipped through her.

"I even tried playing with you," he said as his fingers plucked her nipple, "and your body responded like wildfire, but you didn't wake up." He paused, then continued in a soft drawl, "That might be something I keep in mind… for next time."

Next time. The words echoed in Abby's mind. "Jake, I—"

Her telephone rang, the shrill cry cutting through the room.

Jake swore and reached for the phone.

"No!" Abby jerked up in bed and pulled the sheet to her chin. Jake looked at her, raising one blond brow.

Damn. The man was sexy.

Abby forgot her protest, and just stared at him. The early morning light spilled through her window, bathing him in a soft glow. His blond mane was tousled, his blue gaze slumberous. His chest, that deep expanse of muscle, was deliciously bare. Her fingers itched to touch him, to feel the soft thatch of his chest hair beneath her palms. She sighed, a soft, almost wistful sound. The man ought to be illegal.

The phone rang again, its demanding peal pulling Abby from her muddled thoughts.

Jake reached across her, and his hand touched the receiver.

"No!" She pushed him back. "I—it could be my family."

His lips tightened, but he dropped his arm.

Abby grabbed the phone. "H—hello?"

"Abby?" She immediately recognized Trent's voice. She slanted a quick glance in Jake's direction. As close as he was, he'd be able to hear her whole conversation.

"Yeah, Trent, what is it?"

"What have you done?" His voice was tense, almost high-pitched.

Abby frowned. "Done? I haven't done anything—"

"I know about you and Jake! Dammit, Abby, *I know*! What the hell were you thinking, getting involved with a guy like him? Didn't you learn anything from Sean?"

She stiffened. "Sean has nothing to do with this." Sean had been a mistake. A mistake that she'd made when she'd been a girl of nineteen. A mistake that she'd made when she'd been foolish enough to believe a man could love her, and not her father's money.

"Jake's a user, just like Sean. And he's using you, Abby. He's going to use you, then throw you away—"

Jake snatched the phone from her hand. "Trent, as usual, you don't know what the fuck you're talking about."

Her brother inhaled sharply. "Jake?"

"Who the hell else would it be? Now do me a favor, stop giving your sister shitty brotherly advice. Abby's a grown woman. She can take care of herself."

"What are you doing at my sister's house?" Trent's words were a snarl. Abby winced, easily imaging her brother's beet-red face at that moment.

Jake looked at Abby. It was a heated, lust-filled glance. He swallowed. "None of your damn business."

"If you hurt her, I'll kill you! Do you hear me, Jake? I had to stand by while that jerk Sean broke her heart. I won't let her be hurt like that again! I don't care who you are, you're not going to hurt—"

"As always, it's been anything but a pleasure," Jake snapped, cutting off the other man.

"Jake—"

"Good-bye, Trent." Jake hung up the phone with a soft click.

Abby's heart raced. Trent knew about her and Jake. His timing last night couldn't have been worse.

Trent wouldn't keep quiet. He'd never been able to keep a secret, not once in his whole life. Soon, the entire family would know. She closed her eyes.

"Who…" Jake began very softly, "in the hell is Sean?"

Abby's eyes snapped open. Jake glared at her, his scar appearing a stark white against his skin.

"What?"

"You heard me." His blue gaze narrowed. "Who's Sean? What is he to you?"

"Sean Gallows is my ex-fiancé," she said, waiting for the pain that usually followed that admission. But strangely, she didn't feel pain. She didn't feel anything.

"You were engaged?" His knuckles had tightened around the sheets.

She nodded. "Briefly, during my sophomore year of college."

"What happened." It wasn't a question, it was a demand.

Abby shrugged. She hated telling Jake this story, hated reliving the humiliation that she'd felt. "Does it really matter?"

"Oh, yeah. It matters."

She stood, pulling the sheet with her. She couldn't tell him while they were in bed. Not while he was so close to her. She walked to her settee and grabbed her robe. She donned it quickly, tying the belt with a quick toss of her hand.

"You're armored now," Jake murmured from his position in the bed. "Tell me."

Abby froze. *You're armored now.* Yes, that's exactly what she had been doing. Armoring herself. How had Jake known? She swallowed. Sometimes, Jake saw too much, he *knew* too much about her.

She took a deep breath. "I met Sean my first year at Emory. I fell for him, hard." She'd been completely charmed by his boyish looks and easy smile. So charmed, that she hadn't seen behind his mask.

"You loved him?" Jake asked, his expression tense.

Had she loved him? She shrugged. "I thought I did. I was going to marry him. I planned to live happily ever after with him. I wanted the cozy house and the picket fence." She clenched her hands and shook her head at her own naiveté. "I wanted it all."

"What happened?" Jake sat strangely still on the bed. His hooded gaze was locked on her.

"One day, I dropped by his apartment early. I wanted to surprise him. You know, have dinner and candles waiting for him. Do the whole girlfriend bit." Unfortunately, she'd been the one who'd gotten the surprise that day. "I found him in bed with my roommate." She'd stared at them, feeling as if she would shatter. She hadn't screamed at them, she hadn't raged. She'd just closed the bedroom door and walked away.

Abby closed her eyes, shutting out the memory. "He came to my place later. He told me that he'd only been with me because he wanted to be a partner in my father's business. But I was such a—an i—ice q—queen—" She stopped, shaking. Why was she shaking? What was wrong with her?

Then Jake was there, pulling her into his arms. Warming her, chasing the chill from her body.

Abby pressed her lips together and straightened her shoulders. But she didn't pull away from Jake, from his strength. Because in that moment, she needed him, needed his touch. "He said I was frigid. That he'd been going crazy being with me, that he had to have a real woman. But he said that he'd stay with me, that he'd still marry me. After all, he had big plans for my father's business." She could still see Sean, see his confident expression as he'd told her that he'd overlook her faults and stay with her anyway.

"I hope you told the bastard to go to hell."

Abby's lips curved. "I did." Sean had left, screaming at her that she'd made a mistake, that she would come after him, begging him to take her back. After all, no one else would want her. *"No man would want a frigid lay like you!"*

But she'd never gone back to him. And she never would.

"He was wrong, you know." Jake's warm fingers wrapped around her chin and forced her head up, forced her to meet his probing stare. "You aren't frigid."

"I thought I was," she admitted, her voice soft. "I-I never…enjoyed being with Sean. I-I never really wanted anyone, until I met you." With her words, she knew she'd laid herself bare before him, probably told him things that she shouldn't. It was a huge risk, opening herself this way to him. How would he respond?

Jake inhaled sharply. His naked cock pressed against her thigh. Big. Hot. Hard.

"Woman, do you know what you do to me when you say something like that?"

Her body clenched, her sex grew moist. *Nope, definitely not frigid.* Oh, if Sean could see her now. The two-timing bastard would be stunned. "No, what do I do to you?"

His lips pressed down against hers, his tongue thrusting into her mouth. He pulled back, whispering, "You make me want to fuck you."

A surprised peal of laughter slipped past her lips and desire stirred in her belly.

She forgot about Sean, forgot about the past. All of her focus centered on Jake. *Jake.*

She shouldn't want him again. Not after last night. They'd made love countless times. He'd driven into her body, and she'd climaxed so many times that she'd actually lost count. Her body should be too tired, too satisfied.

But the hunger, the need, roared through her. And she wanted him. Hard and fast.

She wanted to burn. To melt the ice that had surrounded her for so long.

His hand was on her breast. Teasing her nipple. Plucking the tight peak.

Her body ached. She was hot, yearning… for him. She wanted him inside her. *Now.*

Her hands reached down and locked around his silken length. He felt hard, and so warm, against her. She stared at his cock and wondered what it would be like to taste him.

He thrust forward, his length sliding against her hands. Her fingers tightened, and he groaned, closing his eyes briefly.

"Jake—" Did that high, needy voice really belong to the cool and controlled Abigail McGill?

Jake seemed to sense what she wanted, what she needed. His arms locked around her and he picked her up, then took two huge steps toward the bed. He tossed her onto the mattress.

Abby landed with her legs spread. The robe was a tangle around her thighs, exposing her to his hot gaze.

"I'm not in the mood to play," he said, his voice a hoarse growl. "If you're not ready for me, say so now."

His face was dark, tight with strain. The muscles of his arms and chest gleamed. His eyes, dear God, his eyes seemed to burn with lust.

Her laughter of moments ago was forgotten. She could only stare up at him, her chest rising rapidly.

She should have been afraid. He looked like he wanted to eat her alive.

Yes, she should have been afraid. But, instead, she was hungry.

Abby reached for him.

Jake shoved her robe out of the way. His cock pushed against her folds, big and heavy. He pulled back, just an inch, then thrust his full length into her.

Abby bit back a scream.

"You're mine," he gritted, his hips pumping frantically against her. "And I'm going to have all of you, everything!"

Abby's legs lifted, locking around his bucking hips. Pleasure streaked through her.

His mouth locked on her breast. Sucked. Bit lightly. Tormented her.

"Say my name," he demanded. "Say it!"

Abby's head thrashed as the pleasure lashed her. It was so good. So—

"Who am I?" Jake pulled back, holding his cock at the moist entrance of her body.

"Jake!" She arched her hips, struggling to pull him back inside.

"I'm the only one who makes you feel this way, right, Abby?" He wasn't moving. The tip of his cock pressed against her. Strong. Throbbing.

"Yes!" She needed him inside. Deep inside. *Now!*

"No one else. No one else, ever. Do you hear me? No one!" He pulled completely away from her, and Abby's eyes snapped open. He couldn't leave her, not when she needed him so much!

He ripped open the condom packet with his teeth. His face was flushed, and his fingers trembled.

Abby's hands rose—

"No!" His jaw clenched. "If you touch me, I'll explode. And I don't want to do that until I'm in *you.*" He rolled the condom on, his face locked in tense concentration.

She itched to touch him, to stroke him. Despite his warning, she lifted her hands—

Jake grabbed her wrists, forcing her arms down on either side of her head. And he forced his cock deep, deep into her.

Abby moaned, arching her back, sliding him in another delicious inch.

His fingers tightened around her wrists. A growl rumbled in his throat.

As Abby stared into his burning gaze, she saw him lose control.

Jake's hips thrust against her. His cock pushed into her. Hard. Fast. Deep.

Her legs wrapped around him, pulling him in tighter, deeper.

Her hands clenched into tight fists. It was too much. Too much. It had to end—

Abby screamed as her climax slammed through her. Every nerve in her body tingled, and her inner muscles clenched around his strong cock.

"So good." Jake's teeth were clenched. "You feel so damn good!" His fingers tightened around her wrists. His thighs pushed her legs farther apart. "Abby!"

His hips jerked against her. He groaned, the sound heavy with pleasure. He climaxed inside her, shaking. She held him, deliberately tightening around his thick length.

His hands left her wrists, rose up, and his fingers entwined with hers.

His heart pounded against hers. Hard. Fast.

His breath was heavy, labored.

And the scent of their lovemaking hung in the air.

As she sprawled there, her body cushioned beneath Jake's hard length, Abby felt completely satiated. Completely secure.

Jake raised his head and gazed down at her. He didn't say a word. Just stared, his blue gaze intense. Then he kissed her, a soft, gentle touch of his lips.

He slid to the side and cradled her in his arms.

As if she'd been doing it for years, Abby nestled herself into his embrace. One thought slipped through her mind. *I only have six more days with him.*

Then he would leave her, for he was a man of his word. Jake would walk away from her. Their bargain would be over.

And her life would never be the same.

The thought chilled her.

Chapter Five

"Do you know what you're doing?"

Jake looked up at the sound of his cousin's growling voice.

Mike Collins, tall, tan and currently glowering, stood in his office doorway.

Jake held up the Peters file. "Negotiating a buyout?"

One golden brow lifted. "Cute, cuz. Real cute." He sauntered in the room, shutting the door with a quick flick of his hand. "I mean with the woman."

The Peters file was instantly forgotten. Jake stiffened. "The *woman* has a name."

"I know. It's the same name as that company we should have bought and made a nice profit from." Without an invitation, Mike sat down in the leather seat across from Jake. He shook his head. "I can't believe you, of all people, would blow a deal… for a woman."

"I didn't blow the deal." His anger began to boil. "I never blow deals." He had brought himself up from nothing, brought his entire family up, by the strength of his will. He didn't back down from competitors, and he sure as hell didn't blow business deals.

Anyone else might have faltered at Jake's icy soft tone, but Mike was as close as a brother to him. Mike leaned forward, his lips pulling into a frown. "Then tell me what happened. Tell me why Steele Industries doesn't have a few extra zeroes in its bank account today."

"Because we didn't need the damn zeroes!" Because he'd needed something else. Someone else.

Mike whistled softly. "I'll be damned."

"What?" He didn't like the way Mike eyed him. As if the other man had just solved a particularly challenging puzzle…

"You really did do it for her, didn't you?"

His lips pressed into a thin line. He fought the urge to throw his cousin out of the office, out of the building.

Mike shook his head. "She must be one hell of a lay."

Jake was across the desk before Mike had time to draw another breath. He jerked his cousin out of the chair, his hands clenching the fabric of Mike's suit.

Mike stared at him, wide-eyed. He swallowed, his Adam's apple bobbing. "Don't ever… say anything… like that again." Mike licked his lips and nodded frantically.

"Ever," he repeated, fighting the urge to slam his fist into the smaller man. Family or not, if Mike so much as whispered Abby's name with a hint of disrespect in his tone, the younger man would go down. Hard.

"I—I won't," Mike said, his voice sounding like a squeak.

Jake dropped his hands and took a deep breath.

Mike took a few steps back, carefully placing the leather chair between him and Jake. "I—I didn't know it was like… that."

Blue eyes narrowed. "Like what?"

Mike gulped. "Uh, you know, um… I didn't know it was serious. Sorry, man. I'll… just… um… go now."

"You do that."

His cousin scrambled from the room, almost tripping in his haste.

Jake pinched the bridge of his nose and took a deep breath, striving to keep calm. Dammit, time was running out.

The weekend had vanished in a blur of sex and satisfaction. He'd been inside Abby so deep, so many times, that he'd felt like he was a part of her.

The days were passing, fading too fast. Now, he only had three days left with Abby. *Three days*, then his damn bargain would be over. And she would walk away from him.

He didn't want to give her up. Not today, not three days from now.

Hell, yeah, it was serious. Abby was his. *His*.

He snatched up the phone. He might not have much time left, but the time had, he would use. He punched in her number and waited, yanking off his tie.

She answered on the second ring, her warm, softly drawling voice seeming to pour over the line. "Southern Charms. This is Abby."

He closed his eyes, his cock hardening. That was all it took, just the sound of her voice. Damn, he had it bad.

"Hello? Is anyone there?"

He swallowed. "Get over here."

Abby inhaled sharply. "Jake?"

"Get. Over. Here. Now."

"I'm at work, I—"

"I'm at work, too. I don't care. Get your sweet ass over here."

"I can't—"

No, no, she couldn't refuse him. A strange burning filled his chest. "You're the boss. You can do anything you want." And he prayed that she wanted him.

"Jake—"

"You promised me a week, Abby," he reminded her, his fingers tightening around the phone. "I want my week. I want you. Now." He needed her. He needed

to feel her tighten around him, to feel her take him deep, deep into her body.
Time was running out.

"I'll be there in an hour." Soft, husky words.

"Make it thirty minutes." He hung up the phone, not waiting for her reply.

He was a selfish bastard. He knew it. He also knew Abby deserved someone
a hell of a lot better for a lover.

That was too bad. Abby was his. And he wasn't giving her up, not without
a fight.

Three days left...

Abby had never been to Steele Industries before. She'd seen the high-rise
building. Everyone in Atlanta had seen it in the midst of the busy downtown
sector. But she'd never stepped past the gleaming entrance doors.

Until today.

Abby walked past the security guard, nodding nervously in his direction.
She'd been doing inventory at her shop, and she was dressed casually in a
pair of jeans and a white t-shirt. She felt completely out of place, surrounded
as she was by all of the businessmen and women in their oh-so-professional
tailored suits.

There was a large, circular booth in the middle of the lobby. A woman with
stylishly cut blond hair sat at the desk, her scowling gaze trained on Abby.

Abby lifted her chin and marched toward her.

"May I help you?" The woman's tone indicated that she thought Abby had
obviously wandered into the building my mistake.

Abby's eyes narrowed at that tone. She had grown up surrounded by her
father's staff. She wasn't used to someone disrespecting her, regardless of her
appearance. "I'm here to see Jake Steele." Her own tone was crisp.

The blond cocked one brow. "Mr. Steele is quite busy, I hardly think—"

"You're Abigail McGill!"

Abby turned, startled, to find a tall, handsome blond man staring at her
with a startled gaze.

"Yes, I am." She eyed him cautiously. There was something about him that
seemed familiar to her. Something about his eyes, his blue eyes...

He smiled and held out his hand. "Mike Collins. I'm Jake's cousin."

"Oh, hello!" She reached for his hand, noting with surprise the feel of his
callouses beneath her palm. "I—uh—I didn't know Jake had a cousin." She
winced the moment the words left her mouth.

"There are a few of us." He released her hand and waved vaguely around
the lobby. "Jake keeps us all on our toes, working at the family business."

Abby nodded, not really knowing what response was expected of her.

Mike's gaze traveled down her body. His lips hitched into a strange half-smile. A smile that appeared a little too knowing for Abby's peace of mind. "Does Jake know you're here?"

Glancing back at the avid receptionist, Abby frowned. "I don't think he knows yet." She didn't think little Ms. Perfect Suit had gotten around to calling his office yet.

The woman's lips tightened. "I was trying to explain to this *woman* that Mr. Steele is far too busy to see unscheduled—"

Mike raised a hand, cutting off the woman's speech. "Marsha, if you value your job, you'll send this lady upstairs to Jake's office, and you'll do it now." His gaze was hard. "Otherwise, when Jake finds out what's happened, he'll fire you."

Marsha's eyes widened to almost double their previous size. She lifted a shaking hand and pointed toward the elevator. "Twenty-first floor. Suite 2101."

Abby smiled sweetly. "Thank you." She stalked toward the elevator. Mike followed on her heels.

The shining doors slid open just as she approached them, and Abby stepped inside the mirrored elevator. She lifted her hand to punch the button for the twenty-first floor.

"Allow me." Mike reached his arm around her. A bell sounded and the elevator doors slid closed.

The elevator began to ascend and silence filled the small area.

Abby could feel Mike's eyes upon her. She glanced at him with a raised brow. "Is there something I can help you with?"

"Why are you with Jake?"

"*Excuse me?*"

"You heard me, Ms. McGill."

Abby lifted her chin. "I hardly think it's any of your business."

"I'm family; of course, it's my business."

Abby winced. Apparently, she wasn't the only one with family issues. It looked like Jake might be suffering from his own share of family trouble.

She sighed. This had been a mistake. She should never have come to Steele Industries. She should have ignored Jake's call. And she would have, if she hadn't heard the strange note of desperation in his voice.

Yes, Jake had ordered her to come. But underlying his words, there had been an almost frantic need reflected in his voice. A plea.

And she'd responded to his need, to his plea. She'd left the shop in the hands of her assistant. And she driven, as fast she could, to get to him.

"Are you using him?"

"What?" Abby's head snapped up.

Mike shrugged. "He's loaded, you know. Are you with him for his money?"

"I don't care about Jake's money." And that was the absolute truth. She met his stare without flinching. "I don't want his money."

"Then what is it that you want *do* from him?"

Before she could answer, the elevator chimed, signaling that they'd reached their destination. The doors slid open, and Abby found herself standing face to face with Jake.

He was dressed in a conservatively cut black suit. His hair was combed back. His tie was straight. And his polished black shoes gleamed. He looked like a composed, successful businessman.

Then Abby looked into his eyes, into his feverish gaze, and she saw the true nature of the man. She saw his hunger. His lust. His need.

He was a man on the fine edge of control.

He grabbed her wrist, pulling her from the elevator and next to his side. He glared at Mike. "What the hell were you doing with her?"

Mike smiled and held up his hands. "Easy, cuz. I was just escorting your lady to you."

"Then you're job is done, isn't it?" Jake's hold on her tightened. "I've got her now."

"Yeah, but will you be able to keep her?" Mike asked softly. "Be careful, Jake. I think she might be one worth holding." He saluted his cousin and stepped back.

The doors slid closed and Mike disappeared.

Chapter Six

"Come on." Jake pulled Abby down the tastefully decorated hallway. They bustled past a startled looking man with horn-rimmed glasses. The fellow's mouth hung wide-open and he watched them with surprise etched onto his thin face.

"Henry, hold all my calls." Jake opened the door to his office and pushed Abby inside. "Something's come up."

"Ah, yes, sir, I—"

Jake shut the door on his assistant's stumbling words.

Abby stood frozen in the middle of the room. She paid no attention to the expensive furniture or even the startling view of Atlanta. Her entire focus was on Jake.

He stalked toward her. His hands lifted, locked around her shoulders. "I can't get you out of my mind," he whispered. "I keep thinking about you, fantasizing about what I want to do to you..."

Abby swallowed, and held her body carefully still. She had the strange feeling that if she moved, he would pounce on her. Literally.

"Do you want to know about my fantasies, Abby? Do you want to know what I think about? How I think about you?"

Did she? Did she dare? Abby slowly nodded.

His right hand slipped down, cupping her breast. His cheeks were flushed. His eyes dilated.

"I think about taking you, here—on the desk. On the couch. In the elevator. In any damn place that I can get you. I want to strip you, to hold you, naked, and lick every inch of you." He licked his lips. His fingers toyed with her nipple. "I want to sit in my chair, and I want you to ride me. I want you to milk the seed from my body." His voice was a growl.

Abby's knees shook. This was a Jake that she hadn't seen before. She didn't quite know what he was going to say or *do* next.

"Sometimes, I fantasize about having you on your knees. About you taking my cock into your mouth, sucking me—"

Abby gasped. She'd never done that. Not to Sean. Not to Jake. She'd always been too nervous, too shy. And she really hadn't wanted to do that with Sean. But with Jake... "I've never—"

He froze. His nostrils flared. "Not even with that other bastard?"

"N—no."

Her gaze fell to the front of his pants. His erection bulged, pressing strongly toward her. And she wondered, what would he taste like?

Both of his hands were on her shoulders again, and he was pushed her down, pushed with gentle, but determined, force.

"Jake—" She couldn't look away from his erection. So big. So strong. Could she do it? Could she take him into her mouth?

She was on her knees now, his cock directly in front of her. She reached up to touch him through the soft fabric. He jerked against her. His fingers tightened around her shoulders.

"Suck me, Abby," he ordered. "Take my cock into your mouth and suck me."

Her hands shook as she unhooked the button of his pants, as she slowly lowered the zipper. Bare, golden flesh appeared before her. Jake didn't wear underwear, he didn't like the confinement. She continued lowering the zipper with extra care, knowing that his thick length was there, waiting for her.

She pushed the pants down, and his erection flexed, jerking toward her. Abby's fingers wrapped around him, tightening around his cock.

Jake groaned. "Take me in, Abby..."

But she hesitated. What if she didn't do it right? What if he didn't like—

Abby bit her lip and looked up at Jake. "I—I don't know how." Humiliation burned through her.

Jake's eyes blazed. "Lick me," he ordered, his voice little more than a rumble. "I'll show you the rest."

She leaned forward, aware of a heavy ache between her thighs. Her tongue snaked out and touched his tip, tasting the light drop of moisture that appeared on the head of his cock.

Jake's hands lifted and clenched in her hair. "Again."

Abby swallowed, tasting a spicy flavor on her tongue. She opened her mouth, and her lips touched him, closing around his broad tip. And she licked.

Jake shuddered. "More. Take me in deeper."

She lifted her hand and closed her fingers around the base of his shaft. And she began to suck. And lick.

Jake growled and thrust his hips, sending his cock deeper into her mouth. His fingers tightened in her hair, and he began to move her in time with his thrusts.

Abby forgot about feeling nervous. She forgot about being awkward. Her tongue, her lips, her entire mouth caressed him. She licked. She sucked. She stroked. And she pulled his length into her mouth, loving the feel of him, loving the sounds he made.

She felt powerful. Desirable. Jake wanted her. His voice was thick, broken by desire. His strong body trembled against hers.

She was giving him pleasure. She was giving Jake his fantasy.

"Oh, God, Abby—"

A brief knock sounded at the door. Abby's eyes widened and she began to pull back.

"Don't fucking move," Jake snapped, his hands fisting in her hair. Just as the door began to open, he snapped, "If you want to keep breathing, you'll stay on the other side of that damn door!" His hips thrust against her, his cock sliding over her tongue. "I'm—" a deep shudder, "in a p—private meeting."

Someone gasped. The door slammed closed, and footsteps retreated down the hall in a fast thunder.

Had the person on the other side of the door seen or heard them? If that person—

Jake pulled her to her feet and jerked her shirt over her head. Then his hands were on her jeans, yanking the top button loose and shoving down the zipper. "I want you naked. Now."

He kicked out of his pants and lunged for the door. Abby blinked, wondering what he was doing. Then he turned the lock with a quick jerk of his wrist.

Jake looked back at her. "Why are you still dressed?"

"I, uh—" Abby's hands went to the clasp of her bra. Before the garment hit the floor, Jake had her nipple in his mouth.

Abby kicked off her tennis shoes. Jake shoved down her jeans. Then he pulled her behind his desk.

"Jake?"

He smiled and sat down in his black leather chair. "Fantasy time, remember?"

He reached for Abby's panties, and with one hard yank, he ripped the material away. Then he grabbed Abby's hips and pulled her on top of him. "I want you to ride me."

⁂

Abby straddled him, and his cock brushed against her clit. She was wet, creamy, and it was all Jake could do not to thrust, hard and deep, into her pussy.

He reached down, and his fingers slid over her slick folds. She was ready for him. Good. Because he couldn't wait much longer.

God, the feel of her tongue and her sweet lips on him had almost been more than he could take. It had been heaven. Hell. A second longer, and he would have spilled himself into her mouth.

But he didn't want to come in her mouth. He wanted to come in her tight little body.

He reached into his top drawer and grabbed the condom he'd optimistically placed there yesterday. He'd put it there, just in case he'd been lucky enough to have Abby in his office.

He pulled the condom out, preparing to put it on, but Abby placed her hand on top of his, stilling him.

"No, Jake."

For a moment, he was certain his heart stopped. Abby was refusing him? She was turning him away? No, no she couldn't—

But how could he stop her? If she didn't want him, he wouldn't force her to take him into her body. He'd already forced himself into her life enough.

Despair knifed through him.

Abby took the condom from his fingers and placed it on his desk. "I don't want that, I just want you."

Jake stared up at her beautiful face, stunned.

"I want to feel you inside me, Jake. Just you."

He didn't need a second invitation. Jake thrust, burying his cock in to the hilt.

Her legs tightened around him, and her cunt squeezed him, fist-tight and so wet and creamy, he thought he would lose his mind.

Abby lifted her hips, starting a slow, easy rhythm.

Jake growled. He wasn't in the mood for slow and easy. His fingers locked around her waist.

The seductive sound of her laughter wrapped around him.

She began to move. Faster. Harder. "Is this what you wanted?" Her voice was a purr.

Hell, yes, it was what he wanted. But he wanted it even faster, even harder. His fingers clenched around her, and he took control, thrusting harder, moving her body, pulling her into his rhythm. He drove them relentlessly toward climax. He wanted to feel her orgasm. Wanted to feel her milking his cock.

And he wanted to come inside her tight little pussy.

His climax built. His balls tightened, his spine tingled. So close...

Abby bit off a choked scream. Her body tightened, flexed around him.

"You feel so damn good," he growled. Then he exploded, pounding his cock into her. Spilling his seed deep into her body.

Abby collapsed onto him, her dark mane wrapping around him. His arms closed around her as Jake held her against his chest. He held her there, cradled against his heart.

Three more days.

Would he be able to let her go? Would he be able to convince her to stay?

Chapter Seven

The next afternoon, Abby stood in her shop, straightening a display shelf and trying to keep her mind off Jake.

But it was no use. She couldn't stop thinking about him, couldn't stop thinking about how good it had felt to hold him, to kiss him, to make love with him.

They only had two days left. Just two more days. And then it would be over —

"There's something you need to know about your lover."

Abby whirled at the sound of her father's voice.

He stood just inside the doorway of Southern Charms, dressed in an austere black suit and wearing a dark scowl.

It took a moment for his words to register, then Abby blushed as she glanced back at the two avid customers who waited at the counter.

"Dad, I hardly think this is the time —"

"He's using you, Abby. He's screwing you to get back at me. He couldn't take my business, so now he's trying to take my daughter."

Tiny pinpricks of heat pierced the skin of her face. There was a dull ringing in her ears. Abby swallowed, shaking her head. Why was her father saying these things? Why—

"Um, Abby—" The soft voice belonged to her assistant, Trisha. "I'll take care of these ladies. Why don't you and your father go into the back to… um… talk?"

She nodded once, fiercely grateful to Trisha for her interference. Then she turned on her heel and hurried toward the stockroom. She didn't even glance back to see if her father followed her.

But the heavy tread of his footsteps told her that she didn't have to worry. After all, Martin McGill never left a fight before he was damn good and ready.

He shut the door to the stockroom with a sharp snap.

Abby took a deep breath and slowly turned to face him.

Lines of strain marred her father's normally handsome face, and his green eyes were heavy with some unnamed emotion. Anger? Disappointment? Abby couldn't tell, not for certain.

"Girl, I hope you have a damn good explanation for what you've been doing with Jake Steele."

She braced her shoulders and lifted her chin. "I'm not a *girl*, Father." She was a mature woman, and she didn't have to explain her actions to him. It was long past time her father realized that.

He scowled.

"And I don't appreciate you coming into my business and causing a scene. I would never do that to you, and I expect the same courtesy." Her knees trembled, but her voice was ice cold.

"He's using you!" Her father's voice was an angry snarl. "He doesn't care about you! He only wants to hurt me."

Abby swallowed the denial that sprang to her lips.

"Has he ever said that he cares? Ever said that he loves you?" Martin pressed ruthlessly.

She shook her head.

"Don't you see? He couldn't take McGill Properties, so he's striking out. He's trying to take you!"

No, no, Jake wasn't that kind of man.

"I beat him at his own game, and now he wants revenge—"

"You didn't beat him," Abby said softly. "He backed off the deal."

Martin blinked. "What?"

Abby's lips twisted into a parody of a smile. "When have you ever known of Jake Steele to lose a deal? He decided against the buyout, Dad. You didn't beat him. He chose to back off."

"Why?" Genuine confusion was in the one word. Martin obviously couldn't conceive of someone willingly giving up the chance to land a huge business deal. "Why would a guy like Jake do that?"

For me. The words were on the tip of her tongue. Jake had said he'd backed off for her. Was that true? Had he really turned down the deal just for her sake?

Her expression must have reflected her thoughts because Martin gave a short bark of laughter and said, "You think he did it for you." He shook his head. "Baby, men don't do that. They don't throw away millions just for a woman."

"I know that," she whispered, even as a part of her hoped that she was wrong. Hoped that Jake really had backed off the deal, just for her.

Martin paced around the small room, tension evident in the stiff line of his shoulders. "He wants something. The bastard has to be up to something. He—"

"You know, I really take offense to being called a bastard." Jake stood just inside the now open door. A lazy smile curved his lips. "My parents were, after all, legally wed."

Martin stiffened. Abby just stared at Jake, her heart pounding.

Martin crossed the room, putting his body between Jake and Abby. "Stay away from my daughter!"

Jake arched one golden brow.

Martin's lips tightened. "She doesn't want you near her. She doesn't—"

"Doesn't she?" Jake almost purred. "Why don't we ask Abby what she wants?" He lifted his hand, motioning toward her. "Tell us, Abby. Tell us both exactly what it is that you want."

"She wants you to leave her alo—" Martin began.

"I didn't ask you," Jake snapped, his jaw tightening.

Abby stepped around her father. Her gaze met Jake's dark stare.

"What do you want?" He asked her. "*Who* do you want?"

Her father grabbed her arm. "Dammit, Abby, he's using you! Just like Sean. He's going to hurt you—"

"That may be true," she said, pulling her arm free from his tight hold.

Jake looked stricken. "No, I—"

"But I want to be with him," she finished, her voice clear. She gazed determinedly into her father's stunned face. "I love you, Dad. But I'm going to be with Jake."

"You would choose *him* over your own family?"

Abby shook her head, a tight ball in her chest. "I don't want to choose between you." She took a deep breath. "But I'm not going to let you tell me what to do with my private life." And she meant it. She was through letting her family dictate her behavior.

Her father's face was a dark red. "When he tosses you aside, and believe me, he will, you're going to regret this!"

She flinched.

Her father turned and stormed from the room.

Silence, heavy and thick, descended over the small space.

Abby exhaled slowly. The thing she'd dreaded, the thing she'd feared, had finally happened. Her father had found out about Jake. He'd been enraged, just as she'd expected. He'd demanded that she leave Jake.

But she hadn't.

"Why?" Jake asked softly.

"What I do," she paused, pressed her lips together, then continued, "and who I do it with, that's not his business."

"Your family's going to be furious."

She nodded.

Jake walked toward her, the sound of his footsteps filling the small room. He stopped less than a foot away from her. The heat of his body seemed to reach out to her, to wrap around her.

"Your father was wrong, you know."

Abby's gaze lifted.

"I'm not using you." His stare burned into her. "You and me, we're not about some business deal. We're not about revenge."

She wet her lips. "What are we about?"

"Don't you know?" He asked, his head lowering. "Haven't you figured it out by now?"

His lips were a breath away from hers. She smelled his crisp masculine scent, saw the tiny flecks of gold in the depths of his blue eyes.

And she saw his desire.

Abby stumbled away from his. "Sex? Is it just about sex?"

He followed her, like a predator stalking his prey. "Sex is part of it."

She turned away from him.

Jake grabbed her arm and spun her back around. "But if I just wanted sex, I wouldn't be here. I wouldn't have given up that deal. I wouldn't have acted like an asshole and blackmailed you into this week."

Abby stared at him, stunned.

"Don't you get it?" He shook her once, lightly. "I want *you*." His mouth crashed down on hers.

Abby's arms wrapped around him. Her lips parted, and her tongue met his.

His hands seemed to be everywhere at once. Sliding down her back. Caressing her buttocks. Stroking between her thighs.

Jake tore his mouth from hers. "Yesterday, when we made love, I-I didn't use anything—"

"I didn't want you to," she said, her voice husky.

"Why?"

"Because..." She took a quick breath. Her breasts pressed against his chest. "I wanted to feel you, just you... and—"

"And now?"

She smiled. "I only want you." The thought of having Jake's baby didn't scare her anymore... it thrilled her.

He growled and scooped her up into his arms. "Good, because, baby, you're about to get me."

He carried her to the back of the room and eased her down onto the inventory table. He pushed up her skirt and began to rub the lacy edge of her panties with his broad fingers.

Abby moaned, closing her eyes.

"I'm going to fuck you," he said, his words dark and promising. "And I'm going to make you forget any man you had before me. I'm going to make you forget everyone... and everything... but me."

He jerked her panties down. Abby gasped as his fingers plunged deep.

"I'm going to do all that to you," Jake continued in that ragged drawl, "because that's what you do to me. I can't think of anything...but you."

Abby spread her legs and pulled him closer.

"God, you're so wet." He leaned down and began to lick her neck. "You drive me crazy." He bit down, his teeth lightly scoring her skin.

Abby arched her back, heat and need streaking through her. Her legs lifted, wrapping around him. The soft material of his pants rubbed against her.

"I can't get enough of you," he whispered, nuzzling her neck. "No matter what I do, it's not enough!"

As he said those words, Jake realized how much he truly needed Abby. She was in his blood. In his soul. He would never get her out of his system. Never.

He tossed aside his coat and tie, and kicked out of his pants. Then his hands returned instantly to her. *Abby.* He needed Abby. Needed to feel her warmth closing around him, making him a part of her.

He pushed the head of his cock against her, rubbing lightly. Her warm cream coated him. He shuddered. He didn't know how much longer he could wait. He wanted to thrust into her, deep into her.

But he had to tell her... had to make her understand... "Abby, this isn't about the deal."

Her eyes opened, heavy with desire. "What?"

"You and me. This is just about you and me. Forget the damn bargain." His jaw was clenched and it took all of his strength not to force his cock, deep and heavy, into her.

She arched her hips, and her delicious, creamy entrance seemed to beg for him.

But he had to make her understand. "I never would have.., ah... God, Abby, don't do that, you're making me crazy." He took a deep breath, locking his muscles. "I... never would have taken your father's company... even if... oh, baby that feels so good... you hadn't given me the... week!" The woman was going to make him beg. The movement of her hips against his was driving him insane.

Abby licked her lips, her delicate pink tongue moving quickly. "I know."

What? She knew? Then why —

Her legs lifted, and she pushed her body against his.

Jake was lost. He slammed forward, his cock filling her in one long, hard thrust.

They both moaned.

His body moved, plunging deeper and deeper. Her legs clenched around his cock. Abby tossed her head back and moaned, gasping in time with his deep thrusts. A light flush covered her cheeks.

She was truly the most beautiful thing he'd ever seen.

And she was his.

She bucked beneath him, gasping, and her delicate muscles clenched around him as she climaxed.

He lifted her hips, and kept thrusting. Hard. Fast.

She milked him, pulling his cock deep into her warm body.

His own orgasm bore down on him, growing ever closer, but he fought it. He didn't want it to end. *Not yet.* He was too close to Abby. *A part of her—*

But it felt too good. She felt too good. And he couldn't hold back anymore.

A wave of pleasure scorched through him, and he shuddered, pumping into her tight heat.

Abby's arms hugged him close.

And he fell into paradise.

One last coherent thought flashed through his lust-crazed brain: *No way in hell am I letting this woman go.*

Chapter Eight

Jake roused slowly. He knew the weight of his body had to be crushing Abby, and that was the only reason he finally found the strength to move. He pulled her up to the edge of the table, and pressed her against his chest, holding her against his heart.

And he said something he never thought he'd say. "Marry me."

Abby's head snapped back, nearly clipping him in the chin. "What?"

He exhaled slowly, aware that this was probably the most important moment of his life. "You heard me. I want you to marry me."

Her mouth dropped open.

"Dammit!" He winced. "I'm screwing this up, aren't I? I'm supposed to do the whole bit with candlelight and flowers. Women like that, right?"

She just stared at him, her lips parted, her eyes wide.

"I was going to do it all. Hell, I stopped by just to ask you out to dinner. For a real date. And I was going to do the whole bit there." But then he'd walked in on Abby and her father and his brilliant plan had gone to pieces.

He started talking again, fast. "I'll do it, okay? I'll do it all. I'll give you the flowers and the candles. I'll give you any damn thing you want." He swallowed. "Just say you'll marry me."

But Abby didn't say a word. Fear knifed through him.

"Abby…"

She glanced around the room, her face looked almost ashen. "I-I need my clothes. I have to get my clothes." She pushed away from him and scrambled to find her skirt.

This wasn't going well. Jake closed his eyes and counted to ten.

When his eyes opened, he saw that Abby had donned her skirt and she was jerking on her blouse. Or what was left of her blouse. He winced.

"Abby, baby—"

She wrenched away from him.

Jake stiffened. No, this was definitely not going well. He should have stuck to Plan A.

"I've got to go." Abby's green eyes looked feverish. "I have to… We'll talk later, okay?" She hurried across the room, her back ramrod straight.

"Wait!" He couldn't let her go, not like this. "Dammit, I asked you to marry me!" The least she could do was give him an answer. A "Yes, please" or a "No, thanks, but go to hell." Something, *anything*.

Abby stopped, her hand on the doorknob. She took a deep breath, and then she turned to face him. "Why do you want to marry me?"

Jake blinked. "What?" Didn't she know? Couldn't she see?

Abby swallowed to clear the lump in her throat. "You heard me." She waited, desperate for his response.

"I want you, that's why! I need you—"

Abby made a sound of protest and turned back to the door. It was just as she'd thought. He wanted her, but he didn't love her. He didn't—

She yanked open the door and hurried into the store. She needed to get away from him. She was too raw now, too emotional. Her entire body seemed to ache with love for him, but all he felt was lust. Need. Hunger.

"Wait! Abby!"

She spun around, unmindful of the dozen or so browsing shoppers. "Leave me alone, Jake. Just leave me alone." Before she did something she would regret. Like screaming at him. Like raging that he should love her, as much as she loved him.

Because she did love him. She'd loved Jake from that very first night. From the first moment she'd seen him, touched him. And everyday, her feelings had grown. That was why she'd given herself to him. She didn't just want Jake. She yearned for him. She *loved* him.

But he didn't love her.

Her father had been right. Jake had wound up hurting her, and it was a pain far more savage than that inflicted by Sean's casual cruelty.

Now she just wanted to get away, to lick her wounds, to hide.

Abby pushed open the shop's door and nearly ran outside. The hot, oppressive summer air slammed into her, just as Jake's strong arms wrapped around her. He spun her around, forcing her to face him.

"It's not ending like this." His gaze swirled with emotion. "I can't let it end like this, I love you too much—"

Abby stared at him, stunned. "What?"

"I'll do anything, Abby. Just say it. Tell me what to do, but don't leave me!" There was a desperate plea in his voice and, with numb disbelief, Abby realized she could feel his body shaking against hers.

"I know we're going to have trouble with your folks. But I can bring them around. Just give me time. I can convince them that I'll be good to you. Please, Abby, just—"

"You love me?" She asked, breaking into his rambling words.

Jake blinked and halted his mad speech.

"Do you love me?" Abby repeated, hope flaring in her breast. *Please, please let him say—*

"Of course, I love you." He looked shocked by the very idea that she might have thought otherwise. "Woman, I gave up a million dollar deal for you!"

A huge grin split Abby's lips. "You love me?"

His hands lifted, cradling her face. "Listen carefully, Abby McGill. I, Jake Steele, am completely in love with you. I've been in love with you from the moment I glanced up at that damn boring gallery opening and saw you standing next to the buffet table." His eyes shined. "You were wearing that green dress and standing to the side, looking like some kind of lost fairy princess. I took one look at you, and I knew I was staring at my future."

Tears filled her eyes, but she blinked them back. Happiness filled her. "Didn't you think you should have mentioned that little fact to me sooner?"

He shook his head slowly. "I couldn't do it. You were scared enough as it was. If I'd told you, I might have lost you." He swallowed. "It wasn't a chance I wanted to take."

"So you blackmailed me?"

Jake flushed. "I was desperate. I just wanted a chance with you, to show you how it good we could be together. I didn't want you to leave me."

Her lips trembled, then curved into a faint smile. "Crazy man! If I'd known that you loved me, there would have been no way I would have ever left your side."

He stilled. "What are you saying? Will you—"

Abby kissed him. A soft, gentle kiss. A kiss of promise. "I love you, Jake."

His arms tightened around her. "Are you sure? Because if you're not, I don't know what I'd—"

"I'm sure." And she was. Jake was *her future*. "I think I loved you from the moment I looked up at that 'damn boring gallery opening' and saw you walking toward me. You looked so mysterious and sexy. And I thought, why would a guy like that be interested in a woman like me?"

"Because you're amazing. You're beautiful, you're smart, you're kind—"

She laughed. "You really must love me."

His expression was completely serious. "I do."

Her heart pounded. "I love you." It felt good to say the words. So good. So right

"Thank God!" He buried his face in the tumble of her hair. "Woman, you've been driving me crazy! I was so afraid that you would leave me."

"No, I won't leave you." She would stay with him. Forever.

He pulled back, his face lit with hope. "Will you marry me?"

Her lips curved. "Just try to stop me." Abby had finally found the man of her dreams, the one man who she could truly trust, and she couldn't wait to spend her life with him.

"I swear, Abby, I'll make you happy—"

She touched cheek. "You already do, Jake. You already do."

Epilogue

"Are you sure about this, Abby? You know, you don't have to go through with the wedding." Martin gazed anxiously at his daughter.

Abby adjusted her veil and smiled. "I'm sure, Dad. I love Jake."

Martin sighed. "I know, baby." He took her hand in his. "But he's a got a reputation. He's dangerous, bad—"

And, soon, he would be all hers. "I know what I'm doing. Trust me."

His fingers tightened around hers. "I just want you to be happy."

"I am." Happier than she'd ever been in her life.

"If he hurts you, he's a dead man," Trent said as he walked into the room and stopped beside them. He wore a black tux similar to her father's, and his face was set in the same anxious expression as Martin's.

"I know what I'm doing," she repeated with quite confidence. "Jake's the one for me."

Her father leaned forward and kissed her cheek. "I love you, baby," he said softly. He swallowed, and Abby could have sworn she saw a tear in his eye. "And if that scoundrel makes you happy, then so be it."

Abby's lips curved. Jake had been going out of his way in the last two months to bring Martin over to his side. And while her father still wasn't what you'd call "best friends" with her husband-to-be, the two men were gradually getting on more companionable terms. *Gradually* being the keyword.

The faint sound of ringing bells drifted into the room. *It was time.* "Come on, Dad. Jake's waiting."

Trent opened the door and ushered them outside.

A loud chorus of music filled the church hall. Abby's father began to lead her down the flower-strewn aisle.

She realized her father's hand trembled as he held her. Her fingers tightened around his.

Up ahead, Jake waited for her. He stood, tall and proud, at the foot of the altar. And his gaze, his brilliant blue gaze, was filled with love, with promise.

Just a few more feet. Just a few feet away...

Her future waited for her.

About the Author:

I've wanted to be a writer for as long as I can remember. As a child, I wrote short stories all the time for my number one fan—my mother (who, of course, never, ever had anything negative to say about my fabulous misspelled work!). As I grew older, I still wrote, but the stories became longer, more complex.

After reading my first romance novel, I quickly became addicted to the genre. Now, happy endings, alpha heroes, and feisty heroines are a natural part of my life.

I would love to hear from my readers. Please visit my website at: www.cynthiaeden.com *or you may send me an email at:* info@cynthiaeden.com.

Bunko

❦

by Sheri Gilmore

To My Reader:

Creating fantasies has always been one of my favorite pastimes. I wrote my first novel, a sci-fi, when I was eight years old. Although it wasn't published, the editor who had the privilege of reading all my pencil scratches was kind enough to encourage me to "keep trying." I cannot thank him/her enough. I hope that my creations will give you, my reader, a sense of hope, happiness, adventure, and desire. If that happens, I am a success.

Chapter One

"He has got to be the most irritating man I have ever worked for." Tu let the dice slide from her hand. The spotted cubes hit the table with a *thud*, and her partner, Stacy, counted the point.

"One."

Tu picked the dice up again. "I mean, every time I submit a project, he changes the specs on me."

"Roll."

"Huh? Oh, yeah." Tu shook the dice in her hand, then let them fall.

"Bunko!" Stacy said, raising both hands above her head in victory.

Groans from the other tables echoed around the room. Women gathered their dice, pencils, and paper used to keep score.

"Snacks are in here, girls." Rickey, their hostess, waved everyone toward the kitchen. "Get settled and we'll tally the scores."

"What for? Tu has been on a roll tonight with six bunkos," one woman mumbled.

"That's my partner." Stacy patted Tu's shoulder on the way to the guacamole dip.

Tu smiled, but wished someone would answer her questions about her boss. The man drove her crazy. Instead of playing bunko, she needed to be at the office working on this *new*, new project Jack had given her earlier in the day.

"So, what's your boss... Joe, is it?... what's his problem?" Rickey asked. She munched on a salted nut, handing Tu a margarita.

"Thanks." Tu gulped the salty drink so it wouldn't spill. "It's Jack. Jack Noblin. The hardest man in the world—"

"Hey, honey, a hard man is good to find." The blender roared, causing June to shout.

Wild laughter hooted across the tiny apartment kitchen, and Tu had to join her friends at the pun their co-player had made. She nodded and held up her hand to silence the raucous group. Most of them were older than her and Stacy, and had families. She'd met them six months ago when she'd moved to New Orleans. They had made her feel right at home the first night Stacy had dragged her to their weekly game of bunko.

"I thought that line was 'a good man is hard to find'?" Tu asked, smiling at her friends.

"Not these days. I'm lucky if Warren can wake up long enough to give me a three second kiss, much less a hard-on." Nancy, a mother of three, sighed.

Giggles erupted, flowing as easily around the kitchen bar as the tequila.

"Wow, marriage sounds boring." Tu frowned. She hoped her sex-life didn't end when she said "I do." Of course, her love-life wasn't so hot at the present, either. She snorted. "We're getting off the subject, anyway. How do I tell Jack to get off my back?"

"Maybe he *wants* to be on your back. Ever think of that?" Melanie, a lady with a quick sense of humor winked at her.

"Yeah." Lucy agreed and moved around Melanie to get to the margaritas.

"What? Jack, the yuppie, with his button-up oxfords and paisley-print ties?" Tu shook her head. "Not in a million years is he trying to make a connection with me."

"Girl, how old are you?" Melanie asked.

"I'm twenty-five; what's that got to do with anything?"

"You're young and sometimes you can miss the big picture," June said.

"I've had a couple of relationships. I think I know when a man is interested."

"Yeah, how?" Rickey winked at another woman beside her.

"Well… they call all the time with stupid questions, just to keep the contact up with the girl."

"Yeah, has he done that?"

Tu frowned. Jack did come by her desk a lot. Last week he called her at home three times with changes he said were "important." "Yeah, but it was business."

"Any way they can disguise it, honey. He may say it's business, but what he wants is to get into your pants," Lucy said.

"What's he look like? A real geek?" Nancy asked.

"No! I mean, when I first met him I found him attractive." Tu shrugged. "He has gorgeous blue eyes and he's tall. About six-four, I think."

"Oooo… I like 'em tall," Melanie said.

"Um-hmm," several others agreed.

Tu smiled. She liked tall men, too, and big. At five feet, the sense of being overpowered by her man turned her on, but they never seemed to notice her. Every tall man she had ever been attracted to had always been paired with a woman who looked like a model with long legs, long blond hair and big, blue eyes.

"Go on. What color hair?"

"Forget hair, Suzanne. Does he have an ass?" Penny asked.

"Does he ever!" Stacy said through a mouthful of pretzels.

"Stacy!" Tu's mouth gaped. She'd never known Stacy found Jack cute, or otherwise.

Stacy shrugged. "What can I say? I'm normal. The man is built like a running back. Tall, lean, and the tightest buns I've ever seen. Makes me want to take a bite, ummm."

"Oh, my God." A tinge of something coiled in the pit of her stomach, as Tu studied her friend. She frowned and shook her head, realizing it was jealousy.

"Sounds like you got competition, girl." Penny nudged her. "Better start letting dat man know you realize he's alive, or he's gonna move on down da field."

"Yep, sweetie, if he looks that good, there's going to be a lot of cheerleaders waiting on the sidelines for him," June said.

"Dat's right, Tu. You wanna make him score dat first touchdown with you. Grab his balls and run, babe!" Penny nodded and grinned, causing her bauble earrings to bounce and sway.

"Penny!" Everyone turned to the oldest female in their group, laughing.

"I'm old, but I still know how to play," Penny said with a wink.

⁂

Okay, Jack, keep it professional. Obviously, Miss Tran isn't interested, so don't make an ass out of yourself.

"Miss Tran..." *Holy shit!* Jack dropped the file folder he'd been carrying. Computer printouts scattered and fell to cover the cubicle floor, but he couldn't move. His cock hardened with the visual impact of Tu Tran, his top computer programmer, in a soft, clingy, red dress.

The movement of the office chair drew his gaze to a pair of firm, toned legs, as she turned toward him. It was a sight he'd only seen in his dreams due to the fact her usual office attire consisted of faded jeans and sweatshirts. The reality almost made him come.

He choked back a groan when her shifting weight caused the dress to ride high onto her thighs. For a petite girl, she had perfect proportions, which the dress molded—the most edible breasts that he'd imagined cupping in the palms of his hands a dozen times.

I could almost wrap my hands around her twice. He caught himself when his arms lifted from his side. Dragging his gaze down to her feet, he gulped at the sight of a pair of red, high-heeled, sandals. Her toes wiggled, emphasizing the red-painted nails.

A lump formed in this throat. He pulled hard on his tie. Sweat beaded across his forehead. His hand eased to adjust the crotch of his khakis into a less constricting bind, but he caught himself, again, before he'd completed the motion. He cleared his throat.

"Um... excuse me." He bent to retrieve the papers he'd dropped. "I, uh, I wanted to show you last month's report."

He looked up and realized his mistake. From this angle, his view settled level with her hips. He forced his gaze to make contact with her face, and had to bite his tongue to suppress the groan that worked its way up into his throat to escape.

Gorgeous just didn't begin to describe what sat in front of him. The tomboy he'd been fantasizing about for the last several months had disappeared to be replaced by an Asian goddess with red lips the color of her dress. The application of eye shadow and mascara emphasized exotic, brown eyes. An entire new series of fantasies took shape in his mind for his private perusal later that night when he would be alone.

At that moment she uncrossed her legs, and the skirt of the dress rose higher. His gaze shifted to be snared by the sight of red, silk panties. He tried to look away, but couldn't.

"Would you like me to help you?" Her words flowed warm, like the silk of those panties, over his skin.

Would I ever! He shook his head; looked back at her face and… blinked.

Pouty, red lips parted into a seductive smile to expose tiny, white teeth. In his mind, Jack could feel those same teeth nip across his skin, latching onto his dick, then…

"Mr. Noblin?"

"Huh?" He focused on reality. "Oh. Yes, yes that would be great. I didn't mean to make such a mess, but… Are you going on a lunch date?"

Where had that come from? He mentally slapped himself in the forehead. Now, she would think he was interested in her private life. *You are, you fool! What if she's on her way to screw some guy during her lunch hour, while you've wasted three months with stupid games to get her to notice you?*

"No, why?"

"Oh, I just wondered. You don't usually wear a dress to work, or wear makeup." *Great! Now you're telling her she normally looks like a sack of potatoes.* Which was a lie. He loved the way she looked every day, with or without clothes. He raked his hand through his hair at the thought of Tu Tran naked. *Damn!*

"Well, I—"

"Look, it's none of my business. Forget I asked, okay? If you have time in your busy social schedule, could you possibly get this report done today?" Jack cringed at the sharpness of his tone and the look on her face. Her smile faded to be replaced by the customary frown she wore whenever they were together. Obviously, she wasn't interested in him.

Chapter Two

Unbelievable! She'd give anything to tell the arrogant, sonofabitch to stuff his report, but she needed her job. It had taken her two months to find this position. She couldn't afford to be unemployed with a new condo and new car.

She bit the inside of her lip, leaning forward to pick up the report.

Why did I listen to those crazy women, anyway? Getting dressed up, all sexy, just to have him cut me down again. Well, this would be the last time she'd go out on a limb for any man. If they wanted her, they'd have to take her like she was, blue jeans and all. It had taken her three days to dredge up enough nerve to dress up, but it hadn't worked. The signals weren't what her friends at bunko had thought. She looked at her boss's retreating backside and swallowed.

Too, bad. He really did have a fine ass.

❋⟪♡⟫❋

"Well, how did it go? Did he like the dress and makeup?"

"Are you kidding? He was so busy barking orders about his precious report, he didn't even notice."

Someone coughed, like they were choking, at the table across the partition from them, but Tu ignored them, hoping someone else at the restaurant knew the Heimlich maneuver if the poor soul choked. She had problems of her own. She stabbed one of the shrimp on her plate.

"He's so anal. I bet the only position he knows is missionary style." She popped the shrimp into her mouth, and the coughing grew louder. She frowned, but continued speaking through the intrusion.

"I can just hear him. 'No, move this way. No, lie still. A little more to the right.'"

Stacy doubled over with laughter at Tu's imitation of Jack's deep, New Orleans accent. Tu laughed, too. If she didn't laugh, she might just cry. He'd disappointed her when he hadn't noticed the changes she'd made for him.

"You, know, I might just go trollin' tonight."

"What? You've turned down my suggestions about finding a *fuck buddy* since you moved here. What gives?"

"Jack Noblin, that's what. With all that talk the other night about how he might be attracted to me, I got zero to nil sleep all week with all the yummy sexual things I wanted to do to him and vice versa."

"Yeah? Like what?" Stacy's gaze widened in an eager expression.

Tu twirled her pasta around her plate and smiled at Stacy. She shrugged and looked around the restaurant. No one could hear them over the hum of the lunch crowd. She leaned forward. "Well, I was hoping he'd call me into his office and plop me up on that big, wide desk of his, you know?"

"Go on." Stacy's mouth lay open in a pant.

"I was going to surprise him with my panties. They're crotchless."

"Get outta here! You?"

"Yeah, I bought them when Sam and I were dating, but he's like Jack, not interested in anything kinky, or fun."

"Bummer."

"Yeah. Story of my life." A wave of depression washed over her. "I've got all this wild, sexual need inside me, but nobody to wipe it on. Know what I mean?"

"Um," Stacy said. Both grew silent, took several sips from their bottled drinks, and sighed.

Tu slammed her beer on the table. "You know what? I'm tired of living without good sex. If I can't have a meaningful relationship with a guy, I'm going to find a *friend* to take the edge off with every now and then."

"That's my girl. I'm with you all the way." Stacy held up her beer. "Cheers."

"Cheers."

The sound of their bottles, clinking in agreement, mingled with their giggles.

※(☉)※

Fuck buddy, huh? He'd show her *fuck buddy.*

Jack remained seated behind the wooden partition, which separated his table from Tu's. He'd been on the verge of revealing his presence when her friend had asked her if *he* had noticed her dress. He wanted to know more about the guy, who could get Tu Tran so interested, she'd dress up. Hell, he'd spewed beer all over his plate when he realized the two women were talking about him.

If Tu had ever been interested, he'd never noticed. He'd singled her out numerous times over the past month without any indication from her she found him attractive. Not one smile did she give him. Until today. Two days *after* he'd decided to look elsewhere for some fun. *Fun.* He'd show her fun.

He waited a good twenty minutes before he left the restaurant and returned to the office. He couldn't take a chance on her seeing him. He made his way around to the back elevators. When the doors closed, he punched the number of his floor so hard, his finger throbbed.

Yeah, he had a surprise or two for Miss Tu Tran. All that talk about him not knowing anything but the missionary position. "Hah! I'll have her know my favorite position will be in her tight... little... ass."

He didn't realize he'd spoken out loud, but the surprised gasps of two little, old ladies startled him. They huddled together against the far left wall of the elevator, eyeing him like he was a serial rapist.

Heat rose from beneath his collar, spreading across his cheeks. He adjusted his tie, averting his gaze to his right. A young man in his early twenties gave him a slow wink, puckering his lips into a kiss.

Damn!

The elevator *pinged* and the doors opened. The young man gave him one last wink and walked out. The women edged to the opening.

"Ladies." He nodded and gave them a tight smile. He moved his hand to hold the door for them, but they gave a little screech and rushed out.

Jack gritted his teeth to prevent himself from cussing. By the end of the day, half the building would think he was gay, and the other half would think he was a sexual predator. "Tu Tran, payback is going to be hell."

ﾒ❦✾

"Okay, give me... oh... say two hours and I'll meet you there. Yeah, great. Be scoping out the guys for me. Bye!" Tu giggled and twirled her chair around. After five months of celibacy, the prospect of sex had her hot and ready. She hugged herself, feeling so happy, she could sing. "Tonight... hummm... is the night... hummm... gonna make everrrrythinnng... feeeeel... alright."

"I hate to interrupt your recording session, but do you think you could step into my office before you leave?"

"Oh." She clutched her chest. "You scared the hell out of me!"

"Sorry."

Jack Noblin didn't look sorry. If anything, his expression was smug. Tu turned her back to him. The sound of his footsteps faded as he walked away from the cubicle.

She rolled her gaze to the ceiling. *I am not working late tonight. He can forget it!* Grabbing her purse, she strode to his office. At the sight of the closed door, she hesitated. *That's odd.*

She knocked and waited.

No response.

Knocking again, louder, she glanced around. Everyone else had gone for the day. Maybe he thought she hadn't intended to acknowledge his request when she'd turned her back on him. Tu tried the handle, and the knob turned. With a shrug she pushed the door wide enough to go through.

"Mr. Noblin?"

She walked a little farther and stopped when she noticed a light shining under the restroom door. With an impatient sigh and quick peek at her watch, she plopped into the plush leather chair in front of his desk. *If he makes me late—*

Flinging her purse into the opposite chair, the desk she'd told Stacy about caught Tu's attention. The wood gleamed so dark and smooth that a person could see their reflection in the polish. She closed her eyes and imagined being tied to the top. Spread out for Jack Noblin's pleasure.

She snorted, opening her eyes. No sense in wasting thoughts on that prospect, but leaning forward, she couldn't help the masochistic urge to rub her hands over the wood's perfection.

Cool to the touch, a ripple of need shafted from her clit into stomach where it twisted into a knot. A whimper of desire escaped her lips, but evaporated as the lights went out, casting the entire room in darkness.

Tu sat still for several seconds, waiting for Jack to come out of the restroom. When he didn't, and the lights didn't come back on, she shifted in her chair.

Great! Now, she would have to feel her way out of here and pray the emergency lights in the outer office were activated, so she could make her way to the stairs. She stood.

"Where are you going?" The words slithered, warm and coaxing, over her neck.

The skin on her arms tingled with goose bumps at the sound of the deep, masculine voice. She knew who spoke, but the sound of Jack's voice in the pitch black made her weak at the knees.

"I don't know." She sounded out of breath, like she'd been running. In fact, she placed a hand on her chest where her heartbeat pounded hard against her ribs. She turned in the direction she'd heard his voice.

"Then, why don't you stay for..."—his fingers feathered across her hand, still on the desk— "... a while."

Tu sucked in a deep breath at the sensation of his skin against hers. Moisture pooled, trickling through the open seams of the crotchless panties. *Dear God, I'm going to come at the sound of his voice.*

She pictured his long, tapered fingers, as they trailed over her hands, then up and down her arms to her wrists. Once there, he tightened his grip and pulled her closer to his body. His erection pressed long, hard, and thick into her lower back.

She gasped.

His laugh sounded husky against her ear, a mere whisper in the dark, and she shivered. "Does it scare you?"

"No." She wondered why they whispered when no one else could hear them. The cleaning crew never got here this early.

"Good, because I want you to get to know it up close and personal." He kissed her temple and moved his hips in an up and back motion. His erection rubbed along the crevice of her buttocks.

Clenching her fingers against the hot waves of primal instinct telling her to throw him onto the floor and have her way, Tu forced an objection from between her teeth. "J-Jack, I don't know about this."

She would have never guessed Jack Noblin would behave in this fashion.

"Sure you do." He nibbled her earlobe. "I heard you and Stacy talking at lunch."

Tu tensed. *Oh, my God.*

His hands squeezed her wrists for a second. "It's okay, Tu. I've been trying to catch your interest for a month, but you never seemed to notice me *in that way.*" He leaned around her toward the desk.

Objects shuffled and bumped, while he hastily shoved them out of the way. He made a satisfied sound in his throat. "There we go."

"What?"

"You'll see. Now, come around here..." —he led her around the desk— "... and sit right there." He pushed her butt against the edge of the cool wood. She wasn't quite tall enough to sit, but that didn't deter him from his goal. He moved in front of her, but kept a grip on her wrists with one hand.

The rustle of their clothes brushing together tickled her ears, but when his mouth fastened to hers with a flick of his tongue against her teeth and lips, her nipples constricted into hardened points, scrubbing against the material of her dress.

The unexpected sensation shot through her system, straight to her clit. She jumped, pulling back. "Oh."

"You like?" His lips followed her retreat, nibbling and biting.

"I-I don't know." *Hell, yes, she liked.*

"Then, let's try this again."

Her heart beat faster with fear and excitement at her fantasy of being *his* prisoner, but before she could voice her desire, his large hands spanned her waist, lifting her onto the desktop. His face drew level with hers. A puff of his breath, hot and minty, fanned her face, forcing a wave of desire to swamp her sensitized nerves.

If he didn't hurry up and kiss her, she was going to crawl the wall. The burning ache between her legs increased, flaming into an inferno. Tu wiggled her hips against the desk. She needed some action. A "mewing" sound echoed around them, and she realized it came from her. She bit her lip, almost ashamed of her response, but not quite.

"Miss Impatient, hmm?" Jack's hands slid back to her waist and he eased her farther onto the desk.

The rough caress of his hands over her body sent a thrill of pure lust through her. Tu lifted her hands to the collar of his shirt. Her fingers tightened around the material as she tried to ease closer to his heat. When his hand trailed up her back and tunneled beneath her hair, massaging her neck, Tu leaned her head into his touch and moaned.

He shifted closer, and his lips brushed hers in a light caress. She parted her lips, closing her eyes in anticipation of their first kiss, but it never came. She opened her eyes and tried to read his expression in the dark, but couldn't.

His chest moved with a deep chuckle. "I think I'm going to like making you wait."

Chapter Three

Make her wait, hell! He didn't think *he* could wait. His hands shook, a thin blanket of sweat coated his body, and his crotch felt like he needed a fire extinguisher to put out the flames at any second. It wasn't every day a guy lived out one of his sexual fantasies.

Jack positioned her hips on the desktop and stretched her legs out, careful to let his fingertips graze the inside of her thighs. If he kept her distracted, maybe she wouldn't notice how nervous he was.

She moaned again, and he thought he'd come from the sound. To Tran excited was one orgasmic experience, and he wondered what she sounded like when she came. The thought made him harder. He pushed her back onto the desk and grabbed her wrists, pulling them away from their bodies. Kissing her hard, he let his fingers explore the little curves he'd been admiring for weeks.

He'd spent all afternoon fantasizing about this little tryst. He'd called the cleaning crew and informed them to take the night off due to his need to work *overtime* without any distractions. He'd even run down the street to the nearest drugstore and bought a box of condoms. Jack reached into the side drawer. *Yep, right where he'd left them.* He'd bought enough to go all night. He laughed. *And, we won't be in the missionary position, not once.*

"Oh, come on, Jack, I'm ready for some action."

He groaned at the sound of his name on her lips. He couldn't take the wait any longer. With a groan, he slid his hands up her bare arms, caught her wrists, pulling them tight above her head.

She cried out with the sudden movement. Jack hoped he hadn't hurt her, but on second thought, maybe a little pain would be fun. He thought of the leather, beaded cat 'o nine tails he had hidden in his bedside drawer at home, and he pulled her arms higher. He smiled when her breath hissed from her lips. He leaned down and nuzzled her neck. "I want you to hold on to the edge of the desk with both hands and don't let go."

He'd checked her dress over from the safety of his office earlier. He knew a back zipper would release the snug fit from her body, and with a flick of his letter opener, he could cut the straps and slide the silky material down her body and legs with relative ease.

When he knew she gripped the desk behind her head like he'd instructed,

Jack retrieved the letter opener. He moved over her with his lips a mere half-inch from her mouth, but he didn't kiss her. He'd make her beg before he gave in to her. A little payback for what she'd said at lunch.

She gave a frustrated groan and raised her head to his, but he pulled back. "Jack!"

"Tu."

"Kiss me, dammit."

He could hear her demand come from between clenched teeth, and smiled. "Not yet, Miss Tu." He unzipped the dress. Sliding his hand up, he wrapped a finger through the thin spaghetti strap. "You've been driving me crazy for the last two months."

He trailed the letter opener over the skin above her breasts

A gasp escaped her lips, and her eyes widened in the dim light of the office.

"It's my turn." With a quick flick of his wrist the material cut free, and he moved to the second strap. Her body tensed.

As the opener slid beneath the strap, her muscles quivered and corded in her abdomen. Jack hesitated over the dress, but decided to leave it on for the moment. He trailed his fingers down her legs, then over the thin straps of her shoes to tap the end of one sharp heel. His erection surged, and he closed his eyes against his secret fetish for high-heels. Before the end of this night, he would have her wrap those legs around his waist and dig her heels into his back. Sweat beaded across his lip at the prospect.

Gritting his teeth, he circled his hand around one of her ankles. He spread her legs wider, then rose from his squatted position at the side of the desk. "Now, don't move. I'm going to take my time. I want to hear you beg me to take you in every position you've ever wondered about, *except* missionary."

Her breaths panted, short and ragged. "You heard… that part, too?"

"I definitely heard that part, and plan to change your mind about my sexual positioning preferences." He couldn't stop the hard note in his voice from seeping into his words. She had really wounded his ego with that remark.

He sank his teeth into the soft flesh of her side, liking how she arched into him in response.

"I-I never had a clue you were like this."

"Like what?" he asked, flicking his tongue over the same spot he had bitten.

"Well, you know…" —she swallowed hard in the still room—"… kinky."

"You have no idea." His voice sounded authoritative and sinister. He smiled at the evil tone, adding to the sexual tension swirling around them. He pulled at the buttons on his shirt.

Hmm. He could get into this dominance stuff.

Damn! She could get into this dominance stuff. When Jack had pulled her arms up tight, she had wanted to come. And, his voice… oh, my God! Moisture from her sex eased down to tickle the cleft between her buttocks. How could she tell him she wanted him to take her where those warm juices mingled without sounding like a slut?

Listening to the rustle of clothing, Tu sensed him moving in the darkness. She swallowed hard and squeezed her pelvic muscles tight against the quiver in her clit. The touch of his long, cool fingers on her ankles at a point above her shoe strap made her jump. His lips followed his fingers, traveling up her calves, first one leg, then the other.

She pulled against the edge of the desk and twisted her hands, but she couldn't move far without releasing her grip. She knew she could if she wanted, but she didn't want to. Her curiosity craved to see where this fantasy would lead.

His tongue flicked at an area on the underside of her knee and tiny quivers shot up her thigh to her abdomen. Her groan, a sound of agony and pleasure wrapped together, escaped her lips. "Jaaaack…"

Tingling spread over her skin from her feet to her head. Her heart beat crashed against her chest. If he didn't hurry up and *do something*, she would die. Tu pulled harder against the invisible rope that held her hands prisoner above her head. "Jack, pleeease."

At that second, his tongue and lips latched onto the sensitive area of her inner thigh, and her hips jerked off the surface of the desk, forcing the hem of her dress higher up her thighs. Large hands grasped her hips, holding her in place while he feasted on her skin.

Tu arched her neck and head against the tremors that spread from her abdomen down to her feet, but right when she reached the verge of orgasm, Jack pulled back.

"Not yet." He eased away from the side of the desk. He laughed, feathering his fingers across her abdomen beneath her dress. "You're such a hot, little number. We need to cool you off."

Tu gritted her teeth. *Damn him.* He only had to move his hand lower, or swipe his tongue across her panties, and she'd go over the edge. Instead, each of his hands settled on the inside of her thighs, spreading her legs wider. The palm of his right hand rested, large and warm, on her pubis.

Tu gasped at the extreme heat through the thin barrier of her silk panties. Her muscles contracted and flexed in anticipation of him placing those long, thick fingers inside her body.

One finger skimmed beneath the edge of the panties to trace along the outside folds of her vulva. Up one side and down the other, he teased her. The sensations melded into a rhythm. His thumb eased beneath the silk and circled over her most erogenous spot.

"Ummm, that's good." She spread her legs apart as far as she could, so he'd have better access. "Faster, Jack."

He did better. His hot tongue swirled across her panties and clit, and she clutched the edge of the desk and pulled hard. Jack's tongue continued to flick through the thin material.

Her mind swirled with the need to come, and she sobbed, "Yes. God, that feels so good."

"Hmm, I want to hear you scream when you orgasm." He pulled back away from her clit, but leaned forward to press a trail of kisses across her abdomen. "Makes me hard as a brick and two inches longer."

Tu laughed. "Yeah? Just how long are you?"

"Long enough." A note of pride was evident in his voice.

She gulped, then shivered, hoping he was exaggerating, but not. He had to make her come soon, or she'd take matters into her own hands.

"Don't worry, you'll be able to take me." His large body eased up onto the desk between her legs, nibbling with his mouth up the length of her body. The scratch of his clothes against the inside of her thighs made her squirm further. "We'll go nice and slow until that sweet little puss gobbles me up."

His mouth covered hers, and their tongues swirled together. His lips nipped and sucked, teasing her to the point of no return. She tasted him for the first time, and moaned. "Do-Do you taste this good all over?"

He stilled. "What do you mean?"

She heard the laughter in his voice. "I want us to go down on each other at the same time, and I was wondering if your cock was salty, like I like them."

His erection throbbed against her belly at her words.

"First, I have to get us out of these clothes." His words continued, but her thoughts and fantasies swirled out of proportion at the thought of them living her fantasies on top of Jack's desk.

Her mind snapped back to catch the end of what he'd been saying.

"… if you can handle me." His fingers curled around the curve of her hip, digging into the flesh of her buttock.

Tu squirmed. "What did you—?"

"Jack?"

Tu and Jack stilled at the same instant the feminine voice echoed from the doorway. An eternity passed before Jack muttered "Shit" under his breath.

He scrambled off her to the front of the desk just as the overhead light came on with a *click.*

"Oh… my goodness." The woman sounded surprised, but laughed. "Jack."

"Donna, let me explain."

Chapter Four

"Donna? I think you need to be explaining a few things to me!"

Jack shut his eyes against the anger in Tu's voice. He knew he had screwed up big time. He'd forgotten the date he'd made with his old girlfriend two days ago when he'd decided Tu wasn't interested in him. The sight of Tu's dress combined with what he'd heard at lunch had blown his mind. In his lapse of restraint he'd forgotten to call Donna and cancel their date tonight.

"Tu, it's not what you think." With his hands up in a pleading gesture, he turned his body halfway toward her.

Her fists were clenched and her dress lay hiked-up around her upper thighs. The sight of the red high-heels had him glancing back up her body to meet her narrowed gaze. A black eyebrow arched as if to say, "Really? Tell me another lie."

He flinched. *I'm in deep shit.* Not knowing what to say to Tu, he turned back to his ex-girlfriend. "Donna. I forgot to call and cancel our date."

He followed the tall blond's gaze to see his erection outlined through his khakis, then to what she could see of Tu, which was quite a bit, stretched out across his desk.

Donna smiled. "I can see why it might have slipped your mind."

Jack's shoulders relaxed. *Okay, she understands. Great.*

"I didn't know you went for... short... women."

Behind him Tu's heels scraped and gouged furrows across his desk. "Let me up, and I'll show her short."

"Tu." Jack placed a hand on her shoulder to keep her in place, turning from one woman to the other. The tension returned with full force to his shoulders. "Donna, that was uncalled for." He knew the blame for this mess fell on him, but Donna didn't have to be so nasty.

"I'm not going to apologize." Donna pulled out her keys and snapped her purse shut. "When you're through playing with your *secretary*, call me."

"Secretary?" The heels scraped louder, and the door shut with a bang.

"Tu—"

"Let... me... off... this... desk. Now!"

Jack released a sigh, and decided he'd better let her cool off before he tried to explain about his ex-girlfriend. He released the grip to her shoulder. When she stood, he caught the slight musky scent of recent arousal and his cock hardened further. He stepped toward her.

"Don't get any ideas, buster."

Heat spread across his cheeks and he cursed his fair skin. He couldn't control how his body responded to hers. Hell, he'd tried for the last two months, and look where it had led him. He glanced down at his unbuttoned shirt, saw his white undershirt, and shook his head.

The irony hit hard. Here he was fully dressed, with a hard-on bigger than Texas, while in the middle of his office an Asian beauty had lain across his desk, practically naked. Now, she hated his guts. The trust she may have felt with him had been crushed.

"Don't worry, Miss Tran. You're safe." He leaned over her and placed the letter opener in the top drawer. "For now."

When she stood, he stepped several feet away in case his body overrode his mind and he reached for her. He looked into her beautiful, almond-shaped eyes, reflecting anger and hurt.

He didn't blame her. "I'm sorry, Tu. I really did forget to cancel my date with Donna. I started planning all this today after I saw your dress."

Wrong thing to say, buddy!

She clutched her dress to her chest, and he backed away to give her some extra space. Her throat worked up and down, like she swallowed hard, and Jack could swear tears glistened in her eyes.

Ah, man. Now, he did feel like crap. He hated when a woman cried. He never knew if he should hold her, or run like hell. In this case, he'd bet he shouldn't touch her.

Tu didn't say a word. She held her head high.

Okay, I was right. She doesn't want me to touch her. Fine. He clenched his jaw and slid a hand through his hair. He turned to button his shirt. He couldn't have a serious conversation with her half-dressed.

She must have had the same thought, because the sound of her arranging her dress forced images of the silky material sliding over her smooth skin into his mind. He flinched at the pain from his over tight pants when he tucked his shirt into the waistband.

A drawer slid open and he turned to watch her. With shaky fingers, she took two safety pins and adjusted the cut straps. When she finished she walked around the desk to pick up her purse. She didn't hesitate in her movements, and reached the door in four steps. When she turned the knob, she faced him, but wouldn't meet his gaze. "Well, have a good weekend. I'll see you on Monday."

"Tu—"

"Goodnight, Mr. Noblin." Her tone sounded final, and Jack decided not to push her, but one way or another she would be in his bed before long.

"I thought you'd be here already. It's been three hours. Where have you been?"

"I-I couldn't decide what to wear." No way could she tell Stacy about her encounter with Jack and his female friend. The embarrassment alone would kill what ego she had left.

Tu remembered Donna, now. Jack had dated her several months ago. She thought they were history. She hadn't realized he didn't have a problem sleeping with one woman while dating another. Tu snorted and adjusted her mask. Too bad for him that she did. If he wanted her, then the blond bimbo had to go.

What was she saying? She had no intention of letting what had happened a couple of hours ago continue beyond those few brief moments, so she didn't need worry about it. She might like kinky, but she didn't like sharing her man with someone like *Barbie* with her fake boobs, fake tan, and bleached blond hair. She motioned to the bartender. "Give me a beer."

When she'd paid for the bottle, she looked around the club at the possible prospects for the night. She'd show *him*. She'd get her a real stud to be her *fuck huddy*. "What have you got for me, Stacy?"

Stacy stood next to her and wiggled her hips to the music. "Hmm…" —she took a swig of her beer—"… I've been looking, but it's hard to see their faces with these Mardi Gras masks on."

"Well, look at their bodies. I'm not studying their faces. The lights will be off."

"Oh. Okay. In that case the guy over there by the pool table." Stacy angled her head, smiling and wagging her eyebrows over the top of her mask. "He's been here for about an hour, and hasn't hit on anyone. Looks yummy from the back view, but I can't see the front."

Tu turned her head to the side. The view revealed tight buttocks hugged, lovingly, by faded denim. An occasional tear could be noted in all the *right* places. Heat curled low in her abdomen. "Nice ass."

"Yeah, I thought you'd like him." Stacy giggled, focusing her attention on a cute one dressed in a green outfit like a joker with a purple and gold mask painted on his face.

"What about you?" Tu asked, wondering again at her friend's choice of men.

"W-What?" Stacy asked, keeping her eyes on the clown.

Tu looked toward the ceiling, and blew out a slow breath. Her friend could be a ditz some times. "Have you found yourself a guy?"

"Not yet." Stacy turned back to her with what looked like a lot of effort.

Tu shook her head. "What about that one? She frowned and gave a quick nod toward the harlequin, who was getting away.

Stacy shrugged. "Nah, too comical."

"You want the guy you chose for me?" Tu asked, crossing her mental fingers that Stacy didn't.

"No. He's a little on the rough side. I'm not sure you should get involved with someone like that, Tu."

"Why on earth not?" Tu let her gaze travel over the length of long legs, firm buttocks and back, to the wide shoulders, as the guy bent over the table to shoot.

"He's dangerous looking." Stacy's serious features didn't faze Tu.

"Exactly. Here's the plan. We'll go over there together and put our quarters on the table for the next match. Maybe he'll notice one of us."

"I hope not me!"

Tu grabbed Stacy's arm, pulling her friend behind her, as they eased through the crowd toward the pool tables. Suddenly, Tu hoped the guy would pick Stacy. He rated *major stud muffin*, but she didn't feel in the mood anymore. What had happened earlier still had her angry.

No, it wasn't anger. She bit her lip and hesitated before stepping up onto the raised area where the pool tables were positioned. *My feelings are hurt more than anything.* Besides the fact she'd been cheated out of an orgasm, she had wanted Jack to be *the one*.

She gave herself a mental shake. *But, he's not.*

Her foot connected with the second step and her momentum pushed her forward. Reaching the table, Tu dug several quarters out of her jeans pocket and placed them on the side to mark she had the next game without glancing at the group of men around the table.

A warm hand, strong and masculine, covered hers at the same time a very male body pressed close behind her. His height dwarfed her diminutive stature, giving her the impression of being overpowered. She shivered.

Warmth and the scent of spicy cologne wrapped around her, while his erection throbbed against her lower back. Her clit responded with an excited twitch, acknowledging the sexual awareness of his body.

"If you want to play games, then you need to come on home with me, babe."

Tu's spine stiffened at the husky voice in her ear, but didn't pull her hand away. She glanced at Stacy, who watched them with a curious expression on her face. She caught her friend's eye. Stacy frowned, but nodded. Tu relaxed.

"What kind of games are you talking about?" she asked, without turning. If Stacy said the guy was "okay," then she didn't have a problem with him. Besides, it might be fun to flirt a little. She didn't have to go home with him.

"The kind grown-ups play when they want to have sex."

Well, the guy earned kudos for getting straight to the point. "And, do you want to play a game with me?" Tu turned with a smile, which faded, then stared. A chill shot down her spine at the sight of the ugliest, scariest mask she'd ever seen.

The red face had a large, prominent nose with flared nostrils. Fanged teeth filled the wide mouth, except for a hole, large enough for his tongue to fit through and allow him to talk and drink, or other, more erotic things.

Whoa, baby. Tu bit her lip to hold her giggle at the impromptu thought and continued her perusal. What caught her attention most were the mask's pointed ears and horns above the vicious scowl of the eyes. She hoped he wouldn't demand any human sacrifices. With eye sockets, dark and recessed, she couldn't see the color of the man's eyes, but she felt his intense stare. A thrill of unexpected anticipation flowed through her.

This man and Jack Noblin were polar opposites. Even if Jack had surprised her in more ways than one tonight, this one made the hair on her arms stand on end, and she knew she'd found her *fuck buddy*.

The mask tilted at an angle, like a wolf checking out the captured mouse he was about to throw around for fun right before he ate it. "You know I do."

Chapter Five

"Two."

"Dat's tree, Tu. We hit dem twos five minutes ago. Where you be, *Cher*?" Penny asked.

"Probably thinking about her new friend, Dev," Stacy said, shaking the dice hard and throwing them across the table. "Bunko!"

"Ahhhh." All the women moaned in unison, except Stacy and Tu, who gave each other a high five.

"You two won last week. What's the deal?" Rickey asked.

"I dunno. Ask Tu. She's the lucky one this week," Stacy said, grabbing a bag of pretzels.

"Okay, Tu, who's Dev, and how come you're so hot?" Pam asked in between bites of taco salad.

Tu laughed. "I'm not *hot*." She narrowed her gaze at Stacy, but either her friend didn't see the look, or she ignored Tu's glare. She didn't want to discuss *Dev*. He was her secret. The stuff they had done together would make a porn star look like a choir girl.

Correction. He is a secret. She didn't know anymore about him than she did the first few minutes she'd met him this past weekend. The only thing she knew for certain was his agility around a girl's bed and body. There could be no other word for the man, except "phenomenal." She shivered every time she thought of the positions he'd introduced to her, which had the same mind-blowing results—the greatest orgasms she'd ever had.

"Earth to Tu. Come back down, girl." Rickey snapped her fingers in front of Tu's face.

Tu blinked, then looked around at everyone's expectant gaze. Heat rose up her neck and spread across her face. "Uh, sorry, I was just... thinking."

"Uh huh. Wanna share?" Penny asked. "We were de ones who told you to make a move on Joe... Wait a minute. Who's Dev? Dat's not your boss!"

"Jack. That's my boss, and, well, that didn't work out. Stacy and I went out the other night and I met someone." The blush throbbed hotter. "He's real... nice."

Stacy snorted, then coughed when she choked. Rickey patted her on the back with a frown. "Are you real involved with this guy?" she asked.

"W-water. I need water," Stacy said, stumbling into the kitchen.

Coward! Tu watched her friend's retreat and felt herself surrounded by the older women in the bunko group. She shifted her weight from one foot to the other.

"Well, kinda. I mean, sorta involved, yeah." She nodded and then shook her head, not sure what she meant.

"Oh, kiddo, you gotta be careful," Penny said, and put an arm around her shoulders. "Dey be a lot of weirdos in dis city."

"Yeah, Tu, hon. He might look normal, but could be a real freakazoid underneath," Melanie said.

You might could say that about him. After all she still didn't know his name. *Dev* was short for *Devil*, and she'd gotten that from the mask he wore when they had been together the other night, which was weird and sexy at the same time. She didn't know where he lived, what his phone number was, or what kind of vehicle he drove.

Okay, okay, he's a freakazoid, but... Damn, the boy could make her come like... well, like no other man she'd ever been with. "Look, I know you all are trying to look after me, and I really appreciate it."

She held her hands up, but close to her body to stop her friends' rambling, and looked at the floor. "I'm a big girl, and I think I can handle a no strings attached relationship. In fact, that's what I need right now."

Penny nodded and looked around the group. "He's a *fuck buddy.*"

"Penny!" Everyone shouted in unison. Laughter mingled with gasps of shock.

"Well, actually..." —everyone turned back to her—"... I call him my *fuck buddy,*" Tu said with a squeak, then coughed at the shocked expressions she received.

⁂

Tu watched Jack cross the main floor and enter his office. She'd refused to answer his calls to her house the last few days, and the only time they'd spoken since the incident on his desk had been when he gave her new specs for the project she was working on. He hadn't been rude, or even suggestive toward her at work. Just businesslike, as if the entire incident had never happened.

Tu looked at the spreadsheet on her desk and frowned at the code, not really seeing it, but his hands. A suspicion had formed in her mind earlier that morning when Jack had handed her some new specs. His hands had looked familiar.

She shifted in her chair, glancing at the windows of Jack's office. *Nah, it's just my imagination.* She picked up a pencil and tapped it against the report.

Dev's hands are bigger. What are you talking about? Dev is bigger all over! Moisture pooled in the crotch of her panties, and she had to cross her legs to stem the flood of desire. She closed her eyes and performed some deep breathing exercises. In, out. In, out. She moved her hands in a circular motion to help the technique. There, much—

"Ahem."

Tu gasped and her eyes opened wide. Jack leaned against the wall of her cubicle with a strange look on his face, which disappeared when their eyes met.

"You scared me!"

"Sorry." He shoved his hands into his pockets. "I need you to forget the changes to the AP module I mentioned this morning. I've got some new specifications to add to the list."

Her nostrils flared, and she peered at him through narrowed eyes. "Sorry? You're not sorry one damn bit. You're trying to make my life here a living night—" She slapped a hand over her mouth, horrified at what she'd accused him of.

A flash of anger crossed his face, but after a second it disappeared into the smooth, calm features she saw every day.

"Tu, I know you're upset with me, but I am not trying to make your life miserable. This is work and I know we both can be professional."

She nodded. Shame coursed through her, and here he stood, taking everything in stride. Inspecting him closer, her eyebrow rose.

Jack's stance was anything but nonchalant at the moment. His long legs paced the narrow space of her cubicle. His hands were still in his pockets, jingling his change with increased agitation. A muscle ticked along his jaw and his mouth had set into a thin line.

So, he is mad. She didn't blame him. Tu rubbed a hand across her face and took a deep breath. If she didn't get a grip she'd be in the unemployment line this afternoon. "J-Jack, I'm sorry, really. I'm not getting a lot of sleep, and this project is driving me crazy. I'll have the new requirements implemented into the program today. I promise."

Tu hated to grovel, but what could she do? This was her job, and she was letting Dev interfere. She'd have to cool their relationship down a bit. *Relationship?* She snorted. They didn't have a relationship. They had enjoyed one night of satisfying sex. She shook her head.

"Am I interrupting something?"

"Oh." She sat up. "No. I'm just trying to figure out how to… make some changes." She patted the report and smiled up at Jack. She prayed he bought the line. It sounded pretty lame to her.

Her mind wandered when she realized she didn't have Dev's number to call and tell him she couldn't see him anymore. He had asked if he could come by sometime and she'd agreed. She looked at Jack.

He wasn't smiling, and his expression looked wary, but concerned. The next second he hunched down beside her chair so close she could feel his breath against her cheek.

Tu scooted back in her chair.

His hand brushed her shoulder. "What's wrong?"

"N-nothing."

"Look, about the other night, I'm sorry, really."

"No, no, it's not that, Jack." Tu glanced at his hand, which lay across her desk top to her side, without him noticing. She studied it closely, but she couldn't remember Dev. It was Jack's touch and kiss from the other night that she recalled.

She found herself breathing in Jack's scent to see if he smelled like Dev, but he didn't. The spicy cologne that Dev wore was overpowering, while Jack smelled like lemony-scented soap, clean and fresh.

Tu swallowed her frustration. The two men were extreme opposites, and she wanted both of them. She gasped. *What kind of slut-puppy am I?*

"Go out for dinner and a movie with me?"

"Excuse me?"

Jack's thumb brushed the nape of her neck. He leaned closer. His lips tickled the lobe of her ear, and little shivers of desire skittered across her skin. "I asked if you'd go out with me, and let me apologize for the other night."

"When?"

"Tonight. Nothing fancy. Just relaxed."

᙮᙭(ᵔᵕᵔ)᙭᙮

Tonight? Was he crazy? Jack ran a hand through his hair. He'd sworn off Miss Tran for any serious relationship after he'd seen her in action at that club down on Bourbon Street the other night. It had taken her all of ten minutes to accept some pick up line from a stranger and drag him back to her place. The things she'd done to that guy would make a porn star blush.

Five minutes later he pulled up to her curb and parked. The quiet of the street at this early hour surprised him. The neighborhood lay close to City Park, which thrummed with a heartbeat all its own twenty-four hours a day. He got out and flashed the security alarm before he looked around. Mossy oaks lined the sidewalks, and the flicker of the old, gas streetlights twinkled in the early dusk. *Nice place.*

The wrought iron gate squeaked a little when he entered, and a big, lazy cat lifted his head to stare at the intruder, then rolled over onto his back, closing his eyes.

"That's strange."

Jack stopped at the sound of Tu's voice above him and looked up. His heart skipped a beat at the sight of her long, black hair pulled over one shoulder in a braid. Her customary sweatshirt had been replaced by some type of clingy, sleeveless, turquoise job. The scooped neckline, revealing a wide expanse of skin, had him drooling.

Her casual, comfortable stance with her hip propped against the rail, barefooted, and holding a large mug of coffee, had him fighting the impulse to suggest they forget the movie and just kick back on her balcony. "What's strange?" He reached a hand out to scratch under the cat's neck.

"Whiskers only allows people he's met before to pet him."

Jack shrugged. "Guess he knows I'm harmless."

Steam rose from the cup she held and the rich aroma wafted down to tease his nostrils. She took a sip, but kept her gaze locked on him. "Are you?"

Her words were soft, but Jack thought he detected a note of doubt in her question. Before he could answer, she pushed away from the rail.

"Let me grab my shoes and purse, then we can go."

So, she's not inviting me inside. What had he expected? They were back to square one. He'd have to really mind his manners to win her trust again. He sighed, not sure if what he felt could be called frustration or resignation. Either one, he knew he wouldn't be making love to Tu tonight, like his overactive imagination had dreamed about all afternoon.

In less than three minutes she stood beside him.

"That was quick."

"Oh?"

"I mean most women I have dated take at least twenty minutes to put their lipstick on."

She smiled. "Ah, but I'm not most women."

"No, you're not." He let his gaze travel over her petite form and nodded. "What you see is what you get, huh?"

"Most of the time." Her eyebrow rose. "Do I pass inspection, or should I have opted for the dress and killer heels again?"

Jack threw his head back and laughed before he gave her a mock bow. "You're perfect the way you are, Miss Tran."

Both eyebrows lifted in response. A tiny twitch at the corner of her mouth indicated she was trying not to laugh, too. Jack resisted the urge to lean down and taste those sweet lips. He had to be a gentleman and show her he could be trusted. With a flourish, he opened her gate and indicated his car. "Your carriage awaits, my lady."

"Hmm, nice car, Jack."

"It's okay." Jack opened the door to his 1968 Mustang, placing a hand on the small on her back. The blouse rode up on one hip, exposing the skin on her back. The silky texture slid like molten lava beneath his fingertips. He fought the urge to wrap his arms around her and claim her mouth.

Her gaze met his for a second, and he held his breath. She hadn't given him permission to touch her.

"Thanks."

When she smiled, the tension eased from his shoulders. Her breath tickled his chin, and he found himself smiling back at her. He leaned closer, as she lowered her body into the seat, and she patted his arm, like a sister.

He frowned. That hadn't been the response he'd expected or wanted. He had hoped she'd make the first move and kiss him. She hadn't.

"You're welcome." He fought the surge of disappointment. *Easy, boy, you've gotten this far, don't blow it now.* With a deep breath, he stood and strode around the car. The knowledge that there wouldn't be a chance in hell that *he'd* be sleeping in her bed after this date, or maybe even the next one was pushed into the dark recesses of his mind. Would the *other* guy be welcome if he called, or showed up?

He glanced up and watched a cloud drift across the moon. A lonely saxophone played somewhere within the park. Jack released a sigh, as long and mournful as the wailing instrument.

"Where're we going?" she asked after they'd taken their seats in Jack's black Mustang and were pulling out into New Orleans' traffic.

"Tujague's."

"Tujague's!" Tu couldn't hold in her excitement. She had lived here for almost a year, but hadn't ever had the opportunity to visit the famous restaurant. She bit her lip.

"Yeah." He said it calmly, but she saw his frown. "What's wrong with it?"

"Well, it's so—touristy." She couldn't think of another word for the restaurant located in the middle of the oldest part of the city, called the Quarter. When Jack had mentioned taking her out to dinner, she'd envisioned something more sedate and sophisticated. The thought of him enjoying the Quarter was a novelty to her.

Wild things happened in that part of town, especially at night. She wondered if Jack was one of those men, who were cool on the surface and boiling hot underneath. She glanced at him from beneath her lashes, hiding a smile. She was definitely going to find out.

"One of my friends' family owns the place. Have you ever been there?" he asked, glancing her way occasionally as he maneuvered his vehicle through the heavy city traffic heading to the Vieux Carre and Decatur Street.

"No, I haven't had a good chance to go to the Quarter since I moved here," she answered. "I mean I've visited that area, but not with anyone who wanted to really explore."

"What? You've been here for over six months, and you haven't investigated the Quarter?" he laughed. "We'll have to remedy that."

They continued driving in silence to Decatur Street past the Jax Brewery and Jackson Square. She saw several horse-drawn carriages for hire before Jack pulled the car into a parking lot beginning to fill with the many tourists who visited the French Quarter year round. Opening the car door, the sounds of Bourbon Street drifted to her ears with trumpets, saxophones, and voices laughing into the night air. The smell, musty and dank, of the Mississippi River wafted up and over the levee just feet from their vehicle.

"Come on, let's get something to eat," Jack said, smiling down at her.

Helping her out of the car, he grabbed her hand as they hurried across the busy street to avoid the traffic. Much to her surprise, Jack continued to hold her hand when they reached the other side. Losing herself again to the feel of his hand covering hers, she bumped into his broad back when he suddenly stopped.

"Here we are." He pulled her around in front of his big body so she could see the restaurant, her smile fading as she stared at an old, narrow, brick building with a wooden sign bearing the name "Tujague's" swinging from a post above the doorway, and another red and white neon sign extending above the rooftop. The restaurant was situated on the end of a long row of French and Spanish styled buildings with wrought iron balconies on the upper floors reminiscent of an older era.

"This is… nice," she said, trying to keep a pleasant note in her voice, while thinking the place was a dump. She wondered how big the roaches were! New Orleans sat below sea level and stayed damp, leaving the perfect environment to incubate the ancient pests, especially in the older buildings of the Quarter. She swallowed the lump lodged in her throat and allowed Jack to guide her into the structure.

The inside was worse than the outside! Facing them as they walked in the door, was a long bar curving into an "L" shape with various types of people dressed in jeans and tee shirts, lined up at the counter drinking beer and mixed drinks. Against the windows to their right were several small, wooden tables for two. With a sense of dread Tu waited to see if one of the tables had their name on reserve. They couldn't eat here.

On the walls, she saw faded and peeling wallpaper with old black and white, framed photographs hanging, and a television set situated high above the bar. Where some of the frames had been removed the wallpaper was a brighter color, revealing the outline of previous pictures, which had occupied the space. Low-hung ceiling fans spun slowly in the humid air, trying to make up for the lack of air conditioning. Already, Tu could feel the back of her silk blouse clinging to her skin.

As the blades spun, Tu began to smell a mixture of beer, cigarettes, and the musty, dampness of the old building wafting towards her nose. Surprisingly, there was another odor she noticed—the aroma of food. Not just greasy, burgers and fries, which she would have normally associated with a place looking like this, but a delicious smell, making her mouth water in anticipation. Her stomach growled.

After Jack let her "feel the atmosphere," he led her to the left, walking past another line of tables Tu hadn't noticed. When they reached a pair of swinging doors, he turned to her, grinning with what she could only describe as wicked humor.

What was he up to? Tu narrowed her gaze.

Slowly, he pushed the doors open and ushered her inside.

Tu's jaw dropped as she stared in amazement at the tuxedo-clad maitre d' smiling and showing them to their table. Pulling her chair back for her, Jack leaned over her shoulder.

"Close your mouth, Tu, you're starting to drool." His warm breath whispered across her ear, and she quickly closed her mouth, looking around to see if anyone had noticed the gauche way she'd reacted to the "other side." White tablecloths covered about twelve tables sporting fine china, crystal, and silverware across their surface. Above the tables, hung gorgeous and elaborately designed chandeliers, casting a dim, romantic light over the entire room. Entering her vision was another waiter wearing a tuxedo.

"Welcome to Tujague's. Tonight our meal consists of several courses..."

Tu looked at Jack, raising her eyebrows as the waiter continued to list the gourmet foods to be served to them this evening.

What a contrast, she thought. Who would've ever guessed these two rooms existed within the same walls. "... ending with our special dessert of bananas flambé," finished the waiter with a small flourish of his hand.

"Thank you," Jack said to the waiter with a polite smile, causing Tu to spiral out of her daze and focus on what he was asking the waiter. "Could you bring us a bottle of your best wine before our meal is served?"

Jack had kept his eyes intent on her the whole time they'd been entering the restaurant, and Tu could see the humor reflected back at her astonishment.

"You really had me going there for a minute." She moved her knife closer to her plate and adjusted her napkin across her lap. "Of course, you knew what I was thinking when I saw the outside of this place." She laughed, hearing the soft sound escape her lips.

Jack's eyes narrowed and he looked at her so long she forgot what she was saying.

"You look beautiful tonight, Tu," he told her suddenly, the humor retreating from his eyes, leaving them serious and dark. Feeling her smile slip from her face, she was caught in his intent gaze, mesmerized.

Someone coughed; Tu blinked, breaking the spell, as the waiter stood beside Jack with a bottle of red wine. The man opened the bottle with a flourish, pouring the rich liquor into their wine glasses.

Hoping no one noticed how absorbed they'd been with each other, Tu cleared her throat and looked around the room. There was a family sitting beside them, the parents counting in their pockets for change as they looked at their bill for the evening's meal while the three children looked at their plates in undisguised horror. They must not be accustomed to "fine dining." Thinking of her lifelong aversion to certain foods, Tu tried to hide a smile at their expressions.

"So, really. What do you think of my favorite restaurant?" Jack asked, bringing her attention back to him. She could tell he was trying to steer the conversation to more neutral ground. Had their powerful gaze caused him discomfort? She surely hoped so.

Just show me a good time, and let me enjoy myself tonight, she tried to tell him telepathically. He needed to become more comfortable in her company. She wanted to trust him. "I think it's fantastic, so far. The contrast between the two rooms is amazing," she answered, sensing him trying to make her relax. Maybe they wanted the same thing.

From that point, the meal and evening progressed easily. Silverware and glasses clinked, and people spoke in hushed voices as the two discussed everything from politics and religion, to horses and classical music.

"Not that I listen to classical all the time, but I do like Vivaldi," stated Tu with a laugh. "Usually, I listen to alternative rock." She was leaning forward with one arm resting on the table while her forefinger traced the rim of her coffee cup. Jack watched her as she spoke; his eyes alert, but smiling. Tu thought how relaxed he looked in a woman's company. Her finger slowed on the rim as a feeling close to jealousy crept up on her.

This definitely wasn't a new experience for him. He probably spent several weeks on and off in the company of a woman he found attractive, usually in bed after the preliminary few dates. Maybe he'd never found a woman intellectually stimulating, as well as physically stimulating, where he just wanted to talk to her. The thoughts whirled in her head. She'd learned tonight she and Jack had many of the same likes and dislikes, and found she didn't want to share him with anyone else. She wanted tonight to be unique and special. After a few seconds of quiet, she noticed Jack preoccupied with his own thoughts, as well.

Glancing up, quickly, he smiled. "Sorry, I got lost in a thought."

Tu hoped the thoughts were of her, and not some bimbo he'd brought here before tonight. "How about going down to Jackson Square and catching a carriage ride before we return home?" he asked, signaling the waiter to bring them their check.

"I think a carriage ride would be great." Her heart quickened when he'd said "we return home." Not caring what had transpired between him and other women, she decided to take advantage of this moment. If she wanted him, she'd have to show him. No sense in playing games. Tu let him see the look of need in her eyes when he completed signing the bill.

Slowly, never losing eye contact, he returned his wallet to his jacket pocket. "What do you want to do after our ride?" he asked on a slight husky note.

Her breath caught. Unlike Dev, Jack was giving her the option to prolong their date, or take the evening on to whatever climax she chose. She was the one in control. "I-I don't know, yet."

His lips tightened, but he nodded. "That's okay. We'll go slow and play it by ear."

"Sounds good." Silently, she cursed herself. Forget coyness. Deep down she still wanted to have sex with this man. He made her feel special. If only Dev cared about her like this, she would be able to make a firm decision about Jack.

A thought wound through her subconscious, making her remember her long ago dream of having him fall for her. She quickly squashed the idea. It hadn't worked. She only wanted one thing at the moment—a no-obligation type of relationship. The type she had with Dev.

Jack came around to pull her chair out, as always, exhibiting good manners. She didn't know how he managed his cool, polite demeanor when she saw such a fire burning from his eyes and felt the heat in his fingers as he held her arm while she stood and they left the restaurant. When they reached the sidewalk outside, he leaned his head close to her ear, pulling her body against his.

"Your wish is my command." The softly whispered words nipped her ear lobe just as his lips bit further down on the sensitive skin of her neck. Jack hugged her against his side, and they continued walking toward Jackson Square to catch a carriage.

Although the carriage was parked only a block away, the trip felt like a mile as the warmth of his body seeped through her blouse to her sensitive skin. By the time they reached the square, her breathing felt ragged, and Jack had to lift her up onto the padded carriage seat before joining her in the hot velvet darkness of the New Orleans' night.

With the driver facing away from them and seated about two feet above on the driver's seat, the high walls of the carriage hid their bodies from the eyes of the passersby. Jack's arms went around her, pulling her into his embrace. One hand pushed up her neck into her hair, as his lips found hers with a gentle kiss that Tu felt all the way to her toes.

The carriage hit a pothole, causing the carriage to bump hard. Jack's tooth caught her lip.

"Ouch!" Tu pulled back from his embrace, putting her finger to her throbbing lip. She could taste something warm and metallic in her mouth.

"Here. Let me help," he offered. Before she knew what he intended, Jack leaned forward and licked the blood from her injured lip softly and slowly with his tongue.

Tu shivered, keeping her eyes open and staring into his. Her clit tightened with red-hot need.

"I didn't mean to hurt you." He transferred his gaze from her eyes to her lips, then back.

Her breath caught at the blazing passion she saw there. Who could ever think this man was cold? The look on his face could melt the North Pole. *Oh, God, I'm in trouble.*

She'd forgotten how aroused he could get. "You didn't hurt me on purpose." She pushed away from him. "It's better now." A roaring sensation assailed her ears at the same time her heart pounded against her ribs. Was she crazy? Why wasn't she jumping his bones? She knew she wanted him, but she realized she was scared of getting hurt again. With Dev she thought she knew the score. "Look, Jack, I think we need to slow down a bit here. I'm not sure what I'm doing…"

"You don't want me to make love to you?" Jack asked, moving closer to trace a slow pattern with his finger around her ear and down her neck to the dip in her neckline. When his hand brushed against the fabric covering her breast, she trembled.

Was it fear? He looked into her eyes through the darkness, and saw her need mixed with uncertainty. He smiled. He'd just have to convince her they wanted the same thing. Moving his hand lower, he asked her again, "What do you want, Tu?"

The hem of her blouse lay loose at her waist. He couldn't resist allowing his fingertips to caress the softness beneath the silk. Moving closer, he felt her tremble again before she said, "I don't know."

His groin tightened at her answer. She hadn't said "no."

Not taking a chance on her making a negative decision, he pulled her in tight against his side while he let his other fingers slide beneath the hem of her blouse and up to find the dampness between her breasts. Rubbing her nipples with his thumb and forefinger, he lowered himself onto the floorboard of the carriage between her legs, hidden by the darkness.

Without losing contact with her, he pushed her blouse up over her breasts, exposing the creamy skin revealed by her flimsy bra.

Pulling the lace down with his forefinger, so his mouth could gain access, he stifled a groan of pure delight when he inhaled the musky fragrance of her body. Feeling her hands push at his head and shoulders in weak protest, Jack quickly released his tongue against her heated flesh, causing Tu to emit a gasping sound from deep in her throat.

Jack smiled as he continued to lathe her nipples with quick flicks, then with a sucking action, which had her bucking off the seat and tightening her grasp on his hair.

A few more seconds, he felt her thighs tighten around his body, and she gave one last strangled gasp before Jack knew she had climaxed. As her thighs relaxed he moved onto the seat and caught her mouth to his so he could keep her in a heightened state of awareness of him.

Instead of her staying pliant in his hands, her kisses grew stronger and bolder. Remembering how aggressive she'd been a few nights before, Jack couldn't wait to see what she had in store for him.

Keeping her mouth on his, her hands unbuttoned his shirt, before she moved to his waist to undo his belt and pants. When he tried to stop her, she pushed his hands away, sliding to the floorboard between his legs. Her mouth covered his shaft over his briefs. He sat up, but she pushed him back, giving him a smile from her crouched position that took his breath away.

He couldn't give in. She'd hate him in the morning. "Tu. You have to stop."

She hesitated, glancing up at him with a look of disbelief on her face. "What?"

It took all his will-power, but he managed to grasp her upper arms and pull her beside him on the seat. "We're in a public place." His action or words didn't perturb her in the least.

She moved her mouth back to his lips only to travel down his throat and chest, causing him to lay his head back against the seat and enjoy the sensual pleasure of her hot lips and nipping little teeth on his skin.

A streak of light from a streetlamp flashed across her face, revealing an impish grin before she pulled his pants closed over the hardness of his arousal.

"You really are a shy boy, Jack Noblin." The fingernails of her left hand bit into his thigh, while the fingers of her right hand stroked the sensitive skin along his neck.

Gritting his teeth, he tried to resist the urge to show her what he really wanted to do to her. Instead, his fingers tightened in her hair, pulling her head back and exposing her slender neck for his perusal and enjoyment.

Her hands grasped his thighs firmly, as she sucked in a surprised breath.

He leaned forward, flicking his tongue up the column of her neck to her ear where he whispered, "One day, Tu. I'm going to show you the real me." His voice sounded gruff and hoarse. Beside him, Tu relaxed into him, and he released her hair. They completed the ride in a companionable silence.

Slowly, the sounds of the outside world filtered back to him, and Jack looked up at the driver, who seemed not to have noticed anything amiss. Thank goodness. Either the man was good at his job and wanted a decent tip, or Tu hadn't groaned in ecstasy like he'd imagined.

They drew to a halt at a stop sign across from the point they parked the car. Jack kissed the top of her head as he stroked her hair. What was he going to do with her?

Great sex was a good thing. At least they wouldn't be bored with each other right off the bat. Buttoning his shirt, he told the driver to let them off there.

"I need to get you home."

Her eyebrow rose. "So soon? What about the movie?"

Glancing at his watch, he said, "It's getting late, and we have work tomorrow." He didn't care if he had a meeting with the president of the company. If he didn't get her home soon, he would ruin what rapport they had built over the last several hours. Besides, he had plans for the rest of the night. Every fantasy he'd ever had about Tu Tran was about to be explored in the privacy of his shower. Looking down into her flushed face, he smiled. "I'll see you tomorrow."

She frowned and blinked her confusion, but nodded. "Okay."

Chapter Six

"Who are you?"

Tu played with the tip of a white horn, while Dev's tongue circled down and around her abdomen. The sensations he produced weren't enough to distract her from what she wanted to know.

His talented tongue stopped, and he lifted his head.

Tu felt his eyes on her, but again she was unable to see their color.

Dev sighed and propped his chin on one hand. With the other he traced random patterns on her belly, which made her muscles contract. "Why?"

"We've screwed each other's brains out twice, we still haven't exchanged names, and…"—she pulled his horn—"… you're still wearing a mask."

"We don't need to know names for what we're doing, and the mask is part of the fantasy I want to create for you. You know it turns you on."

His hand slipped lower, and her pelvic muscles tightened. He'd spent the last hour licking her clit, but her body wanted more. *No, I want more.* "You know *my* name."

Tu scooted off the bed and out of his reach. She moved across the room to an overstuffed chair she used for reading. When she stood behind the protection of the furniture, she turned to him. Her breasts were in view, and she shouldn't have been self-conscious about the fact, since he knew her body better than anyone, but she was. She could feel his gaze touch each nipple, and the peaks hardened with the knowledge he looked at her.

Tu pulled the afghan from the old chair and wrapped the material around her shoulders. She sensed, more than saw, Dev stiffen in offense.

With a lazy stretch his long frame eased off the bed to stand tall and straight. The broad shoulders tapered to narrow hips and muscular thighs.

She'd been shocked the first time she'd seen him naked, but the massive organ that lay against his dark curls made her mouth water. She zeroed in on the glint of the bedroom light off the silver stud he wore through the foreskin of his shaft. *Umm, the things that little device does to my body!*

Tu had a hard time not to go to him now, and touch every crevice and curve of his physique, like she'd done several times the last time they'd been together. She lowered her eyelashes and looked at his feet, then bit her lip on a groan. Even his feet were beautiful and talented.

The other night she had gotten her wish to perform a *sixty-nine* with him. When they had finished, they had each reclined at opposite ends of the bed. She had tickled him with her foot, and he'd punished her by rubbing her clit with his toes until she came.

Tu swallowed hard at the memory and tried to look somewhere else besides him, but his mere size and presence filled the room to overflowing.

"You're trying to hide from me, but it isn't going to work."

Her gaze snapped back to his face, but all she saw was the mask.

"*Who* is hiding from *whom* in this..." —she waved her hand between them—"...relationship?"

His hands clenched into fists, but he relaxed them before he walked toward her. Her fingers dug into the material of the chair, but she forced herself not to move away from him. She knew nothing about this man, except he'd completely seduced her in bed and could scare and fascinate her at the same time.

Flashes of the kitchen table and the balcony rail scooted through her mind, and she bit her lip. He didn't do too shabby out of bed, either.

He reached her in three strides, while she daydreamed, and with one foot, he pushed the ottoman out of the way. Kneeling into the soft cushions of the chair, he crossed his arms over the back. A spring creaked in the old chair with the weight of his body. He leaned forward. Centimeters from her face, his breath made a panting sound through the hole of the mask and fanned hot across her cheek.

Seconds turned to eons for Tu. Beads of sweat broke across her skin. She trembled, and when his fingers caressed her cheek, she jumped. They had never discussed anything past which sexual position they were going to experiment with next. Her questions put them in uncharted territory, and she didn't know how to respond. What had been a natural, relaxed atmosphere shifted to one charged with doubt and uncertainty.

"Do we have a relationship?" The mask muffled his voice, but she heard the undercurrent in his soft-spoken words. By his tone, he didn't want this conversation, and would make her regret she'd brought it up. She knew he could be rough, and menacing, but he'd never really hurt her.

"I-I don't know." She shook her head. "Do you want to be in a relation-ship?"

"Depends on what you mean when you say that word." He eased away, but wrapped a hand around her wrist.

He didn't force her around the chair, but the pressure on her arm told her she should comply with what he wanted. Tu eased to the side by the arm, studying him, as he turned to settle his large frame into the comfort of the cushions. When he was situated, he glanced at her.

His eyes were nothing but deep, black holes in wicked grooves of the mask.

A slight niggle of fear rose from within her psyche followed closely by a warm expansion of heat in between her legs. She acknowledged he was dangerous, but something inside her, something just as dark as the man in front of her, awoke and craved what he might impose on her body and mind.

With a sudden tug of his arm, she fell across his lap.

Squirming to sit up, his arms wrapped tighter around her, pulling her into a cradled position against his naked chest. His tongue snaked out from the mask and he flicked the tip across her cheek.

"If we're talking about a *one on one* type of thing, *Cher*, then we already have a problem. Don't we?"

There was no way he could know! Tu's heart skipped a beat. "I'm not sure what you mean."

"Now, babe, don't start with the lies, or this *thing* between us will definitely fizzle fast." His hand eased beneath the afghan, fondling her breast with feather-like caresses.

Her nipples tightened. Tiny tremors spread from her breast to her groin, causing her to suck in her breath hard and close her eyes.

"Who was the guy you went out with tonight?"

Tu stiffened and tried to break his hold on her, but his other arm pinned her body closer to him. The hand on her breast slid down her abdomen and settled in the curls between her legs. He had wanted to shave her, but, so far, she'd refused his request.

"You were spying on me?" Tu cringed at the panting quality of her voice. When he slipped one long finger into her slick folds, like he did, she could barely remember her name. The imposing gloom of the darkened room swirled into a kaleidoscope of grays and black.

Dev hesitated for a second, then shrugged. He pushed his finger deeper.

Tu gasped, opening her eyes wide. She should protest, but damn he made her feel good. She couldn't refuse him now, just as she hadn't been able to refuse to let him in when he'd shone up on her doorstep a couple of hours after Jack had dropped her off.

Staring at him for a moment, she'd dropped her hand, allowing him access to her house and her body. A slight niggle of guilt surfaced at betraying Jack, but she pushed it to the back of her mind. Jack had refused to come in; Dev had not.

Dev's eyes gleamed behind the mask, like some pagan god inspecting his sacrifice.

She spread her legs wider to allow him better access.

He laughed, curling his finger inside her, connecting with that elusive spot she could never reach on her own. "You walked into the same restaurant I happened to be visiting. What was I supposed to do?"

His fingertip hit her G-spot again.

Tu moaned, letting her head fall back over his arm. "I don't know. I guess it would... have been..." —she arched her back with a whimper—"...a little awkward if you'd come over and... introduced yourself."

"Exactly." He pushed another finger into her body, angling into her higher.

Tu couldn't stop the cry of pleasure that escaped, and she wanted to clutch his shoulders, but the grip he had on her arms wouldn't ease. Instead, she leaned forward and bit his shoulder, hard.

"Ow, you little witch!" With a swift turn, his fingers left her body, pulling her up where she straddled his thighs.

Her back pressed into his chest. Wiry hairs pricked her skin whenever she bucked against his hold. "You could have mentioned the fact you'd seen me when you showed up tonight."

She squirmed harder, then stilled as his erection swelled against her bottom. "That's the problem. *You* come and go as you please. *You* know my name and what I look like, but I don't have a clue about you, except from the neck down."

"I thought that's how you wanted this *relationship* to be, sweets." He stood, carrying her, with one arm around her chest and the other around her waist, two steps to the ottoman. Once there, he plopped her face down across the cushion.

Tu squirmed to get her knees beneath her, but Dev dragged the stool back toward the chair.

"Your exact term for us, if I remember correctly, was *fuck buddies*. 'No ties. No commitment.'" He repeated her rules verbatim from the first night they'd met.

The ottoman stopped. He leaned forward, pinning her with his body.

Tu pushed against his hold with her elbows.

With a grunt, he shoved her down with one large hand. Thick thighs squeezed tight, trapping her legs between the chair and the edge of the ottoman. "Damn, you're strong for such a little girl."

"I... am... not... a... little girl." She clenched her teeth, bucking her hips, but she couldn't break his hold. She lay panting with his weight on top of her. He had her trapped, and the realization made her mad. Tu screamed.

Dev laughed. "The word *relationship* means there has to be trust between two people."

With her body crushed beneath him, she breathed the scent of her sex through her nostrils. She wanted him. "Take the damn mask off, so I can see *who* is screwing me."

"You know who you're with, *Cher.*" His tone held a quiet hint of steel.

Jealousy? *Nah.* "I thought I had guessed earlier today, but I was mistaken when he asked me out tonight."

His body stiffened, but he didn't say anything.

"You don't ask me to go anywhere. You just come over for one thing, and one thing only. Sex."

"Would you rather be with that sap I saw you with tonight?"

"Jack is not a sap! He's kind and sweet." Her acceptance of Jack's requests lately confused her. While she craved Dev's touch, she'd still wanted to go out with Jack. So, which man did she want? Jack had been so gentlemanly the last few days to make up for the night in his office. She sighed. If only Dev could harness a little of that kindness.

"Sweet, huh?" There it was again, that slight hint of jealousy. "Is that what you want?"

Turning her head to the side against the ottoman, her lover traced a finger down her nose and across her cheek to tickle her ear with a light caress. Tu closed her eyes to enjoy his fingers sifting through her hair, like a loom sifted through strands of silk, then fall against her skin. She shivered. Truth was, she didn't want "sweet."

She opened her eyes and followed the motions of his fingers, as he worked the muscles in her shoulder. The contrast between his fairness and her darkness accentuated their differences.

He hit a particularly sensitive spot; she emitted a small cry of pain that turned to a moan of ecstasy when the kneading turned into a feathery stroking. They might be opposites, but they sure as hell attracted. If she could combine Jack with what Dev did to her, she'd have exactly the man she wanted.

With a groan, Dev bent his head and licked her shoulder hard through the opening of the mask. His erection pressing into her lower back told her more than his groan how excited he was.

"If you took that damned thing off, you could bite me like I want."

"Bite you, huh?" He laughed, slipping his hand beneath her, pinching her nipple hard enough it resembled a bite.

She cried out, squirming, but he refused to let her go.

"I've got something better in mind, wild girl." He licked her ear. "Do you trust me?"

"W-What do you mean?" Did she trust either of the men she was attracted to? Jack had already lied to her. Even though Dev had been up front in what he wanted from her, he still refused to share anything personal about himself.

She smiled at the wariness and fear in her voice. The smile died. She should be. He was a virtual stranger, who had her in a very precarious position. For all she knew, he could be a serial rapist.

His hands slipped to her hips, easing around the front of her pelvis.

Tu held her breath, waiting for the second of sweet-agony when he would slip his finger into her pussy. A line of juice trickled down her inner thigh. *Come on, already.*

Then, it happened. Sliding slow and deep with his middle finger, he worked his thumb over her clit, faster and harder. Her body shook and her hips moved against his rhythm.

"You like it rough, don't you?" he whispered, pulling her back against him with his left hand while the right hand worked in and out of her body. "Um hmm, hot and wet."

Their actions created a slurping sound that radiated along the edges of her mind. She buried her head into the cushion, refusing to answer. Any embarrassment she experienced couldn't outweigh the way he made her crave the sex he could give her. *Wild, free...* she groaned... *uninhibited.*

"No need to answer. Your body's speaking for you, babe." He pushed into her deeper, then pulled his finger, quickly, from her body.

Her body jerked in reaction, as her juices splashed between her thighs. Heat flamed hotter across her cheeks at the knowledge this stranger had of her. The intensity of his gaze burned her skin, even though she couldn't see him watching her.

"You know you blush all over. Why are you embarrassed of what I make you crave?"

Opening her mouth to respond, she bit her lip. She couldn't answer. How could you tell someone that your own embarrassment turned you on?

"Do you want *all* of me?" he asked in a soft voice.

All of him? She frowned. There was a dangerous note in that quiet question that she couldn't comprehend.

His question rang clear when he moved his fingers from her vagina to her ass, slicking her anus with her own juices. She stiffened at the same time her heart rate accelerated and a fresh coat of sweat beaded across the small of her back. She'd never done this.

He leaned forward as if to give her a reassuring kiss, but the mask prevented his lips from touching much of her skin. Instead, he whispered in her ear. "A *relationship* means you trust me enough to give *all* of your body without reservation, and you trust me to give you the same."

He pushed the tip of his erection into the wet, ready, flesh of her vagina, then pulled out, easing up to her ass. "Now, I need an answer. Do you trust me?"

Her breathing grew shallow and ragged. Her face buried into the ottoman, again, but she knew he could hear her nervous swallow. She should say "no."

"I know a part of you wants to say 'yes'." His weight pressed her further into the cushion. "You want to experience a facet of sex you've always ached to know about, but have been taught to treat as taboo." He rubbed his cock up and down between her buttocks, increasing the heat and juices pooling between her legs. "Admit it, Tu. I am the one who can give you everything you've always wanted sexually."

She thought of Jack and how she'd driven him crazy earlier and how he'd accepted her torture, because he knew she had wanted to pay him back for hurting her the other night. If she and Jack were to grow, then she would have to refuse Dev, but her darker side, which she kept hidden, rebelled. Tonight, *it* wanted to come out and play.

"Yes." The half that wanted Jack screamed "no," but the one who wanted Dev smiled with a victory punch into the air.

Dev placed a hand on her back, holding her in place. She couldn't see his other hand, but felt it lift.

A *squishing* sounded close. The realization that he used her juices and his saliva to cover his sex forced a new flood of moisture between her legs. They were really going to do this. *Oh, God. Oh, God.*

She'd made her choice, and he wouldn't hurt her, intentionally, but she knew he wouldn't be like Jack, letting her renege in the eye of a storm. No, Dev would hold her to her decision and enjoy the pain right along with her.

"Loosen up, baby. It'll hurt worse if you're tense." He stroked her back to help her relax, as he eased his weight onto her. "Push out against me."

The pressure of the silver, penile stud he wore, entering her body, made her gasp, but her inner wildness broke free. She had loved the feel of the metal in her—she paused over the vulgar word—*pussy.* Just allowing herself the freedom to think it, increased her desire, she knew this invasion was what she wanted. With Dev she could be everything she'd been taught not to be. With Dev the inner vixen could be released.

Without warning, her sphincter muscles contracted from the fullness of his shaft, but he didn't pull back. A moment of fear forced her newfound elation to falter. "Dev, I don't know about—"

"There's no way to avoid the pain you're going to feel at first." He pushed his way through the barrier.

Tu stiffened, opening her mouth on a silent scream. She'd known it would hurt, but the burning was unexpected. Her hands gripped around the cushion so tightly her fingernails tore the material. Unable to hold her breath any longer, she sucked air into her mouth with a *hiss.*

"Y-You okay?" he asked through what sounded like clenched teeth.

She nodded, but didn't dare speak. Sweat coated her body and dripped from her temples. Dev pushed farther into her heat, and she couldn't help but cry out. The room swirled around her, as the pain and pleasure mingled to create an ecstasy she'd never experienced. Behind her he laughed.

"I can't decide which is better. Your ass, or that sweet little cave of yours," he said against her ear before he licked her neck through the hole in the mask.

Taking deep, steady breaths, she concentrated on forcing her muscles to relax.

"That's right, babe." He rubbed her back. "The pain only lasts a few seconds until you get used to me."

Her muscles relaxed with a rush of heat that effused throughout her entire body. His cock sank full-length into her ass. She groaned at the fullness of him.

Dev sucked in a deep breath. "Ah, God, I gotta move."

He didn't give her a chance to object, but pushed his hips forward, harder and faster.

Tu clutched the ottoman, panting. Her moans should have told him she was enjoying this as much as he. She mumbled something, but wasn't sure what. A wild urge for him to be rougher rose within her.

"What did you say?" he asked, without losing a beat. He must have read her mind, because he leaned forward, wrapping a hand in her long hair and pulling her head back hard.

"M-More!" The words burst from her throat, raw and primal. She bucked her hips into his thrust, urging him to give her what she needed.

Jack would've been afraid of hurting her, but she heard Dev laugh. "Your wish is my command." His fingers dug into the flesh of her hips.

Tu's anticipation that had escalated at his dominating manner crashed. "W-What did you say?" she asked, tensing at his words. Her legs felt like jelly, they were so weak.

"What?" He grunted, pausing for a second at her question, as sweat pooled between their bodies.

The muscles in her buttocks tightened, forcing her to remember her lust. Tu shook her head. "It's just that someone else said the same thing to me recently."

"Shit, Tu, it's a common enough phrase." His grip tightened. "Can I continue?"

Tu heard the sarcasm. She pushed her doubts and suspicions to the side with an uneasy laugh. "Yeah." She sure wasn't going to tell him her other lover had been the one to say the exact words he'd just used with her. *Stop thinking of Jack and concentrate on Dev!*

He kept her head pulled back, while he drove his body deeper, rocking the ottoman and their bodies across the floor with the power of his thrusts.

The restlessness crept beneath her skin, increasing her need to orgasm. She released the side of the ottoman, slipping her hand to her clit. Rubbing the hard nub in sync with Dev's thrusts, she rode the edge. It was there, but wouldn't come. Tu screamed her frustration. "More!"

"Damnation, woman, you like to fuck," he said, but gave her what she demanded, pounding harder. When the climax hit, they came in unison, throwing their heads back and screaming, "Yeesss!"

⁂

Whiskers jumped onto the balcony rail and peered into the darkened room at the two lovers sprawled naked across the over-stuffed chair. Moonlight streamed across the floor to wrap around their bodies like a blanket.

The figure in the red mask moved, but the cat didn't *hiss.* Tu lifted her head from Dev's chest to watch her pet arch his back in a lazy stretch before jumping to the patio below. She sighed and looked toward the hidden face of her lover.

He scares me, Whiskers. Why not you? She sighed. Not with the normal fear someone would feel toward an unknown evil, but from the standpoint he made her crave all those things she'd been taught were "bad" and she'd never done before. She tried to move away, lifting his arm away from her body, but Dev's embrace tightened. She stiffened. *I'm in the grip of the devil, and I like it.*

"Where are you going?" he asked in a groggy, muffled voice.

"Dev, I have to get some sleep. I have to work tomorrow." Again, she tried to rise, but he refused to release her. "Dev—"

"I'm not through with you yet, babe." His hand trailed down her arm to tickle the hair between her legs, cutting off her protest. "You wanted me to teach you everything about unbelievable sex, remember?"

A moan escaped her lips, but her excitement grew. She spread her legs beneath his probing fingers.

Chapter Seven

Tu took a break from keying the changes into her new program. Muscles she'd forgotten she had burned and throbbed. She massaged her neck. After two attempts to find a comfortable position, she stood up and stretched. Her vertebrae popped with a loud *snap*.

"Oh, God, that feels good." Almost as good as when Dev had taken her from behind. *Hmm, not quite as good as that.* She smiled at the memory.

She spread her legs farther apart and lifted her arms up, then across the back of her neck. She performed a slow rotation of her hips, bending over to let her head and arms dangle between her legs. The sight of a pair of male legs encased in khaki pants made her freeze. Her gaze traveled up the long legs and stopped at the crotch. She angled her head and grinned. *Impressive bulge, Jack.*

"Uh, hey Tu." His feet shifted. "I'll come back when you're through with your aerobics."

Tu knew that tone. Even with a hard-on, Jack wasn't happy, and she had a good idea it had something to do with her cool treatment of him this morning. He'd tried to talk to her about their date last night, first in the elevator, then again at the vending machine. Both times she'd made some excuse and changed the subject.

Oh, they'd had a great time over dinner and the carriage ride. Her attraction for him had increased, but when she asked if he would come inside when he dropped her off, he had refused. In a moment of pique, she had turned her head away when he'd tried to kiss her goodnight. His warm lips had fallen on her cheek. His disappointment made her feel like a piece of used gum on the bottom of a shoe, because they'd gotten to know each other, and she liked him a lot.

In fact —she bit her lip—more than a lot. She straightened. "Jack. It's okay. Don't leave. We need to talk." What if he really wanted Donna? Men like Jack didn't choose petite, Asian girls. Oh, she was okay for the occasional romp in the sheets, but when it came down to something serious, she never got to "meet the parents."

Besides the trust issue, there was Dev. On some secret level, she wanted her relationship with him to broaden. He gave her the kind of sex she'd always craved. She couldn't tell him not to come over anymore. Besides, she never knew when he would decide to show up at her place anyway. She didn't want to take a chance on him and Jack meeting. If they did, she'd either lose both of them, or have to choose under stress.

She turned to look at Jack with his brown loafers, khaki pants, and button-down oxford shirt tucked so neatly into his belt. The all-American guy—smart, good-looking, with a good sense of humor—the kind her mom would be proud to have as a son-in-law. She just wasn't sure she was ready to do that yet.

She had the best of two worlds with Dev as her fantasy lover, and Jack as her friend. Oh, she knew he wanted to take their friendship further, but the possibility Jack wouldn't *measure up* lingered in her mind. Deep down, she knew if he didn't, she'd be disappointed, and the special connection they did share would be gone.

She attempted a reassuring smile.

He hesitated. A wary expression flashed across his face, but disappeared after a second to be replaced by a smile. "Sorry about earlier. I never even said 'good morning' before I started talking about last night."

"I was just stretching my back. I-I must have… slept wrong." She sure as hell wasn't going to tell him the real reason her back and butt were sore.

Her cheeks grew warm, as his eyes narrowed on her face after he looked at her from head to toe. His auburn brows drew together in a frown, but he didn't comment on what she said.

She bit back a groan, hoping he didn't think she was taunting him after her rejections. Tu sighed and rubbed her temple. This was getting complicated. "Uh, you wanted to see me?"

His expression cleared to be replaced by his business mask. Not a flicker of emotion crossed his face, and Tu wondered how he could switch gears from the warm, friendly man, who joked and laughed one minute, then turn into this deadpan robot the next. She shook her head. *The many faces of Eve…*

Tu blinked as the image of Dev's mask surfaced and missed what Jack said. "I-I'm sorry, Jack. I didn't hear you."

"For crying out loud, Tu, wake up." The scowl on his face grew darker. "What's wrong with you?" His voice sounded like a growl, and for a second Tu stared at him. He sounded a lot like Dev when he had dominated her. Her skin rose with goose bumps. Her gaze and ears focused on Jack.

"I said I have a luncheon with the CEO today, and need that report completed by eleven. Is that going to be a problem for you?"

"No." She shook her head, frowning.

There it was again—the way he stressed his words when he became irritated. His mannerisms were similar, too. All intense and forceful. She didn't normally see Jack like that, because she always thought of him as the good-natured yuppie. Right now, the uptight and aggressive attitude aroused but confused her.

"Good."

With his back stiff, he walked out of her cubicle and back to his office. He moved with the same animal grace, like a slow prowl, she'd observed in Dev. The goose bumps along her arms increased. A pool of moisture formed in the crotch of her panties.

"Good grief, get a grip." She scrubbed her face and ran a hand through her hair, which she'd left long today. Dev said he liked it long, and—

"Stop right there, and get your butt in gear." She must be crazy, comparing her boss to her lover. There were no similarities. They were night and day. She needed to decide between the two men soon. This double-dating and sneaking around between men had her nerve-endings frayed to the max.

Tu took one last look at Jack. The blinds were open over the glass walls of his office. He looked up and their gazes met. The shaft of awareness that arrowed through her stabbed with an alacrity that had her clutching her stomach. It was the same effect Dev held over her.

She turned away. *I can't choose right this minute.*

❧🐙❧

Well, he'd made it back to his office without grabbing her and kissing her silly. Jack snatched up the phone and hit a few buttons. He had one more number to punch into the pad when he looked up and met Tu's gaze. An electrical current shot through him.

Gripping the receiver, the number evaporated in his mind.

They stared at each other for what felt like minutes, but when she broke the contact, he realized only seconds had passed. That was enough.

A recording repeated over and over, "The number you have dialed cannot be reached."

Jack slammed the phone down. "You're damned straight about that."

He crossed over to the blinds across the front wall of his office. With a quick twist of his wrist, the one-inch slates closed with a snap. He sat back down, puffing his cheeks on a deep exhalation. Releasing the trapped air of tension, he rubbed a hand across his face. Stubble pricked his fingers, but he didn't care. Hell, he could have a whole week's worth of beard and he wouldn't give a damn.

He flopped back into the leather chair, picked up his letter opener and stabbed the tip into the blotter on his desk. He hadn't slept a wink the night before, or the night before that. "This is madness, Jack. You gotta be more aggressive and tell her exactly what you want, man. She's slipping through your fingers."

He snorted and threw the opener across the room where it sank a couple inches into a bulletin-board with a *twang*. The metal wagged back and forth from the force of the hit, and the image of Tu's ass this morning, while she'd been bent over, rotating her hips.

His fists clenched. The fantasy of Tu's body beneath his, while his cock pounded in and out of her sweet—"Enough, already!"

She was driving him crazy. This jittery indecisiveness must be what an addict went through when he or she craved their substance of abuse. The more he stayed around Tu, the more he craved her. He'd never known a woman, who could turn him on so much.

"That, ladies and gentlemen is what we call the ball-breaker." He swiveled his chair to face the outside window, but couldn't focus on the scene below him. Tu's face filled his mind.

He groaned. If she didn't give in to him soon, he'd have to admit defeat and move on. He didn't like dangling on the end of a rope if Tu's plan included teasing and tormenting him. He'd give her one more chance and play *Mr. Nice*.

≈⁂(☉☉)⁂≈

"I can't have dinner with you, Jack—"

"Why the hell not?"

The shock and anger on her face made him clear his throat and adjust his tie. "Sorry. I didn't mean to sound so belligerent." *The hell he didn't.* She probably planned to spend the evening with that other guy. She tried to hide the fact that she was seeing someone, but the entire office could read between the lines with her yawns, circles beneath her eyes, and lack of concentration. His jaw tightened when he remembered all the nights he'd taken a cold shower because thoughts of her raced through his mind.

She nodded her head and thumped a stack of papers together on her desk before she handed them to him. "Here's the new report you asked for."

He took the file and thumbed through it, not really caring if the data was accurate or not. Jealousy flared deep within his gut. He wanted to know if she planned on seeing the other man in her life.

Tu stood, retrieving her purse, a cloth bag that hung down her shoulder to her hip. The purse was simple, but the knitting twisted into an intricate design—beautiful, like her.

He smiled, blocking her path when she made to move around him. He couldn't prevent the caress he smoothed across her cheek with the back of his hand.

"Jack, I—" She looked up at him with almond eyes, as her pupils dilated and her nostrils flared.

He knew she wasn't immune to him. His body responded with a sharp pain in his groin. He ignored it. "How about tomorrow night if you're not busy?"

She shook her head. "I'm sorry. I play Bunko on Wednesday nights."

"Bunko! What's that?" There he went again with the antagonism. He groaned inwardly, but refused to move out of her way.

Her body stiffened beneath the hand he had wrapped around her upper arm. She glanced at his hand with a lifted eyebrow, but he didn't release her. Instead he loosened his grip enough for his fingers to slide up and down the inside of her arm.

She gasped. "It's a dice game played with several groups. In this case twelve women. We play every week on Wednesdays."

He'd wondered where she went every week. Whenever he called on Wednesday nights, she was always late getting home, but he would never ask her where she'd been. It wasn't that he wasn't interested in her life away from him. The problem was he wanted to know everything about her. He just wished that she would concentrate on *him* without outside distractions from games, work, or other lovers.

"That sounds interesting, but not as interesting as what could happen between us if you'd let it." He whispered, reminding her of their attraction. If he kept it up front where she had to see and acknowledge the chemistry, maybe she'd let him closer.

"Jack—" Her mouth opened, then closed. It was like she wanted to tell him something, but couldn't. He saw the confusion on her face, and prayed she wasn't like Donna. His ex had been astute when it came to lying about her involvement with someone else at the same time she dated him. He would have never known, except he'd walked in on them one day. He needed Tu to be honest with him if she didn't want him.

His patience snapped. "Are you seeing someone else? Is that why you won't let us explore this thing between us?"

"Yes. I'm seeing someone, and unlike you, I'd feel guilty if I slept with anyone else."

He couldn't ignore the hurt in her voice. "I've explained about Donna, Tu. She's just a friend. We're not dating."

She nodded. "It's just that I don't like dating more than one person at a time, Jack."

"So, what were we doing the other night?" His grip tightened. "Were you just trying to humor me?"

"We're friends, and I like you a lot."

Jack dropped his hand. A piece of plastic jutted from the edge of her cubicle wall. He twisted it hard. *Friends.*

This called for desperate measures. He needed to discuss serious relationships here, and she had just classified their acquaintance in a category which sounded a death toll in the dating world to any man who heard the word. "Does he feel the same way about you?"

"W-What do you mean?"

Deciding to take advantage of the indecision in her voice, he leaned down so close that their noses almost touched. Her eyes widened, and he heard a catch in her breathing. "Is this guy you're sleeping with, seeing other women besides you?"

"No! I mean, Dev doesn't have time to see other women."

Jack raised an eyebrow. He resisted the urge to shout that the other guy she was dating was *him*. He watched a flash of uncertainty cross her face. He'd planted a seed of doubt in her mind and he wanted to watch the growth. He smiled. "Well, he must know a good thing when he sees it." He stood back up and turned to leave. "I know I do when I look at you."

Pausing at her cubicle door, regret spiraled through his gut for a moment that he caused her to doubt her lover. She looked lost.

The thought of losing her overrode his tenderness. "We have something special, Tu, and you'd be a fool to throw it away on a man who just wants you for sex."

Her head lifted. Defiance sparked in her eyes. "You don't?"

His jaw clenched at the reference to the incident on his desk. "No, not *just* sex. You're warm, beautiful, intelligent, and have the best sense of humor I've ever known in a woman."

He paused, watching her throat convulse in a hard swallow. "I want you for you."

With that, he turned and left to let her think about his words. He wouldn't chase her anymore, as either Jack, or Dev. The next move would have to be hers.

Chapter Eight

"Bunko!"

Stacy groaned. "That's three in a row, Lucy."

"Yeah, I know," Lucy said. "This is great."

"Yeah, great," Stacy mumbled and raked the dice towards her. "Hey, what's wrong with you?"

Tu glanced up, quickly, at her friend, then back to the table. "Nothing. I haven't been getting much sleep, lately."

"Oooo, hot date, huh?"

"Not exactly." Tu hadn't shared much information with Stacy about Dev or Jack, over the last week. She wanted to decide between the two men without anyone else's input, but after no phone calls, or late-night visits from either man, she needed some advice. "Dev didn't show up any the rest of this week, like he said."

Stacy shrugged. "Maybe he had to work or something."

"Um, maybe." Tu picked up the dice and rolled.

"One."

"Did he call?" Suzanne asked.

Tu hesitated, remembering other people were able to hear her conversation. She took a deep breath and shook her head.

"All week! Doesn't sound like a man in love. Is he dating someone else?" Penny asked from the table next to theirs.

Tu bit her lip. "As... frisky... as he is, he probably is seeing other women."

She didn't want to believe what Jack had suggested, but knew the probability was high. Dev had made it plain he only wanted to have sex with her. He'd never asked her not to see other men, or suggested he wouldn't see other women. She'd just assumed they were exclusive.

"Ooo, do tell," Penny said.

"Forget that. You think something happened to him, Tu?" Suzanne asked.

"He's getting bored," Rickey called from across the room.

Everyone went into shocked silence. Concern and pity consumed their expressions.

"Rickey's only saying what I've been thinking, especially after the last night we saw each other."

"What happened?" Stacy asked.

"You didn't tell him you loved him, did you?" Rickey asked.

Tu shook her head, sinking further down into her chair. "No, worse. I asked him if we had a relationship."

"Girrrrl, why did you do dat? You know you don't ask no *fuck buddy* something like dat," Penny said.

"I know, but—I've let him... do things to me no one else ever has. There has to be more to this than just sex!"

Everyone nodded their heads, but no one made a comment. The only sounds were the clicking of the dice, as each player took their roll and their partner counted.

Tu tried to concentrate on the game. Her friends weren't here to listen to her troubles. They were here to play bunko and escape the routine of daily life.

Routine? Hah!

She doubted she'd be able to wade through the mounting chaotic mess she'd made of her life. She thought about all the things Jack had said to her and admitted she missed talking to him. They were more than friends, but what did she do about Dev?

Don't forget he was at that restaurant when you and Jack were there. Tu didn't see Dev as the type of man to go to a place like that alone. She had tried remembering the other customers that night, in case she had seen his face, but couldn't. All she had been focused on was Jack.

"That's not all," she said. The occupants of the room grew quiet. She didn't have to see their faces to know that they were focusing their eyes on her. The stares cut into her skin, like lasers.

"What do you mean?" Rickey asked.

"I don't like the sound of this," Lucy said.

"Me, neither," Stacy said through a mouthful of cheese puffs.

Tu twisted her hands together, not sure she should confess her dating duality. Finally, she gave in. "I've been seeing Jack for the last month."

Several gasps echoed together. Tu cringed, but continued. "He wants to get serious, but I'm not sure I want to give Dev up yet."

Several of her buddies rolled their eyes and shook their heads.

"I mean, Jack did make a move on me in his office while his date was in the reception area, waiting on him!"

"Honey, he explained that, didn't he?" June asked. "Sounds like the guy is trying to make a commitment. Does this Dev character want a commitment?"

Tu shrugged her shoulders and fought back the hurt she felt at Dev's abandonment after all she'd given him of herself. Hurt turned to anger, and anger to resolution. "I'll show him. I'm going out with Jack tomorrow night, and when Dev shows up at my door, thinking he can get some anytime he pleases,

I won't be available."

"Dere you go. Show him what's for, Tu," Penny said with a downward punch of her fist and a quick wink of support.

"Now, don't go and do something you're going to regret," Rickey said, leveling a frown at Penny. "Just because you're mad at Dev doesn't mean you should lead Jack on."

"Lead him on? He knows I'm seeing someone else." Tu shrugged. "He asked me out to dinner and I refused. I'm going to ask him if his offer still stands, and if it does, then I'm going to have dinner with him. That's all."

"Riiiight," Lucy said before she passed the dice to Penny. The game continued.

"Yes, that's right. Just dinner. What else could he think it'd be?"

"Bunko!" Penny shouted.

What else does she want this to be? Jack's fingers tapped against the stem of his wine glass as he watched Tu make her way back to their table from the ladies' room. His gaze traveled up and down her slight frame, and his dick stiffened. She looked sexier than he'd ever seen her.

She had pulled her silky, black hair high on her head to reveal the creamy skin of her neck. Her shoulders were bare, except for two thin spaghetti straps that barely held her dress up. Some kind of shimmery, blue material clung to her breasts and outlined her body to the spot where her legs escaped the delicate silk to travel, bare, to her tiny feet, which were encased in spiked heels.

He angled his head, but couldn't see one line. No way she wore a bra or panties under the skintight dress. *Whoa.*

His mouth went dry, and he shifted his weight in the chair. If she didn't let him make love to her tonight, he was in trouble. He had conveniently not called her up at home the last few days, hoping she'd miss the camaraderie they'd experienced a week ago.

Face it, bud, you're addicted to her. Jack took a gulp of water from the glass on the table. Swallowing the cold liquid, he closed his eyes against the vision in front of him. He had to stay in control. Tu wanted a man to be in charge of her.

His knuckles tightened against the water glass. Where was that self-confident side he used at work when he needed it? Why couldn't his two halves work together? They both wanted the same thing—her.

He opened his eyes just in time to watch Tu bend her knees and slide the smooth curve of her ass into her seat. He bit his lip on a groan. *Damn.*

"I'm sorry, did you say something?"

He cleared his throat. "Uh, no, my throat is a little sore, that's all."

She turned all concerned in a heartbeat. "I feel terrible asking you to take me out when you're sick."

"No, really, I'm fine. It's just a tickle."

"If you want to call it a night, I'll understand." She patted his arm. "Really."

Jack studied her. "What's wrong, Tu? Feeling guilty about the boyfriend?"

She jerked her hand away and picked up her menu. "No, I just didn't want you to feel like you had to take me out." Her voice sounded muffled behind the tall plastic bound pages, and she hid her face from his scrutiny.

"Quit hiding, and let's get one thing straight, Miss Tran." He pulled the menu from her grasp, experiencing a moment of victory at the flare of surprise on her face. "*I* asked you out, not vice versa. This is not a charity meal, and I'm not taking pity on you."

His eyes bored into hers. "Whatever little plan of revenge you've got up your sleeve toward the guy, drop it now."

"I don't know what you mean." Her shock evaporated to be replaced by a flash of anger. Her chin rose and her lips drew into a tight line. She reached for the butter knife with one hand and a roll with the other, but Jack wrapped his fingers around her wrist with the knife. His grip wasn't strong enough to hurt her, but she couldn't move unless he let her. Her eyes flashed venom, but he held on.

"Yes, you do." He stroked his forefinger across the sensitive flesh of her inner arm.

Her hand jerked with a spasm of reaction, but he didn't release her.

Leaning closer so the other patrons didn't hear what was for her ears alone, his eyes never left hers. "When I slide my cock into your wet, little glide, Miss Tran, I want you to know who's screwing you. I..."

He tightened his grip when she would have pulled away. "... also want you to be with me because you want to, not because you're trying to get even with some prick that obviously has dumped you for you to be here with me."

This time he let her jerk her arm back. Oh, she was mad alright. He fought to control the jolt of pure lust that wanted to escape at the magnificence of her fury.

Her cheeks were stained a bright red, and her nostrils flared.

Their eyes clashed, but she was the first to lower her gaze. She placed the knife beside her plate. Her hand trembled enough that the silverware clinked against the china. With the task accomplished, she sat back in her chair and folded her hands into her lap like a demure, innocent girl.

Jack tensed. If he ever made the mistake to think her demure or innocent, the little she-cat would shred him, and he'd never have a chance to win her over. The time to make her *his* lover had passed a week ago, but she'd thought he'd been playing her for a fool the night Donna had walked in on them.

No, the next move was Tu's. She'd have to ask him to fuck her. That way, she claimed the seduction, not him. He'd be damned if she would take him into her body on a whim of retribution.

"You're right, Jack." Her voice was quiet, but firm. Her gaze came up to meet his. "I don't want to hide from you."

"What *do* you want?" Jack gazed around at the other tables, hoping he looked like he was bored and could care less if she took him up on his offer or not. Underneath, his heart beat like a drum and heat gathered around his collar. If his tie got any tighter he'd choke, but he resisted the urge to adjust the knot. He had to look cool and—

"I want you to take me home with you." Her voice caught. "I-I want you to have sex with me."

"Because..." He let the words fade, but waved a hand in the air for her to continue. He refused to make this easy on her. She had to tell him she wanted *him*.

"I don't know why, but it's not revenge."

Jack let out a sigh, pushing his chair back, but Tu grabbed his arm.

"It may have been the reason at first, but I am attracted to you." Her voice held a desperate note, and her almond-shaped eyes pleaded with him.

A tiny twinge of compassion threatened, but Jack knew he had to strengthen his resolve and stay firm.

She spoke again with her eyes downcast. Her voice was no more than a husky whisper. "When you grabbed my wrist I almost came."

"Waiter, bring the check." Jack finished his wine in a single gulp. With one hand wrapped around her wrist, he pulled her to her feet.

Halfway to the exit, she stumbled, and he caught her with an arm around her waist. Patrons at nearby tables paused in their meals to observe them.

Tu resisted when he proceeded to pull her beside him. "Jack, people are staring at us."

She had both feet planted in stubborn refusal to move. Jack looked at the interested expressions of the restaurant's clientele and staff, and sighed. He placed his lips against her hair. "We'll continue this discussion at my place."

Tu looked up with a frown on her face, and Jack raised his eyebrows up and down to make her understand his need for haste. His cock grew another inch when she let her angry stare move down his body to his crotch.

"Oh," she said, and pulled him out the door.

Chapter Nine

Tu's tongue slid up the inside of Jack's thigh. At the sound of his sigh she smiled. If he enjoyed this, then she knew he'd enjoy what she planned to do to him even more. The hair on his legs tickled her nose, but she moved forward.

When she reached his balls she licked the underside and watched the sacs draw tight with reaction. The fact he shaved his groin had surprised her, to say the least. She thought back to the night in his office, and giggled. Who would've thought Jack, the yuppie, could be so kinky?

She lifted her head. Her breath caught.

His eyes were dark and intense, as he watched what she did to him. For a second, she thought of Dev's gaze, but she shook the memory loose. This bed held no place for him. This was Jack's house and Jack's bed.

His fingers tightened in her hair. "Don't, Tu." His voice, husky with desire, held a warning she understood. He knew what she was thinking, and wasn't willing to share her with someone else.

"I'm not." She smiled. "Tonight I'm going to look at the face of my lover, and not wonder who the man is I'm giving my body to."

He frowned, and she realized he didn't know what she was talking about. There was no way Jack could know Dev wore a mask and was unwilling to share not only his face, but his name, or any other personal information with her.

Well, not anymore. She was worth more than a roll in the sack whenever Dev decided to visit. She wanted a man to share everything with, not just his body. The next time he came around, he was going to answer a few questions, or he was going to leave without any.

"I said 'don't'."

Tu squealed at the force Jack exerted on her to lift her on top of him.

"You said you wanted *me*, not him, tonight." His mouth took hers in a fierce kiss before she could tell him she was thinking about him, and how glad she'd decided to come home with him.

His teeth bit the soft flesh of her bottom lip, then suckled the wound when she cried out in pain. The flick of his tongue against hers made her clit quiver, and a flood of moisture eased down her inner thigh.

"Does he kiss you like this, Tu?"

"N-No." Her body shuddered.

"What about this?" His hands and arms lifted her enough to allow his mouth access to her breasts, where his teeth clamped onto her nipple.

Tu threw her head back. "No!"

White, hot desire shot from her breast to her womb. Her thighs tightened around his waist at the first contractions of orgasm. He didn't respond, but rolled her onto her back without releasing her breast. The bite became a suckle, and the tide of her orgasm eased, but only slightly.

She had to give Jack credit. He knew how to make the sensation ebb and flow with first a slow, swirling suckle around her nipple and a deep, hot lick down to the underside of her breast, then back up for a fast, sharp tug at her nipple again, until she clung to him and panted his name.

"J-Jack!"

"Not yet, Miss Tu." He rose, pulling his shirt over his head.

She marveled at the smooth skin of his chest, sleek and muscled.

With an impatient toss, the shirt landed in the corner. He locked onto her with an intense gaze. "I want to know what he doesn't do to you."

"Why?" Her mind felt foggy, but she thought they weren't going to discuss Dev. This was their time together, and she didn't want to think about anyone but Jack.

"Because, those are the things I'm going to do to you, so there won't be any comparisons between your lovers."

Tu shivered. Excitement built in her lower abdomen. She had her fantasies with Dev, but now she could have a few with Jack, too. Dev always took control of the situation and instigated what they did together. Tu knew Jack would let her be in charge for a change.

Ooo, you're a wicked girl, Tu Tran. She wiggled her hips against the pressure of his, but he ignored her hints to put his erection inside her.

"Of course, you could dump him for me." His voice held a suggestive note in the joking quality.

Tu tensed. "Jack, I—"

"Shh, don't talk, just feel." His head lowered to her breast once more, and she closed her eyes at the delicious swirl of his tongue and lips across her skin.

This was definitely one thing Dev didn't do, because of that damned mask. She'd never felt his lips on her body. Tongue, yeah, but no lips or teeth. God, how she craved the bite of teeth against her skin. Hell, he'd never even kissed her, and she loved to be kissed.

"Kiss me, Jack."

He raised his head from her stomach where he'd been circling her belly button with his tongue. "I thought that's what I was doing."

Tu giggled. "I mean on my mouth, silly."

"Hmm, I'll kiss your lips…" —he eased between her legs—"… then, I'll kiss your mouth."

Tu gasped, bringing her knees up at the contact of his mouth on her sensitive skin. Liquid heat enveloped her clit, forcing it to harden. She moaned and thrust her fingers into his hair to massage his scalp to the rhythm of his teeth and tongue. Again, she reached the verge of an orgasm, and again, he eased off.

Damn! He read her body like he'd been playing with her for years. Even Dev hadn't been this good the first time they'd been together.

Screw Dev. He didn't belong here! She wanted Jack to finish what he'd started. Her fingers wound into his auburn hair, pushing his head back down to her body, but he had other ideas.

"No, baby." He moved his body up hers.

"Oh, Jack, come on." She clamped her thighs around his waist to stop his progress. "That was sooo... good. Please finish. I was almost there."

Jack wanted to, but he couldn't chance her coming. He really did want to do all the things Dev hadn't done to her yet, but if she came too fast, he'd have to make love to her. The possibility that she'd recognize him scared him to death.

If he could excite her to the point that she was so wild with desire, she wouldn't know his dick felt the same as Dev's. Of course, he'd taken care of a few minor details before this date, like shaving his chest and pubic hair, and removing his penile piercing. No one in their wildest dreams would associate a penile piercing with good boy, Jack. He said a silent prayer of thanks to Donna for the one reminder of his drunken, wilder days with her, if it continued to please Tu.

He knew the cold metal of the ring sent Tu over the edge, but he wanted her to like *his* cock without embellishment, so he'd removed the hardware he wore as Dev. He was just plain old Jack, now.

"Shh, I'm going to take care of you, don't worry." He continued up her body, gave her nipple a tweak with his teeth that made her squeal, and finally reached her mouth. "Now, about that kiss."

Without delay he circled her lips with his tongue. The smell of her sex lingered beneath his nose, and he knew she could taste and smell herself. That turned him on like nothing else, and he groaned as his body lengthened another inch.

When she whined with frustration at the little nips and nibbles he was giving her, he increased the pressure of his mouth on hers, kissing her deeply. Their tongues mated and danced inside her mouth and his. Jack groaned at the powerful, heady sensation from the taste of her. Ambrosia.

"Ummm, Tu, you taste so good." He'd been dying to kiss her for the last two weeks, but with that mask...

He rolled onto his back, bringing her atop his body. His hands stroked up and down her arms in a lazy, relaxed motion. His cock throbbed between her legs, and she reached down to stroke him with the same rhythm he used on her.

She cupped his shaft in her hand and moved up, then down while her thumb worked its way over the bulb. The friction had his teeth clenched within seconds.

"If you don't stop, I'm going to come all over the front of your pretty stomach."

"That's okay."

Her gaze met his. He sucked in a sharp breath at the desire etched into her face.

"I want you to." With that she leaned toward him, covering his mouth with hers, never missing a stroke with her hand.

Jack pumped into her hand faster and clamped an arm around her waist to keep her from being thrown off. His tongue and lips feasted on hers in a hungry duel. God, she was so sweet, so rich, so—

"Ahhh...!"

White, hot semen squirted into her hands, and her grip slid without effort over his skin. The squish, squish sound was music to his ears. He opened his eyes. Her face appeared half an inch from his. He smiled.

She responded with a grin, kissing him with a fast peck on the lips before she rolled off him. Laying on her back, she spread her legs. "Now, do me."

"Do you, huh?" He knew she was a little firecracker, but he wanted to take things slow and easy tonight. *Dev* worked fast, but not Jack.

"Yep."

He rolled onto his side, propping on his elbow with his cheek on his hand. With one forefinger he traced an imaginary line from her nose and chin, down the valley of her breasts, and into the curls of the apex between her legs. They were soaked, indicating her readiness for him, but he couldn't bring himself to enter her. He had an obligation to tell her about Dev.

Easing a finger into the soft folds, he slicked himself with her juices. He liked the look on her face when he pushed into her deeper with two fingers.

Her eyes closed, as she arched her neck and back with a smile on her lips.

His thumb found her clit. Rubbing the hardened nub in a circle, he pressed into her heat deeper.

Her eyes flew open with gasp. She grabbed his wrist, but he sat up, capturing her hands with his free one, bringing them over her head. He knew what she liked, what she needed, and he wanted to be the one to give it to her.

A low, guttural moan issued from her chest and throat.

"Tell me your most secret fantasy."

She shook her head.

He leaned forward, kissing her hard at the same time he added a third finger into the soft, moistness of her core.

She sucked in a breath with a *hiss*.

"What do you want, Tu?"

At that moment, her muscles clenched around his fingers, and she screamed her orgasm, bucking her hips hard against his hand. He released her wrists, but continued to work his fingers in and out. Her spasms eased, and he kissed her forehead. "That's my girl. Easy, now, I've got you."

She drew a ragged breath, and he withdrew his hand.

The surprise he experienced when she caught his fingers in hers and licked each one clean made his body tighten, but not as much as the moment she looked into his eyes and said, "My most secret desire is to be tied up and at the mercy of whatever my lover wants to do to me."

Chapter Ten

I've died and gone to heaven. Jack's heart stopped at her sensual confession. If she'd touched him at that moment, he would have come.

He shouldn't have been surprised by her admission. The night in his office and the night Dev had taken her from behind, had hinted at the kind of passion she liked. Maybe that had unleashed this particular fantasy within her. He frowned, not sure he wanted to give Dev even a small iota of credit for Tu's desires.

Get a grip, Jack. You're jealous of yourself, man! Yeah, but Tu didn't know that. Yet.

"Jack?" She eased onto her knees in front of him and touched his arm. "Did I shock you?"

She had an expression of dread on her face when he looked at her. Letting his fingers trail across her cheek, he smiled. "I'm not shocked, just surprised."

He leaned forward and kissed her with a light, gentle kiss he hoped would ease her sudden anxiety. All the time she'd spent with him as Dev, not once had she told him something so personal. Maybe he hadn't been the only one wearing some form of a mask. "It takes a lot of trust to tell someone your innermost secrets, Tu."

She nodded, but her lips trembled.

"Does that mean you trust me?" He held his breath, terrified that even though she agreed, she still might be unsure of him. She had trusted Dev, but would she trust him?

The trembling disappeared, and she met his gaze without a flinch. "I do trust you, Jack."

"Even when I told you Donna and I were finished?"

"Yes. I understand that you had given up on dating me and had called her in a moment of... desperation."

"That's frustration." He threaded a hand through her hair. The texture feathered through his fingers like silk.

Tu snorted and turned away to climb off the bed. "Oh, I don't know. As big a bitch as she seemed to be, I'd have to say you were pretty desperate to get some."

Jack grabbed her from behind and tickled her. Tu gave a startled yelp and fell back into his arms. They tumbled onto the bed, laughing. He tickled her again, and she drew her arms close to her body with a shrill squeal.

"I like to hear you laugh." That was something else she'd never done with Dev. He pulled her into his arms, and they lay together in a companionable silence for several minutes, stroking and kissing.

"Um, this is nice." She sounded satisfied, snuggling closer.

"Yeah." He felt like a big, fat cat who'd eaten a huge dinner and was ready for a nap. He shuddered when he felt her fingers wrap around him. Or, maybe he had room for a little dessert.

Jack rolled Tu beneath him and kissed her. It was time to tell her who he was. If they were going to have any type of relationship, they had to be honest with each other. She'd already shared with him.

He lifted up, pulling her legs around him. She'd left her shoes on and her blue spiked heels scraped his back, but he didn't care. He knew he needed to confess, but first, he wanted to indulge in one of his secret fantasies and feel those heels dig into his skin, deep, when he made her come. "You've got the longest legs for such a tiny girl."

"Uh huh, and you have the biggest dick for such a yuppie."

Jack forced a frown, trying not to grin. "Yeah, well, this yuppie is about to make you scream his name, so hang on."

Her thighs tightened around his waist and back at the same time he positioned himself to enter her.

Bzzzz. Bzzzz.

"Ah, hell!" Jack rolled his gaze toward the ceiling.

"What's that?" Tu tightened her thighs.

"My beeper. I put it on vibrate. I'm on call tonight." He patted her legs, indicating her need to release him.

"Ignore it. We've got more important business to attend to."

"I can't just ignore it, Tu. You know that." Jack pulled loose from her death grip around his waist, rolling over and reaching for the beeper on the bedside table. With mock censure he asked her, "So, this is what you do when I have you on call?" He looked at the monitor and groaned. "It's my boss." Jack glanced back over his shoulder. "You ignore the damned thing and go about your business?"

She shrugged, causing her breasts to rise.

His cock twitched, as her nipples drew tight. They were the perfect shape for him to latch onto with his teeth and suckle. He gave himself a mental shake, grabbing the phone. She made it hard to focus on the number he dialed, but he managed to get the call through.

"Yeah, this is Jack. How may I help you, sir?"

Tu scooted off the bed and headed for the bathroom down the hall. His cock lengthened at the sight of her pear-shaped ass, and his fingers itched to cup the delicious cheeks. Jack groaned when she gave him a little twitch of her hips. He had big plans for *that* tonight.

"… did you get all that?"

Not yet! "Uh, sorry, sir, the connection faded out. Could you repeat that again?"

He covered the transmitter end of the phone so his boss wouldn't hear Tu's peal of laughter over his distraction. He frowned at her, and she winked before she disappeared through the door.

Damn woman would be the death of him. He stroked the heavy throb of his shaft to ease the pain growing between his legs. His boss called his name, and Jack tried to concentrate on the call, but it was hard… in more ways than one.

꙳ᕲᕤᕬ᷽

Tu hummed a snappy, little tune on her way back from the bathroom. She and Jack were so right for each other. They both liked the same work, the same food, the same great sex… *You can say that again!* They hadn't even had intercourse yet, and the orgasms had been out of this world.

She felt bad about Dev, but knew he wouldn't miss her too much. She and Jack had shared something personal, whereas Dev was strictly about sex. Good sex, but sex just the same. Tu knew she and Jack could have a relationship built on trust and mutual respect. Hell, Dev wouldn't even show his face or share his name.

Halfway down the hall she passed Jack's spare bedroom and her shoe caught in the carpet. *Damned heels. I know a man designed these things.*

She grabbed the door jamb and stooped to adjust the strap, but stopped when a flash of something caught her eye. She peeked through the open door. Boxes and the usual junk people stored in their extra space lay on the bed and floor around the room. The light from the hallway illuminated several items on the bed—an old baseball glove, a stack of faded jeans, and something red.

Tu frowned and squinted, but couldn't make out the object. She moved to the edge of the bed. Her hand reached to take the object, but faltered in mid-air. Her heart skipped a beat.

No, this is just a coincidence! With hands that trembled, she picked up the mask, red with hideous fangs and white devilish horns. Her fingers gripped the rubber so tight her knuckles showed white in the pale light.

The truth sucked the breath from her chest, tightening with each moment of realization. The mask swam in and out of her vision, and she reached with her other hand to hold the bedpost to keep from falling, if she passed out.

"Hey, where'd you—" Jack's words broke off behind her, and she knew he could see what she held. He picked up the baseball glove, as he moved around her.

Tu turned toward him. Tears threatened to spill down her face, but she blinked twice to keep them in place. She didn't know what emotion was stronger inside her, hurt or anger. She took a deep breath. "I believed you when you explained about Donna. What's your explanation for this?"

"Tu, look, I *can* explain."

"Yeah, I'm sure you can, but I don't trust you anymore, Jack." She threw the mask at him, and he caught it in the gut.

Whoosh. His mouth sucked and gulped for air, like a fish out of water.

She hoped the impact had hurt. With her head held high and a tight grip on her tears, Tu strode to Jack's bedroom. Her clothes were scattered around the room, a testament to their earlier excitement. God, —she put a hand to her stomach— he'd played her for a fool, again. A small sob escaped the tightness of her throat, and she stuffed her fist into her mouth.

"Tu, baby, let —" He dropped the glove on the bed, as he wrapped his arms around her to pull her close, but Tu twisted away to face him.

"Don't touch me."

The concern on his face turned to irritation. "You're not being fair, Tu."

"Ha!" She moved to the far side of the bed and grabbed her dress. One leg into the silk shift, she looked up. "You lied to me, Jack, not the other way around. You could have told me who you were the other night when I asked you, but, no, you had to play your little games. Did you and your girlfriend get a good laugh out of this?"

"This doesn't concern Donna, and it wasn't a game," he shouted, then stopped, running an agitated hand through his hair. He turned his back to her and leaned a hand against the door sill. The light from the bedside lamp cast shadows across the taut muscles of his naked back and buttocks.

Tu looked away from temptation.

His voice was muffled when he spoke. "I knew you were mad about Donna that night. I overheard you on the phone with your friend earlier and knew which club you were supposed to meet her at." He shrugged. "I took a chance that's where you'd end up, looking for some *Joe Schmoe* to fuck your brains out."

Tu flinched at the plain, ugly truth of his words.

He turned to her, and she took a step back at the look of determination on his face. "I didn't know what I had to do, Tu, but you weren't going to be in anyone else's bed, but mine."

She gasped. "So, you thought lying to me about who you were would insure that?"

Jack took a step toward her, and Tu threw her hand up into the air. "Don't come any closer."

He stopped. A muscle twitched in a steady spasm along his jaw. "I put the damned mask on, and you didn't have a clue who I was!" Picking up the baseball glove, he threw it across the room with such force that the leather mitt crashed in the center of the dresser, scattering his wallet, comb, and personal items to the floor.

Tu jumped at the violence she thought she'd never witness in her sweet, lovable Jack. Dev, yeah, but not Jack. She shook her head. "I don't know you at all."

"I could have been a serial killer for all you knew, but you didn't waste any time in taking me home and screwing me."

Bewilderment and the tiniest bit of fear turned to anger. "Don't you dare turn this around on me, Jack Noblin." Tu struggled to zip the dress, while stabbing a finger in the air toward him. "I'm not the one, who—"

She stopped and caught her breath. Her tears were on the verge of escape, and if they did, she wouldn't be able to stop them. "You know what? Just forget it, it doesn't matter." She picked up her purse.

Jack stared at her in disbelief. "What, you're just going to leave?"

"Yes, and I'm putting in for a transfer out of your department."

"Who's hiding now, Tu?" he asked. Anger simmered within his narrowed gaze.

Tu moved forward, and Jack stepped out of her way without touching her. When she drew level with him, she stopped without glancing up. Tension radiated from his body, but she didn't care. She had to get away before she embarrassed herself anymore in front of this man. "I can't sleep, or work, with a man I can't trust."

"Did you trust *Dev*?" His question was laced with acid.

Tu almost laughed, but caught herself. He was jealous of her relationship with himself, but who's fault was that? Her chin quivered, but she held her head high. "At least he was honest in what he wanted from me."

༜ℑ⊙℘ℰ

He faced the open window, not really seeing what lay in the darkness of night. A warm, New Orleans breeze brushed across his naked skin. The sound of a siren passed in the distance, but he barely noticed through the thoughts that swirled in his muddled mind. He tried to focus on Tu and what he needed to do to get her back, but the more he thought of her, the more the image of Tu and Dev rose to taunt him.

Tu making it with Dev. Not him, Jack Noblin. She'd made her choice, and even though he and Dev were one, she didn't want *him*. He smacked his fist into his open palm. She'd chosen the other half, which he kept hidden from the rest of the world.

Jack reached for the bourbon he'd been working on since Tu had left, and held the clear bottle up to the light. Three more shots should take care of what remained, and maybe by then he could get her out of his mind.

He snorted. Here he sat at the bottom of a bottle, and his alter-ego ended up the hero. Jack took a swig of whiskey, ignoring the shot-glass. *How ironic is that?* He swallowed the anger mixed with the fiery liquid, ignoring the hot, scalding sensation down his throat.

Dev could only function behind a mask in the darkness of night.

Jack smiled. Then, he frowned, sitting forward as a thought formed through the alcohol haze.

He had a way to bring his two halves together, and give Tu her most secret desire. He turned the bottle up and drained it dry. Instead of the grimace from earlier at the burning sensation, a grin spread across his face.

Chapter Eleven

"I'm not your partner this round, D'awlin," Penny said.

"Huh? Oh, yeah." Tu slid the dice across the table toward Judith. "Sorry."

The dice clicked across the vinyl table cover and landed on odd numbers, but no six. Tu slipped back into her thoughts. She didn't know why she'd bothered coming to the game tonight. All she could think about was Jack, or Dev. Or, Jack.

Dammit! Why couldn't she get them ̶ him out of her head? She hadn't seen or spoken to him in a week.

"Your turn, Tu," Stacy said.

"Huh? Oh, sorry."

"Okay dat's it. Timeout, everyone," Penny said. The older woman stood up with her hands in the shape of a "T."

"What are you doing?" Rickey asked.

"We got a *Jack alert* over here at table tree," Penny said.

That got Tu up and out of her chair. She hadn't meant for her friends to be affected with her personal problems. "Look, I shouldn't have come tonight, girls. I've got a lot on my mind, and—"

"Ridiculous. That's what friends are for," Lucy said. "What's wrong? Did you and Jack have a fight?"

"I bet he found out about Dev," Rickey said. "I told you not to lead him on, Tu."

"I didn't. He's the one who was leading me on!" Tu sat down with a *thud* and crossed her arms over her chest.

"What?" Several voices called in unison. The group moved in like a flock of vultures on fresh meat.

She sighed at the expectant faces of her friends. "I might as well tell you. You will find out sooner or later." Shifting in her chair, she decided there was no easy way for her to admit her own stupidity. "We did have a fight, and I walked out on him and told him I didn't want to see him again."

"Kinda hard to do if you two work together," Suzanne said.

"I transferred out of his department a week ago."

"How'd I miss that?" Stacy choked around the celery stick she crunched.

The expression on her best friend's face told Tu a lot. If Stacy, the head of the gossip mill at work, didn't know about the transfer, Jack must have kept everything pretty hush hush.

"Yeah." Tu released a long sigh. "I found out he and Dev were one in the same."

The group gaped at her with dazed expressions for about three seconds before Penny slammed her fist down on the card table. Everyone jumped. "Castrate dat bastard!"

For once no one in the group censured Penny, and Tu had to bite her lip to keep from laughing. Not that the thought of rendering Jack's masculinity helpless hadn't crossed her mind, but she didn't want to spend time in jail for any man. *They aren't worth it.*

"Violence isn't the answer, girls," Melanie said. "Make him sweat and see what a good thing he let slip through his hands." She gave Tu a hug.

Tu blinked several times to hold back her tears at the concern they were all showing her.

"Yeah, Tu. You need to dress real sexy at work and make sure you're in the cafeteria the same time he is," Lucy said. "Be real sweet and smile like nothing's wrong. That kills them."

"Wouldn't hurt to let him catch you in a passionate throe with a hot, young stud, either."

"Penny!" everyone said.

"Thanks for the advice, but I don't think any of that is going to help me."

"What do you mean?" Melanie asked.

"Oh, no, don't tell me," Rickey said. "You're in love with the jerk."

"No!" The others turned to her with disbelief in their voices and on their faces.

Tu looked down at the table and picked up the dice. She twirled the white and black enamel cubes between her fingers, trying to decide if Rickey were right. She'd been asking herself the same question all week with no answer.

She let the dice fall with a weak attempt at a roll. The two dice on the table revealed sixes, but one die skittered across the vinyl to land on the floor. She quickly bent to retrieve it, and raised her head to find everyone waiting on her response. She held up a six and tried to offer her friends a smile. "Bunko."

One tear trickled down her cheek. She sniffed. Without anything to hold the surge of pent up emotions, the dam broke and she couldn't stop the flood.

❧⟨ᴗᴗ⟩❧

Tu sniffed. "I've got good friends." No one at bunko had accused her of being a fool when she'd broken down and admitted she was in love with Jack. Instead, they had gathered around her and hugged her and wiped her tears.

After several margaritas even Rickey, the most cynical of the group, had told her to look on the bright side. "You can't die from a broken heart, kid."

Tu sighed into the darkness as she tried to unlock the front door to her townhouse. The key wouldn't fit. She tried again, but missed the keyhole. She eased her shoulder around to prop against the jamb, laughing.

"Well, Whiskers, I'm tipsy." She giggled. Her gray tabby, sitting beside her feet and waiting, patiently, to be allowed inside looked up at her with big, yellow eyes and meowed.

"I love you, too." She turned with her forehead against the glass pane and tried the lock again. With the *click*, she breathed a sigh of relief. Although she lived in a veritably safe part of the city, it was never smart for a single girl to be standing around alone in the middle of the night, especially if she were drunk.

With her shoulder, she pushed the door open, and Whiskers ran between her legs. Tu stumbled, but held onto her balance. "Just like a damn male."

She slammed the door and locked it with the deadbolt. "Flash those big baby blues with a smile and sweet words, then when you finally open the door and give them what they want, they walk all over you."

With another grumble she threw her purse onto the table beside the door, and continued into the house without turning any lights on. She just wanted to flop across her king-size bed and go to sleep. She hoped the liquor would help. Three weeks with little or no sleep had finally caught up with her. All she could think about without the hustle and bustle of work was Jack, and his gorgeous eyes, and mouth, and hands.

Tu reached her bed and yawned. Her arms stretched high to lift her sweater over her head. A cool breeze touched her skin. She shivered and reached for her night shirt. Instead of the feel of soft, cool cotton she encountered hard, warm flesh.

The scream in the back of her throat never erupted. A large hand stuffed some sort of gag into her mouth and flung her face down onto her bed.

Tu struggled to get up, but her arms were quickly pinned behind her back. Strong hands bound her wrists with what felt like pantyhose. *God, was she being raped?*

With that thought, Tu twisted and kicked her legs. She experienced a moment of satisfaction when her foot made contact with her assailant's back, and he grunted from the impact. She had no intention of going down without a fight. If she was going to suffer, so was he.

"Now, now, Miss Tran, is that any way to greet your long lost lover?"

Time halted into a slow motion movie. Her breath along with her entire body froze in recognition of the voice.

Finally, she exhaled, and all hell broke loose. Throwing her body at him any way she could, she shouted the words, "You sorry bastard," through the muffled confines of her gag.

The sound of Jack's laughter and the *tsk, tsk* of his tongue made whatever fear she'd felt at first fade to pure, unadulterated anger.

"That's not very ladylike, Tu." He caught her knees, pushing her legs down, and leaned over her. His lips next to her ear, he traced her lobe with his tongue, and Tu couldn't stop the catch in her breath.

She tried to get her knees under her on the mattress, but Jack's full weight along the length of her body pinned her beneath him. Her nostrils flared with the effort to suck much needed oxygen into her lungs. She moaned, but couldn't move. His hot breath fanned her cheek, and his chin rested on her neck. His hands covered hers with both between their bodies.

"Thatsa, girl. We're just gonna have a good time."

Sweat pooled in her lower back and between her breasts at the sound of his gravely voice. The smell of her fear and anger mixed with his... arousal. She shut her eyes and tried not to panic, because she knew what he had in mind.

Think, think. What do I do? She couldn't let Jack fulfill her secret fantasy. She'd be lost in a one-sided love where she wouldn't know if she could trust anything he ever said to her.

He shifted his body and his hands came from between them, and reached for something on the other side of her. The sound of silk against silk teased the one ear she had uncovered. What was he—?

What little light was evident disappeared when he covered her eyes with a silk scarf. Tu bucked and screamed against the blind and gag, but to no avail. His big body held her captive.

His weight eased down, and he grabbed her at the knees, hauling her further onto the bed. He kept a tight grip, and she knew he would be ready for any attempt she might make to escape.

Zzzzz. A sound, like a cord being pulled loose from a container or confinement, echoed through the room. Tu angled her head to try and hear better, but the movement of her hair rustled through the scarf that also covered her ears to limit her auditory abilities.

The touch of some type of nylon rope around her ankles had her screams muffled through the gag once again.

Damn him! She couldn't see, hear, or move. The monster had rendered her helpless against anything he wanted to do to her. Her vulnerability made her shake with the renewed fear he would soon breach all her defenses.

⁂᷾₷(ᵕͨͦ)ᷤ℀

Jack studied his hands, large and shaking, spanning her tiny waist. From the stiffening of her body, he knew she was angry, but scared. The knowledge caused him a moment of guilt. He hesitated, but remembered her secret fantasy. Taking a deep breath, he flipped her over onto her side.

Her knees came up so fast, he couldn't move out of the way. The impact against the inside of his thigh next to his groin made him double over.

"Damnation!" He gritted his teeth. A bead of sweat worked its way across his brow. The pain ebbed, easing away. He looked down and traced her form against the darker colors of her bedspread with his gaze.

Her nostrils were flared, and her hands strained against the hose he'd tied her with, but she couldn't escape. She was *his*, and he was going to make her pay for making him love her.

He blinked and frowned at the realization. Then, nodded in agreement to what his mind and heart acknowledged, but he could tell her until he turned blue in the face, and she wouldn't listen to him. So, he'd have to show her.

Jack caught her hair in one hand and pulled the mass into a tight grip. The moan she emitted made his heart jump. His excitement had been building all day from thoughts of this moment, and he remembered another night in his office, not too long ago, when he'd plotted Miss Tran's retribution. He gave her a rough peck on the cheek. This time he planned on following through without any interruptions. "Play nice, Tu, and I'll give you everything you want."

He straddled her and watched her squirm against his hips. He loosened her hands, intending to pull them above her head. She tried to punch him, but he managed to retie them to the headboard before she could cause too much damage or get away.

He mopped his forehead. For such a small woman, she sure made him work up a sweat. With a shaky hand he reached into his back pocket. Removing his razor, he slipped the cover off and knew a moment's satisfaction at the knowledge that one of the secret fantasies she'd refused him, as *Dev,* would come true tonight.

The metal glinted in the pale moonlight, which filtered through the gauze liners Tu kept over her bedroom windows. Jack turned the razor this way and that. Too bad Miss Tran couldn't see the way the light reflected on the cold steel. *But, she can feel the effect.*

Jack laid the rounded edge of the metal against the soft skin of her belly. With a gentle turn, he circled her navel. His cock tightened, as the muscles in her abdomen fluttered.

He leaned closer, catching a hint of her arousal through the fabric of her skirt. "I think the clothes have to go, D'awlin'." With a quick, but careful jerk, he tore the material open to reveal a pair of white, cotton panties. "Hmm, what do we have here?"

They were plain, but his dick responded to the sight. With his finger, he rubbed the crotch of her panties, pushing between the folds of her vulva until he encountered moisture.

She squirmed and pulled against the ropes.

Easing his mouth down over the point where he knew her clit lay hidden in dark curls, he blew a stream of hot breath through the thin cotton. Tu bucked hard beneath him, cursing through her gag. Again, he thought he could make out what she said.

"… should have let… castrate you… sorry sonofabitch."

He smiled at her ferocious, passionate nature, but decided it was time to tame the little shrew. She acted tough, but from the viewpoint of *Dev,* Jack knew she wanted her man to be in control. He gripped the edge of the panties, hesitating but a second before he ripped the fabric from her hips.

Her knees arched up, hitting him in the back, but not as hard as the first time.

"That's enough of that, missy." Jack worked his weight down over her weapons. When he reached the end of the bed, he looped a piece of cord around each ankle and secured them to the bedposts. That done, he cut the previous cord, which held her legs together. Her bucking slowed to a bare minimum with the tightening of the ankle cords.

With her legs drawn apart to expose the treasure hidden within damp curls, he smoothed his hands up over the fine muscles of her legs, across her abdomen, and finally, to the apex of her thighs. "Try and fight me now, Tu."

The press of his erection against the confines of his jeans was creating a pain he couldn't ignore. With an unsteady hand, he unzipped his pants, and his cock sprang free. He eased his body onto the bed between Tu's splayed legs. The scent of her sex called to him. *Time to play.*

꙾⁎ᗞᏨᏨᏤᏤ⁎꙾

When she got free she was going to kill Jack Noblin with her bare hands, and enjoy every second she had to sit in prison. He'd scared the death out of her, and she intended to make him pay. At least she'd know he was in hell, too, for what he'd put her through.

His weight pushed the mattress down between her legs.

She stilled, but cocked her head to the side, trying to hear what he planned.

The cold metal object returned; she jumped. A thread of anticipation spread through her abdomen. A silent scream echoed through her mind at her treacherous body. She could fight all she wanted, but she couldn't deny that she craved what he was doing to her. Whatever he had in mind, he had her at his mercy, and the knowledge excited her beyond belief.

Moisture pooled on the sheet beneath her, and the touch of his tongue in the wet folds of her cleft made her jerk in pleasant surprise against the binds that held her. She bit the inside of her mouth to prevent herself from begging him to continue.

She might crave his desire and the demands he made of her body, but she didn't have to let him know how much she liked what he did to her. She bit into the gag to stifle a moan.

His long, thick fingers traced up and down her lips, spreading the telltale juices of her arousal over her heated skin. Jack emitted a deep chuckle.

Too late, he knows. He knew how much this turned her on because she was the one who'd told him about her secret fantasy to be tied up and *taken* by her lover.

His hot breath fanned the wetness, cooling the heat between her legs, which consumed her, but only just. Deep within her womb, the need to explode with every touch of his fingers and every swipe of his talented tongue increased. *Damn him.*

He pulled the hair of her pubis up, and a tearing sound caused her to *focus* on his actions. Again, he lifted the hair, and realization struck. Tu bucked against his hand, screaming. "… amn, yo …!"

"What was that, honey? I couldn't hear you." Laughter rang in every word. He patted her thigh. "Easy, now, Tu, I don't want to cut you. This straight-blade is pretty sharp."

Tu panted through the gag and lay still, listening to the scrape of the razor. The bite against her sensitive skin reminded her of how she'd refused to let Dev shave her. Now, Jack carried out one of the fantasies of her secret lover.

He pulled her hair once more, scraping twice. He stopped. Rubbing his fingers across her bared pubis, he spread her lips. The slick of his tongue against her clit was too much.

Tu moaned, clenching her vagina tight in response. God, she needed him inside her. If he didn't give her some relief—

He moved above her, and she held her breath. The scarf pulled free, and she blinked several times, trying to focus on Jack.

He eased the gag from her mouth, but didn't say a word. Neither did she. The look of tenderness on his face had her at a loss for words. She could only look into his eyes filled with… love.

A tear trickled down her cheek. She tried to tell him she loved him, but the words wouldn't come. Instead, she nodded her head and hoped he understood.

He moved forward with a quick thrust, and his cock filled her. The brush of *Dev's* penile piercing caused her to arch into his momentum where a moan gathered deep in her throat to rush forward and be consumed by his mouth and tongue. The taste of her juices blended with the taste of Jack—the taste of their passion for each other.

Over and over he thrust into her body. Sweat covered bodies melded together into a final climax, and Tu threw her head back and screamed at the same time Jack did. Still he thrust into her, like he couldn't get enough. Tu opened her eyes, and he snared her gaze with his. "We belong together."

The intense stare and words belonged to Dev, but also Jack.

Tu swallowed the emotion in her throat, but couldn't do more than nod her head.

He thrust harder. "Tell me you love me, Tu."

"I-I love you." The words were no more than a groan, husky and low.

"Me, or…" —he thrust again—"… Dev?"

Tu smiled, spreading her legs wider. "I have enough room for the both of you."

Jack's pupils dilated, then he collapsed on top of her. Tiny kisses rained across her throat, chin, and finally, her mouth where he kissed her hard before he gentled his caress of her tongue and lips. "Good. That's good, because they *both* love you, and can't go another day without you." He buried his face in the side of her neck and held her tight.

Tu looked at the ceiling, smiled, and whispered, "Bunko!"

About the Author:

Drawn to the art of writing at an early age, Sheri Gilmore decided to combine her love of erotica with her love of romance to create the kind of stories she always wanted to read. Her many interests include reading, photography, cooking, and the study of ancient cultures, religions, and philosophy. She lives with her husband and the youngest of her three children in the Deep South. You can visit Ms. Gilmore at her website www.sherisecrets.com or write her at sgilmore@sherisecrets.com. She loves to hear from her fans.

Hide and Seek

by Chevon Gael

To My Reader:

Nothing is more exciting than discovering something new and untouched. Adrenaline rushes, the senses heighten; the body anticipates adventure. It's infatuation, lust, love at first sight. I've only felt that way about two things; the moment I looked into my future spouse's "Paul Newman-blue" eyes and the first time we both landed on the tiny island of San Andres in the Caribbean. I hope what we found there translates into *Hide And Seek*, a story of two people discovering something wonderful—a love for each other.

My thanks to Bob, 'Mr. Big Juice' and all the great info on his San Andres website. Thanks, Island Buddy, I owe you a coco-loco! Also to Marley and Miller, the best bartenders in San Andres. Special thanks to Mario's snorkling tours—*Hola, Amigo!* And a very special thank-you to the late Mr. Carrington, my favortie octogenarian chef whose grilled shrimp and hours of brilliant conversation I will miss dearly.

<h1 style="text-align:center">Chapter One</h1>

Kyle DeLaurier wasn't in the mood for sex.

But it was all around him, paraded in front of him on the sandy cat walk that was San Luis Beach. He reached for another cold beer from the ice bucket planted in the sand beside the hotel's plastic chaise lounge and continued to observe the array of female forms that swished past him. Tall and tanned, buff and bronzed, their tiny beach thongs, tissue thin in some cases, allowing him a glimpse at the assorted wares. From what he could tell, pubic region shaving and butt cheek tattoos were definitely this year's trends.

The topless beach at the Hotel San Luis on San Andres Island was definitely a crowd pleaser, as were the women who carelessly sauntered back and forth in groups of three or four in front of the rows of lounges—most of which were occupied by men. Kyle leaned back in the white chaise and finished off his beer, totally unmoved, almost bored, by the bevy of beautiful bared female breasts around him.

He tossed the empty beer can back into the plastic bucket and adjusted his sunglasses. Lord, he was hung over. He reached for another can then decided against it. He should have stayed in his hotel room instead of venturing out into the hot Caribbean sun. Ten o'clock in the morning and already his head was pounding. No breakfast, just a little hair of the dog.

But for the first time in a month he decided to try to stay sober today. It was going to be painful. Perhaps it was because the sting of his best friend's death was wearing off. Or maybe it was because the part of him that hurt so much was now sufficiently saturated by copious amounts of imported rum. Whatever the reason behind his decision, it wasn't going to be easy.

He turned his head at the excited sounds of several young men, barely out of their teens, as they set up their towels and umbrellas on the sand. A new crop of university students probably on a reading week junket from Canada or the States, given the time of year and the fact that their pasty white skin stood out amongst the native San Andreans and wintering elderly snowbirds. It was obviously their first time on a topless beach. Kyle chuckled to himself as he watched their expressions change from anxious curiosity, then admiration, to outright lust. Two of the guys backed into each other and stumbled, spilling their bucket of ice across the sand. The impact frightened a tiny sand crab that skittered out from behind a melting ice cube into the refuge of an empty coconut shell.

Poor bastards, he thought! By tonight those kids will be fried and too drunk to notice. Some dark skinned girls from the local Reggae bar, complete with smoking gifts and condoms, will part them from their Yankee cash. Tomorrow morning they'll wake up sore, broke and unable to remember how they got that way.

Kyle watched the same scene unfold day after day. Except for the fact that he decided not to be totally hammered by four in the afternoon he wondered if this day would be any different.

✲ᨀᘛ☙ᨀ✲

Clothing Optional

Darcy McLeod stared at the sign at the edge of the beach and hugged her towel firmly around her shoulders. She shifted her bare feet in the hot sand, more to do with her nervousness than the fact that her winter boot-bound soles felt char-broiled. Besides which she was ruining a perfectly good pedicure. She swallowed, summoned her courage and chanted her mantra, "It's just a job, it's just a job."

She'd done a lot of strange things in the name of her profession. Dressed like a hooker, disguised as a nun, even learned to ski, all in the name of surveillance. A topless beach bunny should be a piece of cake. She didn't mind flashing in private and she could be very creative in the revealing clothing department if she needed to transform herself into a femme fatale in public. But letting it all hang out on a semi-nude beach of mixed company made her stop and think—was the money really worth it?

She'd seen her target leave the hotel that morning as she enjoyed a light breakfast in the open air dining room. He'd come within a few feet of her table. She discreetly lowered her head, choosing not to make eye contact with him just yet. At the same time, she nearly choked on her eggs. This was definitely not the Kyle DeLaurier in the photo she'd been given. The black and white head shot provided to her by DeLaurier Inc. showed the typical, bored suit-type with salon-perfect hair above a clean-shaven, casual smile. The man who passed her this morning wore a don't-fuck-with-me scowl, a deep tan, a red *Speedo*, leather sandals and sunglasses. He was unshaven, unkempt and smelled like stale beer. And this was the man she was supposed to get close to?

Her plan had been to move into his territory at breakfast, perhaps upset a glass of juice in his lap and offer to pay to launder his shirt. Except he wasn't wearing a shirt and he walked right past the dining area. She turned and summoned a waiter for coffee, at the same time she observed DeLaurier as he stopped at the bar, filled a plastic bucket with ice and a six-pack of canned beer, the breakfast of champions. On to plan B. She'd have to think of another way to get his attention. And several good ideas came to her while she walked to the beach. Until she saw the sign.

Darcy watched two young women walk by her. Their thong-style bikini bottoms left little to the imagination. The rest was public domain. She fingered the thin shoulder straps of her blue tank suit. Hell, she might as well be wearing a parka and consider herself formally dressed by comparison. Gradually she slid the towel down her shoulders and wrapped it around her waist. She scanned the beach for any sign of DeLaurier. Finally she spotted him, or rather, she spotted the red bathing suit and unruly hair.

She walked casually by the long line of occupied lounges and kept her fingers crossed. Luck was with her. There were two free spaces near DeLaurier but the two women who passed her earlier were walking toward them.

Needs must, she decided and dashed to the empty seats, claiming one immediately. She dragged it next to DeLaurier who was lying on his stomach, facing toward the ocean. Darcy allowed herself a moment to admire his long, lean legs, muscled back and derriere, snug and tight beneath the red material. Few men could carry off a *Speedo*. He certainly was a hottie! If only he wasn't just another job...

"Excuse me, is this seat taken?" Gawd! That sounded cheesy. A pick-up line as stale as the beer he must have bathed in. But picking him up was exactly what she needed to do.

DeLaurier barely stirred but mumbled something that sounded like, "sure, whatever."

Darcy refused to be put off. Follow the book, is what Spencer always told her. A good private investigator needs to be discreet, cunning and, at times, tenacious. She tried again.

"I mean if your girlfriend is coming down later I can move."

Another grunt. He was facing away from her, his head resting on a wadded up beach towel.

"If you're sure—"

He turned his head toward her suddenly and barked. "Lady, can't you see I'm trying to sleep one off. So take the chair, a beer or whatever else is required for you to shut the fuck up and leave me alone." He turned his head once again and ignored her. Nice.

Okay, Spence. Now what? Establishing contact was easy. Gaining the subject's trust was going to be a little harder. Trust was based on intimacy. Or was it the other way around?

She turned her back on him, unwrapped the towel from around her waist and laid it across the chair. She surveyed her surroundings. The beach stretched a couple of miles in each direction. The shore was cluttered with row upon row of white chaise lounges occupied by a rainbow of bikini bottoms, long, slender brown legs and bared, well-oiled breasts. The scent of coconut oil sun screen permeated the salt-tinged ocean breeze. The only thing that distinguished her from everyone else was the fact that she was still covered from the waist up. Darcy realized she stuck out like a sore thumb. Bad technique for blending in.

She didn't need to attract attention, except for DeLaurier. She couldn't afford to be different.

She licked her nervous lips, tasting honey flavored protective gloss and tried to swallow past the dry patch at the back of her throat. She looped her thumbs under her tank straps and began to slide them down her shoulders. Just then a strong ocean breeze plucked at the wide brim of her straw hat and Darcy realized she was in imminent danger of losing part of her disguise, not to mention her sun protection. Then a thought came to her.

She slid the straps down her shoulders and kept a protective grip on the top of her suit. She plucked the straw hat off her head and placed it over her breasts. Then she dropped the top of her bathing suit. Technically she was now topless.

Darcy detected a small movement behind her. She kept her grip on her hat while she turned to sit down. He was staring at her.

At least she thought he was. It was hard to tell where his eyes were focused behind the dark sunglasses he wore. She did exactly what he demanded earlier and paid no attention to him. She made herself as comfortable as she could with one hand smashing the crown of her hat against her bare breasts. She cautiously reached into her beach bag with her other hand, drew out a romance novel and opened it.

"It figures," he smirked under his breath.

Darcy never took her eyes off her page while she took up the challenge. If this was his way of initiating a conversation then she'd take what she could get. "What figures?"

"You call that reading material?"

"As opposed to…" she nearly said the financial papers. She thought quickly, "some sports rag with the latest steroid scandal? Or perhaps the T&A issue," she replied tartly. He might become suspicious if she got friendly with him too quickly. Never get attached to a subject. It was Spence's 'Golden Rule'.

He rolled onto his side to study her. "Honey, in case you haven't noticed this is a topless beach. Aren't you a little over-dressed?"

Darcy looked down at her attire. Okay—so her boobs were wearing a hat. In the last five minutes she'd seen women wearing bikini bottoms not much wider than dental floss.

"Nope. Besides, the sign said 'Optional'. I'm exercising my option not to burn my nip—er, my skin." Just then a young woman, who obviously didn't care what she burned, interrupted them.

"Is that lounge beside you free, luv?" she asked in an obvious Aussie accent and pointed to the empty chair beside Darcy. What the girl lacked in clothing, tan lines and modesty she made up in long tangles of blonde curls and round, full breasts.

Darcy had to stop herself from staring. "Ah, help yourself."

The girl offered a wide smile as she bent over to pick up the chair. "Thanks, luv." Her bare breasts dangled much too close to Darcy's face. She lowered her head discreetly.

"Want some help?"

Darcy's gaze shot in the direction of the offer. DeLaurier was now sitting up, although he did seem a little unsteady.

Darcy mimicked, "it figures."

"No worries, mate. I can handle it. Australian beach volleyball team." She flexed a toned bicep to prove her point.

"What a surprise," Darcy said dryly.

The girl grasped the lounge by the foot end and dragged it across the sand.

"Now what is wrong with that?" DeLaurier inclined his head in the girl's direction. Darcy followed his wolfish gaze.

"Nothing. Except any closer and she could have put my eye out with those nipples."

He snapped his head back and snorted. "Yeah, like that's a bad thing?"

Darcy weighed his mood and scoffed back, "she'll never pass the pencil test." Then she lowered her head back to her novel, letting the comment sink in.

"Huh?" he shrugged, a confusion breaking across his swarthy stubble.

Darcy peered at him over her the top of her sunglasses. "The pencil test. You know, the great indicator of gravity. Get your girlfriend to explain it to you."

"I don't have a... never mind." He raked his fingers through his uncombed hair. Whether he knew it or not, his looks actually improved. "You have to admit, they are a pretty nice set of tits."

Darcy slapped the book closed in mock disgust. "Oh, puh-lee-e-eze! A young girl like that. They must have cost her a fortune. She'll be regretting that job by the time she's thirty."

"What job?"

"Well isn't it obvious? She's had some 'work' done."

DeLaurier planted his elbows on his knees and propped his chin in his palm. "Work," he parroted.

Darcy sighed, exasperated. Was he just playing with her or had she underestimated the 'duh' factor? If he was playing with her, she was good at playing right back.

"Yeah, you know," she splayed her palms several inches in front of her chest. "Work."

"Oh, you mean a boob job. And what does a boob job have to do with testing a pencil?"

"I believe the polite term is 'breast enhancement'."

"And you can tell this... how?"

Was he genuinely curious or simply baiting her? Nevertheless, a conversation was a conversation. His question deserved an answer, no matter how uncomfortable his brashness made her feel.

"Um, well. For starters, her breasts were too symmetrical. Too round, too high and way too perky. You see, typically a woman's breasts are slightly uneven." Darcy felt herself blush but couldn't tell if her explanation satisfied him. She saw only her reflection in his dark sunglasses.

"Gee and here I thought it was the little white scar on the side."

Darcy fought the urge to dump the ice bucket over his head. "If you were paying that close attention then why did you ask me?"

"Any closer attention and she would have poked my eyes out. Besides, I wanted to hear the part about the pencil."

Darcy made a sound halfway between a sigh and a snort and returned her attention to her book, noisily flipping pages to find her place.

"Hey, I've pissed you off. I'm sorry. Kyle DeLaurier," he held out is hand.

Bingo! Friendly contact established. Darcy put down her book and held out her hand. "Darcy McLeod. And I'm not pissed off. I'm just jet lagged."

"So, Darcy McLeod. Tell me about this pencil test."

Darcy cleared her throat. "I can't believe I'm having this conversation with you."

"Hey, you owe me."

"Owe you?"

Kyle grinned at her for the first time. Really grinned. He had a mile-wide smile that broke up the swarthy features of his face and didn't make him half as ferocious as he seemed, or she'd read about. Stay calm, Darcian. You are not falling victim to the smile that launched a thousand broken hearts, including the very expensive one Kyle DeLaurier apparently left behind in Toronto.

"Yeah, you owe me. You interrupted a perfectly good hangover. My day planner says I'm supposed to spend the day in misery. You chased away my miserable mood and now the rest of my day is in the toilet. Then I get the opportunity to be up close and personal with some tender Aussie booty and you spoil it by telling me it's all artificial. Now you leave me hanging about how to study for a pencil test."

Snake charmer! So that's what Spence warned me about.

Darcy merely smiled as she swung her legs off the lounge, still keeping her grip on the hat. "Beach bar's open. I feel like a juice frosty. Want something?" She motioned to Kyle's ice bucket which was now no more than a couple of empty cans bobbing up and down in melted ice water. "Another 'hair of the dog'?"

Kyle ran a hand through his messy crop of hair which, Darcy noted, was a deep brown accented by bronzy strands probably as a result of his exposure to the sun. "Club soda with lime," he said finally. "That is, if you don't mind."

"Oh, I don't mind," Darcy replied as she stood up. "Just don't let any more buxom young things with boob jobs, er, breast augmentations, take my lounge. They're at a premium this time of the day."

"The breasts or the lounge?" He grinned again. "Lots of ice in the club soda. Pleeeze." He flashed that grin, the grin, again. Darcy was determined to stay immune.

"Right. One club soda with lots of ice. And a lime. Just what the doctor ordered."

᠊ᢌᡧᢍᡃᢞᢥᢝᢞᢥᡟ

Just what the doctor ordered. Kyle watched her saunter over to the beach bar several yards away. The kind of women who could turn a good man bad, whether she knew it or not. Yes, she was out of place compared to the rest of the women at San Luis but it seemed to suit her. In some ways, she was a lot more interesting, mysterious perhaps, with her clothes on. If you called that stupid looking hat *clothes*. Who was she kidding? She was no more at ease bearing her two-somes than he would be in one of those absurd looking banana hammocks he'd seen guys wearing. Nothing more than two shoelaces attached to a condom.

It really was far more interesting to imagine what was under the bathing suit. Other than that heart-shaped bottom when she bent over, or her own perky pair of headlights under that stupid hat. And what about the rest of the treasures that bathing suit bottom was hiding? Perhaps a perfect puff of blonde curls sculpted by one of those cutsie in-the-shower women's razors, or maybe a golden nest of soft tangles untouched by any brand of steel? What if she was more daring than she let on and let her favorite aesthetician go to town with bikini waxing? *Oh happy day!* He couldn't remember the last time he'd had the taste of a smooth split-peach between his lips. Could be an interesting exploration.

Kyle was always the kid who wanted to be surprised at Christmas. None of this list making and brand picking, right down to the price and catalogue number, like his older sister, Monica. Half the fun was the anticipation of slowly peeling off the wrapping, pausing at the threshold of an unopened box and savoring the moment before actually plunging inside. What would it be like, he wondered, to plunge inside Darcy McLeod?

He wished with all his heart that Kevin were still alive and lounging around with him. He would have liked this Darcy girl, despite the fact that he left a wonderful, gorgeous wife and a son who held him in the grip of his two year-old hand. Ms. Darcy McLeod seemed very down to earth and, in spite of his foul mood, they'd managed to have a conversation that didn't revolve around her looks or his money. Correction, his father's money. In the few moments of sobriety he managed to achieve since arriving in San Andres, Kyle realized something about himself.

The first was he didn't like his father. And because of that, he didn't like himself because he'd allowed his old man's badgering to make him into the kind of person he didn't like. A man like his father. A man consumed with money, the idea of money and where he was going to get more of it. Because money meant more to Mason DeLaurier than anything. How to get it and how to keep it. And lately, what would happen to it once he was gone, which, Kyle bitterly hoped would be soon.

So now, here he was, Kyle DeLaurier, CEO of DeLaurier Inc., one of the most affluent and lucrative investment firms on Bay Street, hanging his head on a tiny spit of an island smaller than his family's vacation property in Maine and wondering what to do with his life now that he decided what he didn't want. Men like him weren't supposed to experience mid-life crisis until they hit mid-life. Kyle was barely a hair over 35. Mid-life was something Kevin would never see. Kevin, who'd been with him through high school, then university, then been given a sweetheart job at DeLaurier. The best friend who forgave Kyle for throwing him a bachelor party at the airport stripper bar and not the elegantly staid Boulevard Club, then proudly waited for Gayle to walk down the aisle the next day. Kyle was right beside him, as best man. Kyle was also right beside him the day he died.

He heard Kev's voice in his ear as he reached for another beer. He stopped. Kev wouldn't want to be mourned like this. But somebody had to mourn him, besides Kyle and Kevin's wife and son.

Kyle shook his head. He sure couldn't expect Mason to mourn one of his employees. All Mason cared about was who would cover Kevin's desk. It wasn't Mason's fault the man lost all his money in the last stock down turn. Everyone lost money. But it was Mason who encouraged both Kevin and Kyle privately to invest in a tech stock based on 'reliable' inside information. Who knew the dot com tech world would take such a dive? Kevin lost everything. Devastated, he turned to Kyle for help. But by the time Kyle arranged for an emergency loan, the stress proved too much. Kevin died of a massive heart attack in the middle of a client conference call.

Mason had been furious. The client's business meant everything to Mason. He ordered Kyle to step in and close the deal at the cost of missing Kevin's funeral. It was the last straw. After the funeral Kyle got good and drunk, packed his suitcase, opened the atlas, covered his eyes and stuck his finger in the middle of the page. The page turned out to be the middle of the Caribbean Sea and the tiny island of San Andres was right on the tip of his fingernail.

He hadn't contacted anyone since.

In fact Darcy was the first female contact he'd made since he'd been here. He just didn't have the urge to take what was so blatantly being offered day after day. Half-naked women were becoming as common and monotonous as sand and palm trees. Except for Darcy. And from what he observed she had every intention of remaining unique.

Kyle noticed her immediately as she navigated her way back down through the beach crowd from the bar. He had to cough to keep from laughing. She did indeed have their drinks—one in each hand. But her elbows were glued to her sides trapping the brim of that ridiculous hat and holding it firmly in place. One thing was for sure, Darcy Mcleod had the best posture on the island.

⁂🙶🙷⁂

"I feel soooo stupid right now," Darcy muttered as she picked her way across the hot sand, careful to avoid the sea of bodies below her. With all the chairs occupied people were now camping out on gaudy cotton beach towels. Why hadn't she slipped her top back into place? Why did these people have to lay right in her path? The last thing on earth she wanted was to step on somebody's important body part. Why couldn't Kyle have gone skiing in Vail? With half of her mind on DeLaurier and the other half on keeping her secrets safe, she fell into the very trap she'd been avoiding.

She was forced to detour around the newly erected volleyball net where the Aussie girls were engaged in a healthy co-ed game and quickly attracting a crowd. The on-lookers blocked her view of that portion of the beach where she left DeLaurier.

Darcy inched herself past rows of half-naked bodies. Twice someone bumped into her causing the drinks to slosh over her hands.

"Shit! These drinks will be gone or warm by the time I get back." Of course her real fear was that DeLaurier himself would change his mind and be gone by the time she returned. She reached the edge of the crowd and saw him wave to her. She nearly waved back but remembered her arms glued to her sides and why they were there. In the next instant however, she wasn't so lucky.

Someone behind her yelled, "look out for the ball."

Darcy turned and gasped. The ball was headed straight for her. Unable to dodge an out-of-control volleyball Darcy instinctively crossed both arms in front of her face without thinking.

Instantly, the hat became a victim of gravity. The ball knocked both drinks out of her hand. Her newly bared breasts received a bath in ice and club soda.

Mercifully, someone had grabbed her by the shoulders and turned her around, away from the view of Kyle DeLaurier and into the face of Miss Australian boob job.

"Ow, eh luv. I'm ever so sorry. I'll have me mates get you another chug."

"It's… it's okay," Darcy stuttered. She gasped as the cold ice melted between her cleavage and tiny droplets rolled down her bare midriff. She quickly pulled her bathing suit top back into place.

The girl lowered her sun bronzed face closer to Darcy. "It's okay, luv. They're quite a nice pair. Why don't you just leave 'em out? That bloke beside you won't mind." Then she stepped back and winked at Darcy. "I'm Gretchin. Let me know what you want and have the bartender put it on my tab."

Darcy recovered herself. "Uh, this is an 'all-inclusive' resort."

Gretchin giggled. "Oh yeah. Well, anyway you should sashay back to that hunk while the headlights are still flashing." She cast an obvious glance at Darcy's top. Sure enough, the melted ice was doing it's job.

"Thanks," she replied dryly.

Gretchin tossed her crimped blond hair over her bare shoulders. "No worries. Anyway, I'd… aw, geeze. You're too late."

"Gretchin!" someone yelled and before Darcy could ask her what she meant, the girl dashed back to her game. Too late? Too late for what?

Darcy peered through the increasing throngs of mostly male volleyball fans and down the beach to where she had left her quarry. She located her beach bag on the sand beside the chaise where she'd left it. But the lounge next to hers was empty. Kyle was gone.

Chapter Two

Gone! Shit!

"Oh!" Darcy jumped as someone behind her plunked her hat back on her head. She turned suddenly.

"You lost your hat."

Kyle stood in front of her, hands-on-hips casual stance, rumpled hair, five o'clock shadow. "Thank you. I'm sorry about the drinks."

He grinned. "I'm not."

"Huh?"

"Gave me the chance to get an accurate weather report."

Darcy glanced skyward. The sun was high and not a cloud in sight. He was losing her, fast.

"Fog," he said simply. Then he did something that totally unnerved her. He reached out and ran his index finger along the decolletage of her wet bathing suit. "Fog," he repeated softly.

Gretchin's words echoed in her head. *Headlights.* Duh!

Except that the touch of his finger so close to her skin was creating not a fog but a major blackout. Suddenly her pulse seemed to bypass her heart and head straight for her mons. She shuddered slightly and squeezed her thighs together.

"You cold?" He paused the tip of his finger above the crest of her left breast, his palm dangerously close to hitting the target. Her next deep breath would cause a major collision. Her breasts suddenly felt hard and plumped up while her nipples issued their own invitation.

Headlights nothing. She was sending out high beams. Darcy caught her breath and remembered her role. She didn't have enough insurance for Kyle DeLaurier's kind of collateral damage.

She gently took hold of his hand and removed the hazard. "Not cold. Actually, I feel like the bottoms of my feet have been branded."

He raised his eyebrows as he looked her. "Careful bending over. You could poke somebody's eyes out with those things."

She answered him with a sarcastic, "ha, ha."

"I can get you some ice for your feet then," he offered. "Or some liquid libation to cool you off."

Darcy thought for a moment. The morning had not gone at all well. The whole topless thing had disconcerted and distracted her. If she was ever going to get DeLaurier to trust her then she had to get him off the beach. But she needed to stay coherent. Sun, heat and alcohol made for a dangerous cocktail.

She took him by the hand and began to lead him back to their lounge chairs. "There's a bar near the pool. They have gallons of cold, bottled water on tap. I'm going to soak my feet in the freshwater pool."

"So does that mean you don't want sex on the beach?"

Darcy halted in mid-step. *Think fast, Darcian. You've got him swimming around the net. Keep him there.*

"Ah, well it's a little too crowded here. Don't you think?"

Kyle answered her with a laugh but kept following her in the direction of their lounge chairs. She felt herself turning beet red and not from the sun. She tried again. "Um, does that mean you're an exhibitionist and you're ready to drop down on the sand and do it while the Aussies are making their next serve? Or does that mean we go swimming and do it in the ocean like sea horses?"

"'Sex On The Beach' is a drink."

"I knew that," she said quickly. Yes, it was. She remembered reading the 'drink of the day' feature on the chalkboard by the bar. There were a number of similarly themed drinks also listed.

"In fact, I think I'll have a Screaming Orgasm." She couldn't pat herself on the back for remembering but she did fidget with her hat. They reached the chairs and Darcy packed up her beach bag. Kyle grabbed his towel and slung it around his neck. Darcy led them both across the property to a huge "L" shaped swimming pool. Since most of the action was on the beach, they had their pick of pool side lounges. Darcy made herself comfortable and dug into her beach bag for some sun screen. "Here," she handed the tube of cream to Kyle. "Make yourself useful. Do you mind?"

"Gee, thanks. Don't mind if I do. Didn't think I was burning yet."

She laughed in spite of herself. He was unfailingly charming. She had been warned.

"I meant could you please put some on *my* back."

He took the plastic tube from her and squeezed a generous amount of white cream into the palm of his hand. He made a circling motion with index finger. "Turn around," he instructed. "Now slide your straps down and tell me when you'd like your screaming orgasm."

He wanted to play. He always wanted to play. She'd been warned about that too. As usual, no matter how prepared she thought she was, or how many text books she'd read or how many late nights she'd spent in Spence's car guzzling coffee and gazing bleary-eyed through binoculars, nothing measured up like on-the-job training. She was being forced to deal with DeLaurier at his level. So be it.

"Um... let's see. Oooohhh that feels good." And it did. Whatever other kinds of problems DeLaurier had it certainly wasn't a lack of magic fingers.

This guy was good. Real good.

"Screaming orgasms are supposed to feel good."

Darcy softly chuckled at his playful innuendos. If truth be told, she'd never had a screaming orgasm, alcoholic or otherwise in her entire life. Hers were more like whimpers, over almost before they began. But she knew the fault didn't lie with her. Impatient partners were usually the cause. Left to her own devises, including the battery-operated kind, she did just fine.

"Your shoulders are starting to burn a bit." He stopped to apply more cream to her skin. "Your neck muscles are so tense. You've been working too hard."

Perfect timing. Darcy slipped in her cover. "You know how the real estate business is. It's a buyer's market right now." Spencer thought real estate would blend well with DeLaurier's financial background. It would put her on even footing with him. Put him at ease with chit-chat and small talk. According to his track record, he'd be more inclined to spend more time with her if there were potential gains to be had. A bogus condominium corporation had been set up for just such a circumstance in case DeLaurier decided to go digging.

"But I decided I needed a break."

Kyle agreed. "Good decision, Darcy. And speaking of decisions..."

"All right, all right. My orgasm. Okay, right after your erection, during a double foreplay but before your ejaculation." There, she'd gone through every drink on the menu. He murmured into her ear. "Double foreplays are pretty strong you know."

"I'll take my chances. Hmmm... you missed a spot. In the middle of my back."

"I didn't miss anything. I hate being rushed. I like to be thorough and enjoy my work. I'm very particular about details. Now be quiet and enjoy it."

Enjoy it? No shit, Sherlock. This was the easy part. "What kind of work do you do? No, let me guess. You're a masseuse."

"I am for the next few minutes."

"And before?"

He didn't answer her right away. His silence told her everything. Maybe getting him on a plane back to Toronto wasn't going to be that easy after all. In fact, Spence cautioned her that she might damned well have to drag him back kicking and screaming.

"Let's just say that vacations are for forgetting 'befores'. There, all done." He patted her back lightly and slid her straps back into place. "Now, if we were still on the beach I'd offer to rub down your other exposed parts."

Darcy flashed him a wide smile. "So just what level of SPF do use on nipples?"

He returned her smile. "Yours or mine?"

Darcy fingered the brim of her hat. Briefly, before he plucked it off her head. "Hey, I need that protection."

"You're really into safe sunning, aren't you." He examined the inside of her hat. "A-hah!"

"A-hah?"

"A-hah," he repeated with a self-satisfied grin. "Did you buy this here? If you did, you've been cheated. It says on the inside tag, 'made in the Philippines'. We're a long way from there. Ah, the tourist fantasy is shattered."

Not all my fantasies, she thought.

"May I have my protection back? Our drinks are ready. I saw the bartender signal you."

He handed her back her hat. "That's the way of it," he sighed heavily. "Safe sun, safe sex. Everything is far too safe these days. Nobody wants to take chances, blow with the wind, be surprised at what's around the next corner."

"Sounds like a cavalier attitude." *Just like you.* The thought was safely hidden as Kyle went to get their drinks. He returned almost immediately, time enough for Darcy to regain both her hat and her composure. He handed her her 'Screaming Orgasm' and she thanked him.

"Huh, that's it? That's all? Give a girl a 'screaming orgasm' and a simple thanks is all you get these days. No breakfast, no phone call, no commitment."

Darcy leaned back in her chair and chuckled. If nothing else, he had the damnedest sense of humor. It was going to be hard to keep up with him. But she had to try.

"That's the twenty-first century woman for you. Tell you what, you have dinner with me tonight and I'll tell you how a girl thanks a man for a real screaming orgasm." The challenge was issued along with the invitation. Darcy propped her hand on her knee and waited for him to take the bait. Kyle wasn't going to make it that easy for her.

"And just how many men have you thanked? Actually, let's back up." He paused and took a sip of his drink. A lone diver splashed into the pool near them, soaking Darcy's legs and wetting Kyle's already unruly hair. Darcy slowly, deliberately ran her hands down her bare legs, shaking the water off her fingertips. From behind her sunglasses she could see his gaze following her movements.

"You were saying," she prompted.

He wiped his forehead then brought the plastic cup to his lips. His tongue captured a lone ice cube floating in a mix of pineapple juice and gin. "I was saying that I should have asked you how many of those screaming orgasms you've had."

"You mean at the resort, or in general?"

"Both."

"Let's put it this way," it was her turn to pause and play with the quickly melting ice in her drink. "The drinks are good. Anything else, the jury's still out."

Kyle looked at her and smiled slowly as if considering her answer. "Fair enough," he said finally. "I'd love to join you for supper. Shall we say the seven o'clock sitting? That will give us a chance to go for a walk afterward and enjoy the sunset. Do twenty-first century women still enjoy sunsets?"

Darcy nodded, "This one does."

"Good. I'm going to take a shower and grab the bus into town. I have some business to take care of."

"Oooh! Business. Sounds intriguing." And it did. Darcy wondered what kind of business the errant heir apparent had in San Luis city. "Let me guess. International man of mystery. You're after a spy. No, wait. You're a double zero something on a secret mission and you want to use our rendezvous tonight as a cover. Okay, I'll play the spy girl in the movie. You know, the one everyone ooh's and awe's over but never hears about again."

"Except Halle Berry."

"Or Ursula Andres. But technically they don't count because they were famous before they became spy girls."

"Yeah, but they both kicked ass in a bikini."

"Just don't leave any top secret disks or world altering formulas in my–"she almost said 'room'. "purse. You know, slip them in while I'm eating dinner then try to retrieve them later."

"Later as in while you're asleep."

"Later as in… later."

Kyle chose that moment to touch her arm. Actually he tugged at her wrist to see her watch. Still, the touch affected her as much as his earlier massage. There was that sudden, sharp jolt through her body, sending shockwaves of sensation straight to her mid-section. And below. "Almost eleven. Stores in town shut down at twelve thirty for siesta. Gotta motor. Seven it is, in front of the main dining room." Instead of releasing her wrist, he brought her hand to his lips and kissed her fingertips. There it was again. That sharp tingle that made her bottom wiggle around in her chair. His lips were soft, the kiss firm and purposeful. Those lips could do a lot of damage if they found the wrong places, or was that the right places? He winked at her, then rose from his chair leaving Darcy to wonder if his lips, or another part of him, were responsible for that famous heartbreaker reputation. Yes he was good. Real good.

Darcy leaned back in her chair and smiled. But she was better.

※᠊ᢍᡧᠻᢗᠵᢗᠵ᠊ᢡᢢᢘᢘ

It wasn't the snooze alarm that woke Darcy from her own siesta later that afternoon. It was the annoying ring on her cell phone.

"Yeah," she mumbled and pawed at the cotton sheet tangled around her waist.

"Hold for the mainland, *por favor.*" The heavily accented voice was barely discernable through the static. Darcy had been warned that cellular service was scant and scratchy at best. That's why she opted to keep Spencer informed via e-mail on her lap top. A phone call could mean only one thing; the old man.

"Mason," she sighed and waited for the connection to clear. "What the fu–"

"Miss Darcy? Miss Darcy are you there? Where's my son? Have you found him?"

"Yes and yes, Mr. DeLaurier. I'm here and he's here."

"In your room?" The voice on the other end boomed into her right eardrum.

"No... no sir. Not here in the room. I mean he's here on the island and still safely single. I'm having supper with him tonight."

"Do you think you'll have him back here by the end of next week?"

"Don't worry, sir. He has to leave when his visa expires." Which was only five months from now, but she didn't tell that to the old man. "He'll be back in time for the merger. I guaranteed it, didn't I?"

"Spencer guaranteed it. I want updates daily. Keep me in the loop."

"Sir, Mr., er, Mason. I think it would be better if you didn't call me every four hours, especially when I'm trying to sleep."

"You're sleeping on the job?"

"Mason, everybody is sleeping at this time of the day. That's why they call it a siesta. Now, if you'll excuse me, I'll send my boss an e-mail with a copy to you. Every day. Whether I have something to report or not." With that, she snapped the phone shut and tossed it into the drawer of the night stand. She almost reached over and turned it on again, tempted to run out the battery but stopped. Her professionalism wouldn't allow her to possibly endanger herself just because her client irritated her. San Andres might be five hundred miles off the coast of Colombia but it still belonged to the Colombians. And the military presence on the island could be unpredictable if one stepped out of line, tourist or not. She might very well need that cell phone in an emergency. She glared at the clock. Time for a shower.

While she stood under a lukewarm stream of half salt, half fresh water, she wondered again what kind of business Kyle had in town. San Andres was popular for two things; sand and emeralds. The emeralds mined in the mountains of Colombia were that country's biggest export next to coffee, and big business on a duty free island. She'd seen some of what Colombia's natural resources had to offer in the hotel jewelry store. Big and green—her envy, and the marquis-shaped stone in the centre of the most gorgeous dinner ring she'd ever seen. Big and green was what she needed in her wallet when she saw the price. So much so that she'd declined the jeweler's offer for her to try on the ring, fearing she'd never want to take it off. "Sure, that's how they get ya", she grumbled as she reluctantly walked out of the shop, minus the ring. And the tennis bracelet, and the earrings and the—Darcy shook herself. No use mooning over things she'd never have.

Now, if she caught someone like Kyle DeLaurier with mega bucks who could afford a few trinkets like that... well, that would be a different story. But DeLaurier had a fiancée, sort of, back in Toronto. Bet he could buy her a huge, honking winker like that. If he wanted to. But it didn't sound as if he even wanted the fiancée.

Enough to get himself into trouble with the next biggest Colombian export? She'd seen the huge haciendas in the hills behind the hotel. She'd heard more than one rumor that they were owned by drug lords. Apparently the homes were seldom used except as vacation properties. Hey, even a drug lord needs to take a vacation now and then. If that's what DeLaurier was up to on the island then it was going to take a more experienced investigator, not to mention a few platoons of Marines, to get him out of trouble. And if the situation required the latter then Darcy was sure daddy big-bucks was quite willing to accommodate to get his twenty-six percent back in the country.

That's what Spence called Kyle. The old man's twenty-six percent. As in share of DeLaurier Enterprises. Mason held exactly half of the voting power in the company. Kyle's mother, Mason's ex-wife, held twenty-four. That left Kyle with the magic number for any serious monopoly playing. According to the information she gained from her meeting with Mason, the balance of power was split, with Kyle holding all the cards. Side with mom, ditch the merger and be on the old man's shit list. Side with Mason, ostracize mom and poof! Out of the will. The rich had so many problems. If she were Kyle she'd have done the same thing, pack a bag, disappear and come back after somebody else cleaned up the body parts.

But she wasn't Kyle DeLaurier, the poor, little rich playboy. She was Darcy, the poor—period—who actually worked for a living, even if that living meant fucking up someone else's life.

"Life's a bitch," Darcy sighed and spit out a mouthful of soap suds. "Then you become one!"

She stepped out of the shower and wrapped up in a large, white cotton towel. She had already decided to wear the I-wanna-see-your-cock-get-hard black sheath with silver come-fuck-me heels. She quickly gathered her damp hair and pinned it in a simple up-do to set off the light tan already covering her shoulders. She stepped into a black lace thong, wondering why, exactly, men thought it was a comfortable experience to have an elastic thread stuffed up your butt. A single-strand silver necklace and dangling earrings finished the trap. A little war paint and a spritz of pheromone-inducing perfume and she was done.

She sat down at the writing desk and flipped open her lap-top, thankful her suite was Internet ready. She sent off a quick progress report to Spencer. The clock told her that Spencer was probably in his office finishing off his day's paperwork. She waited five minutes and sure enough, she received a response.

Glad to know the sun hasn't fried your brain. Just remember why you're there. The papers here are really playing up this merger. Kyle's mother is dead set against it. She refuses to vote on the issue. Next Friday is the deadline. The rumor mill is rabid about Kyle's disappearance. The official press release has him vacationing in the south of France. That should keep the bloodhounds off you for a while. If his whereabouts are

leaked and he bolts, we're finished. Hope you didn't spend the advance.
Take care, Darcy.

Regards, Spencer Brightwood

So this is what modern detective work had become, chasing down wayward children. Except this wayward child was a grown man who held a deal worth millions in the simple stroke of a pen. So far, she'd found Kyle to be a careless, sloppy, rummied-out flirt who needed a shave, shower and a severe attitude adjustment. At that moment she didn't know whether it sucked to be him or if this was all a staged practical joke and Kyle himself was having the last laugh.

Darcy switched off her laptop and stood up. She took one last survey of her work in the full mirror on the back of the bathroom door. She applied another coat of lipstick and puckered at her reflection.

"For someone who didn't want to show off her tits, Darcian, you look like a Russian peeler fresh off the corner of Jarvis and Church." Well, not quite. Her hooker's outfit was red with thigh-high black leather boots.

She adjusted her sheath—down in the cleavage and up on the thighs—and pinched her nipples. Pleased with the results she headed out the door, a fully baited man trap complete with headlights.

She arrived at the main dining room fifteen minutes early so she stopped at the lobby bar for a confidence booster. She tried to ignore the pointed glances she received from men. The hotel catered to guests worldwide and Darcy recognized Italian, French and German accents interspersed among the mostly English speaking guests and Spanish-speaking employees.

She didn't have to understand all the languages to know what the blatant stares and inviting smiles meant. That language was universal. She strode over to her favorite forbidden zone, the jewellers, now closed for the evening, and gazed longingly at the window display. She was so busy trying to figure the exchange of 450,000 pesos into Yankee dollars that she didn't notice the reflection of another person behind her. She looked up. It was him, of course. But a barely recognizable him.

For one thing, he'd had a shave and a haircut. He wore... clothes. Real men's attire, tan pants, white shirt and sandals. And he smelled... well, he didn't. No beer, no day-old sweat mixed with a heavy coating of coconut oil. He smelled good. Fresh. Male. Darcy hadn't prepared herself for quite dramatic a change. It was like the 'Fab Five' flew in from New York and did an emergency makeover on Kyle before changing the chintz pillows in the lobby and coordinating the drink menus. She liked the results, regardless of who was responsible, even if it did throw her off balance. What unbalanced her more was the direction of his gaze. Shit, she thought, I don't have headlights, I have neon signs.

"Nice jewels."

"Nice if you can afford them. They're so expensive. And... big."

"You say 'big' like it's a bad thing. I'm a man and I can tell you, size matters."

He sure as hell was a man! Darcy recovered herself and readied her psyche for another round of innuendo. "Well, I'm a woman and I can tell you that there really is such a condition as too much of a good thing."

"Like orgasms? I brought you one from the bar but I see you already have a drink." He was indeed holding two highball glasses to her one martini. She downed the last of her martini and took one of the drinks from him.

"That's the trouble with fast women. They never take the time anymore to enjoy what really matters."

"Like size," she answered over the rim of her glass before taking a sip. She motioned to the display case. "And rings."

"Anything else?"

She leaned against the glass and screwed up her face pretending to labour over her answer. "Hmm. Chocolate. Lobster. Getting sand out of my crotch."

"Ouch! Anything I can do to help?" He grinned and moved closer to her until she barely had room to raise her glass between him.

"Uh-uh. I took care of that myself when I had a shower. Sorry."

The double glass doors of the main dining room opened and supper was announced. Couples and groups moved toward the open doors.

"We'll wait a moment until the hungry hoards get seated," he suggested. "Then I can take care of the first two items on your list."

"I hadn't finished my list," she murmured. "But food takes priority. I'm starved."

"So am I but there's plenty of food so why get caught in the crush?"

"You've dined here before?"

"Actually, I've been on the island for a while so I'm used to the drill. And don't worry, I have an 'in' with the maitre'd. They'll hold my table."

"You must like it here," she probed.

"It's a great place to escape. Cheap, simple, nobody bothers you."

"Sounds like paradise. Care to tell me what you're escaping from? Or is it a who?"

"Shhh!" He put a finger to his lips. Then to hers, a simple, yet intimate action. "International man of mystery, remember?"

Darcy swallowed, feeling the pad of his finger brush against her lower lip. He let it linger for a second before withdrawing it. He looked at the lipstick mark on his finger tip. Then he did something that horned her out. He licked her lipstick off his finger.

"Mmmm. Burgundy is my favorite flavor."

"Glad you like it," she murmured finally. *Give your head a shake, Darce.* "All us spy girls use the same shade. We get a bulk discount." Okay, she wasn't totally lying. She was a spy, sort of, and she got the lipstick as a freebie with nail polish.

"Señor, your table is ready." The maitre'd motioned to them. Darcy turned first, eager to get her pounding heart back to normal. She was the one who was supposed to be in control of the situation. She allowed Kyle to escort her to their table and smiled politely when he held her chair for her. They decided to share a lobster plate and she let him order the wine.

"A light chardonnay should never overpower the lobster," he said.

"Is that a rule?" She planted her elbows on the table, laced her fingers together and propped her chin in her hand.

"I don't live by rules. But I do enjoy good food. And good women."

"Hmm. I see. And which category do I fall under."

He mimicked her chin prop and stared back at her. "I haven't tasted you. Yet."

Darcy maintained her composure, despite the meaning in his words. "So does that make me a good woman?" She dared to redirect her gaze back at him through the candlelight on their table. The dining room lights were dimmed shortly after they were seated. The flickering candlelight was caught in his eyes and reflected back at her.

"Like I said, I haven't tasted you."

"Yet."

"I was just coming to that. I wanted you to finish your list."

"List?"

The lights were dim but so was her brain. He had the damnedest habit of keeping track of every word that came out of her mouth. "Oh, right. Things I need to take more time to enjoy. Let's see," she broke eye contact with him and looked around the room. "Flower arrangements. Like that one in the middle of the dessert table. Orange zinnias, yellow mums and red birds of paradise. Very decorative. I must compliment the manager."

"Please don't go Martha Stewart on me. I mean the sensual things in life. You had an excellent start with chocolate and lobster. Let's continue in that vein."

"Flowers are sensual. Smell. Visual. Touch."

"I didn't realize horticulture was so sexy." Back to sex again. Like it or not, she realized she was going to have to get into his mode and stay there if she wanted him to remain interested in her. The waiter arrived with the wine. Kyle removed his elbows from the table and waited until the man opened the bottle and offered the cork for Kyle's inspection. Kyle nodded. "Just leave the bottle. I'll do the honors." He poured them each a glass. He smiled and raised his glass toward her.

"To sensual horticulture?"

Darcy frowned at his suggestion. "Try again."

"To sex and horticulture. You know, all those horny little bees pollinating all those fertile little flowers."

"Will you behave?" It was hard to be aggravated or annoyed. He had such a charming, boyish way with avoiding anything serious.

"All right. To sex and sensuality. Wasn't that a book or something?"

"That was *Sense and Sensibility.* And yes it was a book."

"All right then. To good books."

"Now, I will drink to that." She took a sip of her wine. The chardonnay was light and fruity on her lips. Quite refreshing.

"Especially ones with pictures that fold out of the centre."

Darcy coughed and reached for her napkin.

"Are you all right? Here, let me help you." He got up and came around to where she sat. He knelt down beside her. She waived him off but kept coughing, holding her napkin in front of her mouth. She was aware that several people nearby were staring at her. Shit! This was embarrassing. After a few seconds, she calmed down enough to be able to take a sip of water. She allowed Kyle to pat her lightly on the back. After a moment or two, the patting turned to a light caress.

He leaned his face close to her ear and apologized. "I'm sorry you choked on my words. That's not what I had in mind."

Darcy lay her bunched napkin in her lap. "In mind for what?"

His lips barely grazed her earlobe. "For dessert." And then louder, "Ah, here comes the lobster." He got up, went over to his side of the table and sat down as if nothing had happened.

Darcy smiled approvingly at him for his choice for their meal. *You'll get yours, you arrogant little prick.*

She managed to make it through the remainder of their meal without incident. She even indulged in chocolate mousse. A reward, she reasoned, for putting up with the hormone spewing maniac on the other side of the table. She would talk to Spence tonight after she got rid of him. She would ask for a raise.

After supper Darcy led him out to the terrace and lighted walkway. There were other couples taking advantage of the gardens and cobblestone walkway so she didn't feel uncomfortable being alone with him even if all he did through dinner was stare at her breasts.

"All that butter is going to sit on my hips. A good walk is just what we need."

"We? I didn't say anything about walking. By the way, why don't you take off those heels and let me carry them before you catch one between a cobblestone and trip."

"Good idea." They stopped and Darcy used his shoulder to balance herself while she removed her shoes.

"Here," she handed the sandals to him. "Thanks."

"Don't thank me. I'm looking out for myself."

She stopped him. "Excuse me?" She faced him in the twilight. There was a saucy sort of grin on his face and his eyes twinkled dangerously. He was amusing himself about something and seemed very eager to share it with her. But Darcy had a feeling she was going to have to beat him with a stick to find out what it was.

He looked around first before he answered her. "What I mean is, if you fell and that gownless evening strap you're wearing got hitched up, it could be embarrassing, if I've bet my cards right."

"Bet them on what?"

He leaned closer to her and placed his hands on her shoulders. Her shoes still dangled from one hand and he was careful when he touched her. He lowered his face to hers and Darcy prepared herself for a kiss. But the kiss never happened. Instead he brushed his lips against her right ear and whispered.

"On whether or not you're wearing underwear."

Darcy nearly choked, but not from indignation. He nipped at her ear lobe, disturbing a dangling silver earring. She closed her eyes and shivered at the sensation. He seemed intent on kissing a path all the way down her neck from her ear to her shoulder. The lips of her pussy throbbed. Her bottom tightened impulsively. Her nipples ached to be touched. She pressed her body closer to him and did indeed feel the achieved effect of her dress. Not even the dual thud of her sandals hitting the stone sidewalk broke the spell.

"And by the way, I don't care who walks by. I don't care who's watching. I don't care how long it takes. I'm not going to let you go until you tell me."

Chapter Three

He'd laid his cards on the table. Her options were limited. If she told him, 'yes', he might not believe her and he'd insist that she prove it. If she said, "no sailor, I'm going commando tonight," chances are he'd slip his hand under her dress to find out if she was telling the truth. Either way, it would be the end of her.

"If I tell you, will you believe me?" she whispered against his lips.

"Honey, right now I'll believe anything you say." His hands travelled down to caress her buttocks. "I can't even feel a panty line. Shit, I should have bet my wad."

Darcy let out a nervous chuckle. "We'll discuss your... wad some other time. Face it, stud. You bet the farm and lost it."

He cast her a mock pout, the kind of expression Darcy was sure got him past many a resisting gal. But not this gal!

"Does that mean you'll take pity on a poor, homeless farm-boy without so much as a haystack to roll in?" The vision his words presented nearly caused her throat to close up. Except that hay made her nose red and her skin itch. Right now, she was coming damned close to scratching the kind of itch Kyle was creating whether she wanted to or not.

However, she was known to nibble. And she might just dive right in if he kept holding her too much longer. Especially when he took an even greater advantage and pressed her closer. He then ran his hand between the crease of her buttocks. That damned near finished her off. She was so busy enjoying the pleasurable feelings racing through her she didn't feel him gather the material between his thumb and forefinger until... snap!

"Hey!" She jumped back, effectively breaking their romantic clinch. She planted her hands on her backside and rubbed hard.

"Thong. Well, how about that. I'm wrong. I'll have to mark this on my PDA calendar."

"Congratulations, joker." Asshole was more like it. Why didn't Spence warn her about these kinds of occupational hazards? Kyle might be laughing but the joke just put her on ice.

"I think we have to call it a night."

"Oh?"

Darcy reconsidered her decision when she saw genuine disappointment in his face. "Yeah. I, uh, have to go back to the room and change."

"Into something more comfortable, I hope."

"You might say that." She grabbed the front of his shirt for balance and furtively wriggled out of her thong. Kyle's eyes never left her as she inched the garment down her thighs, over her knees and onto her ankles. Then she gingerly stepped out of the circle of black lace. She dangled the thong between her thumb and forefinger. The tee-strap had given way when he'd snapped it.

"Oops," he murmured sheepishly. "I'm really sorry. That's not exactly the way I wanted to see your underwear." She was on the verge of actually believing he might be embarrassed. She couldn't tell but from the dim lights of the lanterns lining the walkway, his face looked a little red. Of course, he might only have a sunburn.

"You owe me," she said and stabbed her index finger into his chest. His shirt was open. His skin was warm. Darcy fought the desire to run her fingers through the crisp, curling hairs.

Kyle cleared his throat and had the decency to appear uncomfortable. "Yeah, I guess I do. For that, I'm willing to agree and call it a night. But let me take you into town tomorrow and allow me to buy you a replacement."

Darcy thought about his offer for a moment. Unlike a bouquet of flowers, she'd actually have to be present for this apology. Perhaps dragging him around to a string of lingerie stores might be the ideal way to get him to loosen up about his personal life. She could load her arsenal of prompts about returning to Toronto. And if it took a few concealed weapons, so be it. So far he was taking the bait nicely. Nothing like a little private modelling to close the cage. And speaking of close, Kyle was getting a little too close for her comfort. He invaded her comfort zone, violated her space. He covered her hand and pressed it flat against his chest. Darcy swallowed. It was too intimate a touch. It was one thing for him to fondle her ass in the dark on a public walkway; she was in control of what he touched and when. She wanted him to notice her and he did. But it was quite another thing to give up control of the situation.

"You know what you should add to your list?" His warm, wine-scented breath brushed across her lips. His mouth was too close.

She lowered her gaze to his chest where his fingers gently caressed her own. "I live in hope that you'll tell me," she breathed.

"Sex."

"What a surprise," she replied dryly.

"Really, you need the time to enjoy sex. No 'wham-bam-thank-you-ma'am'. You see, great sex is like great art. You need to appreciate the life of the artist to understand his work."

Darcy inhaled slightly, half in impatience, half in anticipation. What was he going to do, talk all night? So far his fingers hadn't walked anywhere she needed to throw up a stop sign. A little less conversation, a little more action. "If you don't hurry up and give me two nickels for your artist paradigm, my nether regions are going to catch pneumonia."

His eyes darkened. "There's a prevention for that, you know. It's called heat."

"I take it you don't mean a blanket and a hot water bottle." How much longer could she keep him at bay?

His mouth twitched before he answered. "I don't know about you but I don't have blankets on my bed. And I prefer my bottled water cold." Cold was absolutely not the way he was making her feel. She could either stay here and continue the coy sparing and subtle nuances that were the hallmarks of their meeting so far or... Or what? Drag him off to her room? Follow behind him while he dug a hotel room key out of his pocket?

Darcy felt her fingers begin to perspire around the mangled thong she still clutched in her hand. Too much, too soon. It was definitely better to just talk the talk—for now.

Her palm tightened around the tiny scrap of black lace. "About your career as a starving artist..."

She felt his chest rise and fall under her fingertip as he gave a sudden, almost impatient sigh and rolled his eyes heavenward.

"Tease," he whispered. Then, he cleared his throat. "Let's see... sex is my medium. Your body, a canvass. My, uh, tools –"

"A-hem."

"My tongue lapping a trail that starts at the base of your neck, down your back and over your ass." Darcy felt a slight shiver, and not from the ocean breeze.

"My fingers painting a path from the cleft of your breasts, following the curve outward and around to gently caress your nipples which I would then nibble without mercy." It was then he leaned forward and nibbled the exposed flesh of her neck. Darcy suddenly gasped. What was she doing and why wasn't she stopping him?

"The tip of my cock insistently nudging your pussy lips apart, eager and anxious to slip inside. And you'd be wet, so wet. The perfect paint for every stroke." He finished by suckling her ear-lobe. Then he lightly kissed her temple. The cocky grin was back and so was the "bet you can't beat that" expression.

She couldn't. She wouldn't even try at this point. But she would put some safe distance between her and her sexual Picasso. Darcy removed her hand from his chest and stepped back. "That's... inspirational."

"Yep. Not exactly the kind of first impression I made with you this morning, right?"

Darcy couldn't help but smile at the truth of the situation. "You did come across as more of more of a burned-out rummy than a frustrated artiste."

"I'll bet."

"You should stop betting. You've lost once already."

"I don't have much to lose."

"Really?" Maybe he didn't, but the man who hired her had every reason to believe he'd lose millions if Kyle didn't come home, not to mention a sort-of fiancée.

"Neither do you. Between the undies and that leather apron you're wearing. I don't consider jewellery and footwear as clothing."

"Thanks to you I don't even have the undies. And accessories come in pretty handy when you're playing strip poker." She held up the crushed thong in her hand. She thought about bouncing it up and down in her hand or dangling it in front of him but she knew he wouldn't take a refusal for that kind of invitation.

"Play a lot of strip poker, do you?" He flashed her the kind of grin that told her he was hoping.

"I've won my share of hands," she admitted. She didn't spend all those nights in the surveillance van with Spence just filing her nails. Except the only thing in the kitty when she played with him were quarters or a stash of 2-for-1 pizza coupons.

"And where do you put these hands when you win them?" His eyes twinkled dangerously.

"Ha-ha. If they were your hands, where do you think I'd put them?" Yes! He was speechless. He blinked a few times. His jaw twitched and his mouth moved but no words came out. A slow smile spread across his face as his gaze raked her up and down. Finally he said, "I could think of a few places."

"Took you long enough. I was beginning to think you had a smart answer for everything."

"I know when it's time to keep my mouth shut."

"Do you?" She moved closer to him. Something exciting churned in her stomach. That first kiss started it. Or was it simply the atmosphere? The tropical weather. Was it merely humidity or was it real heat? The kind of heat that's given off from a powerful explosion when two volatile substances are suddenly mixed.

She stepped in and lightly nipped his open mouth. It was the danger, she reminded herself. The thrill of the chase, of cornering her prey. Only at this moment, she felt like the prey. He'd certainly pursued her enough today. But wasn't that the plan?

"Yes," she breathed without thinking.

"Yes? That was easy. My room's on the second floor."

Darcy snapped herself out of it. "I mean, no. Not that."

"Tease," he accused softly before placing his arms around her and pulling her into his embrace. The kiss deepened. No soft, playful nips and interrupted nibbles. This was a full-fledged, 'my room's on the second floor' reminder.

Darcy opened her mouth to his tongue. She suckled it with the kind of hunger that she knew would get satisfied on the second floor. Right now, she had to decide how much longer she was going to revel in the thrill his mouth was giving her. If this were purely a pursuit of pleasure, she'd plant his hand against her crotch so fast it would make his hormones spin. God knew, hers were. Her clit pulsed and begged for the touch of his fingers, her nipples ached to be sucked. She'd back him behind the giant azalia and wrap one of her legs around his hip and give him the benefit of how wet he was making her. A quick flick of her fingers and his dick would be free. All she'd have to do was give one little hop, mount that bad boy and... *yeehaaaw*!

To hell with strip poker, all bets were off.

Ticka... ticka... ticka...

"Did you hear that?" It was Kyle who stopped the party.

She wanted to shout, "yes, that's every nerve in my body humming." Instead, she took a deep breath to clear her head. Suddenly, Kyle's arms tightened around her.

"Don't move," he cautioned softly. She didn't. She could tell by the change in his voice and the way his body stilled that something was wrong. Her mind immediately went back to work. They were on a tropical island. Snake? Spider? Eek-gads, she hoped not. Rats and garter snakes she could handle, but the tiniest spider made her itch for her 9 mil Glock. In a pinch however, a baseball bat or a very *big* fly swatter would do.

"Do you like crabs?" he asked.

Darcy kept her gaze fixed on the azalia behind him. "Depends on how they're cooked. Or is this a trick question?"

"No, but there's one on the sidewalk here." There was just the fraction of caution in his voice.

Darcy relaxed and looked over. Yep, it was a crab. A big, white crab, out for an evening stroll. She turned toward it and planted one hand on her hip. "You mean that thing?" She started to laugh.

"You mean you're not scared?" There was a note of genuine surprise in his voice.

"Not at all. I–" She was about to say, "*I hit The Crab Shack on Yonge Street every Saturday night.*" But then there'd be questions about her life, her other life. Kyle might wonder why a savvy real estate broker would patronize a grungy joint like that. Quickly she covered her butt. "I've seen them here on the menu. We're on a tropical island and crabs come out at night. Don't you, little fella," she took a small step toward it. The crab moved furtively toward the bushes. Its two foreclaws slowly opened in defence of its territory, which, right now, was the walkway. "Damn! Wish I'd brought my camera."

Kyle clapped his hands and crab ran into the rimmed underbrush of miniature palms and hibiscus.

"I'm impressed, Darcy. I love a woman who can handle herself in the face of danger. And here I was hoping to demonstrate my bravado by picking you up and carrying you away from the threat of crustacean nightmares."

"I think there are worse things for me to fear at night than crab legs."

"Ah, you mean the two-legged kind."

"Exactly. Claws mean nothing when there exists a creature more fearsome, more volatile, with the fastest hands in the tropics, able to paint the town red and probably make the local pharmacist smile every time he comes in to buy a gross of condoms."

He gave her a wide-eyed, innocent stare. "Surely the lady can't mean me?"

Darcy slipped into her shoes. "'Fraid so, Romeo. Besides," she paused and pointed in the direction of the crab's retreat. "Three's a crowd."

Kyle frowned at her actions. "Remind me to corral that little sucker and herd him into the nearest soup pot. He's worse than a cold shower."

"I think we should call it a night, anyway. What time do you want to go to town?" she asked, eager to get Kyle's mind back on track. It worked. He folded his arms across his chest and stared down at his sandals.

"How about ten. I like to get in a swim first. Maybe breakfast?", he asked hopefully.

"If you're asking me to join you then, yes. Breakfast at the Tiki Buffet, seven sharp." She turned and started to walk toward her bungalow. "And don't be early," she called over her shoulder. "I don't like a man who comes too early."

Kyle watched her walk away. Every instinct inside him wanted to follow her. His groin still throbbed, aided by the memory of the taste of her skin, the unspoken promises of their kiss. What a woman! Afraid to show her tits on the beach but could face down a crab the size of a Buick. Maybe tomorrow he'd tell her that he did get to see the show this morning.

He'd squeezed through the volleyball crowd just in time to see her stupid hat hit the sand. What a shame she chose to hide such natural charms. And what a wonderful contrast against all the expensive, gravity-defying inserts around her. Those deep, rosy nipples standing up to catch the sea breeze, planted in the middle of dark areolas, all set off by the milky-white plumpness of her breasts. Yes, her body was a work of art!

His mouth watered at the thought of running his tongue across those nipples. His fingers itched to fondle her breasts to a desirable hardness. He made up his mind as he walked back toward his room. What Darcy McLeod hesitated to share with the world, he'd find a way to make her willing to share with him.

And she was willing. Not even she could deny the evidence tonight when she wriggled out of her thong. Any fool could see she was ready and wet for him. Even a blind man could pick up the scent of her slick pussy. As for him? Damn straight he was hot and hard for her. He'd been holding her so close. It wasn't like he had to whip it out and hang a neon sign on it saying, "my cock is ready for action."

Until that crab and its rotten timing! He sighed. Oh, well. Better to be interrupted by them than have a case of them. In a way he couldn't blame the voyeuristic critter for wanting to get a little closer to her. He wanted the same thing.

He climbed the stairs to his second floor suite deciding that celibacy was highly overrated.

Chapter Four

Kyle stopped in at the hotel manager's office shortly before meeting Darcy for breakfast. Oliver Daas, a dark-skinned San Andrean and manager of the hotel greeted Kyle.

"Eh, Kyle, mon! You come to use my phone again. When we goin' fishin' next?"

Kyle propped himself on the corner of Oliver's desk. "Anytime you say, Olie. Right now I'm doing a little fishing of my own."

"Ya, mon. I see you with her last night at supper. *Sweet thing!*"

Kyle grinned. "I think so, too. Having breakfast with her this morning."

Olie winked at him. "Why you not call for room service? I serve the two of you in bed." He gave Kyle a sly grin, displaying a dazzling row of white teeth, a couple of them capped in bright gold.

"It wasn't that kind of a night, Olie. I slept alone. This one's a lady."

Oliver nodded his head, despite his doubtful expression. "Ya. I could see by the way she dress. She fishing with the right kind of bait."

Kyle slid the phone across the desk and began to dial. "Has anyone ever told you you have a suspicious mind?"

"No more than you, my friend. I'm going to get a coffee."

"I was wondering when you'd scram and give me a little privacy."

Olie removed himself from behind his desk. "Give my regards to your pretty mama, if that's who you're calling."

Kyle called in first to his office voice-mail and made notes. Message from father, message from mother. Urgent message from father. Message from Tiffany's father. Message from Tiffany. He deleted all except the one from his mother. He hung up and dialed again.

"Yes, operator, I'll hold for a connection." The island connections could be unpredictable. Weather, equipment, atmosphere, San Andres was still a third world country by North American standards. He turned his attention back to the line.

"Hi mom."

"Kyle? Is that you?" The voice on the other end was barely audible.

"I'm at your hotel in San Andres. I'm staying in your suite."

"So, you're not in France. Does anyone know?"

"Just Oliver. What's the news?"

"Your father's having a shit fit. He's combing the globe for you. All the press knows is that you're on vacation. They're really playing it up too. A last fling for the millionaire playboy. Tiffany wants me to give her a shower. I don't know what to tell her. I may not agree with why you're marrying her but I don't want to hurt her feelings."

Kyle was too far away to tell Frances that hurting Tiff was his job, not hers, assuming that his fiancée had any feelings beyond which mansion in Forest Hills they were going to occupy.

"Don't tell her anything. I've come down here to sort things out. I just want to do what's right."

"Do what's right for yourself son, not Mason. That's what I've always told you." His mother's words rang true even if they were coming from three thousand miles away. Kyle wished he could see her reassuring face. For now, her voice would have to do.

"I want a marriage like Kevin had, not some politically correct, financially feasible contract. I know it may sound trite, mother, but I really do want love."

"And you don't love Tiffany, that's for sure. Anyone who looks at the two of you can see that."

That's what mothers were for, to tell you the truth and temper the harsh reality with sage advice. She wanted what was best for her son and she knew from the beginning that Tiffany Garrett-Shawcross, only daughter of billionaire shipping baron Joshua Shawcross was not the woman for her son. Kyle knew it too. Despite all this, Mason threw Tiffany into his path and all but promised Joshua that the marriage would guarantee that Joshua's ships would transport Mason's lumber around the world with one stroke of a pen. And that pen would be signing the wedding register as well as the shipping contract.

"Listen, mom. Thanks for letting me hide out here. I'll keep in touch."

"I hope you find your heart, son. And don't let Mason intimidate you."

Kyle thought about her last statement. "Dad can't bug me if he can't find me."

"I've heard he's hired a detective or something. He means business, Kyle. And so do I. Mason can do what he wants with his own life but I think this whole deal with Shawcross stinks. He's clear-cutting valuable forests and I won't go along with any business deal that condones stripping our country's natural resources. I won't agree to it. And if you go along with him, I'll be very disappointed. You'll hurt me and you'll hurt yourself. All because Mason can't think beyond the next dollar."

Kyle allowed his mind to drift. He rolled his eyes and shook his head. He'd heard the arguments a dozen times before. His mother plain out didn't want him to side with Mason on this deal. She even hinted that his position in her will could be usurped by Monica if he sided against her. He knew she didn't really mean it. She was upset. Yet her displeasure hadn't waned, her refusal to vote for the merger created a huge rift with the board of directors. She stood her ground and watched Mason manipulate the board until they finally voted her out.

"I'll take care of dad when I get back. Try not to kill each other until then, okay?"

"All right, dear. Try to relax and have some fun. I'll expect the bill."

He heard her sigh loudly, after which, he said 'good-bye.' He hung up the phone and left Olie's office. He walked to the breakfast buffet but didn't see Darcy. He checked his watch. He was just a little early, so he helped himself to some coffee and sat down to wait for her. He stirred thick cream and two heaping spoonfuls of raw brown sugar into the cup and watched the black, strong coffee turn to a rich, caramel color. His mother's words swirled around in his head. No, he didn't agree with his father's plans for the lumber. Several hundred thousand acres of northern Quebec land had come with Frances MacDonald, an heiress of 'old money'. As long as Arthur MacDonald was alive, the land was safe. Mason built a hunting lodge there and Kyle and his high school friends used to go up there and party and hunt moose in season.

Then Arthur died and the land went to Frances. That's when Mason decided to branch out his holdings to include lumber. Cheap to cut, cheap to transport but the hassle and cost of renewing the shipping contracts with Shawcross year after year was taking its toll on DeLaurier profits. More profits meant more money to buy land—lots of it. There was land in Kyle's name, Monica's name and now, probably Tiffany as well.

But something happened when Mason sent his developers to Kyle's land in the Northwest Territories. The aggregate testing showed the land rich in minerals, especially and unbelievably enough, diamonds. Plentiful, exquisite in quality and easy to refine. It was the excavation costs that blew the whole idea out of the water. Except for Kyle. He was willing to gamble and invest his own fortunes on setting up an excavation operation, if Mason was willing to underwrite the shortfall. But when Mason saw the figures he almost had to reach for oxygen.

"Are you out of your fucking mind? This is your mother's doing. She's on this tree-hugging kick. She put this stupid idea into your head. Well, you can forget about it."

"But it's my land and it's my money," Kyle argued. "You have nothing to lose." But his reasoning settled on deaf ears. The argument did do one thing, however. Kyle refused to let his father near the property with so much as a boy scout and a penknife. The land would stay intact. That was over five years ago. He knew Mason was eyeing the property again—as if Kyle couldn't see right through Tiffany's offer to buy the land outright. His old man was persistent, if not subtle.

He blew the steam from his coffee and wondered if Darcy liked diamonds. Or emeralds. Or both. He saw her last night, gazing longingly into the shop window, hungrily devouring the display in the lobby. He should find out if she had a few extra days to spend here. He'd take her right to the source. Still, he thought as he checked his watch again, if all went well then the source would be here any day.

᠅᠁(ᢗᢒ)ᢘ᠁

Darcy waited in the shadow of a large palm by the staff entrance. She could see Kyle sipping on a coffee and staring into space. She wondered about the phone call he made this morning and if it had anything to do with him checking the lobby bulletin board where the flights to and from Colombia were posted. The alcove near the manager's office was deserted so Darcy strolled by and paused outside the closed door. She pretended to read a tour magazine in front of the closed door and decided what she would tell the manager, should he return.

She wondered if Kyle was talking to Tiffany. She must have come by toward the end of the conversation as she could barely make out the words, "love you too" before she heard him hang up the phone. She dashed into the nearby ladies room before he opened the office door. She opened the bathroom door just a tiny crack and saw him checking the flight schedules.

Maybe he was going home after all. Bonus. A job quickly done and a few days in paradise. Once he left for the buffet, she wandered out and checked the bulletin board and discovered that only the Colombian flights were posted. Her mind went back to Kyle's admitted 'business in town' yesterday. The uneasy possibility that the Colombian flight might contain more than a shipment of coffee again nagged at her. It wouldn't be the first time some spoiled, rich kid with a lot of time and money to blow—blow being the operative word—decided to dabble in a bit of illegal trafficking. Yet, on the surface, Kyle didn't seem the type. She'd have to watch him more carefully.

She composed herself and walked into the buffet dining room to join him. He smiled at her, an electric smile that jolted her as if she'd just received a severe carpet shock. She swallowed to try to settle the giddy jumping in her stomach. It wasn't him, he reminded herself, she just needed an omelette and a wake-up coffee to steady her low blood sugar.

"How'd you sleep?" he asked and rose to pull open a chair for her.

"Fine." *Lousy, thanks to you.* "You?"

"Great. Until the rain this morning. Good thing it was only a short shower. Looks like we'll have good weather for strolling around town."

"Yes," she agreed, still thinking of her throbbing clit the night before and how she finally took matters into her own hand. Even after the initial bang subsided, it was only a physical release. In truth, she spent a restless night tossing and turning. Every time she closed her eyes she felt Kyle's lips nibbling her neck, his hands caressing her bottom, his cock rubbing up against her. The thought of another day verbally sparring with Kyle's non-stop sexual innuendos was almost more than she could bear. If she wasn't careful, she'd have to jump him simply to get it over with so she could carry on with her job. But getting Kyle in the sack hadn't been part of the job description. It could set a dangerous precedent. On the other hand, what man would admit that a woman used sex to trap him? The chances were good that Spencer would never hear about it.

"Breakfast?" he asked, drawing her concentration back to him.

"Cheese omelette and a gallon of Colombian coffee."

"Wired or tired?"

"Both. My bed's a little soft," she lied.

"I can see where that might be a problem. I much prefer going to bed if it's nice and hard."

Well, shit me! It's starting again.

"Perhaps you should ask the front desk if they can put you in another room. Or a different bed."

Like yours, for instance? Darcy carefully set down a glass of papaya juice and looked him straight in the eye. "Are you programmed to do that?"

"What?" He assumed an innocent face.

"That. Every time you open your mouth, those wise-cracking, leading, ulterior-motive remarks just roll off your tongue."

He sat back in his chair and crossed his arms over his chest. "Miss McLeod, I'll have you know I've been told I'm very good with my tongue."

Darcy covered her face with her hands and groaned. "It's too early for this."

"You're not a morning person I take it. I'll have to remember that. Next to your name in my PDA in quotes—Darcy—only gets lucky at night."

She looked over at him. "Hey, who says? I get lucky any time I damned well feel like it."

"Ah the great thing about being a woman. Batteries."

"I might throw something at you yet."

Kyle leaned across the table. "C'mon. Smile. That's it. You're almost there—what—not quite—YES! There it is. A smile."

Luckily their breakfast together was short. Afterwards they boarded a shuttle for San Luis City. Their transportation was an old school bus that had seen at least four previous lives. There was only room enough for two people on the seat and only if they squeezed close together, which didn't seem to bother Kyle at all. Darcy sat next to the open window aware that Kyle's arm was around her and his knee was pressed against her bare leg. They both wore shorts, Kyle in beige with a matching polo shirt and Darcy in a white with a cotton halter. Her outfit, like everything else, was cunningly chosen to keep Kyle's attention. More so in the bright sun than in the shaded dining room, her dark nipples shadowed nicely against the white material. More than once she noticed Kyle's gaze rivetted in the right direction.

If he could drive her crazy with words, she could do it visually. Men were primitive creatures that way, their brains were hard-wired so that whatever their eyes saw bypassed their logic and went directly to their testicles.

Darcy slipped on her sunglasses and gazed out the window, taking advantage of the ocean breeze. The main—and only—paved highway ran along the shore line from the hotel in south San Andres into the city centre. The ride was only about 20 minutes, plenty of time for them to drive each other crazy.

Kyle leaned in close to her. "Did you bring them?"

"Bring what?"

"What we're going into town to replace," he whispered low into her ear and brushed the tiny earlobe with his lips. The gesture sent shivers along her spine. Her mons twitched and she pressed her thighs together to stem the rising awareness. Her headlights blinked. He was such a dog!

"I don't need them with me. I can tell what fits just by looking."

"You mean you're not going try anything on for size? Gee whiz! I was hoping you'd model for me." He gave her disappointed sniff and an exaggerated pout.

Darcy patted his cheek. "Awe. Poor Kyle. Cheer up. I'll let you pay for them."

Kyle squeezed his eyes closed and gave her that severe inhale-through-gritted-teeth, seething with displeasure look. "I knew it. Take copious advantage of me then throw me away like a used condom! Is there no sense of romance left in the world?"

"Oh, stop." She swatted his knee.

"A little higher," he begged.

"No."

"Fine. Then it's my turn."

"What?—"

And before she could protest, he kissed her, full-lipped and open-mouthed. His one arm still hugged her tightly. His other arm crossed the polite border between them. He rested his hand on her bare upper thigh. The touch of his warm fingers turned on a switch inside her. She felt her heart skip into a gallop. Several drops of anticipation escaped the twitching folds of her vulva and dampened her bikini panties. Suddenly his thumb brushed her crotch. Her thighs acquiesced and parted slightly. His fingers played at the seams of her shorts. She knew the material was damp with her own wetness seeping from inside her. His fingers played at the base of her mound, toyed with each lip, pronounced by the front seam fitting snug against her crotch. Her clit was swelling against his fingertips creating an unbearable ache. In their present situation there was no relief for her, certainly none for him.

Suddenly the bus hit a huge pothole and lurched sideways. Darcy and Kyle broke apart. Darcy could feel her skin, hot and flushed from his eager foreplay. Kyle still had one arm around her shoulder. The hand that had a few seconds ago mercilessly teased her now rested in his lap. Then he did something that pushed one of her major buttons.

He raised his hand to his face and passed his fingers under his nose. To an onlooker it might look like he was scratching his upper lip. But she knew what he was doing. He was breathing her scent off his fingers. His eyes darkened for a moment. And if that wasn't bad enough, his tongue snaked out between his lips and slowly licked his index finger. He looked at her and whispered. "Delicious!"

Then his chest heaved as he took a deep, reclaiming breath. It was as if he was telling her—enough—for now.

"We're nearly here," he announced and politely took hold of her hand.

So was I!

"Let's go forward. These busses don't give you a lot of warning."

They eased through the narrow aisle and stood waiting for the bus to come to a halt, which it did, rather suddenly. The door opened and the bus emptied.

Downtown San Luis was alive early in the morning, as most stores closed between noon and three for siesta. The salt-tinged air was already humid. The smells of coffee, fried plantain and baked goods hung in the air. The public works department was dumping hot asphalt to mend city streets. Clouds of oily smoke puffed out the backs of motor scooters. The smell of the sea was everywhere. The stores had huge awnings cranked out to their fullest to protect customers from the intense sun. Everyone rushing past them was armed with bottles of water.

Kyle had a firm grip on her hand as he lead her through the crowded sidewalk to a section of Avenue Bolivar to New Point Plaza. Here were the more upscale shops compared to the usual beach-side kiosks and tourist establishments selling coconut shell crafts, beach towels and water shoes.

"I don't know whether to be impressed or jealous that you know exactly where you're going," she said when they finally arrived at a women's lingerie shop.

"It's easy to get around here. It's a very small island. Every street eventually ends at the sea. No need to worry if you ever get lost. Just get to the main shore road and flag down a shuttle. There is no schedule here. The busses run every 20 minutes—more or less. In we go," he opened the door with a flourish and waived her into the shop.

Darcy looked around at the racks and shelves filled with tempting confections of silk and satin. She cocked her head toward the ceiling where soft music floated from a round speaker.

"You just can't beat Burt Bacharach elevator music for shopping," she sighed.

Kyle sat down in a tub-shaped leather chair and hummed *This Guy's In Love With You.*

Darcy glared at him over her sunglasses.

"Sorry," he muttered. "Just caught up in the moment."

"Why don't you sit there out of harm's way while I browse." She removed her sunglasses and tucked them into her purse. She came over to where Kyle sat and handed him her purse.

He looked at the purse, then at her. He put one hand on his hip and tapped his chin with his index finger. "Not my color," he quipped.

"Never mind. Just please keep an eye on this so I won't leave it in the dressing room. A woman losing a purse is a national catastrophe. All my travellers cheques and what few pesos I have are in there."

Darcy combed the racks looking at thongs, teddies, bras, garters and horribly expensive negligees. She knew she could never afford anything so pricy or lavish but decided to get back at Kyle by teasing him. She plucked out one design after another and feigned modelling in front of a mirror, deliberately avoiding Kyle's interested gaze. It was small payback, she knew, but it was the best she could do under the circumstances. She glanced at his reflection in the mirror.

Goddamned him! Why did he have to be so frigging perfect? He looked good, he smelled good, he tasted great and felt even better when he touched her. She almost wished there was a flaw, something that she could focus on to sidetrack her from the dangerous road their foreplay was taking them. But hard as she tried, Darcy could find nothing to dampen her raging hormones. Not a wart, or a unibrow, tattoo or body piercing in sight. Hell, the jerk didn't even have the decency to commit fashion suicide by wearing socks with his sandals.

Maybe the great flaw was hidden, like pecker-rot, or some homicidal psychosis.

He smiled at her and winked. Maybe not.

But Darcy had a plan. Never go into the field without a plan, cautioned Spence. It was time to uncork the plan. She gathered up five or six of the most expensive, revealing creations and whirled past him into the dressing room.

"Think I'll try these on for color," she quipped as she pulled a chintz curtain across an empty dressing room entrance. She quickly removed her halter top and lopped it over the top rail, in his plain sight. Then she stuck her head out from behind the curtain. "But don't go away," she shook her finger at him, admonishing him like a naughty schoolboy. "I might need a second opinion."

Kyle shook his head and chuckled softly as Darcy slid the curtain back into place. Once she was safely in the dressing room, and he was sure she'd be occupied for a few minutes, Kyle went over to the cashier. "Does Mrs. Frances DeLaurier still have an account here?" He pulled out his wallet and showed the girl an assortment of credit cards. He tossed her one. "Run this through and keep it open. Anything she wants—" he inclined his head toward the dressing room where Darcy was changing—"put it through on my card. Also, I may call in later to add more on this bill. Is that all right?"

"I will speak to the manager." The girl disappeared through a mirrored doorway. She immediately returned with an older, dark-skinned woman.

"Señor Kyle. I am Mrs. Daviot. I have had the pleasure to serve Mrs. Frances in the past. Anything you wish to purchase I will put on her bill. Is she joining you this trip?"

Kyle shook his head. "No, unfortunately my mother couldn't make it. I think she's planning to spend a month at her hotel next January. I will tell her you asked after her. And by the way, just put any purchases on my credit card. My mother doesn't have to know I was here."

Mrs. Daviot raised a speculative eyebrow but said nothing except, "Gracias, Señor. Is there anything else I can do for you today?"

Kyle saw the curtain flutter out of the corner of his eye. There was now a small gap between the safety of the dressing room and any immediate voyeurs, which, at the moment, consisted only of himself. No doubt a calculated tactic, and very much appreciated. She really did mean to get him back for all the teasing he'd put her through.

The gap revealed a portion of the dressing room mirror. Darcy had her naked back—and the very naked rest of her body—toward the mirror. She was bending over and stepping into a peach silk, thong-style teddy. Oh, God—that ass! That beautiful heart-shaped ass. Firm, round, begging for his fingers to dig in while he rode her. She bent right over, her legs slightly parted revealing her lovely split peach framed by golden curls. The glistening folds of her flesh winked at him, a teasing invitation that demanded acceptance. If she thought for one minute that she was extracting revenge for last night then... it was working. A fire deep in his belly made his blood boil. His trousers felt overly snug in the crotch. She was too good to ignore this time. If she wanted to play hide and seek then so be it. He wasn't going to spend another night with his fist wrapped around his cock

He suddenly cleared his throat and turned his attention back to the manager who was waiting for an answer to her very loaded question. He smiled politely and handed her a U.S. hundred dollar bill and did what he did best. He shot from the hip.

"Yes. You and your clerk can lock up and go to lunch."

Chapter Five

Darcy peered into the mirror, trying to catch a glimpse of Kyle through the strategic curtain opening. Where the hell was he and what the hell was keeping him? She could only stand in the buff under the air conditioning for so long. It was bad for a girl's health. Come to think of it, so was Kyle.

She'd seen him leaning across the check-out counter and talking to the sales girl, then the owner. She bent over and stepped into the teddy, but seeing the price tag she changed her mind in favor of a peach-colored silk thong—one she intended to buy as it was about the only affordable scrap of cloth in the store—and when she stood up Kyle was gone from her view.

Darcy barely had time to refocus when the curtain swung back with a 'whoosh' from the opposite side. There stood Kyle DeLaurier, carefully admiring the goods.

"About time," she snapped and parked her hands on her hips. She tried to remain cool and detached from the sudden intrusion. She only hoped he couldn't hear her knees knocking or her heart pounding.

"I hope you're buying that, now that you've—um—broken it in." He stepped inside the dressing room and closed the curtain. His gaze fell to the narrow triangle covering her mons.

She followed his reference then realized what he meant. There was a slight discoloration in the fabric from her own wetness. She realized suddenly her little tease had not only backfired, it was in danger of blowing up in her face. She tried to ignore him.

"What about the staff?" she questioned and returned her gaze to the mirror and tried not to look as flustered as she felt.

"Getting harder by the minute."

Darcy growled and rolled her eyes. "I mean the ladies who work here." Letting him cop a feel on a crowded bus was one thing but playing personal fashionista in close proximity of the owner was quite different altogether.

He stepped up behind her and placed his hands on her shoulders. His fingers were warm, but not sweaty and exuded a slight pressure. A strange, delightful tingle threaded her skin.

"They've gone to lunch and locked up. Lucky us."

Darcy regarded him in the mirror with raised eyebrows. "How much did your 'luck' cost you?"

"Not a cent. This one's on the house."

"You do know that 'lunch' as they call it lasts for about three hours."

He kissed her left shoulder and murmured. "Good for the digestion." Then the hollow of her neck. "Mmm... so are you. The low-carb woman. All protein, no calories. Perfect lunch for my diet." He reached around and patted her flat stomach. She only thought about stopping him when the patting turned into a light caress. "I even get dessert after the main course."

She let out a nervous chuckle. "I didn't realize I was on the menu."

"It's an all inclusive resort."

"Nice try."

"I think so. Is it working?"

"Jury's still out."

"I don't think so. My verdict is, you're guilty as hell." Yes, she was. Guilty of enjoying the path of kisses up and down the side of her neck. Guilty of the pleasure that caused her nipples to stand up and beg for attention.

"I have all the evidence I need, right here."

'Here' was where he placed his hand—over the damp, peachy fabric between her legs. Tried and convicted. Short and sweet, save the taxpayers' money. She knew she wasn't going to like her sentence in the morning, especially since she'd written it herself.

"Turn around."

She did. She faced her judge, her jury, her jailor. Her executioner. She knew she could flatten his ass with one neatly placed punch, grab her clothes, rip down the flimsy curtain, wrap it around her and high tail it out of there. Somehow, that scenario didn't play out as well as Kyle slipping his hands between her legs and allowing his fingers to slide into the panty. She moaned softly when he touched her, aware her own confession was complete. He toyed with her curls, circled her outer lips, teased her to readiness. It took her only a moment to realize she was stuck with the peach silk thong now whether she liked it or not.

Shit, she thought! *Why didn't I just cuff him and ship him air freight back to Toronto?*

"Well, looked what popped up to say hello. It's the accidental cli-tourist."

Darcy buried her head in his chest and tried to stifle the laughter. It didn't work. Twitters leaked out despite her attempts to muffle the sound. She felt him shaking her shoulders, trying to get her attention.

"Darcy, look at me. This is a serious moment."

It wasn't, according to the smile on his face and the twinkle in his eye. But his hands were serious. Serious as sex as he moved from her shoulders to her bare breasts.

"I shouldn't let you do this."

"Don't worry, I can afford it. I'll pay for the panties, anything you want. Just kiss me."

"No!" she shook her head, determined to catch a clear thought before it was too late. But it was already too late, she realized. And not because she was naked in a change room with the son of her boss' very rich client. It was too late from the first moment he scowled at her from under his hangover and snapped at her with his stale beer-breath.

There was something dangerous about Kyle, something that rang her inner warning chimes. Something about his sexy smile, his musky male scent and the rugged stomped-on-and-kicked-in-the-ass first impression he made. He was a chameleon with a dozen faces and one big, fat, 'fuck you world' attitude. Right now, however, he was a man. An aroused man by the feel of his body pressed against her. A man ready to do what aroused men did best. Ready to do what she narrowly avoided last night.

"You don't want to kiss me?"

"No... no, I mean, you don't have to buy me anything."

"Ooh," he grinned like a red heart joker on a deck of playing cards. "*Suavemente, besame.*"

"Yeah, suave, all right."

"Say '*si, si*'."

She couldn't. But then she couldn't stop the whistling sound coming from between her lips, either.

"*Si*, Señorita?"

"*Si... si...*" *See, see me blow a huge bonus.*

"*Besse me.*"

Kiss me! Kiss my job good-bye!

His lips hovered over hers. It was her last chance to run for safety. But safety was not why Darcy was in this business and running away was not in her profile.

She flung her arms around him suddenly and pressed her body against him. She grabbed his hair, forcing his mouth down on hers. She kissed him greedily, recklessly with all the force of her pent-up desire. He responded without hesitation. His hands roved up and down her back, over her buttocks, pausing to give each one a passionate squeeze.

He interrupted the kiss briefly. "Jeez, woman. When you say '*si*' you really mean it!"

"*Tengo hambre.*"

"*¡Estoy listo!*"

She was hungry. And he was ready! She pressed her abdomen into the protruding stiffness beneath his pants. Her hands moved to his belt. Her fingers fumbled recklessly with the buckle. The buttons, the zipper, the band on his white briefs, all annoying roadblocks on the way to her ultimate destination.

He stayed her fingers. "Easy does it, sweetheart. We've got all afternoon."

"And all night."

"You're hopeful."

"Viagara's cheap."

"So am I, but I can be had by the right pair of hands."

"Shut up, cowboy. I'm horny!"

"No shit, Sherlock."

Darcy froze. "Wha—what did you say?"

"I meant 'no kidding' you're horny."

"Oh." Her moment of caution slipped away faster than the strings of her thong slid down her legs. "OH!" she breathed as her fingers slid beneath his briefs and closed around his erection. What a treat! A man with a big, thick, hard, hot cock. Locked and loaded, just the way she liked to work. Only this weapon had nothing to do with self-preservation, unless he wasn't prepared to use it, then he was in for a shit-kicking.

"Something tells me this bad boy is gonna feel real good."

"And something tells me I'm going to slide right into something warm and wet and nice and tight."

"Well, then lets stop talking about it and start doing it."

Darcy'd had enough of foreplay. She'd had nearly two days of it. She wanted to get laid and she wanted it now. She yanked his pants down to his ankles. She hurriedly kissed whatever her mouth came into contact with. A navel surrounded by a wisp of dark hair. The slit of his cock, weeping in anticipation, his balls warm and musky. The insides of his tanned, muscular thighs. She squeezed the hard cheeks of his ass as she made a quick pass over them.

"Hey, lady, you gonna buy or you just gonna finger the merchandise?"

Darcy chuckled as she stood up and turned around to face the mirror. She bent over the armless courtesy chair. "I trust you don't need a demo."

"No fucking way! C'mere."

He snuggled in behind her and pressed his erection against her bottom. She felt him bend slightly and capture his pants from the floor. It took her a moment to realize what was causing his delay. She heard the plastic packet crinkle as he opened it. In the mirror she could see him deftly roll the condom over his penis. Then he bent his knees slightly and aimed his now-sheathed cock. Darcy felt it press against her. She adjusted her stance slightly to enable him to enter her easily. She grasped the sides of the velvet seat as his round, bulbous tip sat poised to slip inside her.

When it did, she gasped out loud. "Geezus! Kyle!"

"Yeah!" He filled her with one great thrust. He paused for a moment then reached around and cupped both her breasts as they hung freely in her current position. His warm breath came heavy across her back.

"What a great ass you have! Great tits! A gorgeous pussy! Oh, god, you feel good."

She squeezed him then and he groaned out loud. "You're— amazing. I never thought... I never dreamed..." Then he let one hand slide down to her mons. His fingers toyed with her opening, rimming her outer lips with her own wetness. Then he went for the gold. He began to thrust again, creating a collage of sensation. He massaged her clit in time with his thrusts. Darcy closed her eyes and let her head drop forward like a limp doll. This was sex the way she imagined it would be with him. Hot and hard, dangerous and dirty. Fast and loose. He pommelled against her and she could hear his balls slapping with every thrust. His fingers were no slouch either. He was hitting the spot all right. His fingers buffeted her clit in tiny circles.

She was close to her climax. She knew he could feel it too.

"That's it," he coaxed, his mouth desperately close to her ear. "I can feel you tense. Let it happen. Come for me. Let me feel you cum all over my cock." She needed no further urging. Her legs began to shake as the sensations vibrated through her body. She gave in and let her orgasm overtake her completely. Not a mere gasp, or a barely-there hiss of awareness but a genuine cry of exhilaration. She slammed against him, eager to savour every last inch of him.

That's when she felt him shudder deep inside her. He leaned his head on her back to muffle a cry of orgasmic delight even as she felt the spasms of hot cum wash deep inside her. Suddenly he grabbed her around her waist and she found herself sinking to the floor with him. She landed on top of him as they lay on the carpeted dressing room floor.

"Dizzy," he panted.

"Yeah, me too," she agreed.

"The-the ceiling. It's spinning," came a faint, breathless declaration.

"Uh-uh," she murmured. "It's the floor."

There was a brief moment, then a long sigh before he answered her. "Maybe it was an earthquake."

Darcy smiled weakly into his chest. "As in 'the earth moved'?" She felt a gentle ruffle on the top of her head where his warm breath settled on her hair. Yes, it was cliche. Yes, it was trite. But no statement could have been truer spoken.

"I always thought that was a myth." His voice was a velvety, deep pitch. Subdued, yet full of satisfaction.

"What about me?" It was hard to lie on top of him and carry on post-coital banter with his fingers drawing swirls across her bare buttocks.

"Oh, you definitely are a figment of my imagination. Just the kind of woman me and my right hand would fantasize about every Saturday night." He gave her a possessive squeeze, just to make sure she knew he was still on his game.

Darcy nuzzled her cheek against the dark mat of curling hair on his chest. "And you are a dream lover. Something my mind brewed up between last night's lobster tails and the Spanish coffee. Or a ghost from one of those mystery flicks with the 'gotcha' ending. You know, 'I see naked people'."

His chest rumbled beneath her. "That's going to be true soon enough if we don't get up. One of the staff might decide to end their siesta early. Besides, I want more of this—later. Now, kiss me."

She did. And she was glad she did. This kiss was a warm, cuddling kind of 'thank you' kiss. There was passion in that kiss.

"Mmm... more," he begged.

Darcy chuckled softly. Keep 'em wanting more. She'd never had a lover who wanted more of anything from her. Except cab fare and that didn't count. "Tonight. Right now, I think we better get off the floor. I think you have a garment tag sticking out from under your back."

"Oh yeah? What am I worth?"

"More than my budget allows. Trust me."

"Okay. Whatever you say." After a minute he added, "promise?"

She murmured a muffled, "hmph," her ears still echoing from the blood pounding, her fingers and toes still pulsing from Kyle's wondrous lovemaking. She was perfectly content to curl up on top of him and slide into a long, relaxing sleep. But they were in a store, not a hotel room and Kyle couldn't possibly be comfortable in his current position.

The impatient tapping on her back confirmed her musings. "Promise?"

"I promise, Romeo."

"Hey, I'm the international spy. Remember?"

"Listen lover, most spies I see make love to the girl with a gun under the pillow and then kick the shit out of the bad guy. You couldn't kick the shit out of a coconut right now."

"That's your fault, spy girl. You've got some kind of cock-draining, secret pussy weapon down there. I don't know what it is but if you ever bottle it you'll make fortune."

"Wuss," she sighed into his chest.

He was right about one thing, though. Right now, even she didn't have the strength to kick the shit out of a coconut if their lives depended on it.

꙳ၷ(ꗏ)ၡ꙳

Three hours and four bags of lingerie later, they left downtown San Luis. Instead of taking the resort shuttle bus, Kyle flagged down a cab. They stashed the bags in the trunk and Kyle insisted she stretch out on the back seat. He was growing on her like moss. For a loner like Darcy she thought it might be irritating. Most of the time if she knew she had to put up with a clingy client she always asked Spence if she could shoot them first.

Right now, with her head in his lap and Kyle's hand maintaining a firm, territorial grip just under her right breast she was feeling almost lulled into a domestic kind of security. She hadn't had a lot of time for boyfriends since she joined Spence. The old man never had any attraction to her and she was merely the junior ingenue of the outfit. They were chums, buddies. In fact, Spence encouraged her to talk about her personal life the way two men might discuss casual sex in a bar over a couple of beers.

"Get your humping out of the way now, kid. On the job you need your head. I've seen good cops, veteran private eyes, even the best-trained covert ops feds blow their careers all to hell over a lousy piece of ass, or a piece of lousy ass, take your pick. Even if you have to go to the bathroom and jack off, get it done and get back to work. You lose your focus and you could lose your life." Then he took her weapon out of her holster and laid it on the table. Before she could stop him, he plunged his big, gnarly, size fifteen ring finger hand up her skirt and cupped her panties.

He tapped her Glock. "Pistol." Then he squeezed her crotch. "Gun. One is for fighting, one is for fun. Never forget it."

That was his little test to see if the newbies could stick it out. Either they got all flustered and threatened to report him or, like Darcy, they had the guts to stare him in the eye coolly and snap, "get your paw off my privates, private, before I shoot you."

"Technically, I'm a colonel," he put in smoothly, not even batting an eye.

That's when he hired her. Good thing too, since leaving the Metro Toronto Police Force a few months earlier shot any pension expectation all to hell. Just two measly years as a street cop. It wasn't that she couldn't handle being a cop; she loved it. It was all the shitty rules and regulations that kept her from doing her job. She drew a real rotten apple for her first post, assigned to "Outer Scarberia" the polite term for the suburb of Scarborough. A real wicked melting pot of racial nests and the problems that went with them. The Tamil Tigers were constantly shooting up the Sri Lankans, the Jamaicans fought amongst themselves, the East Indians ran when they saw a uniform coming and the hard-core middle east sects ignored you completely if you were a woman.

Darcy couldn't help the young women found dead as a result of 'honor' killings. A five-year-old Pakistani tot was beheaded by her father because she was 'disrespectful'. He sat in the defendant's box and simply shrugged when pronounced guilty. No remorse, no emotion. That's just the way it was in their culture.

But it was her city, a city out of control. There were streets of witnesses to drive-by shootings but nobody saw a thing. She'd had enough. Luckily she landed a transfer to downtown 52 Division. Her youth and looks made her a perfect fit for the undercover task force cracking down on prostitution and the Jarvis Street brothels masquerading as illegal massage parlors.

Even that wasn't getting her job satisfaction. Some of the busts revealed twelve-year-old Russian girls smuggled in to lend freshness to the trade. Add to that, transvestite hookers, kiddie porn and the odd homicide. Still, rules was rules. You couldn't kick the shit out of some kid's pimp, you couldn't rescue every waif on the street. So she quit. Handed in her badge and gun and got her P.I. licence and threw her lot in with Spence, who sent her on tame investigations for insurance frauds, credit card scams and babysitting sons of nauseatingly rich clients—who just happened to have great equipment and knew what to do with it.

"A penny for your thoughts, sweet thing."

I should have shot you!

"I was just thinking that a screaming orgasm would taste great right now.

Then a dip in the pool. Then dinner. Then–"

"You get your drink, hon, everything else is negotiable."

"For what?" She batted her eyes innocently.

Typical man, wants to get laid again. Okay, no turning back now.

"Later." He smiled knowingly down at her. She looked into that smile. That sex-struck smile, those deep, lingering eyes. Hungry eyes that coveted her every movement, silently worshipped every natural attribute she possessed. Those strong, expert fingers that gently grazed the fabric over her breasts and set a fire of sensations raging across her skin. Yes, his body was becoming honed to hers. Familiar, possessive. Dangerous.

Don't look at me like that. You're going to really hate me in a few days.

"Your hotel, señor."

Not as much as I'm going to hate myself.

"Up you get, sweetheart. We're home."

Darcy smiled at him as she allowed him to help her up and out of the cab. Home. Where she could return to the relative security of spying on cheating husbands and suspicious wives. Home to her rented condo overlooking the waterfront, a long way off from the massive properties on the Bridal Path where spoiled kids like Kyle DeLaurier had rock stars and pro hockey players for neighbours.

That was Kyle's world and she promised to return him to it. A world in which she surely didn't belong.

Chapter Six

"I'm not answering that frigging phone."

Darcy returned to her room and dumped her gifts from Kyle on the adjoining bed. She was in the middle of sorting through the sea of naughty treasures when the high-pitched ring interrupted her.

It might be Spence. She'd missed her afternoon e-mail due to her little shopping spree with Kyle. Her money was on Mason. She fished through her handbag and answered the call.

"I'm sorry I can hardly hear you. Please speak up." Damn, what a lousy connection.

"I said, 'how's it going, kid'?"

"Spence. Yeah, fine." She propped the phone between her ear and shoulder and continued to sift through the rainbow of lace and silk. She frowned, not entirely focussed on her conversation. Where the hell was the black thong?

"You don't sound fine. You seem... distracted."

"I am, and I am."

"Don't tell me the millionaire playboy is getting to you."

Darcy cleared her throat. Now there was an understatement!

"He's fine, Spence. Got him in my sights."

Yeah, staring nose to dick was pretty close sights.

"So, what's the problem?"

"Uh... I just misplaced something. A personal item. Not to worry. I'll call you when I have something to report, okay?"

There was a pause. She always hated the way Spence could sense hesitation. It meant indecision. Worse, it meant she was hiding something.

"Yeah, fine. Carry on."

Carry on! Yes, she was doing that. And an enormous success at it she was too. She flipped the phone closed and tossed it on the bed. It landed in the middle of the silky pile. Damn! Where was that thong? She saw the sales clerk put it in one of the bags. It was the one item she wanted to keep. She intended on returning everything else when this was all over. A knock at her door interrupted her.

She moved to slide the lock back, figuring it was Kyle since he said he'd bring her the much-needed drink. She opened the door, prepared a smart-ass comment designed to counter-balance him when...

"What-the-hell-is–THAT?"

Yeah, he was there all right. Wearing the same red trunks he'd worn yesterday and holding a tall, frosted glass in his hand—and a barbeque skewer clenched between his teeth. Worse, he was wearing her black thong—across his left eye.

"Harrrr, lass. This be the Caribbean, and I be a pirate!"

Darcy dragged him inside. God forbid anyone should see him skulking outside her door. "Okay, is this your idea of kinky?"

He removed the skewer from between his teeth and handed her the drink, which she downed immediately. "And please take off my panties. You'll give the locals the wrong idea."

Kyle flopped down on the empty bed—her bed, she noted.

"Okay, I'm ready. Strip."

Darcy set the glass on the night stand. "Giving up on foreplay already? You must think I'm real easy after this afternoon."

"On the contrary, sweetheart. I'm merely getting comfortable. That boutique floor was okay, but I'm into real, hard-core, post-coital afterglow. I also believe in scented candles, satin sheets, herb-oil massages, joy-jelly and items which require batteries. But in a pinch, I'll make do with a sleeping bag, a flashlight, some margarine and a peeled cucumber."

What the hell, she decided and sat down on the bed beside him. "Okay, Darcy McLeod 101. First, I don't do camping. Okay? My idea of roughing it is having to wait for room service. Second, I like to pick out my own toys. With or without batteries. Third, I am NOT a vegetarian. My greens remain in my salad. Fourth–"

"Fourth, you talk too much."

"It has been said of me. Fourth—I am in desperate need of a siesta so scoot over."

"You're taking a nap?"

Darcy unbuttoned her blouse, liking the way Kyle's eyes changed from surprise to heated interest.

"Do you mind? You can join me if you like."

He leaned back against the pillows and cradled his head in his hands. "I thought you'd like to model some of that oh-so-sexy wardrobe for me."

"I think I've done enough modelling for one day. You must be beat yourself, Kyle. Between your business this morning, the trip into town, our, ah, extra-curricular activity in the dressing room and this heat, you'll never make it to supper."

He suddenly bolted upright. "Shit me! I almost forgot about supper. I planned for us to have a quiet little romantic supper tonight at an exquisite, out-of-the-way island restaurant."

"Sounds wonderful."

"Problem is, I have to see someone about business."

"The same business as this morning?"

"As a matter of fact, yes. Say, you're good for a spy-girl newbie."

Darcy almost bit her tongue but shrugged instead. "Just lucky, I guess."

Kyle winked at her. "Twice in one day. Anyway, I'd promised I'd have supper with him tonight. You don't mind, do you? I am sorry about the timing. We'll go out tomorrow night, I promise."

Darcy stared at him for a minute, wondering where to take this next. She was supposed to keep him out of trouble until she could get him back home for his wedding. How could she keep tabs on him without seeming like a cling-on? On the other hand, the wedding was the least of her worries if Kyle wound up rotting in some Colombian shit-hole prison.

"Tomorrow night is good. I have no plans other than to catch some sun and do some snorkelling."

"Tell you what, I won't be too late. I'll meet you down at the Soca bar later on. We'll hit the disco, then the casino."

"Sounds like I better get my rest."

He leaned across the bed and trapped her in his embrace. He felt good against her. Bare chest to naked breasts. Warm, sexy. Dangerous. He held her close and kissed her deeply while fondling her breasts. As expected, she reacted to him immediately. The war inside her started. Sure, it would be nice to start something wonderful, but why start if he couldn't finish it? If she kept him here, she might very well be keeping him out of trouble. On the other hand, if he missed his appointment, he might end up being pissed with her. The best thing to do was throw the decision back in his lap.

"You sure you want to leave me? I know one part doesn't."

He reluctantly broke away from her. "Now see what you've done." He pointed to the obvious result of their intimate tussle. "My pirate ship is ready to sail. The mizzenmast has risen."

"Tell you what, you can tie me up and make me walk the plank later tonight."

He flashed her a wolfish grin. "Argh, matey! Friggin' in the riggin'. That be a date."

"Aye, aye captain."

⁂

Forty-five minutes later. Darcy was changed and ready to go too. She tied a bandana over her hair, donned sunglasses and slipped into a shapeless, multi-coloured caftan. Everyone was wearing them over their bathing suits so she was sure she'd blend in. She wandered over to the main lobby where the cab pool met, sat down at a crowded bar and ordered a soda.

A few moments later, she spotted Kyle as he came down the spiral staircase from the second floor. Something of interest she did take note of was that he came from the general direction of an area marked "Employees Only." What the hell was he up to? She hoped for her sake he wasn't shagging one of the showgirls, since the casino was also on the second floor.

He went through the front doors and hailed a cab. She waited until he got in before she left the lobby and grabbed a cab from the rear of the line. She was about to get in when a battered, blue Chevy cut off her cab and a dark, shiny-skinned native yelled out the window.

"Hey, ma'am, I drive you. I give you good tour. Brightwood special."

Darcy jerked her head up. In her business, there were instincts, clues and flashing lights that didn't necessarily belong to marked cruisers. This was a red, neon blinker. She by-passed her original driver and hopped into the Chevy.

"Follow that cab," she instructed and tossed the driver an American fifty.

His eyes lit up at the bill and he gave her a curt nod. "Yes, ma'am," he responded in a lilting Island tongue. From what she'd researched, the driver appeared to be a native San Andrean. The black islanders were descended from slaves bound for Jamaica and knew the tiny island like their own mothers. They were the only ones allowed to own property on San Andres and it was more than likely land that had been in their family for generations. If Kyle's 'business' took him off the beaten path, her guide could be circumspect in following him. He could also provide some necessary information such as who was the owner of Kyle's destination.

The only other property owners were representatives of the Government of mainland Colombia and, of course, the drug lords who either bought or leased the land from the San Andreans. Darcy glanced at her watch. Government offices were closed and Kyle's cab was heading away from the downtown core and hotel zone.

"He turning up Pepper Hill, ma'am. They tell you about Pepper Hill?"

'They' meaning the hotel staff at orientation. "Yes. Mr. Daas gave us the skinny on where not to go."

The man laughed. "Dat be my cousin, Olie. You want I should follow?"

"Yes."

The driver cast her a doubtful glance via the rear view mirror. "Okay, ma'am. I do like Mr. Spence say and keep you safe. But I think maybe you slide down a bit so no one see you. Single white woman too much temptation for bad kinda peoples."

Good plan. She took his advice. Pepper Hill was one of those places like Regent Park back home. You sped through the neighbourhood with Navy Seal-like manoeuvres and hoped your windshield didn't shatter. In marked cars it was different. You expected someone to shoot the cherry off your cruiser. If Kyle was going to Pepper Hill it could only mean one thing. He just might not make it to the church on time.

Her driver, who finally identified himself as Rocco, pulled off the gravel road around the bend and out of sight from an enormous hacienda-style home surrounded by a high, black wrought iron fence ringed with barbed wire.

"We wait now," instructed Rocco.

"Who lives there?"

Rocco blinked, his white eyes shining like a cat in the dark. Despite the extreme humidity, he wasn't sweating. In fact, he wore a polo shirt buttoned up to the neck and black cotton slacks.

"Big shot from the mainland. Place used to belong to drug money but the government shut it down and take the property then sell it at auction."

"You know this big shot?"

"Yes, ma'am. Señor Juan Valdez."

"Tell me you're kidding."

"No. Juan Diego Garcia Valdez."

"By any chance is he into coffee?"

Rocco laughed. "No, ma'am. He into exporting something though. I pick up a fare here two nights ago. Three ladies from your resort, blonde, funny accent, big boobs."

"They wouldn't by any chance be from Australia."

"Yeah, ma'am. Dat's it. That one gal, she had on a short dress, bare back, not much on underneath. One of the men, he slip his hand under her skirt. She got a nice tat on her ass. When she get in I ask her, 'Hey, lady what's dat creature?'. She say, 'Dat's my roo'."

"Terrific. And stop calling me ma'am. If you know Spence then you know who I am and why I'm here."

Rocco chuckled. "Yes, Miss Darcy. Spence, he tell me, 'Rocco, you keep my Darcy safe, just like you keep me safe in the war."

Darcy didn't speculate on which 'war' Spence was referring to. He was old enough to have fought in Nam but she also knew he'd seen some military action in other parts of the world, Haiti, the Middle East, the Persian Gulf. Spence was what one might call a diversified personality. She didn't ask questions and he didn't volunteer information. When she first started with him, she'd had to field calls that came from some real hot-beds of trouble across the globe. He'd get a call, say, 'yep, I got it. Be there in 24', pack a small gym bag and be gone for weeks leaving her to 'man the fort, Darce.' Then he'd take off for a while. Again, she never asked where he'd been or what he'd done, even when he showed up limping or sporting an impressive rack of stitches across his forehead. Only that their bank account was sweeter because of it.

So, if Spence trusted Rocco, it was a given that she trusted him too.

"Got any back-up in case we run into some 'bad peoples', Rocco?"

The big man reached over and opened his glove compartment. Yahoo! A .381 special with a five inch barrel. Sweet!

"This gal, 'Lolita'." He reached in and patted the gun stock. "She young, but deadly. A virgin. Never been fired, except on the range, but she primed and ready."

"Thanks, Rocco. Now tell me more about your fare the other night."

"Nothing to tell, really. Girls come down from house, gate open. The big fish, the bodyguards, one is my cousin you know, they escort them to my cab.

I can tell the boys is packin'. It 98 degrees and they coats buttoned tight. I see the outline when they walk back up the stairs. A little show of force to anyone who might be prowling around. But nobody gives them trouble."

"And we know what this Juan Valdez does?"

"Importing. Exporting. I see him in town sometimes leaving the bank. Always with the big, black briefcase handcuffed to his wrist."

"Hmm. Interesting. I'd like to find out what he's guarding so carefully and why our boy is having late night suppers with him."

"He not alone tonight. My cousin took the same three girls there," he nodded toward the house, "in time for cocktails this afternoon."

At the mention of another cousin, Darcy smirked. Rocco had more cousins than a Texas politician. On further thought, however, her smirk pruned into a frown. So, Miss Aussie with a kangaroo chiselled onto her butt was bouncing around inside that house with her flap open for every Joey, Dick or Kyle to jump into. As long as her roo didn't jump onto Kyle's dingo, she could live with it. After all, this was only a job.

She caught herself suddenly at the thought that invaded her. Why in hell was she suddenly feeling territorial about Kyle? Job aside, it was still his life. If he wasn't willing to be dragged peacefully to the alter and jumped her in the dressing room to prove it then why should she be concerned about him in the same space with Gretchin? As usual, she qualified her answer with practicality; STDs, VD, AIDS, etc.

Condoms—much more than party favors. Although she personally disliked them, she was glad Kyle kept his good and handy.

Another thought took root and sprouted. Now that she had slept with Kyle, he was going to expect it. To deny him might make him suspicious. She couldn't suddenly cool off their affair, it would piss him off and drive him away. That was the last thing she wanted to do.

Her concentration was broken by a call over Rocco's radio. Rocco turned to her. "Someone in the house call for a cab to take Mr. Kyle back to the resort. We better hot foot it on back there."

"You got that right. Step on it, Rocco."

᠅ᢀᡫᡰᢏᢎᡫᢊᠮᠼ

She made it back to the hotel mere moments before Kyle. It wasn't nearly enough time to shower, change and get to the Soca bar. She hadn't had supper yet either and was starved. The bar had the usual snacks so she grabbed a napkin and dumped a handful of pretzels and potato chips on it. She was busy munching away when she saw Kyle approaching through the crowd—with Gretchin on his arm.

To his credit, his face lit up when he saw her. He slipped Gretchin's hand off his arm and they parted ways.

"Hey, gorgeous. Mmm… you look good enough to eat." He nibbled her neck behind her ear. A delicious tingle swam across her and she shivered. Damn it all! She wore a simple cotton sun dress, modest but tied halter-style at the neck. Kyle busied himself by playing with the knot.

"Enjoy your supper?"

"Not half as much as if you'd been there. I even passed up a scrumptious-looking kiwi dessert." He leaned and whispered in her ear. "If I want something soft, wet and covered with fur, I can think of better things to sink my, er, teeth, into. And my tongue. And my nose. And my–"

Darcy covered his mouth with her fingers. "I get it, cowboy."

He softly bit the end of her index finger. "You will. But later. What are you drinking?"

It was clear by now that whatever interest he'd had in Gretchin wasn't immediately sexual. Perhaps she was just one of these forever party girls who sidled up to the first handsome guy they saw and fawned all over them.

"A 'Big O'. Want one?" she asked innocently and fluttered her eyelashes at him.

Kyle arched his brows. "Does a bear shit in the woods? Is the Pope Catholic?"

"Do you want a drink?"

"That too. Bartender, I'll have what she's having."

"I see Gretchin managed to find you."

She had to squeeze it in. She couldn't let it go. Curiosity and the cat. Jealous? Not her.

"Yeah, we shared a cab back to the resort. That broad was so hammered," he stopped and shook his head. "She was all over me in the cab. And her perfume was strong enough to choke a horse."

"Really." She thought she said that with a little too much enthusiasm. "I mean, I'm glad she made it back. These islands can be as dangerous as any city street back home if you don't use your common sense."

"True enough." The bartender brought his drink. He plucked a chip off her napkin. "Please don't tell me this is your supper."

"I over-slept. I'll grab a sandwich later at the midnight buffet."

"Who says you'll still be up by then?"

"I expect to be awake."

He grinned. "Me too. Hey, I have an 'in' with the chef. Let's mosey over to the kitchen and see what we can mooch."

"You have an 'in' with everybody, the bartenders, the maitre'd, now the chef. It's like you own the place, or something."

Kyle felt his mouth twitching. How he'd love to tell her! Everything. He'd come down here to clear his mind of one woman and found the perfect cure – another woman. But not just any woman. Darcy was whole, earthy, no bullshit. She was the way he remembered his mother had been once before she let Mason's bullying, badgering and eventual infidelity turn her into a hard, joyless person. From a stay-at-home trophy wife to an independent business woman.

Only after her children were grown was she having what Monica called, 'a life.' Yes, she was still fighting with Mason. But now it was because she believed in something substantial. Her fight had meaning. She had principles and she was standing behind them, even if it meant alienating her only son. Yep, mom was a pip!

She'd like Darcy. She'd approve of him marrying someone like Darcy. Someone, in many ways, like herself. Ordinary. No falseness. Whenever he thought of Darcy now, he imagined the gloriously sexy, young woman with her nose pressed against the jewellery store window, her crystalline blue eyes hungrily devouring the rings and necklaces.

Tiffany had a closet full of gems. And Versace dresses, Manolos and Jimmy Choos. Luxury cars, liposuction (although she staunchly denied it) and a full set of DaVinci veneers making her smile as glossy and superficial as the rest of her. Kyle didn't see himself as part of her collection. Never could.

Darcy's cute nose had an irregular curve at the very tip. Her tummy had an appendectomy scar. Her slender hands were tipped with short, no-nonsense nails. Her fingers would look great modelling a custom setting around a hand-picked emerald. She sat beside him, her natural lips devoid of colour and clamped around a straw sipping her 'Big O'. He carried through on a sudden impulse and leaned over to kiss the tiny bump on the end of her imperfect nose. A wide smile, unbleached and unblemished, shot a heated arrow into his gut. And Kyle had always gone with his gut. At that moment he realized exactly why he'd come to San Andres.

He realized he'd made up his mind.

He also realized his decision was going to rock the world back home, not to mention his own.

Chapter Seven

"Wake up, gorgeous."

It was Kyle, leaning over her naked body and smelling like after-sex. Of course that's what their night had been all about after leaving the bar. Actually, it started before that. The local Reggae band opened up the dance floor at eleven and they'd soca'd, mambo'd and swayed for nearly an hour before the heat, not the temperature, became unbearable.

They walked up the stairs to the second floor with Kyle embracing a very bad imitation of Bob Marley in her ear...

"...in my single bed, we'll share some shelter..."

Si, si!

Only it wasn't a single bed, it was a queen size bed which made her wonder how he garnered such treatment as most of the rooms at the resort held two doubles. Ah, to have money! She'd been much too busy to bother scrutinizing the decor.

Add to that he kept at least one hand clamped on an intimate part of her body, oblivious to the stares of other guests, most of whom merely smiled slyly in their direction or whistled. Darcy usually didn't mind this but it was the obvious comments from the single guys half in the crock that irked her.

"Way to dip your wick, dude!"

If she'd been alone, she'd have decked the assholes.

She gazed up at Kyle through sleepy eyes. "Hey, you. That was some midnight buffet!"

Kyle wiped a hand around his mouth. "I can still taste you. Yummy!"

"What's on the breakfast menu?"

He grinned.

"Besides that."

Kyle tore off the single Egyptian cotton sheet. Again, preferential treatment. "A little nature hike. And I do mean the nature kind."

Darcy wrapped her arms around him. "I was going to say, this is a pretty confined trail and only two specimens to observe."

"You've never been snorkelling out on the reef, have you."

"Nope. Didn't even bring my gear."

"That's okay, I have—"

She put her hand over his mouth. "Let me guess. An 'in' at the dive shop."

He bent his head and kissed her. "Beautiful and psychic. A rare mix."

"Okay, snorkelling it is. Who's our guide?"

"Me."

"Really? I'd never have taken you for the fishy kind."

"I'm a regular 'Mr. Limpett'."

"Uh, my thigh says all evidence to the contrary."

"I didn't say 'limp'."

"But you forgot 'Incredible'."

No she didn't. How could she after last night? *I'm so totally fucked!* Obviously she'd missed this chapter in the surveillance handbook. She'd surveilled to the n'th degree. Examined, almost microscopically, every inch of his rock-hard body. She had so much of Kyle's DNA plastered over—and inside—her she could almost hear The Who rockin' away while a cloud of fine, black powder settled over the distinguished ridges of their fingerprints. If she died on the spot, she'd leave a glowing tornado of evidence swirling around the room through mists of luminol. And if he touched her again the way he was touching her now, she just might do that—die quite happily.

"I thought you wanted to catch the tide this morning."

Reluctantly, he rolled off of her.

"I do. I want to show you my island. I want to show you everything. I love it so much here. The people, the atmosphere, the weather."

"The topless beach," she chimed in.

He smiled. "That too. Er, not that I noticed."

Darcy reached behind her, grabbed her pillow and playfully tossed it at him. "Now do you understand the pencil test?"

She hoped so. She'd spent a good thirty minutes last night trying to explain that if you held a pencil under a droopy breast, the pencil could defy gravity. Her pencils kept dropping to rounds of repeated demonstrations egged on by calls of "show me again." Then the teacher called for a pop quiz. The student was a quick study.

And speaking of students, hers was already out of bed and stretching in glorious liberation in front of her.

"Why do men do that?"

"Arrrgghh!" he yawned. "Do what?"

"Reach down and scratch their balls?"

"It's a guy thing."

Darcy followed his actions. "Don't worry, cowboy. They're still there."

"Good. I thought you were going to bite them off last night."

"I almost did." She arched her brows and shot him a cocky grin. "It's a girl thing."

"Yeah, like getting off the Titanic first. Never having to shave everyday. Having younger lovers without looking ridiculous. Women have it made."

"Yeah, like monthlies, menopause, pregnancy, giving birth and, my personal fav, Brazilian waxing."

"Okay—let's not go there."

"Right. Breakfast in half an hour?"

She dressed hurriedly while Kyle was showering. In the morning light she had the chance to observe his room a little closer. It was a woman's room. Pastel shades, a beauty vanity, one of those old style sofas with only one arm rest. Way too much closet space. It made her wonder just who he'd usurped to park his butt in here. She hadn't had a chance to see many of the hotel's other suites. This room could be reserved for very special clients. Yeah, that's money working again. Darcy shook her head as she slid on her shoes, wondering what surprises Kyle had in store for her today.

⁂

"What did he mean, 'watch out for sharks'?"

Darcy allowed Kyle to lead her out of the dive shop while she protested every step of the way.

"Calm down." He was laughing at her. Sharks—real ones—were serious shit. "José was messing with your head. He wouldn't send us to places with sharks. He wants repeat customers."

Darcy nearly hit him with the mask.

He lead her to a dune buggy that looked like it had been through the Gaza Strip grand prix. She noticed that about San Andres transit. The public busses looked like they survived the Detroit riots of the 60's. The taxis had registrations starting with San Francesco, then Tijuana and finally Bogota. Even the bicycles had that just-blown-into-a-WWII-foxhole ambiance about them.

She stood outside the passenger side for a moment. She had to, the door was welded shut.

"Just hop in, like this." He demonstrated his Beach Boy leap with ease. Darcy also noted the lack of mirrors, seat belts and any type of canopy. "Hurry up, gorgeous. I have to have this baby back before sunset. No lights."

"Does the horn work?"

"Sure."

"Great. It'll be the last thing I hear before I'm designated tourist road kill."

"Hey, don't knock it until you try it. Get in before I use up a battery start. I've only got about thirty."

They used half that trying to get it started. Finally the engine caught. Darcy stowed their gear in the rumble seat then gingerly climbed in.

"YIPES! Black vinyl. Hot sun. Bare skin."

She quickly grabbed a towel and placed it under her. Once they were out on the highway, second degree burns were the least of her worries. She clung to the door rail as the buggy, minus a set of shocks, bounced precariously without the least inclination. She wondered how fast they were really going as none of the instrument panels functioned. She didn't know how Kyle could tell if they had enough gas.

"Easy. When we stop, we're out."

Darcy nodded into the wind. Of course. Ask a stupid question...

But then, it was an island seven miles long and three miles wide. They could always walk, or flag a bus, or borrow a burrow.

Kyle took them only fifteen minutes away from the resort but it was enough highway time to last her a lifetime. Unlike Toronto city traffic where you parked on the Parkway and nobody rushed anywhere during rush hour, San Andres didn't have a posted speed limit out of town. Most of the vehicles didn't have signals that worked anyway so everyone went on the horn system. Two honks to pass. Three if you knew someone's sister. A raised hand with a pointed index finger indicated 'stop' whereas four fingers extended meant 'wazzup'.

At last Kyle pulled off the main road to a small driveway parallel to a beach.

"La Picina Natural. The Natural Pool. Wait until you see the fish."

He wasn't kidding. The 'pool' was actually a cup-shaped formation carved out of a limestone cliff in the ocean. The ages of tides, winds and ocean waves created the pool. The water on that side of the island had a higher salt content and therefore effected more buoyancy. It also attracted hundreds of species of tropical fish. Darcy stared into the pool, amazed.

"My God! Look at them. It's just teeming down there." She turned to Kyle. "And you expect me to jump into the middle of all those fish? They look hungry."

"They are." Kyle led her to a bamboo and rope ladder used to climb into the pool. He had already adjusted his mask over his face and was testing the adherence of his snorkel. He climbed down the ladder until he was waist deep in the water before slipping into his rubber swim fins. Once they were in place, he called up to her.

"Watch. I'm going to feed them." With that, he produced some crumbled bread from the plastic bag holding his fins. He threw chunks of bread into the wavy water. Instantly the water became a virtual whirlpool of activity, not unlike piranha. And Kyle dove right into the middle of it.

Darcy felt the shock ripple through her. She darted forward to the edge of the ladder, straining to see Kyle among the hundreds of fish fighting for a morsel of bread. She breathed a sigh of relief when she saw him surface on the other side of the pool.

"You've gotta get in here, Darce. It's amazing."

No, I don't. Still, the fascination of the fish churning the clear blue water proved to be too much temptation. She placed the mask over her face and positioned the snorkel. She'd already decided to follow Kyle's example and put her fins on once she got into the water. Slowly she eased herself down the ladder. The unusual warmth of the water hit her immediately. She spied Kyle looking at her.

"Warm, huh. It's the ocean current. San Andres is part of a protected biosphere. The algae and the vegetation are unique to this area. That's why the fish love it."

"Not to mention the hotel fare," she called back.

Despite her slipping into the water, the hoards of fish basically ignored her. They created tiny currents as they whizzed past her. Some of the braver ones inspected her fins. One plucky little fellow had the nerve to bump into the nipple poking out from her bikini top. Eventually she made her way over to Kyle.

"That's incredible. They act like they don't care whether I'm here or not. It's like being inside an aquarium."

"Ready for an insider's view?"

She nodded.

"Okay, snorkel in. Take my hand, deep breath and follow me. Let's find *Nemo*." Instantly she was plunged into another world. Below the surface hundreds of colors swirled by her. Clown fish, blue stripes, Angel fish, groupers. Dozens she couldn't identify. Kyle had given her a brief lesson on how to breathe through the snorkel. She followed him through the water, paying attention when he tapped her arm and pointed at some unusual species. At last he motioned her to 'heads up'. It was then she noticed they'd left the area of the limestone pool. She followed him onto a secluded beach and tried to navigate his path as he frog-stepped out of the water. Finally, she gave up and slipped off her fins. She sank to her ankles in soft, pinkish sand.

He had already taken off his mask and snorkel and was shaking out his fins. Darcy followed his example. He plopped down on the warm, white sand. She joined him.

"Isn't it beautiful?" she said at last.

He turned to look at her. "It sure is."

"That's classic, bordering on cliche."

"I don't give a shit, it's true. It's all beautiful. The ocean, the island, the company. I don't want to leave it."

He'd opened a door. Finally, he was thinking of going home.

"Then don't."

"I have to. I have… responsibilities back home."

Did she hear right? Could it be that simple?

"Ah, yes. The real world. Corporate road kill, cubicle monkeys, relatives we'd like to hire contract killers to take out. Friends who becomes enemies and enemies who suck you dry and toss your carcass on the heap of humanity."

"You sound like you know my old man." His voice took on a bitter edge. Maybe it wasn't that simple.

"Ah, parental issues. You can skip over it if you want to."

He shook his head. Dried sand flew, followed by a warm ocean breeze that was drying them fast.

"You're from Toronto. I'm sure you're acquainted with the name 'DeLaurier'."

At last, an opening. "Oh, you mean *those* DeLauriers? The nauseatingly rich ones?"

"Guilty."

"I won't hold your oceans of cash against you." But she would if she could.

"No. Please do. I sure as hell do. Money isn't all it's cracked up to be."

"It is when you don't have it."

He looked at her then. His eyes hardened, his brows furrowed. "Is it worth your best friend's life?"

Darcy fell back on her elbows. This was something new, something Spence didn't give her a heads up about. "Want to tell me?" she asked gently.

He did. And as she followed his tale, she began to understand about his liquid breakfasts and mid-morning hangovers. After he finished telling her about Kevin she found him sprawled on the sand with his head resting on her bare stomach.

"And now my father's made a deal with Joshua Shawcross and I'm the sweetener, the dangling carrot in front of Tiffany."

"Isn't that supposed to be the other way around? The opposing family usually offers the daughter as a sacrifice."

He threw a handful of sand toward the ocean. "Nope. I'm the sucker. My mother—you'd love her, she's like you—she's dead set against it. Wants me to quit my dad. She's really pissed at him. I don't want to get on her bad side. She can be just as cut-throat as him when she wants to be."

He then told her about the feud between his parents. Darcy lay there, with the sun baking her body and the wind whipping her hair around and thought about this poor little rich boy.

In a way she didn't envy him being a pawn between two parents' battle of wills. In fact, she could almost empathize.

As a child her own parents had done the same thing to her. Only it wasn't material bribes they used to divide her loyalties, it was the emotional ones. Manipulating, damaging and very effective. Her father blamed his drinking on her mother walking out and, subsequently, accusing Darcy of allowing her mother to 'make' her hate him. Her mother invented a myriad of medical ills to keep Darcy close, having various 'attacks' of nerves, pains and 'spells' either the night before or the day of Darcy leaving to visit her father. Her own guilt caused her to abandon her father to care for her mother. In the end she quit them both and struck out to find her own life.

And life in the police force suited her disposition just fine. Methodical, organized, where things were black-and-white, rules and discipline were the order of the day and where an emotionally cold person could operate and view the daily assaults on the human condition without becoming 'involved'. And for a while it worked. But after a couple of years of walking into domestic situations and seeing children being as emotionally abused as she had been she realized something else. She'd been hiding, using the uniform as a way to avoid dealing with her own weaknesses. People saw her as a symbol of strength and authority, a figure of support in times of trouble. She saw herself as a fake.

The trouble was that in wanting to help others, to 'Serve and Protect', first she had to take a long, hard look at helping herself. Her original leave of absence did nothing to reconcile her with a father she couldn't find and a mother who'd remarried and moved across the country. What she did find was the zen of Spencer Brightwood, the sober father-figure who took her under his wing, took her basic police training and fine-tuned it to deal with the imperfections of his clients. Spencer, her teacher, father-confessor, friend—employer.

She returned her thoughts to the man lying in the sand.

"So why don't you marry the girl, vote with dad, then divorce her and quit him? Seems like a logical solution to an illogical problem."

"That's very pragmatic."

"That's what you like about me."

"It sounds so... so..."

"Antiseptic? Cold?"

"Yes. Exactly."

"Kyle, does she love you?" Left field question, but she had to ask. She had to be sure. Keeping her head on straight for the next few days depended on it.

To her surprise and relief, he burst out laughing. "Hell, no! The idea of love never entered into the negotiations. In fact, I believe her initial response was, 'I can live in Forest Hills if you can'."

Darcy whistled. "Forest Hills, nice area. I used to drive through there a lot at night."

"Really? Casing the joint, were you? Or were you looking to crash a ball like in *True Lies*?"

Darcy gulped and stopped toying with Kyle's hair. She couldn't exactly explain that her nightly visits were in a cruiser and at the request of the residents who demanded the noise level in their exclusive community be kept to a minimum, all trespassers be prosecuted and those guilty of not picking up after their dogs be rightly and properly fined. Quickly she imposed her cover.

"Real estate. Remember, that's what I'm taking a break from."

"Makes sense."

He'd reached over and was caressing her bare legs. His other arm was flung above his head. His fingers toyed with the hip band on her bikini.

"Anyway, Kyle, getting back to my original solution."

"About me trying to please all of the people all of the time—yeah, well I've discovered I'm not into taking the coward's way out. I'm not going to marry Tiffany. I don't love her."

Her stomach fluttered at those words. Her inner self responded with a wide smile. A sudden *zing* shot from her head to her heart. She was happy for him—honest. And while she was being honest, she was happy for herself. For one thing, she could stop hiding the guilt she felt about sleeping with another woman's fiancé. With one sentence, he'd popped the growing guilt balloon.

"Well, that's… truthful. And you're right, you can't please all the people all the time." Boy, wasn't she an authority on that!

"I know. Whatever I do, somebody is going to get hurt."

"And what about Kyle? What does he want?"

There was silence between them. A lingering silence that made Darcy smile. He wanted to tell her—something. Left alone long enough with a few well chosen words to keep them company, a suspect usually recanted and came clean. She had that gut instinct about Kyle.

"Better own up. We spy girls have ways to make you talk." Truly, a little prompting didn't hurt.

He turned his head toward her and shaded his eyes against the sun. "Okay. I'll have to tell someone sooner or later. I've made up my mind. I'm going into business for myself. Screw my old man. Tiffany can buy herself something nice to ease her broken heart."

Now that was the first adult thing that came out of his mouth all day. He'd obviously decided to stop whining and do something. Problem was, she had a feeling the 'something' wasn't part of her goal.

"I have some land up north. We're talking waaaay up north, where the moose and the caribou play. I've had some preliminary mineral sampling done."

"And?"

"Wanna buy a stake in a diamond mine?"

Darcy sat up on her elbows, astounded by this news. "You're kidding, right."

"Nope. Thar's ice in them thar hills. And I'm going to find it, refine it and export it. Did you know that Canada is the third largest diamond producer in the world?"

"No. I must have missed that bulletin on MSN."

"It's true. Problem is, I have to raise the capital to start mining. My father laughed me off the first time I mentioned it to him and refused to back me. He also hinted that no one else would loan me the money either. After all, he's the mighty Mason DeLaurier. He holds, and pulls, a lot of strings in the city's financial community. I can't—I won't—ask my mom for the money, not even as a loan. I want to do this on my own. So I'm here trying to raise some cash."

Darcy nearly choked on the alarms. Drugs were fast cash. Surely, Kyle couldn't be that desperate. She had to find out.

"Ah, and that would be your 'business' in town and the mysterious supper I was stood up for."

"Yep. I went to see a fairy godfather of sorts to see if he could manage a little magic dust."

Oh, SHIT!

Godfather—as in crime? Dust—as in cocaine?

"Are you sure you know what you're doing?"

"No. But that's the beauty of being an entrepreneur. Yas gots to take risks."

Not these kinds of risks.

As much as she adored Kyle the man, loved spending time with him—in bed and out—she was sure now more than ever that the best thing she could do for him was get him the hell out of here. All she promised to do was get him back to Toronto before the deadline to vote on the merger. She didn't have to spend every waking minute afterwards seeing to it that Romeo got to the alter to marry his Juliet. As far as she was concerned her contract ended the moment they both stepped off the plane at Pearson International. What Kyle decided to do after that was his own business. If he decided not to vote with Mason, it was out of her hands.

A good conscience had a way of justifying its decisions.

The same way she justified sleeping with Kyle, the minute he told her he didn't love Tiffany and had no intention of marrying her.

The same way she could justify the man slipping his fingers under her bikini bottom. She could feel the temperature suddenly shooting up and it had nothing to do with the mid-day sun.

"I'm sick of talking about myself. *Maclean's Magazine* does enough of that for the both of us. I want to talk about you. Specifically, why you're wearing so many clothes."

The time to talk was over. "These aren't clothes, they're tan line markers."

"Well," he rolled over and kissed her deeply. "Time to play trace the tan lines."

"I don't have any—yet."

"Want some?"

"Nope."

"I was hoping you'd say that."

She didn't help him. She let him have the luxury of removing her bikini top while she bathed in the pleasure of the sensations he created. The bow at her neck was the first casualty. She felt her breasts exposed to the warm, Caribbean sun. The ocean breeze tickled her nipples and they answered by completing the transition from flat, rosy disks to dusky little buttons. Kyle kissed each of her nipples in turn. He took each bud gently between his teeth and played with it. His tongue licked and lapped.

Darcy could hear her own soft moans over the sound of the sea waves breaking several yards away from them.

"I'll bet there's a wet spot in the sand," he teased.

"Mmmm... I'll bet you're right."

She wriggled out of her bikini bottom. "Your turn," she insisted and tugged at his bathing suit. He stood up then and helped her to her feet. How decadent to be naked on a secluded patch of sand, to feel the sea breeze brush her skin, to be completely free and unencumbered by thoughts of civilization. They were in their own tiny paradise here.

Kyle stepped out of his briefs and left them in a puddle next to her bikini.

"Hey, look what someone wrote on the beach."

Darcy leaned over to check out Kyle's artwork. It was a heart drawn in the sand with the letters 'D & K' printed in the middle.

"Gee, that's almost as romantic as carving it into a palm tree."

Kyle ran his fingers through her loose hair. "I mean it, you know. I heart you."

His index finger passed her cheek. Darcy reached out and grabbed it with her lips and nibbled on the tip. "You heart me?"

"That's the best I can do. For now." His eyes spoke sincerity. His touch spoke passion. Only Kyle knew his own heart. Darcy felt both elation and dread. She pushed both away. It was too much intrusion on the moment.

"Then I'll take all I can get. For now."

"Hmm. We're both covered in sand." He reached around and brushed sand off her bottom. "Your little blonde muff is full of sand. That could be painful—for the both of us. Let's take a dip." Then he grabbed her hand and pulled her toward the sea. She ran with him across the sand and they plunged head first into the surf.

She broke the water first and looked around for Kyle. She could see his body moving under the water a short distance from her. She was only waist deep but it was glorious. The gentle pull of the waves rushed around her. Her 'muff' as Kyle called it looked like a pale sea urchin under the water. The swell of waves brushed between the cheeks of her bottom. She lay back and floated. The salt water gave her body a special buoyancy. The sun's rays warmed her and she closed her eyes, intent on basking in complete sensual glow.

She smiled then as a certain hand crept between her legs to capture her mons.

"Wake up, little mermaid."

Kyle took her in his arms and she floated against his chest.

"Remember when we first met and you said something about doing it like seahorses?"

"And you're suggesting…"

"Exactly."

Well, maybe not exactly. Perhaps not the way she suddenly found herself with her legs wrapped around his hips and her slit cradling a certain aperture.

"My little sea-siren," he murmured and pressed her body close. His chest hair was all matted. Water sloshed between them.

"Deep breath and close your eyes," he whispered. Then he kissed her and released his stance. They both plunged under the waves. His mouth covered hers. She could taste salt water in her mouth, along with Kyle's kiss. The kiss was short and they surfaced almost immediately.

"You taste like salt," she said as she wiped her mouth free of water.

"So do you, and I don't mean just your mouth."

"I've heard a woman's vagina described in the same sentence with fish—and not in a good way!"

"Trust me, gorgeous. You're low-carb and high sodium—and in a good way."

He held her closer, gripping her hips. "Ready, baby?"

"Oh, yeah."

He dipped slightly and she slid onto him with ease. She gasped at the sudden swiftness with which he entered her. Fullness and girth replaced tingling emptiness. Ripples of pleasure tortured her senses. There was no contraceptive barrier between them this time. It was skin against skin. Darcy didn't care. At this moment, possibly for the first time since she'd known him, he was completely hers, inside and out.

Joined as one, they moved with ease through the water aided by the swell of waves that rocked them to and fro. It was as if the sea was an active partner, a voyeur, aiding a gentle hand in their lovemaking.

Kyle kissed her exposed skin. His tongue licked the wetness from her cheeks, her neck. There was the sudden stroke of tongue across her lips. She reached out and captured him in a deep, salty kiss.

"This is wild," he confessed. "No wonder so many people have hot tubs."

"Shut up and play with my clit," she ordered

"With pleasure." And it was. He cradled her bottom against him with one hand and slipped his other hand between them. Darcy clung to his shoulders and arched back until her head touched the water.

His finger began a slow, circular massage of her inflamed bud. Kyle slowed his thrusting cock to a pace better suited to letting her catch up with him. Darcy tensed against him, gripping his cock in the clutch of her inner muscles. What had begun as a spark deep in her abdomen suddenly spasmed into a luscious flame that spread through her. The cries of her orgasm were carried away on the waves that broke over her.

That's when she felt Kyle thrust deep inside and pound against her cervix as the surf pounded against the coral and rendered it to sand. He stiffened and drove into her, his cock shuddered against her walls.

At last he slipped from the cradle of her thighs. She could feel his seed washing out of her and spilling into the sea. He pulled her close and held her for several moments. Finally, he let her go.

"My back is burning," he confessed.

"So are my tits."

"Okay, clothes and sunblock."

They swam toward shore and reclaimed their clothing and snorkelling gear.

"Yipes! Darcy, your back and shoulders are burning. Let's get back to the buggy."

Darcy started toward the water, intent on swimming back the way they came.

"Hold it. There's a staircase carved out of the stone. We can get up that way." He pointed to the limestone wall that met the sand at the end of the beach.

"You mean anyone could have come down here?" The thought never occurred to her that anyone swimming by or snorkelling into their little cove could have had an eyeful.

"Don't worry. I bribed the owner not to let anyone down here. I also paid him to watch the buggy while we were gone."

Darcy moistened her sun-baked lips with her tongue. She was still at the edge of the surf, ankle deep in sand. She nodded, thinking once again how he so smoothly disarmed her. "A-hah! Now I understand about the 'extended' lunch at the lingerie store."

Kyle grinned and shrugged. "Hey, what's money if you can't spend it?"

She crossed the sand and took his outstretched hand. It was warm and rough and the memory of those hands expertly kneading her body's most intimate parts into exquisite pleasure made her shiver.

"You're not catching a chill, are you? That's a sure sign of sun-stroke. We better get you back."

His concern for her softened the last of her reserve. Her next words were carried out across the ocean breeze, and to Kyle who turned to look lovingly into her eyes when she blurted out, "Kyle, I heart you too."

⁂

They returned to the hotel shortly before supper and stopped at the front desk where Kyle picked up his messages.

Darcy saw him frown. "What's wrong?"

"It's Juan, my source. My business buddy. He wants to see me tonight. Says it's urgent. I hate to do this again gorgeous, but I have to—say, why don't you come with me to Juan's?"

Second best idea she'd heard all day. She could check out the situation for herself. Her heart rate shot into action mode. Adrenaline rocketed to high alert. It was DEFCON 1 in the private eye business. She'd have to call Spence, let him know what was up and where she was going.

"Sounds good. I'd like to meet your... source. Besides, I'm getting tired of hotel food."

Kyle squeezed her. "Me too. Except for one item on the menu," and kissed the top of her head. "You go get changed, then call me when you're ready. We'll grab a cab."

He sent her off with a playful swat on her behind.

She rushed back to her room to shower. She tried to book a call through the mainland but the lines were tied up. She quickly scribbled a note to Spence to drop off to the hotel business office. She'd get them to send a fax. The next route was e-mail but with the transmission time difference and Internet discrepancies, he might not get the message until tomorrow. If she hadn't been so busy playing fog-up-the-swim-mask with Kyle she could have gotten here earlier. She turned on her laptop. As she'd suspected there was a flashing banner indicating she had mail as soon as she logged in. It was all marked urgent. She opened the first one.

You slept with him, didn't you!

Delete.

Darcy, you should know better.

Delete.

Quit deleting my messages and answer me, dammit!

Jeez! Had Rocco snuck in and installed a mini-cam or something? She was in a hurry and not in the mood to file a number-stroke-letter occurrence report, so she typed in the first thing that came into her mind.

Spence, I'm dealing with a delicate situation. I'm taking the steps I deem necessary to complete the assignment. It's not like there's a P.I. helpline down here. There isn't even an abundance of fresh water!!! Our boy may be in some real trouble so I have to stay with him 24/7. Scan on a Juan Valdez (seriously) and see what you come up with, then take appropriate action. In the meantime, please trust me.

P.S. Rocco says hi.

She didn't have time to detail the 'real trouble'. If she even hinted drugs might be involved she knew Spence would yank her ass out of there faster than she could say *adios*. The thing that disturbed her the most was that Kyle's potential business partners already knew who he was and what he was worth. If drugs weren't the number one issue, and she now believed they might be, then there was the possibility of kidnapping. People were snatched all the time in banana republics and held for ransom. Kyle's captors could get a pretty penny for him. Then they'd kill him.

Her going to bed with Kyle was no longer the issue. Keeping him safe was. It didn't matter that he was supposed to go back home, make up with daddy, close the deal and marry the girl he didn't love. She'd settle for getting him off the island, alive and in one piece.

Because that's what you do when you 'heart' someone.

And it wasn't because it was Kyle. She'd feel that way about anyone she suspected might be in the same kind of danger. If he insisted on taking her to meet Juan, then she was going in with more than just a halter-tied, rayon side-slit Gap cocktail dress and Sears mules. She reached for the phone, buzzed the front desk and issued a page for Rocco.

Chapter Eight

"Darcy McLeod, meet Juan Valdez, my supplier and business partner."

Darcy planted a less than genuine smile on her face and shook hands with the designer-clad, swarthy stranger.

"Señorita McLeod. It is a pleasure to meet you." He then said something in Spanish directly to Kyle and the two men laughed.

Kyle turned to her. "He said that you're welcome here anytime, with or without my ugly face."

Darcy smiled. "Gracias, señor Valdez."

"Just 'Juan' please. May I get you a drink? Some Amaretto, perhaps. On ice."

"Thank you. That would be nice."

Juan excused himself but Darcy's keen eye kept tabs on the four burly men who arrived with him. She could tell in an instant they were all armed, probably the same ones Rocco saw the night he was here to pick up Gretchin. And each man was now babysitting all possible exits to the house. Darcy calmly and carefully moved toward a huge bay window.

"What a beautiful view," she declared and looked from left to right, taking in the fact that the property was surrounded by high, barbed wire fencing. The window itself overlooked an outcropping of rock. She noted the absence of any way to open the window. She surreptitiously glanced at each corner and saw the tempering watermarks and the insignia of the manufacturer, a company she knew to produce bullet proof glass. So, jumping through the window was out of the question.

The only help beyond these walls was a cell phone the size of a tampon and 'Lolita' in her shoulder bag. Which would look really great if the Colombian army decided to swoop down on them. She'd be down here until Spence's grandchildren had grandchildren. She had to come up with something else, and quick. She noticed Juan's private army didn't crowd him when he was dealing with guests. She might be able to take Juan hostage. But then one of them might shoot Kyle. That'd really screw up her evening.

She eyed Kyle. Hmm… maybe. She'd have to think about it for a moment. Rocco did say he'd be around the bend in case she needed him. All she had to do was get her and Kyle off the property. She'd worry about the Alcatrazstyle guard houses when the time came.

Kyle came to stand behind her. She smiled out at the ocean, the embryo of a plan forming in her mind.

"I hope that smile's for me," he said and handed her a drink. She raised the glass to her lips then stopped. It could be laced.

"A toast," she said suddenly, and dragged him away from the window. "Let's drink to Juan and his hospitality."

"*Muy bien!*" added Juan, who motioned for them to gather around a huge glass and ivory centre table. "To *mucho* good times."

"Profitable times," added Kyle.

"Cheers!" cried Darcy and drove her glass into the other two with calculated force.

Instantly, their hands were covered in alcohol. Shards of broken crystal fell onto the glass top table.

Darcy cried out. "OHMIGOD! Oh, oh, I'm so sorry. I'm such a klutz." She grabbed a neatly folded linen napkin off the table and started to dab each man's hand. "I'll pay for the glasses, I promise. Goodness, they're so beautiful. I shouldn't have hit them so hard. Oh, shit! I'm–I'm–" *I'm doing a good job acting like a girly-twit. Please buy it. Pleeze. Pleeze.*

Juan Valdez slowly shook glass off his hand and calmly brushed ice off his shirt front. "I will get a towel," he said and sighed deeply as he disappeared to the kitchen.

"Oh, Kyle. I've pissed him off. I'm so sorry. Maybe we should go. I feel so awful!" She started to pull Kyle toward the door. It had been a mistake coming here in the first place.

But Kyle seemed unusually mild-tempered. Come to think of it, so did Juan. Maybe she wasn't fooling anybody.

"Would you believe Gretchin did the same thing the other night? Tried one of her Aussie toasts and *WHAM!* A trio of 'Masturbations' ended up on the carpet. I keep telling Juan about the virtues of plastic cups but…" he shrugged.

"Plastic! Great idea. I saw some bottled water on the bar. I'll just go for one of those. I mean, after all, how much damage can I possibly do with a plastic bottle?"

Spence demonstrated nineteen fatal hits one afternoon on a gym dummy. He'd taught her eight—proficiently.

"Are you sure?"

"Definitely."

By the time Juan returned Darcy had cracked the seal on a bottle of water. She saw that he'd changed his shirt. He'd brought Kyle a fresh drink.

"I think the next time I am in town I will go to the *supertienda*—the supermarket—and buy these plastic cups. I am truly sorry, Darcy."

"Oh, no. I'm the one who caused all this. I really do apologize. I think I spent too much time in the sun today, right Kyle?"

She didn't miss the smirk on Kyle's face.

"*Si*, the *sol*—sun—is very hot this time of year. We are, after all, only twelve degrees off the equator. Would you like some ice for your... water?"

"No thank you. Twelve, huh. That all?"

"Yes, only our sister island of Providencia is closer. You and señor Kyle must come with me to Providencia some time. I have a private plane and would be most pleased to show it to you. I keep a modest residence there as well."

Of course he did. Rich coke lords could live anywhere they damned well pleased. On the other hand, it would be one of the first places for Spence to send in the troops if it came to that. She couldn't see Juan holding anyone hostage for very long on San Andres. Too much Colombian military presence—and all probably bought and paid for by Juan-boy.

Kyle bolted his drink back and returned the empty glass to the table. Immediately it was refilled. She waited and studied Kyle to see if there were any ill affects from the drink. When she was satisfied he was okay she returned her attention to a plan of escape should they need one.

After a few more moments of small talk, a small brown-skinned servant in dinner whites similar to their hotel staff issued a summons to supper.

Darcy followed the men into the dining room. Where the living room had been brown wicker with overstuffed cushions, the dining room was more formal. More glass tables (don't these people know glass and bullets don't mix?) with fine linen tablecloths laid across them. A tropical flower centerpiece featuring two huge birds of paradise nearly overshadowed the place settings.

Kyle seated Darcy with gentlemanly flair then took a seat across from her. Juan sat at the head of the table.

"I hope you like lobster, Miss McLeod. It is our Caribbean rock lobster, softer shelled than your east coast Maine lobsters, but with a special flavour only found in these waters. It is the ecosystem in the biosphere. The lobsters eat very specific prey."

The little servant brought in a large silver serving tray, displaying no less than four rock lobsters on a bed of rice and vegetables. Each person received a lobster, their own melted butter urn and a hefty portion of pilaf.

More small talk through dinner. Actually there was little talk as both men devoured their meal. She knew the reason for Kyle's appetite. She hoped this wasn't the Colombian version of 'The Last Supper.' Several glasses of dry white wine attended the meal which was completed by citrus sorbets.

"Delicious," she announced.

"*Gracias*, Miss McLeod."

Very rich, very charming. No wonder Kyle gravitated toward him. They were the same personality.

"Darcy, you don't mind if Juan and I talk a little business, do you?"

She moved her chair back. "You'll excuse me, then."

"Oh, no. Please stay, Miss McLeod. There are no secrets among friends."

Sure, that's how they get you. Before she knew it, she'd know too much and it wouldn't be safe for her to leave. Bad enough Kyle was knee deep in doo-doo.

"Did you bring your stash?"

Kyle's question was out there. Darcy had to stop her eyes from widening, although she couldn't help her breath from quickening. How many take-downs had begun with those famous last words?

"I never travel too far without it, señor Kyle. And you, did you bring what I requested?"

Oh, please, for the love of God, Kyle, don't make me wish I was a real cop again. Goddamnit, this isn't fair.

But here it was, a macho game of 'you show me yours' being played out in front of her. She couldn't let Kyle go through with this. He'd ruin his future, his name, his family's name. And this was the man she had funky fish sex with this afternoon. Quietly she picked her shoulder bag up off the floor and made a womanly display of digging through the contents looking for something. Out came the lipstick, then the compact. She asked politely for directions to the bathroom then got up and walked around the end of the table. The guards had disappeared from view during dinner but no doubt were nearby. She walked behind Kyle and slowed. She had one chance.

"Kyle, darling. I have the most terrible headache. I don't have any aspirin in my purse. Do you think you could drive me back to the hotel?"

Juan chose that moment to interject. "Perhaps you would like to rest, Miss McLeod. I offer you the hospitality of my guest bedroom."

"Good idea. Thanks, *amigo*. C'mon, Darcy. I'll take you."

Seeing no other alternative, Darcy decided to go along with the idea. For now. Perhaps once they were alone, she could persuade Kyle to take her back. She followed Kyle to one of the large bedrooms, listening to his concerned lecture about sun stroke.

"You should have said something sooner. I wouldn't have dragged you out tonight. I knew you had too much sun today. What was I thinking?"

He led her to the bed, a large satin-covered property with a curved wicker canopy and sweeping, sheer bed curtains. Decadent. Definitely a playground. Too bad about the timing.

"Here, lie down and rest. I should have slathered you with lotion..."

"Kyle..."

"Do you want an aspirin?"

"Kyle, there's something I have to—"

There was a knock on the door. "Señor Kyle." It was Juan. "A moment, please."

Darcy sank onto the mattress, her shoulders and her confidence sagging.

She should have tried to get them out sooner. She saw the bedroom door close and heard the men's muffled voices. What was going on? She needed to know how deep Kyle was in this so-called 'business'. She leaned forward but was still unable to make out what they were saying. She took a chance, got up and tip-toed to the door. She pressed her ear against the door but heard nothing. Had they gone somewhere? Darcy paced the floor for a few moments before making a decision. She was about to become chronically ill.

She turned as the door opened. It was Kyle.

"Kyle, I'd really like to get back to the hotel. I really feel—"

But Kyle walked past her and went directly to the bed where her purse sat. Before she could stop him, he opened the zipper and dumped the contents on the bed.

"Kyle, don't!" she warned as he reached for the gun. He turned and looked at her, his hand motionless, eyes questioning. After a moment, his gaze drifted back toward the gun.

Darcy nodded in sudden understanding. "Metal detectors," she murmured. "I should have known. Very sophisticated. Very expensive. Prohibitively so. But not for a man with a lot of money."

He raised his eyes toward her. "Your friend down the road—"

"Rocco!"

"You better come up with a good explanation for the gun. Juan's boys are on their way to have a little chat with him."

"Rocco can take care of himself. It's you I'm worried about."

Kyle folded his arms across his chest. "I'll bet you are." His voice was cool, accusing. His face, implacable.

"Kyle, I'll explain later."

"How about now?"

"No! Dammit. We have to leave."

"I'm not going anywhere until you tell me what you're doing running around with a gun in your purse. Guns are illegal on this island, except for the military. Just who the hell are you?"

Her voice rose into frantic whispers. His face hardened with every question.

"Calm down, Kyle. We're getting out of here before Juan reveals more than we want to know. Just tell him you're taking me back to the hotel and we can quietly walk out the front door. You don't need his drugs, or money, or anything else that can cause you to become a chalk outline."

"I'm not going anywhere until you tell me what the hell is going on."

Stubborn fool! He wasn't going to budge. She knew the time had come to tip her hand. She also knew she was about to do irreparable damage to a really good thing. She sat down on the bed and haphazardly shoved her purse contents back inside. She put the gun in last.

"I'm a private investigator hired by Mason to track you down and keep you out of trouble. The gun belongs to Rocco. Rocco belongs to... well, it's a long story."

She ignored Kyle's sudden, sharp intake of breath. "And I intend to keep my word. So you can tell your friend," she indicated to their host beyond the bedroom door, "to take his dust and blow somewhere else."

"Darcy..." Kyle's voice sounded like he was grating her name through clenched jaws.

"Kyle," she warned through gritted teeth, "now is not the time to argue."

"Look, *Miss McLeod...*"

Eeewww! Majorly pissed. So much so that she missed the bedroom door open.

"Emeralds," said Juan who stared at her with a touch of amusement playing around his mouth.

"What?" Darcy started and stared at Juan. She also realized she had company in the way of Juan's guards, who stood behind him.

Kyle leaned down and hissed into her ear. "You heard him Mason's Angel, emeralds. As in looks real good next to my diamonds around a girl's neck. Now sit down before I toss you over my knee and spank your ass raw and that's prior to taking you down to the sea and drowning you. Then, I'll ship your lying tits back to my father. Are we understood?"

"Shit," she whispered, but nodded in acquiescence.

"Good." Then he turned to Juan, "Darcy's going to rest here until our business is finished."

Juan looked at the couple then nodded. He addressed Darcy. "Mario will be outside the door if you need anything. Señor Kyle, bring Miss McLeod's bag with you. I'm sure such a heavy burden on her shoulder cannot be good for her... headache." Juan bowed and left them alone.

Kyle took her purse. "That was not a request. Your purse will be returned when you leave. Juan is shipping the gun back to Rocco. Oh, don't worry. Nothing will happen to Rocco. He's related to half these guys anyway."

Like she had a choice. "Sure. Kyle, I'm so sorry... I– this has all been a misunderstanding and–" her gaze followed Kyle's retreating figure out of the bedroom. She was still apologizing until he closed the door behind him. He wasn't listening.

⁂

It was the longest hour of her life. Finally Kyle appeared and returned her purse, which was a lot lighter. She'd much rather spend the afternoon in the gym with Spence being a Guinea pig for some of his chop socky moves than to have to face Kyle.

"I trust you've been able to come up with a suitable apology." His stony face viewed her with anger and contempt, not that she blamed him. Apologizing to Kyle however was going to take a lot more doing.

"Of course," she said swiftly. "Anything. You've got it. But Kyle–"

"Don't 'but Kyle' me. I don't think we have anything more to say to each other. You can go back to wherever the hell you came from and tell my father that if threatening to disinherit me didn't make me side with him, I sure as shit have no intention of doing so now."

Darcy expected his anger. He was justified and she deserved his rage. Still, she tried to salvage her own situation. "I don't care what's between you and your father. I was hired to act in your best interests. Christ, somebody had to. You were a train wreck the first time I saw you. Who knows what could have happened to you. Some little rich boy snapped up off the street, shipped to Colombia and held for ransom. Do you know how often that happens? Do you know what the survival success rate is even if the ransom is paid? Believe it or not, there are people in this world who care about you, even if you don't care about yourself."

"What about you? Did you care at all, or were you just on my old man's payroll? How much did he pay you to sleep with me?"

It was a slap, and she deserved it. But she was not without her own defense.

"You're still formally engaged to Tiffany what's-her-name, if I recall. I don't see you running to the phone to inform your intended that she'll have to do without her mansion in Forest Hills."

He stared hard at her, his chest heaving with unspent anger.

"And for your information, Romeo, I slept with you because I wanted to. Nobody paid me to whore myself out."

Why not say the 'w' word? He was thinking it. He even implied it. She felt better saying it first.

"You really thought I was going into the drug trade? After all you know about me, you'd think I stoop that low?"

"No. I didn't," she admitted. "But you certainly walked the walk and talked the talk. Juan, your 'supplier'. Your fairy godfather and his magic 'dust'. This fortress, the armed guards. I was a cop once, you know."

"No, I don't know, but that explains a lot of things. Look, I'm tired. I'm thoroughly embarrassed by what happened here tonight. I just barely rescued my deal with Juan by the skin of my teeth. Now I have to go back to the resort, which my mother owns by the way in case you already didn't know, and put up with knowing that you'll be skulking around watching my every move until I decide to leave."

That did it.

"Well, fuck you and you're welcome. Okay already, it was a mistake. But every scenario I laid out for you could have happened pretty boy, so you can just suck it up because until I'm off your old man's payroll, I intend to be your little shadow."

His countenance was becoming more stormy by the minute. He'd stopped pacing and stood there looking at her, fury shooting out every pore. He suddenly sank onto the bed opposite her as if the burden of contained anger was too much for his body to bear. His fists were curled tightly into the decorative cushions.

"Well you can start packing, little shadow because come tomorrow, I'm getting the hell out of Dodge. Now, you can walk out that door and get your cabbie friend around the corner—yes, Juan's boys had a chat with him—to take you back to the hotel. Juan will drive me later. We still have a lot of business to discuss and I have a lot of fences to mend. You do understand about damage control, don't you? Good. Now, if you'll kindly get the hell off my planet, I have to go and control your damage."

※

Rotten and miserable. It was the only way to describe her mood the next morning. It wasn't made any better by Spence yelling at her over the phone.

"You did WHAT?"

She told him. He didn't like it. She expected he'd fire her. He didn't. She sat through a seething lecture of ethics and protocol however that scorched her ears and battered her professional ego.

"I'm sorry."

"Sorry don't get it done. Where is he now?"

That was the second piece of bad news.

"What do you mean, 'he's gone'?"

"Bailed this morning. I checked the airport. The only regular flights in and out of here are the mid-week transports, private and commercial flights from Colombia and the charters leaving tomorrow. He wasn't booked on any of them."

"So, he's still on the island. Mason will be glad to hear that."

"Ah, no."

"No?"

"He hopped a private to Providencia and saw to it that no local pilots would take me. And before you say anything else, I haven't a popsicle's chance in hell of renting a boat either."

That's what you could do when you had money. Rent a store so you could jump your sweetie, rent a beach to shag her, have the run of mom's hotel then strand that lying piece of ass so she'd be reminded about the power of M - O - N - E - Y.

"Well, Darce, today you're luckier than two gays in a butt plug store because Mason called me first thing this morning to say that sonny boy is on his way home. And well before the merger date next week. Congratulations, you earned your bonus. Now get your pretty ass back home. We're getting busy."

Click.

The end.

Once again Eve was booted out of paradise.

"Well, this sucks," she snapped. Too late, the phone was silent. There was nothing left to do now but pack up and try to get a seat on tomorrow's charter.

She by-passed breakfast, went to the hotel's booking office and arranged her flight. When the Soca bar opened promptly at ten, Darcy McLeod was its first customer.

Chapter Nine

March came in like a true lion. Outside the wind howled. Snow piled up on the windowsill of Spencer Brightwood's ground floor office on St. Clair Avenue. A Toronto Transit bus rolled by, spraying unsuspecting sidewalk patrons with cold, brown slush. The atmosphere inside SpenceCo wasn't that different. The paperwork was finished. Kyle DeLaurier was officially out of her life. Darcy was receiving her debriefing lecture from Spence.

"The love boat done sailed, honey. Use your bonus and take a real vacation. I hear cruises are good for single people."

"Piss off, Spence. What's my next assignment?"

She sat in Spence's dark wood-panelled office. Spence had a flare for theatrics. His office looked like it walked out of a 1940s hard-boiled detective movie, complete with a trench coat and fedora hanging on a wooden coatrack. He even had a replica candlestick phone sitting on the ink-stained blotter covering his oak desk. It didn't work but it got laughs from a lot of clients, great conversation piece. The only thing missing was Bogart, the fat man and the black bird.

What the average client didn't know was that the phone contained a tiny mike and the coatrack was wired with a mini cam. Both were connected to the latest spy-ware. Spence was a sucker for toys. He leaned back in his leather swivel chair and parked his feet on his desk.

"I'm serious, Darce. I want you to take a breather. Either that or you can pick up that felt pen over there and march yourself up to my white board and write out 'I will not sleep with the clients' one hundred times."

Darcy sighed but endured his sarcasm. Two weeks back and she was still hearing about her one and only mistake. She crossed her legs and fidgeted under his censure. How confining her navy wool pant suit felt after frolicking naked in the sand. "I'm sorry I'm not perfect like you. Haven't you ever screwed up?"

"Nice choice of words and no, not on the job."

The look that followed warned her she better not go there.

"I could always go back to Metro as a re-tread and spend my days towing illegally parked cars."

Spence regarded her from under his greying, bushy brows and those hawk-like eyes that saw everything and missed nothing. He didn't even twitch his once broken nose at her sorrowful, self-pitying attempt to jump ship. "Don't think so. You've got too much talent, despite your little setback."

Little was a word which qualified as an understatement. Her gaze drifted to the newspaper on Spence's desk. The headline in the business section read, *"DeLaurier-Shawcross Marriage Merger A Go."* She scowled at the picture of Kyle and Tiffany, him standing beside her—both hands in his pockets she noted—while the bride-to-be turned her overly made-up, vapid eyes and full set of DaVinci veneers into the camera lenses. Mason DeLaurier and Joshua Shawcross stood beside them, shaking hands. It was a done deal. Cha-ching!

"So, *shweetheart*, Richy-Rich boinked you, got inside and messed up your head. Nice going. And to think of all the time and money I invested in you. Now his old man wants to steal you away from me."

She tore her gaze away from the picture. "What?" Spence could be a real prick sometimes. Like now, after all the posturing about remaining professional and doing her job he was smirking at her, his scarred upper lip twisting into that 'time-to-throw-another-red-herring-into-the-plot' grin.

"Yep. Got the word this morning. I'm supposed to be thinking over an offer to sell our—meaning your—services to him exclusively as the sole security consultant for all the DeLaurier properties."

"Did you tell him to go boink himself?"

"More or less. I knew what you'd say, especially after today's headlines."

Not just the newspaper but the financial magazines were having a field day. Every day, a new story was released. The marriage/merger was going through, it was stalled, it was postponed. Stock was up, stock was down. The Shawcross people weren't lunching the DeLaurier people. The suits weren't talking. Obviously Kyle, or the lawyers, had made up their mind sometime last night. The big story was staring her in the face.

"Just out of curiosity, what was his offer?"

"Six figures a year plus stock options."

"You're right, I'm much better off barely eeking out a living here with you." Yes, sarcasm worked both ways.

"That's my girl. No selling out to the suits for you."

"That's not the real reason."

But she couldn't tell Spence the real reason. She had read the headlines this morning. Kyle was marrying the girl after all. Her ego wanted to think he was on the rebound. Her heart wanted to believe he was hurting as bad as she was.

"Did you love him?"

Damn, Spence. Was he that good, or was she too easy to read?

She stared down at her nails and shook her head. "I don't know. I loved being with him. I loved hanging out with him. I loved being in the sack with him. He… he made me laugh."

"But you're not laughing now. In fact, I haven't seen you crack a smile since you got back. You've been very distracted. That's why I want you to take some time off. I can't have you distracted. Not on the job."

She protested. "But Spence, I want to go back to work. Don't you see, work is the best thing for me. It'll get him out of my system."

"I take it you don't want to work for Mason."

"Tell him to shove it. Better yet, I'll tell him myself."

"Can I tell him why?"

"Tell him I got a better offer."

Anything was better than being stuck behind a desk calibrating video security software and nosing into the personal lives of DeLaurier employees. Spence told her Mason even had the ignorant audacity to offer her an office on the top floor of the DeLaurier building, just down the hall from Kyle. Now that was throwing salt into an open wound. She could just imagine the small talk at cocktail parties... 'Hi, I'm Darcy, the woman Kyle screwed silly before he married the wife he doesn't love'...

"He sent an advance, a signing bonus. Want to see the check?"

"Shred it."

"Yep, you love him all right."

"Enough already."

"Did you get your invitation to the wedding?"

She held up her middle finger.

"My, my, aren't we testy. I sent my regrets, I'll be out of the country."

"Again?"

Spence shrugged, as he always did when Darcy attempted to question him about one of his little trips.

"Okay, okay. If I get an invitation, I'm sure I'll be busy. I'll send a gift."

"I sent place mats."

"How Martha Stewart of you. I'll get them a—a melon baller or something equally inane."

"Those place mats are made of chain mail. I figure they'll need it once the honeymoon is over. I saw them together when I went over to collect our fee. They communicate through lawyers. I'll bet the lawyers will even do the screwing on the wedding night. I give it four months."

"And you're waiting for me bite, is that it? Sorry to disappoint you."

"Aren't you the least bit interested?"

Of course she was. She was chomping at the bit. She wondered what was truly going on in Kyle's mind. All the plans he made, the intimate dreams he shared with her that day on the beach. His ideas had such potential. He seemed so focussed, so... happy. And then there was Juan's investment. What happened?

"Gossip about lovebirds? No thank you. It's a match made in the boardroom. I'm sure all the lawyers are happy. Besides, Kyle is a big boy and he can make up his own mind." Even if that mind was to marry a woman with all the depth of a nose pore and the personality of a sock puppet.

"I wonder."

"About what?"

"If Kyle did make up his own mind or if he just figured he couldn't do any better."

Darcy bristled. This comment she took personally. "Any better than Tiffany Shawcross, with her haute couture clothes, her nose job and sneaking in and out of the liposuction clinic."

"My, we have been busy since we got back."

Darcy wanted to slap that all-knowing expression off his face but realized he'd have her on the floor and hog-tied to the coat tree before she could spit. Still, she didn't think she could stand his baiting much longer. "I'm being sarcastic."

"You're right on the money kid, as usual."

"So who else should Kyle marry?"

Spence merely shrugged and gave her one of those 'if-you-don't-know-I'm-not-going-to-tell-you' smirks.

"Yeah, whatever."

"Is that your final answer?"

"No lifeline, thanks. I'm going bareback on this one."

"And you don't want to work for Mason."

"Bite me."

"Good. That's exactly what I want you tell Mason when you see him at lunch today."

He handed her back the check while she was busy trying to close her mouth.

"And make sure he picks up the tab."

❧❨♋❩☙

Lunch at La Scala. Hell, she couldn't even afford to tip the parking attendant on her salary. Still the crumpled bribe sat burning a hole in her purse. She didn't care how many zeros were on it, she was giving it back. She couldn't wait to see the look on Mason's face.

But it was Kyle who entered the restaurant. She did a double take at the change in him. Charcoal double-breasted suit, burgundy tie, cashmere overcoat handed off to a waiter, briefcase in tow. He cleaned up nice! At least bridezilla was nowhere in site. She didn't think she could fake her way through latte and shrimp cocktail with her hanging off him.

A line from an old song crossed her mind as she studied him. Yes, the heart actually did go boom! He'd gotten a haircut but he still had his tan. Gone was the cocky 'screw reality, let's get laid and go for a swim' attitude. He was clean-shaven and serious. The last time he cleaned up for her she found herself bent over a chair in a dressing room. But that was about a hundred years ago. So where was the old man?

"I hope you checked your gun at the door."

She looked up at him. She didn't smile. "Well, at least some things never change. Still a smart ass."

"That's the way I am. I don't hide behind lies."

"Neither do I."

"Or deceit."

She decided to ignore him. "Where's Mason?"

"He's not coming."

She stared at him, realization creeping in. "You set this up?"

"Can I sit down or are you going to stand there and snap at me?"

He sat down across from her. He waived off the waiter. "DeLaurier and SpenceCo have business." He glanced at his Rolex. "And I have sixty minutes to waste negotiating with you."

"Ah, yes. Papa spank." She reached into her purse and tossed the crumpled check across the table. "That's papa's answer."

A ghost of a smile attempted to cross his lips, but faded almost as fast. She'd surprised him. Or not.

"I'm glad. I told Mason you'd never go for it."

"Yes, well. All evidence to the contrary, there are some things I don't do for money."

"I told him I'd meet with you, as one last gesture. Prepare to be wined and dined."

"Don't be in too much of a hurry to choose your plastic weapons. I'm not really hungry and, like I said, you got your answer. So, I guess we're done."

"You're a cheap date."

"So you've told me in no uncertain terms."

"If I insulted you Darcy, I'm sorry. I was very angry."

"Don't worry about it. But then again, I'm trained not to give in to emotional frailties."

She could have sworn he winced.

"Is that all you have to say?"

"Yes."

"Fine. But there is one thing I want to know before you leave." He leaned across the table and lowered his voice. "Why did you really go to bed with me?"

There it was, the million dollar—or close to it—question. There was only one way to answer him.

"Because I wanted to, cowboy. That's why. Unlike you, I'm not on a short leash and nobody, but nobody, holds my purse strings."

"Is that why you sent all the lingerie I bought you back to the store?"

He was pissing her off and she was too close to the edge not to do something she'd regret in front of witnesses.

"Send it to Tiffany," she snapped and grabbed her purse and gloves off the table. Kyle clamped his hand down on hers.

"I'm only going to tell you this once, Darcy. I came here today to tell you in person that I am not going to marry Tiffany Shawcross. The stories in the newspapers were planted by Mason in order to pressure me into changing my mind."

Darcy dug into her purse and withdrew the business section. She slapped the newspaper down in front of him with a flourish. "Nice pic," she snapped.

Kyle frowned and threw the newspaper onto an empty chair. "Whether you believe it or not, that photo was taken months ago. Now, please sit down so we can talk." He clutched the sleeve of her jacket.

Darcy shook her head and looked over the top of his handsome head, his neatly groomed hair was a deeper brown but still showed the remnants of sun-kissed streaks of bronze. "We have nothing more to discuss."

"I'll double Mason's offer if you'll come to work for me. And only me."

"Oh for—NO! Now let me go before I deck you."

"I'll charge you," he countered coolly. "I'll take you to court. My very expensive lawyers will sue you and win."

She looked at him, then down at his hand. She still had one free hand and her fingers were already wrapped around her salad fork.

"I'll claim sexual harassment, have you charged and jailed. My underpaid buddies in Metro blues hate suckhole guys like you. You and your suit would never survive a night in the tank. You'd be some biker's bitch faster than our waiter could swipe your card. And don't think you'd get bail. Papers have been known to disappear—for days."

He must have taken her seriously as he removed his hand. "I guess your blue suits trump my Hugo Boss flush."

Darcy claimed her bitter victory and sat down. There were things she still needed to hear—from him. "Did your conscience eat at you enough to tell Tiffy-poo about your little indiscretion?"

His answer surprised her. "As a matter of fact, I did. Believe it or not, she didn't care."

"Oh? Did she have an order of fries on the side while you were gone?"

"Stop it, Darcy. This bitchiness isn't like you."

"What is like me, Kyle? Do you know? You should, we spent enough time together. I think you should be answering the question, 'Why did you climb into my bed' before you start making demands on me. Start with yourself because I don't think you know. I have nothing more to say to you except have a nice life, if you can have one without Mason pulling your strings. I'm sure you'll all be one big happy family."

She got up to leave—again.

"Please don't go. At least have a coffee. It's cold outside."

It was getting pretty cold inside too.

"All right, but under one condition."

"Name it."

She sat down. The waiter appeared and Kyle ordered two coffees.

"Tell me what happened to the Kyle who laid on the beach with me in San Andres and wanted to mine diamonds?"

His face changed then. What had been a cool, combative exterior became a mask of controlled emotions. His gaze drifted from her face to somewhere over her shoulder.

"Some things are better left on far away beaches. It wasn't feasible. That's all."

His answer had all the depth of a school-boy learning by rote. Or a sleeper waking from a wonderful dream and finally having to face reality.

"So, that's it. You're just going to abandon your dreams. You show more devotion to your deceased friends than you do to yourself. I'll bet if Kevin were alive he'd knock some sense into you."

His eyes widened and his jaw twitched. She'd slapped him in an emotionally vulnerable spot. Had she gone too far?

"My private life is no longer any of your concern. Your work is over and you've been paid. As for the corporate end, Darcy, you're not a business person. I've gone over my finances and it won't work. I need funding and Mason made good on his promise to see to it that I can't get it. He'd told every bank in the city that my venture is a bad risk."

"Bastard!" she bit out.

Kyle grunted in agreement.

"There's got to be some way you can make it work, Kyle. You went to all those schools, have all those initials after your name, not to mention the money and a worldwide corporate name behind you. Surely somebody somewhere is willing to take the chance and lend you a few bucks."

He glanced momentarily to the left of their table, as if suddenly mesmerized by the design on the salt-stained carpet. "I've lost interest," he said simply and shrugged.

Darcy pressed her lips into a slim line of disdain. *Liars always look to the left.* She'd learned that in the force. Spence rode straight on that trait too. Confessing suspects either looked directly at you or glanced to the right when trying to recall details. But not liars, they loved the left. It was time to confront him, whether he was ready or not. She needed to hear the truth from him once and for all, even if that truth would probably make her feel like shit for, well months. Or longer. "That's either the biggest lie or the poorest confession I've ever heard. If it really is true, then you have 'commitment phobia' written all over you. First Tiffany, then me, now your diamond mine. If it's a lie then what makes you think I can't accept the real reason? You're trying real hard to throw me off the trail. I guess we're better off leaving our little fling back in paradise."

He looked away from her, left again. "Yeah, I guess."

The coffees arrived. Kyle took his the way she remembered it, two sugars and one cream. She wondered if he remembered the last time they shared a coffee together. Room service. Darcy immediately looked around, anxious to get her mind on another topic. Unfortunately, her thoughts kept going around and around and ending up back on the same subject. There had to be a way for him. There just had to be. His body language, his voice, his eyes. They told her a different story than the one he wanted her to believe.

"I have a little money," she began.

"No!" he snapped.

"Why not?"

"Because I want to do this on my own. Besides, you don't have the kind of capital I need to get started. I'm talking millions, Darcy. And I don't have that kind of money. With the stocks down I can't even sell them to raise enough capital. You see, what I came to tell you is that I've cut ties with my father. He's disinherited me. Bagging you was my 'last gesture' of allegiance and I knew you'd never go for it. So, after today, I'm out of the company. He could even sue me if he felt so inclined."

Bastard! Darcy nearly choked on her coffee. "Can he do that?"

"He can try. The only thing stopping him is my voting with my mother against him."

Darcy's mind worked furiously. "So, let him buy your vote. Buy it with enough money to get you started. I know you, Kyle. I know you can do this and make a success of it. You have it in here," she placed her hand on the breast of her suit jacket near where her heart was. "All you need is somebody on your side. You don't need Mason and his greedy manipulation."

She waited for him to say something. Finally, he did.

"Funny, that's what Kevin once said."

"Was he right?"

"He never lived to find out."

"So why give Mason the satisfaction of giving in? Sounds to me like that's what he wants. To show the world he can own anyone and anything he wants with threats and bribes."

"And what kind of a bribe did you get for sleeping with me?" Direct question, aimed directly at her.

"So that's it," she murmured. "This little lunch isn't about working for you or Mason. It's about your pride. You think bringing you back at any cost meant being paid to crawl into the sack with you. You believed it that night at Juan's and you still believe it, even though I swore up and down it wasn't true. Well, here's a bulletin. I made love to you because I wanted to. Because I care—cared—for you. Because I—" she stumbled over the words, words she was compelled to say but was sure he'd never accept. Nevertheless, she had to say them. "Because I love you."

It was Kyle's turn to look unconvinced. He folded his arms across his chest. He swallowed. "You slept, and fell in love, with another woman's fiancé. Apparently my father couldn't buy you morals any more than he could me."

She gasped. It was more than a hit. It was the deepest cut of all. And it was enough. Darcy slammed her cup down on the saucer so hard, coffee sloshed over the rim of the cup. This time she made a mad swipe for her purse and gloves.

"*Screw you!*" she hissed and sped out of the restaurant.

Kyle turned and watched her retreat. How could he blame her? He became aware of the curious stares of other customers watching their altercation.

He'd best leave too before somebody said something that reached some nosy newspaper reporter. He couldn't afford another headline. He tossed the waiter a twenty, grabbed his coat and walked out the front door.

His car was waiting but he waived off his driver.

"I'm walking back to the office," he called, but found himself walking in the opposite direction.

The cold bit into his uncovered skin. He didn't care. He deserved it. Gone to far? Over the top? Hurt her the way she'd hurt him? Yep. Yep. And, not that he planned to, but he did it anyway. He passed his favorite bookstore without going in. He didn't have time to read. Except maybe a self-help book on how to save a relationship after you severely pissed off the woman you know you can't live without. Did they sell books like that?

He passed the travel agency where he'd bought his ticket to San Andres. It was packed with people looking to escape the frigid weather. He passed a jewellery store and did stop. He stared at the display case and at his reflection. The last time he'd done this Darcy was standing beside him. She wore the black sheath that drove him nuts. He thought then—and still did—how stunning she'd look with a string of diamonds setting off her neckline.

Those could be his stones in the window. Perhaps with a few of Juan's emeralds taking up the slack. He'd even drafted a company logo while in San Andres—DK Diamonds, the DK standing for DeLaurier Karats. Somewhere he still had a cocktail napkin with DK written in a flourishing hand—Darcy & Kyle. Then he remembered the sand heart, the initials inside and his declaration to a woman he knew he was madly in love with, but convinced himself that had nothing to do with it.

The stones in the window winked at him under the bright display lights.

I heart you.

I hurt you.

There had been times these last few days when he caught himself thinking of a way to pull it off, to start the diamond venture. He'd even approached his future father-in-law. But Joshua thought even less of the idea than Mason. Tiffany loved it only because she thought she could have all the diamonds her little heart desired, so he quietly shelved the idea. None of it mattered now.

But more and more, his instincts, his desires were pulling him in another direction. He tried going to his club and working out his frustrations in the gym and later in the pool. The flourescent lighting reflecting off the chlorine-blue water threw him back to their hedonistic day on the private beach. Darcy leaving the sea naked with salt water raining off her skin, the sun catching the water and causing it to glisten—like diamonds. The tiny specks of coral sand clinging to her—a mist of multi-colored gems. Her eyes at night, the candlelight dancing in their depths and the way they grew wide when she was aroused. Darker jewels. Darcy herself, the rarest of them all.

He'd gotten over being angry with her. All it took was to be in the same room with Mason for a few minutes and bang! A match to a can of gasoline.

Lucky for Darcy, Mason took full responsibility for the escapade. Of course, Kyle deliberately overlooked the Darcy sleeping with him part. And from the sounds of things, her boss was just as discreet. It was to her credit that she felt the matter didn't need to be revealed to anyone.

On the other hand, Kyle was itching to tell the world what he'd found. A woman he loved. A woman he needed. A woman he lost. Or had he?

I heart you, too. And I'm sorry. Oh, God! How I'm sorry.

He turned away from the window and started back towards his office. A gust of frigid air slammed him. His hair whipped across his forehead. The collar of his coat jumped toward his cold ears. Tiny drops of sleet cut into his exposed skin. The icy crystals struck him like a frozen slap in the face. Hard. Cold. Like diamonds. He took a few steps before he spotted a cab. It was now or never. He hailed the driver and jumped in.

"Rosedale, please." He gave the driver the exact address and hoped, no prayed, his mother was still talking to him.

⁂

One afternoon a week later, Darcy was in the middle of her last load of laundry when the security buzzer sounded. She didn't feel like having visitors, not on laundry day with her unwashed hair jammed into a lop-sided pony-tail and her only clean clothes a set of ripped grey sweats bearing the faded police academy logo. The concierge in her building informed her that a Mr. DeLaurier was on his way up. Darcy dropped the last of her sun-dresses in a plastic clothes basket and pondered over the reason for his visit. She nodded her head. Of course, another attack from the bribe tribe.

She was taking her mandatory leave and hating every minute of it. Spence had e-mailed her that Mason had tried once again to lure Darcy away from him. Spence laughed in his face and laughed harder when a thoroughly ruffled Mason threatened, 'you'll never work in this town again'. After which Spence closed up the office for a two week 'holiday', then left the country on his secret little visit to who-knows-where to do who-knew-what. Darcy was sure Mason would try again.

"You don't quit, do you Mason," she muttered and kicked the laundry basket.

A few seconds later a knock sounded at her door. Darcy braced herself, composing her attitude and arming her verbal artillery. Couldn't he take no for an answer?

She opened her apartment door. "Look, I don't—Kyle!"

"I'm sorry," he said swiftly and positioned his foot to keep her from closing the door. "Can I come in, Darcy. Please? It's important."

Darcy warily eyed him, her intuitive training taking in the superficial details. He'd visibly changed since she'd seen him. He looked tired, as if he hadn't slept. The growth of a stubble told her he hadn't shaved for a few days, either. If she looked close enough through the open collar of his overcoat, she could swear he still wore the same suit. Something was up.

"You look like a refugee from a rave."

"I've been up all night, almost every night since last week."

Darcy closed her eyes and leaned against the door. "Oh, Kyle. You're not binge-drinking again."

"No! No. I've been working on a few things. Have been since our lunch. Listen, can we talk?"

Famous last words. Well, why not? She motioned him inside. "Take off your boots. Want something hot?"

He nodded and removed his overcoat. "Sure. Just don't go to any trouble. I won't be here long. I've got a flight early tomorrow morning so I have to get home and pack."

"You're leaving?" She tried not to sound alarmed as she hung up his coat. Why should she be after he verbally crucified her.

"I'm sorry," he started. "I need to get that out of the way before we go any further."

Kyle sat down at Darcy's tiny bistro table in the even tinier kitchen. Darcy went to the kitchen sink and began to fill the kettle. "Me too," she said over the rush of tap water.

"I hope that's coffee," he prompted.

"It's only instant but if you're in a hurry, it'll have to do." Gawd! How polite they both sounded, how formal.

"Instant is fine. I just came from my mother's apartment and I'm full of herbal tea." His tone of voice told her that he'd rather have ingested drain cleaner. Darcy could understand that. She hated tea. Being a cop she relied on a constant influx of Tim Horton's coffee to keep her going on night shifts. In fact, the only tea she had in the house was something she got in the mail as a sample. Some lame ass peppermint herb concoction she nearly choked on. After putting the kettle on the stove, she sat down across the table from him.

"Kyle, I need to know. Someone told me recently 'the love boat done sailed'. As far as that goes, is our relationship salvageable or did it sink for good?"

She watched his expression. It had changed from one of hurried anticipation to surprise, tinged with relief.

"On the contrary. I bring you today's paper. They were just delivering it to your building box when I came in." He dug into his overcoat and handed Darcy the business section. Darcy stared at it for a moment, unable to believe the headline.

DeLaurier/Shawcross Merger Falls Through: Mom Nixes Deal

She read a little further.

It's Official: No Marriage For TSE Couple!

At last, it was out in the open. She had to give him credit for that.

Stocks Nosedive! Boy, was she glad she didn't take those.

Kyle DeLaurier To Mine Diamonds In Frozen North. Well, would wonders never cease.

She handed the paper back to Kyle. "I don't understand."

"Is that all you have to say?"

"I don't have an MBA. Give me the stupid person's version of what happened."

Kyle took a deep breath. "I went to see Frances, my mother, last week after La Scala. I told her about the newspaper stories being false and about Mason and I going our separate ways." Darcy took note of the disdainful tone of his voice.

"And..."

"It appears she was very busy while we were lazing around in San Andres and having nasty seahorse sex. She was able to influence enough board members to vote against the merger. So marrying Tiffany would have been a useless exercise in bad taste and a waste of money. Except my mother's on the hook for the church's deposit, but she'll get over it. By the way, she thanks you for returning all the lingerie I bought for you on her account. She thinks you have good taste anyway. And she's impressed you can't be bought."

Darcy's mind worked furiously. Truly timing was everything. If only she and Kyle had been able to stay away for a couple of more weeks, her mission to San Andres might never have been revealed. They would have been able to return and possibly avoid all the hurt they suffered. If only Frances had worked a little faster... if only. But what was done, was done.

"Okay, mom likes me. Let's move on. Why else are you here?"

He frowned at her. "You talk as if you have no part in my life."

She sighed. "I don't. You made that clear at La Scala."

"But we're both sorry."

"But nothing's resolved." She tried to keep the agitation out of her voice. "We need to rebuild some trust here and that's not going to happen with one 'I'm sorry'."

"But, it's a start."

"These things take time."

"Says who? The relationship police? I hope you have a manual because I didn't get one." He was irritated now as well as tired. Kyle had moved fast from the very beginning. It had been a fasten-your-seatbelts ride since the moment she and her hat disrupted his hangover. He was still trying to do all the driving.

"You left San Andres, Kyle. You just... disappeared. You never let me explain. You just took off. We have a ton of unresolved issues here."

"I was hurt."

"I know that. I'm the one who hurt you. Why didn't you just do what other men do when women piss them off? Go to a bar, order a pizza, go fishing, I don't know."

"Neither did I. I'd never been hurt like that before. I didn't know what to think. I felt so..."

"Betrayed?" she offered.

"And angry. I just had to get away and think. I've done a lot of thinking. About me. About you. About us."

"How come you're brutally honest all of a sudden?"

"Because we're back in the real world. Maybe because..."

Darcy watched him fight for the words which, up until now, had been spilling out of him like lava out of an active volcano.

"Because I wanted to see if what we had on the beach could translate to the ice and snow."

Darcy digested his speech. Somehow, the words couldn't get past the lump that had suddenly formed in the back of her throat. He'd left the door open. Time for the burning question. "Is there still an 'us'?"

"That's up to you. That's why I wanted to come here and try to set things straight before I leave. I'm going back to San Andres to see Mr. Valdez about buying into the company. Here." He shoved an envelope across the table.

Darcy stared at it. "What's this?"

"An apology, a chance to set things right. Call it a leap of faith. I don't want your money but if you still want to throw in with me," he tapped the envelope, "whether or not you act on what's in here could change the future, for both of us."

Darcy hesitated before she picked up the envelope. Kyle had 'I Dare You' written all over his face. Darcy opened the envelope in front of him, which is what she knew he wanted. He wanted to see her reaction to the mysterious 'Pandora's Box' in a number ten off white. She steeled herself and slid on her surveillance face. "An airline ticket." She looked at him, puzzled. "I just finished washing sand out of my clothes, my hair and other parts of my body I prefer not to mention." She slid the ticket back in the envelope. "I'll think about it."

"It's an open-ended ticket but don't take too long. However, I have to be out of the country in about twelve hours, so I'll say good-bye, Darcy."

He rose and went to the door. Darcy got his coat from the hall closet while he bent to put on his boots. She took the chain off her door and opened it for him. He took his coat from her and she handed him his portfolio. Suddenly he dropped both. His arms were around her faster than she could draw breath. Then his lips were on hers and she couldn't breathe. Her arms locked around him and he pressed her body against him. His mouth devoured hers. Their tongues danced a furious routine. Their kiss was interrupted and punctuated by tiny snippets of conversations, pieces of words. Things that only made sense to them.

"Oh, God! How I missed you. I'm so sorry."

"I'm sorry, Kyle. Please believe me, I never wanted to hurt you."

They continued to pay tribute to one another by close fondling. He, molding his hands around her buttocks; she, pressing her breasts into his chest. The elevator pinged. The whistling kettle changed to a demanding scream. Reluctantly, Darcy pushed herself away from him.

She pressed her cheek into his shirt. "If we start, you'll miss your flight."

"I know," he whispered and kissed the top of her head.

Darcy raised her face to him. "You have to go." She bent down and retrieved his things.

"I hope you make the right choice, Darce." Then he turned and was strolling quickly down the corridor. Darcy waived to him before he entered the elevator, then closed her door. She walked to the kitchen, swearing softly at the kettle before she took it off the burner.

The right choice. She knew the right choice was a gamble. Her whole life resting on the toss of one card. Or an airline ticket.

It was remarkable how alike relationships and diamonds were. One day you're an old lump of coal, then, after a few million years of pressure you're either crushed or you harden and sparkle. They were diamonds in the rough, her and Kyle. And they'd had enough pressure in the past few weeks to crush them forever, or turn them both into the rarest of stones. In that moment, Darcy made her choice.

She wasn't just going to sparkle. She was going to shine.

Chapter Ten

Darcy looked around the familiar suite that Kyle had taken once again. Of course she knew this time it belonged to Frances.

"It's deja vu all over again," she muttered and placed her suitcase on the stand beside Kyle's. She then noticed something strange. The sofa in the sitting area was filled with bags from the lingerie store in San Luis. Somebody was optimistic.

She went over and rummaged through each bag. Yep, it was all here. All except for the one black thong. She wondered if Kyle had kept it as a token of their time together. The way some serial killers keep trophies of their victims? She returned to the bedroom. Okay. Now what?

She jumped at the knock at the door. Her heart pounded. She almost whizzed in her walking shorts. She wasn't ready to face him—yet.

"Room service, señorita."

Whew! Darcy breathed a sigh of relief. She opened the door and accepted a tray laden with fresh fruit and a bottle of champagne with two glasses.

There was a monthly magazine on the desk featuring the highlights of the resort's winter season. Darcy smiled and chuckled out loud. Gretchin was on the cover modelling the tiniest of bikinis. As usual, her cups runneth over. She thumbed through the features.

"Aussie wins best tan contest. Aussie wins best bikini contest. Aussie signed by Hollywood agent. Surprise me."

Slowly she smiled. Then she grinned. A second later she was diving into her suitcase. She slipped on her bikini and hastily scratched a note for Kyle to meet her on the beach. This time she left her hat behind.

Meet me on the beach.

Vague but effective. Darcy was here all right, the rest was up to him. He returned to the room and discovered he'd missed her by at least an hour. The champagne hadn't been touched and the bottle was sweating. Well, that made two of them. Only he knew the cause of his nervousness. Ice buckets—not just bar decor. He'd order up some ice later. He changed from light tan shirt and slacks to his red swim briefs. Although it was mid-afternoon and the beach was usually packed, he knew it would be easy to spot Darcy, just look for the girl wearing a hat but not on her head.

He strolled the beach line, his gaze skimming chair after chair. Nothing. He went to the water's edge to see if he could see her swimming. Nada. Next he'd try the bar near the beach sports net. There was a rowdy crowd gathered around watching a co-ed game of topless volleyball. He ordered a large soda with lime and glanced over to the game.

Same old. Same old. Tits. Ass. Tans. Tats. Darcy…

"JEEZUS!"

She was getting ready to make a serve. Across the net, several men were getting ready to make a play. The guy beside her was getting ready to make a pass. Kyle pushed his way through the crowd of onlookers. And they were all looking at his Darcy. And her bare breasts. His breasts, slicked up with suntan oil and jutting out for all the world to see. For old men to ogle, for young men to fantasize about—and maybe a few women in the crowd for that matter.

She made a toss in the air, jumped and slammed her palm against the ball. A whistle sounded. Someone cried "foul." But all he could see was his private property bouncing up in the air and settling with a perky jiggle when she landed. Enough!

Kyle ran straight into the field of play, scooped her up and tossed her over his shoulder. He carried her off the beach court. As he passed the bar he grabbed a dry beach towel and wrapped it around her.

Darcy made a scene of kicking and yelling—and laughing (the bitch!) but he refused to let her go until they were safely inside his room. He dumped her on the bed.

"What the hell were you thinking?" he yelled.

And the smart ass broad had the balls to lie there, point at him and laugh hysterically. Finally she calmed down.

"Well, hello to you too. I had a wardrobe malfunction. I forgot my hat."

She was laughing. And smiling. She wasn't railing at him or storming off like she did in La Scala. Kyle paced the floor in front of the bed. He stopped a couple of times, opened his mouth, then closed it. Pointed his finger at her then wound up scratching his head. Finally he gave up and went to the mini-fridge and pulled out a bottle of water. He took a long swig then passed it to her.

"Here. You look thirsty." He knew he was being curt with her and he didn't care. Didn't she know what she was doing? She was his. What came naturally with her was his. Except he realized he'd forgotten the most important part. She was totally in ignorance of his belongings.

He sat down beside her and poured some water into a plastic cup and raised it high. "Cheers," he said in a dull monotone.

"Cheers." She sidled up to him and hugged him.

"I heart you, too," he said.

"I haven't said 'I heart you'."

"But you will. You were thinking it. I was only saving you the embarrassment of having to say it first."

"Let's start with 'I'm sorry' and progress."

"I can't. I'm in therapy. A very wise woman once told me I was a commitmentphobe. I'm trying to break the cycle and just say 'no'. You can call this cold turkey."

"I'd say you've made a good start. And speaking of starts... I'm Darcy McLeod, ex-cop currently on leave of absence private detective and sometimes super-spy companion. Pleased to meet you."

He humored her and shook her hand. "Kyle DeLaurier, former heir to my father's fortune. Currently up-to-my-ears-in-loans entrepreneur and sometimes super-spy. Don't blow my cover. I'm in diamonds."

"What a coincidence. I'd like to be. I'm considering a career change. Got any openings in your new company?"

He rubbed his chin and looked at her. "Well, I hear diamonds need a lot of security. Send me a resume."

"Done."

She hoped so. Done with fighting. Done with picking at each other. Darcy put her glass on the night stand and set out to prove it.

"Did I ever say I was sorry?"

"That night at Juan's house. About a hundred times. And a million times since."

"Were you listening?"

"No."

"Are you listening now?"

"Yes."

"Can I go back to the game?"

"Hell no."

"Gee, I was hoping you'd say that."

"These," he leaned down and cupped each of her breasts, "are mine. And only mine. Mine to see, mine to touch, mine to taste. Mmm... and they do taste good, although a little like coconut oil. Too many trans fatty acids."

Darcy leaned back on a pillow. How wonderful it was to have Kyle touch her again. She missed him, terribly. Missed his humor, his charm, his gorgeous bod making wild, passionate love to her, bugging the shit out of her.

"I only came down here for one reason, you know."

"I don't care why. I'm just glad you're here."

"So I guess you don't want to hear that I'm in love with you." It was getting harder and harder to concentrate. Kyle was busy sliding her bikini briefs down her legs.

"Hmph. Hmm. Umm." He kept licking and nibbling her nipples.

A luscious tingle created a haze of pleasure. She heard her own voice becoming soft and dreamy. "Translated that means either you're in love with me too, or shut up and grab a condom from the top drawer."

"Both. Can we have sex now?"

"Mmm. Thought you'd never ask. But don't worry about the condom, unless you did the nasty with some other woman you're in love with. Then I'll have to insist."

Kyle stopped what he was doing and propped his head on his hand. "I didn't," he admitted. "I couldn't. Not with you running around in my mind and the memory of our time together playing bumper cars with my hormones. Although I did kiss her once, just to say good-bye. Coldest sensation I ever experienced. Now you, on the other hand, are hot enough to burn the short and curlies off a guy's *cajones.*"

She laughed softly. "Don't worry, cowboy. When we get to the frozen north, you're going to need all the insulation your cajones can get. Wouldn't want to freeze the family jewels."

"Amen to that. Especially since they're not worth zip anymore. Still love me?"

"Yep. Now will you continue so I can prove it?"

And he did. He started by nuzzling her neck. The stubble of his cheek grazed the hollow at her shoulders. She ran her fingers across his tanned shoulders, taking satisfaction in their muscular contours. He kissed a path and stamped his territory from her cleavage all the way down her bare tummy and across her abdomen.

He reached her nest of curls and plunged his nose into her scent. "God you smell so good. I couldn't get you out of my mind. Or my mouth. Or my nose. I wanted everything and everyone to smell like you. You're a natural aphrodisiac or something. Something wicked and addictive. And the taste of your skin—I could live on that alone."

His confession startled her as much as it pleased her. Now she needed to open her heart.

"I missed you so much, Kyle. I've never had a man make love to me the way you do. And I never want another man."

"Good because you'll have a hard time getting rid of me. And speaking of hard... I've got something that's been aching for you, gorgeous."

He mounted her then and she felt his need stabbing the top of her left thigh. She wrapped her arms around him and pressed her body into his, luxuriating in the feel that was everything male against her skin. Her nipples responded at the chafing of his chest. She arched her back and pressed her mons against his crotch. She felt the need to show him how much she desired him.

Kyle began a slow slide down her body, his tongue lapping at every inch of bare skin leaving a burning fire in its wake. At last he came to her mons and slipped his tongue between her outer lips. He licked her lightly, teasing, taunting.

"Delicious," he murmured and continued torturing her. He plucked at the folds of her labia and suckled each side, nearly driving her out of her mind with pleasure.

"Lick my clit," she panted.

"Patience, gorgeous. Good things come to those who wait."

Darcy didn't think she could wait much longer. Blood raced through every vein in her body ready to implode if she didn't get release. At last he turned his attention to her waiting bud. She could feel it swell under his careful ministrations. He knew the landscape, he'd been there before. He knew just what made her tick. And her ticking bomb was ready to explode. He licked the fuse, rolled the charge between his teeth. He set the final blast by inserting two large fingers inside her slick channel. His fingertips primed her G-spot.

The detonation rocketed from her vaginal wall to her clitoris. The spasms raced from her vulva down her legs like a bullet and ricocheted back up her abdomen until even her eyelashes tingled. The force of her orgasm sent her reeling. She gasped. She cried his name. She thrashed her head until she was dizzy.

The experience was barely over before he mounted her, positioned the velvety tip of his hard cock between her lips and thrust himself inside her. The feel of him filling her, the way her snugness accepted him, as if she were made for only him fuelled her for another mind-blowing climax. His rod pummelled her pussy. She heard the sucking sound of her incredible wetness against him every time he withdrew and plunged inside her. She wrapped her legs around him, urging him deeper, harder.

His face radiated sheer ecstasy. His eyes were half-closed, the pupils wide and dark from the drug-like pleasure racing through him. He was getting his fix of her as surely as any junkie was answering the knock of his Jones at the door.

Finally he stiffened above her and a small, strangled cry escaped his throat. She squeezed his rod, thrilling in the quick jerks of him spilling hot fluid deep inside her. Then she found him on top of her, his breath coming in small, rapid gasps in her ear. Eventually he settled in beside her and his breathing became slow and even again.

The room was silent except for the rhythmic *whap whap whap* of the ceiling fan blades above them. Darcy glanced at the clock. It was siesta time. Tourists pulled their tots from the pool and put them down for a nap. Resort guests retreated to the shade of the pool bar. And two people in love carried the heat of the Caribbean sun into their room.

"I need a Screaming Orgasm," came the muffled voice beside her.

"I think you just had one."

"No fair. You had a Long, Slow Screw."

"I'll let you treat me to Sex On The Beach later."

He turned and grinned at her. "Yeah, and after we can have a drink."

She smiled at him then. "Are we back?"

"Did we ever leave?"

"No, and I don't think we ever will. But no more hide and seek. Where you go, I go and vice versa."

"Deal. I'd shake your hand only I'm exhausted. By the way, do you mind waiting for a diamond ring? I'd like to put one of my own on your finger, but I'm broke right now."

She kissed him gently. "I don't need a ring, but I'll wait. I hear diamonds in the rough are worth waiting for."

"So are real jewels. But in the meantime..." He climbed off the bed and stretched. He went to the ice bucket now containing three inches of cool water and the long-forgotten bottle of champagne and brought it over to the bed.

Darcy wasn't exactly thirsty for champagne but her mouth was so dry she'd drink anything right now. She stared at the bottle. Her keen observation skills immediately alarmed her about what was amiss.

"Kyle, that bottle's been tampered with. The seal has been sloppily reapplied and that cork looks like it was expelled and pushed back in already."

"Okay, Officer McLeod, calm down. I'm the guilty party. I should have known I'd never be able to put one past you."

He pulled off the foil seal and pushed out the cork. He turned his back to her for a moment while he filled the glasses, which he looked like he was having difficulty in achieving. After a moment he handed her a glass of champagne but was careful to keep his palm wrapped around most of the glass, almost to conceal it.

"What are you up to?"

"My, suspicious aren't we. You'll have to lose some of that or else I'll never be able to surprise you with anything. Here's your glass."

He handed the glass to her. "Now look at me while I make a toast." He pruned his mouth with an exaggerated effort and closed one eye in pretended deep thought.

Darcy stifled a yawn. "Wake me when you make up your mind."

"Okay, skip the toast. I'm not up to clever anecdotes after I've had my pipes cleaned."

Darcy rolled her eyes. "Ever the romantic." A second later her sarcasm was put to the test. As she put the glass to her lips she noticed something lodged in the bottom. Something square and green.

"Oh-my-god... it's... it's..."

"An advance from Juan. And the beginning of your engagement ring. I want you to pick the setting—eventually. And I want to showcase that emerald with our new diamonds. Your ring will be the first design out of our company. And you get to name it."

She set the glass down on the night stand and fished the emerald out of the glass. She shook it a couple of times. Droplets of champagne flew between them. She placed the jewel in the palm of her hand.

"It's wet."

"Great name! 'Wet'—like the way you get with me."

"You're positively lurid. And is this supposed to be a proposal? No down on the knees, magic phrases, just 'here's part of your ring'. Well, here's part of my answer—oh!"

"'Oh' what?"

"You get the 'kay' later."

"Promise?"

"Yep."

"How much later?"

"In time for your mother not to lose her deposit."

He took a giant gulp of his drink and set the glass on the floor. "You know, you don't have to do that. We can get married anywhere, anytime. You pick the place, the day, the time."

Darcy stared at him over the rim of her glass trying to decide whether or not to call his bluff. She knew she'd have to give in to the church wedding rigmarole eventually. But for now they could do it their way, laid back and easy going, just the way she knew Kyle would want to. "Okay, how about tomorrow on the beach. Olie can find us a minister. He and Rocco and his dozens of cousins can stand up for us."

She knew she'd said the right thing when his eyebrows shot up and a huge smile softened his face. "That's exactly what I hoped you'd say. I can see you'll be no slouch when it comes to making the major decisions in this company."

Darcy leaned over his naked body and joined her glass on the floor next to his. She still had the emerald clutched in her hand. "Not all the major decisions, cowboy. We still have a lot of planning and work to do to get this partnership off the ground. Let's throw some clothes on, go to the bar, then hit the pool."

Kyle pulled her onto his lap and kissed her. "Let's not and say we did. Here— " he took the stone from her hand. "I'll put this in the safe downstairs until we're ready to leave."

"Now that's sensible. Want to see something else that's sane and sensible?"

"Such as..."

Darcy climbed off his lap and out of bed. Naked, she walked to the window and peeked through the slats of the closed vertical blinds. She crooked her finger for him to join her. He gave a reluctant sigh and sullenly slipped out of bed. She mimicked his pout as he crossed the room. Then he was beside her, fondling her buttocks and slipping his hand between her legs.

"What's so important that you had to drag me out of bed?"

She pointed to the children's play area where a set of swings and a huge sandbox sat near a wading pool. He squinted through the blind, then nodded slowly. He wrapped his arms around her and pressed her naked body against him.

He murmured softly, next to her ear. "Someone's been playing in the sand again."

She turned her face slightly and caught his kiss. "I mean it. Really."

"I know, love. I heart you, too."

About the Author:

Chevon Gael lives in a small town north of Toronto, Ontario. Close enough to experience the city, yet far enough to indulge in her two greatest passions; skiing and writing. Her third greatest passion is her spouse and personal hero, Brian, a Mountie! Both enjoy being at the beck and catterwall of Buddy, a black tabby with a large appetite.

Seduction of the Muse

by Charlotte Featherstone

To My Reader:

I love writing tortured heroes and I hope you'll find Aidan, the Duke of Rutherford a delectable specimen of passion, lust and sensitivity. Enjoy of the fantasy.

Chapter One

September 1808
London, England

He couldn't say when his obsession with Emily came into being. It had seemed so long now, like she had been a part of him all his life. It had been nearly a year since she had ceased being simply Emily, Jane's friend, and became his Emily instead.

As his gaze strayed to the clock atop the mantel, he wondered how he had allowed himself to become so easily infatuated with someone like Emily Beaumont. She was a virgin, a lady of breeding and social standing. She was not the sort to dally with, and the odd dalliance was all he could give her—for her sake.

His palms grew damp, and when he heard the front door creak open yet again, he ran his hands down his woolen trousers in an attempt to release some of the pent-up anticipation that was coursing through him. Voices, husky and feminine, washed over him and he felt his body tighten with anticipation. What good fortune to have overheard Emily talking with her friend. What luck to be able to be the one who would awaken her to the delights of sexual pleasure. Had he known what his precious Emily truly longed for, he would have made plans for her seduction months ago.

The feminine voices moved closer and he heard Emily's nervous laughter echoing off the coved ceilings of the foyer. What was she thinking? Was she on edge, or was she excited by the prospect of sharing her body with a stranger?

She appeared in the door of the salon with the madame of the house. Her face was heavily veiled, but he could see her moss-green eyes sparkling behind the black netting. Her body, so familiar to him, was shielded beneath a black cape, hiding the breasts he knew would be inching seductively above the edge of her bodice.

Sinking further into his chair and allowing the shadows of the night to engulf him, he studied the woman he was going to seduce. She was nervous; he could see it in her eyes, in the way she chewed her bottom lip. Her posture was ramrod straight, and her fingers gripped the silk of her skirts. As her eyes scanned the salon and everything in it, he wondered if she would bolt and run.

Or perhaps, he thought, allowing his gaze to roam throughout the salon, she would find someone else to her liking.

The notion sliced through his gut. He had not waited more than a year to have her, only to lose this chance. He would not let her choose another. He would be her lover this night. He would make certain of that.

"I employ the most attractive of men, and I ensure that they are highly skilled in their art. Every man here is, I assure you, expert in all forms of pleasure to suit every woman's tastes and fantasies," Madame Wilson said with pride.

Emily swallowed hard and surveyed the assembled men. Dark or fair, tall and broad or sleekly lithe, they were assembled in the adjoining salon engaged in such activities as playing cards, reading by candlelight or lounging negligently on the numerous settees that fringed the perimeter of the room. Some were dressed as gentlemen, others as sailors or hired hands. Still others appeared to be bookish man-of-affair types, while a few reminded her of dark and brooding romantic poets. The beauty before her was unimaginable, and she would not have believed such a place existed had she not witnessed the illicit decadence with her own eyes.

For years the whereabouts and legitimacy of The Temple of Flora had been speculated upon and yet here she was, standing in the very real and tastefully decorated foyer of Mary Wilson's brothel for women. The Temple of Flora was rumored to be the place to indulge in one's passions at the hands of men who were masters at pleasing women. After thirty years of virginity and far too long nursing a hopeless passion, Lady Emily Beaumont was ready to heed the desires of Mother Nature.

"Come, my dear," Miss Wilson murmured. "I shall show you to the boudoirs."

As Emily followed the madame down the carpeted hall, Emily wondered if this was the right course to take. After all, she had her reputation to consider. She had not survived in society this long by playing fast with her good name. But there was no denying that she was restless with her life. She wanted more. She wanted to know what it was like to be intimate with a man.

Of course, she had only ever wanted one man in particular, but that had been years ago and he hadn't paid her any heed. Too many years pining for that man had brought her here tonight, to The Temple of Flora, for a taste of pleasure at the hands of an experienced master.

"This is the smallest of the rooms," Miss Wilson remarked when they stopped before a paneled door. "Had I known your intent to visit this evening, I could have arranged for you to have your pick of rooms. However, we are rather busy, and I am afraid you will have to make do with this one."

Miss Wilson opened the door and ushered her in with an elegant wave of her hand. Emily nodded and tried to act nonchalant about the whole business. Strolling to a curtained window, the madame pulled on the velvet cord. Up came the red drapes to reveal a window. Peering through it, Emily saw that it was the same salon as she had viewed upon her arrival, only the position of the window gave her a different view.

The salon, just as richly and elegantly appointed as the boudoirs, was liberally filled with chairs and settees and a huge hearth in which a fire blazed. There were card tables where the men played whist or hazard and side tables filled with decanters of liquor. Her gaze jumped from man to man, and she wondered how she would ever make such a monumental decision. She had never seen so many handsome men in one room before.

"Take your time, my dear. Look them over, decide which is worthy of you tonight. They cannot see you through the window. Feel confident in perusing them. When you have fixed on your prize, ring the bell for the chambermaid. You have only to point out your object of desire and he shall be brought to you."

Movement through the window caught Emily's eye, and her gaze searched the shadowed corner until she saw a tall man, his face concealed by shifting shadows, uncurl his frame from a chair. All she could see of his face were his gray eyes, and he stared intently at the window as if he could see her. She stood momentarily transfixed by those eyes and then with a gasp of alarm she stepped back, away from the window and the man's burning gaze. There was pain in those eyes, she thought, glancing back at the man, and suddenly she could not help but think of another pair of eyes that haunted her thoughts.

She knew then, that she could not go through with this. She thought she could put the man of her dreams out of her thoughts and allow herself to be touched by another, but it appeared she could not. She should run and not look back. But then the door closed behind the madame, leaving her all alone with her thoughts and her unconsummated desires.

"All is ready," Mary Wilson whispered in the darkened hall.

Emerging from the shadows, he stepped forward and reached for the latch on the door. "And you are certain it is the right woman? She was heavily veiled when she arrived."

"It is the woman you want," Madame Wilson sniffed. "Have no fear."

Her pale fingers, covered in sparkling gems, reached out into the darkness and he fished in his waistcoat for the pound notes he had folded in the pocket. "Now then, Madame," he said, reaching for the door. "We are not to be disturbed, and you will not discuss this transaction with anyone. Do you understand?"

She nodded and lifted her skirts, the swish of her satin train the only sound that could be heard throughout the quiet hall. With a rush of elation and sexual eagerness, he opened the door, prepared to enjoy the charms of an enchanting virgin—a virgin he intended to thoroughly claim before the rise of the sun made him skulk back into the dark shadows.

The door opened on a nearly inaudible squeak and Emily anxiously turned her head to the sound. The sizzle of moisture against the flickering candle flame sounded above the closing door before the room was snuffed into darkness.

Blackness cloaked her and the click of a key turning in a lock sent gooseflesh erupting along every pore of her body.

A deep and melodious whisper erupted in the quiet. "I have been waiting for you."

"I think you have the wrong room, sir," she murmured, her voice trembling with fear and perhaps a touch of excitement. "I am afraid I have not requested my night's entertainment."

He ignored her weak protest and snaked his arms around her middle, bringing her flush with his chest, a chest that felt firm and warm beneath his clothing. "You will not have to make any requests this night, for I know how to pleasure you and give you what you want. I am an expert in desire."

He brought her up against the wall, holding her upright with his thighs pressed against hers. His fingers laced through hers, holding their entwined hands against her side, while his other hand trailed down her throat to her décolletage and down over her breasts. He cupped her and she felt his breath hot beneath her ear, smelled the scent of him, spice and claret beneath her nose. His thumb slid over her nipple which hardened painfully beneath her silk gown and he chuckled deep in his throat when she whimpered and squirmed against him.

"I know this is something you desire. I heard you, you know, talking to your friend. What was it you said?" he whispered as his finger slid away from her breast and skated down her belly. "You want to know what it is to feel passion, you want the feel of a man's hands on you. You want to know what it is like to have a man inside you." Her body went rigid and her eyes widened in shock. "Have I gotten it all correct, Emily? Have I left out any parts?" His fingers were now at the junction of her thighs and he was stroking his fingertips against the curls that lay beneath her gown. "What other naughty bits did you refrain from telling your friend?"

Her stomach coiled and tightened, and she felt her blood thrum heavy in her veins. How would he have heard her telling Jane her secrets? That conversation had taken place in the darkened hallway of Mr. Hawgood's Museum of Curiosities. They had been completely alone, she was certain of it, yet he had repeated her words verbatim. How had he discovered her identity, she wondered, even as she whimpered again when he stroked his hand up the length of her body.

"Do I frighten you with my passion, Emily?" he asked as he kissed her throat. "Or does this excite you?" She moaned and her legs weakened when he pressed his lips, then his tongue, to her breasts. "Excites you, doesn't it? I can tell by the way you tremble against me. It is not a shiver of fear, but of desire, a yearning for more. You want to discover the mysteries between men and women. You want to learn why women will risk all to meet their lovers."

"Yes," she hissed when she felt his fingers expertly reach for the edge of her bodice. Slowly he inched it down until her breasts were nearly spilling out of her gown. "I want to know," she cried, arching her back when his nails caressed her breasts, scant inches from her nipples. "Show me. Excite me."

"Are you wet?" he asked, his lips brushing her ear as he whispered the words. His finger traced her jaw beneath her veil and slowly he raised the lace so that it skimmed over her lips and nose and back over her bonnet. He untied her bonnet strings, drawing out the action so that she began to shiver when his fingers touched her skin and his breath caressed her throat. "If I were to touch you, to spread your legs and feel you, would you be ready to come for me? Tell me, just how much are you willing to do to feel this excitement, my sweet?"

She pressed against him, unable to talk or think. How could she when he was even now lowering her bodice so that her breasts were exposed? With his thumb and forefinger, he gently rolled her nipple and automatically she reached for his wrist, knowing she should stop this. But he refused her and instead brought her hand to his trousers and pressed it against the bulge behind the flap.

"Take my cock in your hand, Emily and pleasure me."

Her blood quickened and instead of allowing her to fumble with the buttons, he tore the flap open and she felt his erection spring free. With ruthless determination, he curled her fingers around his thickness and pressed himself into her hand.

"Play with me, Emily," he groaned. "I am quite at your mercy."

She did not know what to do, other than to slide her fingers along the satiny skin. She must have been doing an admirable job, for he groaned and thrust his hips forward, sliding his erection up the length of her palm. Closing her eyes, she let her head rest against the wall and allowed herself to feel his warmth covering the front of her body. His mouth was everywhere, on her throat, the tops of her breasts, her lips. His hands were roaming the contour of her figure and his fingers cupped and stroked every inch of her burning skin. Her heart was pounding so fast she felt lightheaded and yet she could not stop what was happening even if she desired to. This passion, the feel of him surrounding her, the intimacy of his tongue in her mouth as he possessed her lips was nothing she thought ever to experience. It was Heaven, bliss, an erotic sensation she could easily find herself addicted to.

In some cognizant part of her mind she tried to recall the fact that this man was a stranger, someone who made his living by saying the right words and touching the right places. And yet nothing she had ever done felt this right. There was a safeness about this stranger despite the new sensations he was awakening in her. Who was this man who had caused her to abandon all good sense and her reputation?

Fisting her hand in his silky hair, she brought him closer, seeking his heat and his tongue dancing with hers. He growled and brought his hand up to her throat. His thumb rubbed the pulsating vein in her neck, back and forth, lulling her into a dreamlike state, bringing her back to another time and place where a kiss had made her feel this impassioned and wild. But that had been another time, another man.

Tearing his mouth from hers, he thrust his hips forward again and she curled her fingers tighter around his erection. Sliding her hand down, then up, she pleasured him, listening to his sucking breaths, feeling the tightening of his body, forgetting that she had no experience in pleasing a man.

When she had arrived at The Temple, she had no way of knowing how wonderful or liberating it would be to have a man so completely enraptured with her. She could have no way of knowing that words and the feel of a hard male body could make her as bold as a Haymarket Tart. She liked the feeling. She was no longer the shy, timid Emily, but someone else, another creature who was taking over and learning newfound pleasure.

He reached between their bodies and placed his hand atop hers, showing her how to hold him and stroke him. When he increased the rhythm of her strokes, his voice was a ragged rasp. "Tell me, Emily, do you wish to feel me nudging between your thighs? Will you be as willing and wanton when I'm sliding my cock into you?"

"Oh yes," she sighed.

Needing to explore the man who held her entranced, she let her fingers slide into his hair and then glide toward his face. With a sharp breath he pulled away. "The bed," he commanded, reaching for her hand. "I ache with desire. I have waited too long."

His voice was different somehow. More haunting, more familiar. "Do I know you—"

He cut off her words when he lowered his head to her breast and circled her nipple with the tip of his tongue. "No questions tonight, Emily. Only pleasure."

Putting the nagging half-memory behind, she gripped his linen shirt and felt his heat sear her fingers. His skin was hot, his muscles hard and contoured beneath her hands. She sighed when he continued to lave her nipple while he palmed her other breast. Snaking her hands beneath his shirt, she slid her fingers up his smooth skin, kneading the muscles that bunched and tightened. Without warning, he shoved himself out of her arms and reached for her hands. She felt him move away from her at the same time she heard his boot scrape against the floor.

"This is your fantasy, Emily. You don't have to touch me. It is for me touch and pleasure you."

"I've already touched you intimately. Now I want to feel all of you", she said, reaching out again. "Light the candle. I want to see you."

The lock clicked and the door creaked open, and turning in time, Emily saw her mystery lover. His back was to her, but she saw that his shoulders were broad and his hair, a mass of dark waves brushed against the tops of his shoulders. "If your penchant runs to watching, Emily, I'm afraid you will have to choose another, for I am not the sort you would wish to see rutting atop you." And with a solid thunk the door shut soundly behind him.

$$\mathscr{C}hapter\ \mathscr{T}wo$$

November 1808
Richmond, England

I dream of her. I want her more with each passing night. I can no longer go on as I am, desiring to taste her lips, craving the feel of her soft body pressing against mine. I remember all too well the taste of her, the smell of her...
Second Installment of the Dark Lord's Memoir, 'Seduction of the Muse'.

"Please do continue," Emily nodded, waiting for Lord Grey to finish the passage. She was literally sitting on the edge of her seat, waiting to hear every word.

"That is all there is," he said, grimacing as he flipped the newssheet over. "No, I'm afraid you shall have to wait another sennight for more of the infamous Dark Lord's tale of seduction."

"I cannot believe it," Jane huffed, snatching the paper out of her husband's hands. "You waited in a queue for over two hours for this?" Jane scanned the paper then tossed it to Emily. "I daresay the ton will not be amused when they read this. Two months of waiting for more of the Dark Lord's tale and he gives us this? He will soon lose his readers' interest if this is what we can expect from his return to the literary world."

"How wrong you are, my love. This Dark Lord is quite cunning. He knows exactly what sort of delicious details to dangle before the carnivorous Beau Monde. He's feeding them, you see, slow and steady, sure and knowing. No, this Dark Lord is a man who knows what he's about."

"And he can certainly write the most passionate passages, can he not?" Emily peered down at the newssheet. Memories of a stranger's hands and mouth caressing her flesh wound their way into her consciousness. Since the night at the Temple of Flora she had thought of little else except passion. She had a new, intimate perspective in regards to the passions of the soul and the yearnings of the body—*he* had been responsible for making her see and understand those yearnings. Before she had entered The Temple she had been ignorant of the power of pleasure. How that evening had changed her, how the events in that chamber had made her yearn for more—every night now, for months, she had thought of that passionate night and wondered what might have happened had her mysterious stranger not left her.

Shaking off the memory and filling her lungs with a steadying breath, she looked pointedly at the newssheet and felt her heartbeat steadily pound against her ribs. How many times had she read the Dark Lord's memoirs, thinking—feeling that it was she he was thinking of when he was putting his scandalous thoughts to parchment?

"There is no denying that the man is rather skilled with a quill," Jane said with a mischievous grin. "Even me, a happily married woman, has felt her heartbeat quicken a time or two after reading his more passionate musings."

"He does write with an alarming amount of familiarity," Emily said. "To me there is a feeling of intimacy in his work that is not commonly found in novels."

"The man writes with an overwrought flare," Lord Grey grumbled.

"Really, my lord," Emily said defensively, "there is nothing at all offensive about the man. He's passionate and bold and his words ring of a deep desire that few men can own to."

"I'd say you've taken a fancy to the Dark Lord, Emily."

"Well, who could not, my lord?" she said, bristling in her chair and flinging the paper down upon the brocade stool. "I daresay I'm not the only lady in the ton to think so."

"No, obviously not," Lord Grey drawled, picking up the paper once more. "In fact there were more damned ladies waiting in the queue than there were gentlemen. I assume the crush was not for the fashion plates of hunting costumes or the latest designs in rapiers, but instead for the Dark Lord's libidinous prose."

"It's rather strange, isn't it," Jane said while pouring the tea, "that a weekly column intended to titillate the minds and fascination of men has become the most sought-after publication for women. There is a certain frenzy surrounding the Dark Lord that has captured not only the men's interest but the female one as well."

Discreetly clearing her throat, Emily raised the cup to her lips and let her gaze stray out the salon window, watching as the tree limbs, bereft of leaves, waved in the late November breeze.

She was no different from the other women of the ton. The Dark Lord's memoirs had captured her attention also, but not in quite the way her mystery lover at The Temple of Flora had. She could not stop thinking of him, of how familiar his embrace felt, or how she wished she had not turned him from her. She still did not know who he was, despite the obvious fact that he clearly knew her.

"I should see that Aidan is taken some tea," Jane said, her tone suddenly sober.

"Let him come downstairs," Lord Grey muttered while he opened the newssheet.

Swallowing hard, Emily focused on the leaden sky. Pleasant thoughts of her mystery lover floated away, only to be replaced by painful memories of the man she wanted above all others and would never have. Aidan, the Duke of Rutherford. Her heart's greatest desire—her utter despair.

She had secretly loved her best friend's brother since the tender age of fifteen. He had been twenty-two then and the most intriguing man of her acquaintance. She would never forget the moment when her feelings had changed from that of congenial friendship to outright love and adoration.

She had been staying with Jane for the summer. Aidan had been there, entertaining his friends. She came in to the ballroom on a mission to fetch some music sheets from the pianoforte. He was there, shirtless, the muscles of his chest chiseled and glistening with perspiration. He was fencing with his companions and Emily could still hear the clashing of metal and the labored breaths of the men. She could still see Aidan's eyes, a haunting grey-blue, look up from a veil of dark brown waves that had come loose from his queue. Her heart started to pound and her hands shook as she stood frozen to her spot ogling a half-naked Aidan.

She hadn't been able to utter a single word, not even when he had smiled and bowed to her. No, she made strangled, stuttering noises that only made his companions grin and chuckle. Tears welling in her eyes, she fled from the room, humiliated and mortified. But then she heard him, chastising his friends before running out of the room after her. In that moment of his defense of her, Emily had been smitten. Infatuation only deepened until she had completely fallen in love with him. She'd loved him for years, even when she had stood alone in the crowded ballroom of his townhouse and watched him announce his engagement to the outrageously beautiful and much-desired Margaret Thomas.

"Aidan must be parched," Jane murmured once more as she rose from her chair and placed a cup and saucer onto the tray. "He hasn't had breakfast yet."

"Leave it, Jane," Grey commanded as his wife reached for the tea tray. "We've only one infant to take care of."

"How can you say that?" Jane's voice conspicuously lowered an octave. "You're being an insensitive lout."

"I am merely reminding you that your brother is thirty-seven years old. He hasn't needed a nursemaid in quite some time."

"I am not coddling him," Jane insisted with a haughty stamp of her foot that made Emily smile.

"You're mothering him. And you're mother to no one but my son, Jane. Your brother is a man, let him resume that role."

"He's been through an ordeal."

"It's been above a year, at least," Grey said emphatically, sending a shuddering reminder down Emily's spine. "It's past time he came out of the shadows and back into the light of life. I realize that he thinks he's doing the right thing by having his brother oversee the estate. But the truth is, he is avoiding his ducal responsibilities because of his bruised pride, not because of any real infirmity. It is time he saw to the future and went back to his own house. "

It had been more than a year since Emily sat by Aidan's bedside nursing him through the night. A year since she had given in to temptation and lowered her lips to his. Lips that had been full and hard and curved with excruciating pain. In that moment, she couldn't resist those lips, or the chance to take away his pain.

"You're not telling me that I cannot go to my brother, are you?" Jane challenged Grey. "I won't have it. When you agreed he could convalesce in our home, you didn't say anything about making him heal on his own."

Swallowing uneasily, Emily let her gaze stray to the window. It was somewhat uncomfortable to be found in the middle of a quarreling couple, especially when it was Jane and Grey, a couple who were so in tuned to each other that they hardly ever quarreled. But Emily knew that where Aidan was concerned, Jane would fight anyone, even her husband, in order to protect the brother she loved so dearly.

"His injuries have been healed for a year now, Jane," Grey challenged in a firm commanding voice. "It is time for his mind to follow suit."

Emily shuddered again, recalling Aidan's bandaged head, the burns on his back and his left arm and hand. He had been in terrible pain, crying out in agony whenever a treatment was forced upon him, praying for death when he thought he was alone in the room. But he hadn't been alone. She'd been there, soothing him, whispering to him—loving him more than ever. It had been the one and only time she had kissed him, and she promptly left for London the next day, fearing that she could no longer keep from kissing the man she had loved for so long. He had been engaged to Margaret then, and she could not bear to know that once he was healed he would belong to another.

But while his injuries had healed, his mind had not. Aidan had become a recluse, hiding within Jane and Lord Grey's Richmond house. Refusing to be seen, refusing to see her. In the six weeks she had been staying with Jane and her husband and their new baby, Emily had seen nothing of him. Just the briefest glimpse of his broad shoulders as he disappeared amongst shadows as if he were a ghost. He had become a phantom to her and those around him, and she reluctantly concluded that Aidan might very well be lost to her.

"Jane," a familiar voice sounded from the doorway. "My heartiest felicitations."

Whirling in her seat at the sound of Aidan's voice, Emily looked away from the window, only to meet the blue gaze of his twin brother. Her disappointment was acute, and she hid it behind the rim of her cup. It was only Michael after all, not Aidan.

"Michael," Jane cried, jumping up to hug her brother. "We've waited forever for you. Your nephew is nearly six weeks old, you know."

"I had a few things to see to," Michael answered as he hugged his sister. "And to be truthful, I was hoping to give our brother some more time. Has he forgiven me yet for forcing him to see the light?"

A strange expression crossed Jane's features, and Emily couldn't help but notice the nervous glance that Jane sent her way. Michael followed her gaze, and Emily watched as he stiffened in surprise.

"My dear Emily, pray forgive me for not seeing you sooner," he said with a smile. He released Jane and strode to where Emily was seated by the window.

Michael Montgomery, twin to the duke and next in line to inherit the dukedom, was a handsome rogue. He was nearly identical to his elder brother, but with light blue eyes and long brown hair. He was tall and well-muscled, just as Aidan was, but to Emily, Michael lacked Aidan's brooding mystery. Where Michael was lively and jovial, Aidan was cool and distant. Michael was a ready wit and conversed with ease; Aidan, on the other hand, preferred standing alone on the opposite side of the room to watch and listen. Emily had always liked that about Aidan—he had never needed to be the center of attention.

"I daresay, Emily, you look ravishing. You quite take my breath away."

Flushing, Emily allowed Michael to raise her hand to his lips. "You are a shameless flatterer, sir."

He grinned before placing a kiss to her knuckles. Michael had never made her stutter and tremble. She was always at ease with Michael, but never felt that way with Aidan. In the past, whenever they were together an uncomfortable current ran between them. Emily assumed this discomfort indicated that Aidan had somehow discovered her affection for him. The tenseness she always felt emanating from him must stem from his not wanting to hurt her. Aidan had never returned her affections, she knew that.

"So," Michael straightened away from her, drawing her thoughts away from Aidan. "Where is my nephew?"

"I shall ring the bell for nurse," Jane said excitedly. "I cannot wait for you to see him. He's beautiful, brother. A miniature of his father."

Michael smiled dutifully and clasped his hands behind his back, all the while looking about the room as if he were searching it for a means of escape. "Ah, I see you've gotten your hands on the latest installment of the Dark Lord's musings," he groaned. "Don't tell me you indulge my sister with these tales, Grey."

Lord Grey nodded, refusing to look up from his paper. "I do indeed, although I suspect that Emily has more of a taste for the tales than my wife."

"Emily?" Michael turned and appraised her with interest. "Little Emily indulging in wickedness? My dear, you shock me."

"His tales are not so very bad, you know."

"They say his tales of lust and passion border on the gratuitous. It's pornography, my dear."

Emily gasped, but Michael continued on.

"I've heard that the Earl of Chillingworth attempted to bribe the publisher for information about this man. The publisher would not give up the identity of the Dark Lord, but he did say that the upcoming installments were more graphic and shall we say... more visceral than anything that has preceded it. Talk amongst the ton has been rife. Everyone is waiting for the next installment with bated breath."

Emily looked away from Michael's piercing gaze and focused instead on her hands that were folded in her lap. She felt his eyes scouring her, roving along her face then to the décolletage of her breasts. His perusal was bold, interested, and she did not know what to make of it.

"My dear Emily," he drawled, his gaze resting on her tight fitting bodice.

"Allow me to accompany you tonight to the theatre. I fear I am rather eager for your company."

She was certain shock resided in her face, but she hid it from him. Michael had never addressed her so intimately. He had most certainly never looked at her in such a way as he now was.

"Emily?" he asked, taking her hand in his once more. "Might I share the evening with you?"

"I would be delighted," she said, conscious of the way Jane smiled at them. She knew the thoughts running through Jane's mind; they were plain enough to read. Her friend was hoping that she would develop a tendre for Michael. But that was impossible, for it was the other brother who owned her heart. Still, one must not seem impolite in front of one's friends. And the truth was, she hadn't been invited to the theatre in ages, and she did so enjoy the theatre. And wouldn't it be splendid if, by some miracle Aidan discovered her plans for the evening, thereby incurring his jealousy? She smiled over that wistful, misguided thought, even as she relished the idea of Aidan brooding through the halls in a fit of envy.

"The theatre would be lovely," she said, thinking of how she would give anything to have the power over Aidan, the mighty Duke of Rutherford, to make him crazed with lustful jealousy.

"And we shall accompany you," Jane announced.

"And what of our brother?" Michael asked.

"I fear not." Jane glanced uneasily at Grey. "He prefers not to go about in society."

"How very dull," Michael drawled before sliding his gaze once more to Emily. "But then perhaps he's found a more pleasing and vastly more entertaining reason to stay indoors. I know I have."

⁕⋙⟮⁘⟯⋘⁕

Stalking up the carpeted steps, Aidan rounded the curve of the balcony and stood before a pair of red velvet curtains that shielded his box from the rest of the theatre.

"Your Grace," the footman said with surprise before bowing and reaching for the curtain. "Allow me."

"Thank you, no," Aidan mumbled, quickly reaching for the velvet and holding it tightly in place. "I will make as little a scene as possible, I think. I've no wish to disturb the performers."

The young man looked uneasily to the left side of his face before swallowing deeply. "As you wish, your Grace."

Pushing aside the distaste he saw in the footman's expression, Aidan quietly slipped behind the curtain and sat in a chair, angling it so that his presence was shrouded from the couples filling the box beside him. In this position he could not be seen, nor could he see anyone, save for one person—Emily. He had not ventured out into society tonight to take in a play or watch the indelicate activities of the ton. He had risked being seen in society for only one purpose, to see Emily. And she was so bloody close to him, sitting in the next box, leaning against the gilt railing, her lovely eyes glowing in the golden candlelight.

Loosening the length of lace around his throat, he crossed his leg over his knee and settled comfortably into his chair to watch the woman he desired above all others. She looked particularly lovely tonight, dressed in a dove grey silk gown embellished with silver thread and bows. The bodice was tight and form fitting, thrusting her soft breasts into round globes, globes that begged to be touched by a man.

He wanted to run his mouth and chin against their softness, delighting in the smell of her skin, the quiver of flesh beneath his mouth. He visualized his hands reaching for the sleeves of her bodice as he slowly lowered her gown, teasing himself as he exposed her breasts to his gaze and hands, just as he had that night at The Temple of Flora.

Desire filled his loins and he curled his fingers into a fist, ignoring the tautness of the flesh that covered his knuckles. Did Emily ever recall that night? Had she any idea of who her lover was?

It had been two months and he could still taste her, still feel her against him. He regretted that he had to come to her in such a way, hated that he had to hide himself from her. But he was no longer the sort of man who could entice women. He was a monster, not a lover. She would not want him if he were to come to her and declare himself in the light of day.

A flash of black caught his eye and he looked in time to see Michael sitting forward, reaching for Emily's hand and bringing it slowly to his lips. Damn the bastard for being able to sit beside her and touch her. Damn his brother for being able to smell her when it had been an agonizing week since Aidan had allowed himself that pleasure. He had steadfastly avoided Emily since the day she had breezed past him in the hall. She had not seen him standing in the shadows, watching her. But he had seen her, and he had smelled her. The scent of roses on a summer morning had enveloped him, stirring in him a deep, growing hunger that was begging to be fed.

It had not always been this way. There was a time when Emily had barely garnered his notice beyond the niceties required of him. She was his sister's friend, a girl, seven years his junior. She had been plain with hair that was neither blond nor brown. She was short and curvy and his penchant generally ran to tall and slim.

Her bloodlines were impeccable, yet her brother had succeeded only to squander her dowry and run down their estates in the ensuing years. Her brother's neglect had left Emily looking even plainer in gowns that were out-moded and constantly refitted. No, Emily had been unremarkable to him. He had neither liked nor disliked her. Thought her neither beautiful nor ugly. In a phrase, he had thought nothing of her.

But as he looked Emily over, taking in her softly rounded cheeks and green eyes, he realized that he had been a blind, pompous fool when he had failed to notice Emily's qualities. He should have noticed them years ago, and perhaps a part of him had taken notice of her. But he had ruthlessly shoved those thoughts aside and instead pursued the renowned beauties of the ton—the same beauties his friends had wanted and pursued.

It had taken his own humiliation and the destruction of his considerable vanity before he could see Emily through clear eyes. All those nights she had stayed by his bedside, whispering to him, comforting him had made him see her in a new light. He had felt her beauty in every little touch, heard it in every soft, kind word. In his mind he saw her and realized that her beauty was the rarest of kinds.

She had not been the dazzling diamond that Margaret had been. His fiancée had been the most sought-after woman in the ton. With her exotic beauty and lithe, cat-like figure, Margaret had been the type of woman unable to melt into the wallpaper. She had garnered every man's attention and infatuation with her black hair and almond-shaped eyes. She was tall and long-legged with an aura of haughty elegance. He had been taken with her from the minute his eyes had landed on her, and he had decided within that minute that she would one day be his wife.

Coldness and regret settled deep in his chest as his gaze flickered once more over Emily. While Margaret had been stunningly beautiful, she had also been unmercifully selfish and spoiled. He had chosen to ignore that failing, however, hoping that once they were married she would settle and become satisfied with him as her husband and her title of duchess. He had been wrong, of course. Margaret hadn't settled for him, not after she had seen him after his accident.

"A drink, your Grace?" the footman asked, holding a silver tray with a glass of champagne.

He reached for it, suddenly parched and needing the heat of alcohol to warm his insides. Margaret had been a cold, unfeeling bitch, and he would rue the day he had ever asked for her hand in marriage. *Damn that calculating bitch!* And yet he had been miraculously spared the feel of her conniving claws in his flesh. In a perverse irony, he was rather grateful his brother was a proliferate rake, for it had been Michael who had saved him from a lifetime of heartache. After all, Michael had awakened him to Margaret's failings before he had done the unthinkable and married her.

Shutting his eyes, he forced aside the image of Margaret on her knees, his brother's swollen cock pumping in her mouth. He had come upon them in the afternoon. She had been the first person he had sought out after rising from his sickbed, and he had found her in the conservatory entertaining his brother in a way she had never deigned to entertain him.

"Can you bear it?" Michael asked as Margaret's mouth brought him to ecstasy.

"I shall for you, my love. I shall think only of you when I am beneath him."

He had promptly left them, returning to his room and firing off a letter to the deceitful bitch. He had tossed her out of his life as easily as he let her in it, and Michael did just the same, a week later.

Opening his eyes he saw Emily in quiet discourse with his brother, and rage like he had never known flooded his brain. He'd been angry when he'd found his brother with his fiancée, but that anger was nothing comparable to what he was now feeling.

Emily was too good for Michael, too good for him. Michael would toy with her, get what he wanted from her, then leave her heartbroken. And Aidan could not stand to think of Emily's gentle heart being shattered by his reckless brother.

Ever since the night he had nearly taken her in The Temple of Flora, he knew that his fate was tied to hers. He just needed to figure out how he could be a part of her life without having her turn from him in disgust.

Searching his memories, he allowed himself to recall the night he had realized that it was really Emily, not Margaret, his body was clamoring for. It was the night he felt small hands covering his chest, rubbing the pain away, soothing the anguish that always came after a treatment. He felt those tender, comforting hands in his hair, the softness of her voice as she whispered soothingly into his ear. He recalled the tentative touch of her unskilled lips on his. He had tried to believe it was Margaret kissing him. Even through his laudanum haze he had fought the idea that it was really Emily making him feel this way.

That had been the reason he had sought out Margaret when he finally arose from his bed. He needed to wipe away the crazed thoughts of Emily and how she inflamed him with desire. But when he had seen Margaret with Michael, he had been forced to confront the truth—it was not Margaret he was in love with, but Emily.

By the time he had allowed himself to believe it, she was gone. And it was fortunate too, for the day Emily left, his bandages had been removed. Any designs he had for following Emily to London and asking her for her hand in marriage died as the white cloth bandages were peeled from his face.

He remembered that day, sitting in his chair before his dressing table, a mirror up to his face, his lips curling in horror and distaste at the reddened scars that ran from the corner of his left eye to his chin. The burns he could grapple with, they could be covered and disguised. But his face, which resembled that of a monster, could not be hidden. He had promised himself as he traced the scars on his cheek that she would never see him looking like this, like a freak in a traveling show. She would turn from him in disgust, and he could not bear the thought.

But it hadn't kept him from wanting her, or from dreaming about her while he plotted out his erotic seduction of her. And damn him, as frightened as he was of having her turn away from him, that thought was not half as frightening as the prospect that she might find herself ensnared with his rake of a brother. He could not bear the thought of Michael hurting Emily, nor the idea of Michael's hands caressing her flesh. Not even his scarred face was enough to keep him away from Emily when he thought of her being seduced by his brother. That was the real reason he was risking all by being seen; he could not stand to lose her to anyone, least of all his brother, a man whom he knew only too well loved and left his lovers without a thought.

No, if Aidan truly wanted Emily, if he truly needed her, then he must risk everything to have her.

Chapter Three

In the past I have been forced to visit whores to slake my desires. My muse has left me needy. She fuels my desires, she teases me, leaving me in a state of agony that I have no other recourse but to vent my passions upon whores. I am only a man. I have needs.

As sexual congress ensues, I cease to see the woman who works so diligently to arouse me. Instead, I see her, my muse, working to satisfy me until I can no longer resist. I close my eyes and let her take over. It is only then, when my desires are spiraling out of control that I begin to carry out my dreams. My dreams are highly erotic. I should like to tell you one particular dream in which my muse plays the supplicant for me in a house of ill repute. A house that caters to the female appetite and curiosity. It is a temple of sorts. A place to worship the power of carnal pleasures. And in this place I thoroughly, carnally worship her...

Third Installment of the Dark Lord's Memoir, 'Seduction of the Muse'

"What do you mean, that is all?" Emily hissed, tearing the newssheet from Jane's hand. Good God, could it be? Could her mysterious lover be the infamous Dark Lord? No, it wasn't possible, and yet she could not help feeling as though the Dark Lord was writing directly to her. Knowing that no one other than herself was privy to that night, Emily experienced a sensual titillation. *It was their secret.*

"Ssh," Jane whispered, looking about the room to make certain none of the servants had heard them.

"Where did you get this?" Emily asked, her eyes wide as she read the scandalous lines. "I cannot believe this was in the gentleman's review."

"It wasn't." Jane muttered, tearing the paper out of Emily's hands and rifling it beneath numerous papers that littered the table beside them. "I found it amongst my brother's papers after he'd already left the breakfast table. It seems the Dark Lord has ceased writing for the gentleman's review and has now branched out, into his own volume. With memoirs such as that," Jane nodded to the stack of papers, "there is no wonder the review halted his publication. I understand the Dark Lord's volumes can only be found in the gentleman's clubs now. Grey told me the price is exorbitant and the number of volumes purchased has nearly tripled. The men have been clamoring for copies, and it's obvious my brother is no different." Jane fell silent as the door of the breakfast room was thrown open and Lord Grey and Michael entered.

Emily smiled as she met Michael's warm gaze. He had been exceedingly good, not to mention attentive company at the theatre two nights ago, and she greatly enjoyed the easy conversations they shared on their walks through the gardens. He was a very good sort of friend, she realized, and she truly enjoyed his companionship.

"Good day, ladies," Michael said as he stopped before the table and reached for the tea that Jane had just poured. "A frightfully chilly day, is it not?"

"Very," Jane said, smiling mischievously. "One would say it's the perfect sort of morning to spend indoors reading a riveting tale of love and passion."

"How very unsubtle of you, my love," Lord Grey murmured. "I saw you with the Dark Lord's scandalous volume."

Jane merely smiled and allowed her husband to kiss her full on the mouth. "Now then, what have you in your hand?" she asked, reaching around his waist where he concealed something.

"An invitation," he announced waving the missive high in the air. "To Lord Manwaring's yearly masquerade."

"Oh, very exciting." Jane grinned, her eyes dancing between her husband and Emily. "I do hope the entertainment shall prove to be as memorable as last year's."

Grey swooped down and kissed his wife again, and Michael coughed loudly before turning to face her. "Shall you attend, Emily?"

"The invitation does include you, Em," Lord Grey said, showing her the missive.

"I don't have a costume."

"Well, that won't be a problem," Jane announced. Jumping up from her seat, she reached for her wrist and tugged her up from the chair. "Come with me. Mary has a secret room filled with costumes. I'm certain there we can find something for you."

As they left the study and entered the hall, nearly racing to where Jane's lady's maid waited them, Emily was struck by a very strong tingle down her spine. She felt as if she was being watched and she looked over her shoulder only to see the shadowed corners.

"Come," Jane commanded. "We must be quick if Mary is to make you over."

They rounded the corner, and Emily reached out to steady herself against the wall. Her hand brushed something hard and unyielding. "Oh," she cried, freezing mid-stride.

"Forgive me." The deep, rich voice appeared out of nowhere through the dim daylight. "I didn't mean to frighten you."

Her mouth opened then shut, unable to even stutter a sound. It was Aidan standing before her, her hand pressing against his heart, the warmth of his chest penetrating her trembling fingers. His hair was long, much longer and darker than she remembered. The lush waves still rippled to his shoulders, but the sides were thicker. He wore it unbound, the long locks concealing the left side of his face. His eyes, those mysterious gray-blue eyes stared out at her from the shadowed daylight that poured through the French doors, reminding her of another pair of gray eyes—the ones she had seen that night at The Temple of Flora.

"Aidan," Jane said, "How good to see you this morning. I trust you slept well?"

"Yes, thank you," he muttered. "And what of you, Emily? Were your dreams pleasant?"

"I... I..." she swallowed hard and looked at her hand which still lay atop his waistcoat. Suddenly, she pulled her hand away with such swiftness she felt as though she had been branded with a glowing iron.

"Did you dream sweet things, Emily?" he asked, reaching with lightning speed and raising her fingertips to his mouth.

How had he known she'd dreamt of him last night? He could have no knowledge that in her dream he had come to her room and lay down beside her. She could still feel his arms snaking around her waist. She recalled the comforting heat of his naked chest seep through her fine lawn nightgown as he crushed her chest to his and stroked her back with his large palm.

Please, she had pleaded, afraid to open her eyes and have her dream vanish in the darkness. *Kiss me*, she asked over and over, but he only traced her face and the shape of her mouth with his fingertip. *I won't be able to stop at a kiss*, he had replied, his voice deep and husky, calling to her womanly needs. *One kiss*, she pleaded, touching her pursed lips to his throat. Just one, please...

One kiss, he replied, lowering his face to hers so that his breath whispered against her upturned face. *Open for me, Emily, for I want all of you in this kiss*, and then he pressed his mouth against hers, kissing her softly, reverently until she moaned and touched her tongue to his. He deepened the embrace, bruising her lips and clinging to her, kissing her hungrily, devouring her mouth, stroking her tongue with his as he pushed her deeper into the mattress so that she found herself beneath him. Wantonly she kissed him back, clutching at him, as if he would turn to vapor in her arms. She wanted him there with her throughout the night—throughout each and every night.

Beautiful Emily, he murmured against her as he nudged her head back, seeking her throat and unlacing the demure silk ties that held her nightgown together. *I ache for you. I ache to be inside you.* Yes, she had sighed as he slipped her breast free of its linen prison. *I ache for you, too. I want to know what it is like to have you buried deep inside me. I dream of it... yearn for it.*

She had pleaded with him in her dream, nearly begged him to show her passion, but he had refused. And then she had fully awakened to a dark, empty room with only the memories of her vivid dreams to keep her warm.

"Well, come along, Em," Jane said, tugging her away from her frozen spot and the fevered memories in her brain. "We've got work to do if you're going to make a splash at Manwaring's tonight."

"Manwaring?" Aidan asked, his gaze slowly flickered down the front of Emily's plain yellow gown then back up to her face. "Surely you are not going to subject Emily to such a spectacle. Manwaring's soirees are noted to be a dead bore."

"A dead bore? Brother," Jane laughed, tugging Emily along. "You've been out of society for far too long."

Aidan tried for a different tactic, anything to keep Emily away from such a display as one of Manwaring's soirees. "Truly, Jane, you cannot want to go to one of Manrwaring's unpleasant crushes. I believe the accounts of his annual soiree are rather overblown. "

"Unpleasant? Overblown?" Jane asked. "Brother, everyone knows that Manwaring's masquerade is the event of the winter."

Everyone also knew, Aidan thought, as he watched Jane and Emily disappear down the hall, that the reason it was billed the event was because it was nothing more than an orgy for the ton. Manwaring's masquerade was as infamous as it was debauched, and he could not allow his sweet, little Emily to be caught up in such ribald activities.

Sweet little Emily, he thought as he watched her turn the corner. But she was not that sweet. He smiled, recalling how hot she had been in his arms last night. He remembered the scalding heat of that kiss, the fevered mating of tongues and lips as he ravished her mouth with his. He could still feel her supple body trembling with need beneath him and the smell of her arousal. It would have been so easy to lift her gown and sink into her wet, impatient body. She had been eager for his touch and would not have denied him.

It had been so hard to tear himself away from her, to slink back into the dark shadows and watch her sleep the night through. She had slept so deeply that he could not help but wonder what would awaken her. How many times had he made his way back to her bed and stood, watching her sleep, watching as a pale, curved thigh escaped from the bed covers; studying how each slow breath made her breasts rise and fall gently, and listening to those soft breaths as they whispered from swollen, parted lips—lips he wanted so desperately to kiss again. How indulgent he had felt watching her sleep, watching over her. Watching her sleep had endeared her more to him than he ever thought possible.

He'd been so hard, so bloody aroused watching her and thinking of the way she had responded to him—eager, exuberant, unschooled—begging to be properly tutored. And God, he wanted nothing else but to be her tutor in pleasure. But he wanted her awake and willing, knowing that it was him—Aidan—arousing her, not Michael or a dreamy specter or some damned masked stranger at Manwaring's ball.

When I am buried deep inside you, Emily, you will look up at me with your dreamy eyes and see the man who would worship you with everything he has.

I would have you see the man who would pleasure you forever.

She had not awakened when he said those words to her, but instead pressed her face against his hand. *How I love you,* she had whispered, and he had prayed—prayed with every ounce of his being that it was him she had meant to say those words to.

"Ah, there you are," Grey said, standing beside him. "I gathered you already heard?"

"Heard what?" he growled staring after Jane and Emily until they rounded the corner and he could only hear them climbing the steps.

"That she's going to be fed to the wolves tonight."

"I don't know what you mean," he said, clutching his book so tightly he thought his knuckles might break beneath the strain.

"I think you do know what I mean. I know your secret."

"You know nothing, Grey."

"I know you want Emily, don't bother to deny it. I also know that Michael is going to this masquerade and that Jane would welcome a match between him and Emily."

Aidan's gaze lingered on the empty hall where he had last seen Jane tugging Emily by the hand. "You mean that my sister is going to throw Emily to my brother tonight?"

"No, I don't think throw is the right word, but I'm certain that she will do everything in her power to make Emily enticing to Michael. And for my part, I don't believe it will take much for your brother to be encouraged."

Aidan felt his heart come to a grinding halt in his chest. He couldn't breathe when he thought of Emily clutched in Michael's arms.

"Here," Grey said, thrusting a missive against his chest. "Take this and don't mess it up. Don't let your damn pride get in the way of what you want. Live man," Grey said vehemently. "Don't let her go."

Aidan dropped his book on a nearby table before breaking the seal on the missive. "I don't...that is, I can't." But then he recalled how much time Emily had been spending in Michael's company. His brother had been in residence nearly a week, and he had spent much of that time with Emily, wandering the house and the grounds, laughing and talking quietly so that not even Aidan, the man who blended into shadows, could hear them. Every night they had ventured out together, to balls in London and intimate dinners hosted by the best families in Richmond. Each night they had returned home later than the previous evening. Each night he stood at the window waiting to see her, fearing he would catch a glimpse of her locked in an illicit embrace with his brother. Fear gripped his gut as his mind registered the possibility that she had thought he was Michael when he had slipped in bed beside her last night. Had her words been intended for his brother?

"It's a masquerade," Grey said, drawing him out of his dour thoughts. "She doesn't have to know it's you. For once in your life, take what you want."

Aidan stood staring down at the missive, his scarred hand held the ivory

card and he noticed how grotesque it looked against the elegant backdrop of the
black ink. His writing had at one time looked this graceful with curling flour-
ishes he had painstakingly practiced. In disgust, he curled his fingers around
the invitation, crushing the paper with his hand, wishing he could squeeze the
pain from his chest as easily as he did the invitation. He no longer fit into the
glittering world of the ton, where beauty and elegance reined supreme. He no
longer fit in anywhere except the shadows.

"Hello, brother, it has been a while, has it not?"

Aidan looked up from the crinkled paper in his scarred hand to see his
brother step into the dimly lit hall from the salon. Anger turned to rage as he
watched his twin stride confidently up the hall to face him. Michael's long
hair was loose from its queue, hiding a portion of his face. How much they
resembled each other, he realized, staring into his brother's light blue eyes.
Except beneath Michael's brown waves, his face was still whole, still handsome
and unmarked. Still desired.

"Out of the darkness, at last, I see," Michael said, studying him curiously.
His gaze strayed to his left cheek, and Aidan wondered if his brother saw what
he kept hidden behind his long hair.

"I've been here a week and have yet to lay eyes on you. Pray tell me, what
has captured your attention and intrigued you enough to come out of the gloom
and into the light?"

"Nothing that is a concern of yours," he said coolly, bringing himself to
his full height.

"Everything concerns me," Michael replied, holding his gaze steady. "You
are my brother—my twin. We share the same blood—"

"We share nothing!" Aidan hissed. "I am not the man you are. I am not the
sort that goes about and ruins others' happiness."

Michael lifted his chin and folded his arms across his chest. "You would
not have been happy."

"You betrayed me!"

"She is not worth it, brother. Don't let what happened with Margaret destroy you, or us. We have a tie that binds us, a bond that is stronger than most
brothers."

"We did," he snapped making to pass him, but Michael reached out and
tugged at his arm.

"Why would you want someone like her?" he asked. "Someone who would
search out your brother while you lay near death in your sickbed? Why, when
you could have had someone who would have loved you regardless of what
had happened? Who would have placed your head in her lap and held you and
comforted you and whispered words of love in your ear? Why were you willing
to throw your life and happiness away on a woman who wanted nothing more
than a huge estate and unlimited funds?"

Aidan tugged his arm free and straightened his cuff, forcing his gaze away
so that Michael would not see the emotion shining in them. How often had

he wondered the same thing? How had he allowed himself to be blinded by Margaret? How many times had he thanked God that he had seen Margaret with Michael?

"I didn't come to her," Michael said quietly. "She came to me, and I hated her for it. I hated what she was willing to do to you. I hated what she offered."

"But it did not stop you from accepting what she was so enthusiastically giving you," Aidan snarled.

Michael closed his eyes as if he were in pain. "I knew you were there. I knew you would come to find her, to find out if she was the one—" and then he stopped and fixed his gaze on him, watching him with his intelligent, knowing eyes. "I could not allow you to marry a woman who would destroy you. So I allowed her to seduce me, praying you would find us, praying you would hate her enough to turn her away. She was going to destroy you, don't you see," Michael said angrily, reaching for him and gripping him hard on his arm. "You were vulnerable."

"Pity!" He thundered. "You did it out of God damned pity? I would have preferred you allowed her such liberties because you were a red-blooded male ruled by the needs of your cock, not because you were worried over me and my fragile feelings. Jesus, I cannot abide pity. I won't abide it."

"You would not have been happy with her."

The stone dropped from his heart, and he knew that Michael was not the one he wanted to rail at. In truth, he wanted to rail at the world, at the misfortune that had befallen him. It was unfortunate that Michael was here acting as his whipping post, and it was unfair of him to lash out at his brother.

"I realize I would not have been happy with her, Michael, and while I find your method of showing me my intended's true nature perverse, I am thankful for it. I would have regretted the marriage instantly. I would not have been content knowing that she was only suffering through my affections. I want to be wanted—and now that is not possible."

"That is not true—"

"Face reality, brother. I have. No one will want me."

"Aidan," Michael called before he could stalk away. "What of your future? What of the estate? What of the title?"

"You've done an admirable job seeing to the estate since the accident. Have no fear, my anger with you is not so deep that I would see the title go to another. You shall be the next Duke of Rutherford."

"What of heirs, brother? If you do not intend to marry and the title shall fall to me, then I shall have to see to marrying and having children."

"By all means," he snapped, stalking away.

"Then I should like to inform you, Aidan, that I have set my sights on a prospective bride. Someone who will do the title of Duchess proud. Someone who will bear me strong children and love them and me. Someone who will be a comfort at my side and who will warm my bed with passion."

Emily... the name crept in his head and he forced it aside. No, Michael would never choose someone like Emily. Michael could have any woman; he would not pick the woman that Aidan wanted.

"I've grown tired with the rake's life, brother. I want to settle down and feel content with only one woman. I want passion and friendship. I want a woman I want to be with, in and out of bed."

"Who?" he asked quietly, turning at last to face his brother. "Who is this paragon of female virtue that has you willing to sacrifice your rogue appetites for monogamy?"

"Emily Beaumont," Michael said quietly. "Have you any objections, brother?"

The news was like taking a knife through the heart. He could not bear it, could not stand to look at Michael and think of him in bed with Emily. Visions of Emily's lush body moving beneath Michael—beneath the man who looked like him—tormented his mind.

"Have you any objections?" Michael asked again, watching him closely.

Aidan couldn't answer. He was robbed of his voice, his breath, so instead he turned and walked away from his brother.

"When the bloody hell are you going to return to life?" Michael roared. "When are you going to allow yourself to feel?"

Aidan ignored him and turned the corner, stalking up the stairs that led to his chamber.

"I will take her, brother." Michael's words followed him up the stairs, and he felt the weight of them piercing his skin

"And I will be happy with her Aidan, and while you are up in your room and skulking about, and I'm lying satiated between her thighs, and she is holding me to her breasts, I hope your shadows will keep you company and make tolerable any regret you may have over the loss of her."

Chapter Four

Stepping into Manwaring's darkened ballroom, Aidan wished to God that his brother had not decided to wear such an outlandish costume. When he had asked Grey to assist him in his plan, he had nearly choked when his brother-in-law had found him cloistered in his room and dropped the contents of the costume on the bed. Could Michael not have adopted a simple black domino and mask instead of a bloody pirate costume? Bloody hell, the ridiculous feather kept billowing and blowing, dropping red strings onto his nose. He looked like a bloody peacock and he felt as though he stuck out like a sore thumb. Grey was probably even now smirking and grinning like a simpleton.

With a frustrated sigh Aidan tore the hat from his head and set it down atop the table beside him. It was dark enough in the room, Emily would not be able to distinguish him from Michael. Of that he was certain.

Scanning the ballroom, he found his brother, dressed in identical garb, engaged in conversation with his cronies. He watched with satisfaction as the courtesan he had paid to entertain Michael stealthily made her way toward him. Instant interest flared in Michael's eyes and within minutes he was escorting Abigail Layton to a darkened corner. Aidan knew that if he watched a minute longer he'd see his brother disappearing up the stairs, his night's conquest trailing behind him. Bloody hell, the rogue would never change, despite his impassioned declaration that morning in the hall. Wanting one woman, what rubbish. He was supposed to be here with Emily, and yet he was upstairs tupping a whore.

He should be thankful really, that Michael couldn't shake his appetites. If his brother had, he wouldn't find himself able to woo Emily this night. But he had no desire to think any more about his brother. He had only one burning wish and that was to spend the evening with Emily, even if he had to endure playing the part of his twin.

Aidan allowed his gaze to scan the room and he found Emily dancing the minuet with some fool dressed as Julius Caesar. He watched Emily, his hands fisting at his sides, heat and longing infusing his veins as he studied the way she glided elegantly down the line of dancers wearing a scandalous sea foam green concoction that made his blood roar in his ears. She looked like a golden-haired siren arising from the sea amidst filmy silk foam.

He had never seen anything more arousing than the gown that Emily was wearing. The bodice was made of a thin watered silk that he was certain was translucent in the right light. Between the gathered puffs of silk and chiffon were encrusted seed pearls, several strategically placed to conceal the shadow of her areoles and nipples. But instead of disguising them, the pearls only served to draw a man's eye, and his eyes, not to mention his brain, were mesmerized by the teasing possibility he might just get an illicit glimpse.

Reluctantly his gaze left her overflowing bodice and trailed down the length of her gown. The color, a muted green and blue, gave her an ethereal, silvery light that made him blink in wonder. Her hair, which she pulled up high in a chignon looked blonder in the flickering candlelight. Silver netting adorned with pearls covered her hair, completing her Goddess of the Sea costume.

The minuet ended and he watched her curtsey to her partner, the fluffy flounce of her bodice draping invitingly forward, revealing a glimpse of ivory décolletage that begged to be stroked.

Seeing another toga-clad rogue steer himself in her direction, Aidan stepped forward, deftly maneuvering himself in front of the Greek God, and headed for Emily.

"Dance with me."

The voice sent a shiver down her spine and Emily wheeled around and stared up into a pair of eyes that held her bewitched.

"Come," he entreated, tugging her by the hand to where the line formed for another minuet. It was Michael and yet she felt as if she was with another person. He was different tonight. His voice seemed deeper, more haunting than his normal light tone.

"Good evening, my lord pirate," she drawled, curtseying as a violin struck up. "You are a pirate, are you not?"

He said nothing as he stepped forward, taking her hand. His gaze, which was shadowed in the muted light held hers through the openings of his plain black mask. His white ruffled shirt was opened at the throat, revealing a patch of skin that hinted at a muscular chest covered with a sprinkling of hair. She had never seen Michael dressed so informally. He was always one to be immaculately turned out. And yet she much preferred him dressed this way.

"You decided against a hat after all." She smiled, strolling down the line with him and raising herself onto the tips of her jewel encrusted slippers. "Jane was certain you were to be wearing a black hat with a white feather, and Grey was just as certain the feather was to be red."

His gaze held hers, and Emily couldn't help but swallow hard. She felt nervous, almost inadequate when he looked her over. Nonsense. She was being foolish. This was Michael, after all, and there was no need to feel discomposed in his company. So why then when his lips quirked into a lopsided grin did she stutter and choke on her words?

"Do not all pirates wear hats?" she asked, feeling her hand tremble on his as she fought to make conversation.

"I haven't any idea."

"Perhaps you are a buccaneer, then?" she laughed, but the sound became strangled in her throat.

"I am just a man, my sweet. Tell me, what sea nymph are you?"

She looked down at her gown and couldn't help but hear his sharp breath. Looking up from her bodice, she saw that his eyes had turned curiously darker. Almost as gray as... no, she must not do that. She must not compare Michael to Aidan.

"I believe I am supposed to be a mermaid," she answered, looking down at her foamy skirts.

"A siren is more like it," he whispered, before handing her off to another partner.

She watched him and noticed his slow, languid gait as he weaved in and out of the other dancers. She had only ever seen Michael walk with something akin to a general's march—fast and purposeful. Aidan walked with negligent ease, like a jungle cat that had just arisen from sunning himself on a rock. But this was not Aidan; this was Michael. This was also a masquerade, a night for play acting and dressing up. No one was what or who they appeared to be. It was the excitement and the champagne combined with the darkness of the room that was making her confuse Michael with Aidan.

"Do you know what you do to me in this gown?" he asked as they came together once again. She noticed that the familiar twinkle in Michael's teasing gaze was not there this evening. It was not teasing she saw in those glistening eyes, but something else.

"That gown has me thinking very ungentlemanly thoughts."

"Michael," she drawled. "You always were a shameless flatterer."

"Michael." The word was uttered so quietly, so disturbingly, that Emily couldn't help but look back at him over her shoulder.

"I didn't... that is to say...." She couldn't speak, couldn't get the words out, not when he kept staring at her like that.

Aidan wanted to believe that having her in his arms, dancing with her and watching her, was worth any pain it might cause him to hear his brother's name on her lips, but he had been grievously mistaken. Seeing Emily, dressed as she was, listening to her teasing voice that was husky and alluring when she laughed, hearing that same seductive voice whisper his brother's name while he had her standing beside him— it was more then he could bear.

"Michael," she whispered, and then he felt her fingers trembling like butterfly wings against the lace cuff of his shirt. And he knew then that he could not continue the ruse.

"Pray forgive me." Then he bowed before her and promptly left.

Emily stared after the broad back that was ruthlessly and effectively cutting a swath through the crowd. As she watched him, she realized that she was watching a very different man. For this man was not the Michael she had gotten to know this past week. His features were the same, yet there was something about his eyes that were different. It was pain, a haunting emptiness she saw that confused her. He had changed.

Lifting her skirts she recklessly followed him through the crowd of dancers. She saw him leave the room and she followed him down the hall, letting the ring of his boots on the marble tile guide her to him. She passed by a set of stairs and into a darkened hall where only shadows of moonlight lit the path. There appeared to be no exit in the secluded corridor and the sound of boots suddenly ceased.

And then she felt it, a warmth, a soothing comfort engulf her from behind and then he was there, pressing her against the wall as he covered her back with his chest. Her thin gown did nothing to conceal the heat from his body and she felt him, hot and hard pressing against her back.

She had felt this way before. In her dreams she had felt his heat, smelled his scent. She moaned, feeling his hands roam to the front of her gown and creep ever so slowly from her belly, upward. She knew the feel of those hands.

"Remember me, my sweet?"

She trembled when she felt his breath against her ear. His voice was so familiar. She tried to focus on his voice, but his hands were searching her body making thought impossible.

"Do you know who it is making you feel this way?" She nodded, unable to do anything more except that. She felt him tense, felt his fingers press into the tender flesh beneath her breasts. "Do you ever think of that night, Emily? Do you think of what might have happened, or what we might have done to one another?" She whimpered when she felt his finger leave her breast only to trail up her neck and skim to the front of her throat. "I think of that night, Emily. I dream of what I wished to do to you."

She swallowed hard and felt his fingers stroke her throat before lowering achingly to the cleft of her breasts. "Tell me, are you as eager now as you were that night?"

She nodded and he kissed her cheek, his finger sliding down the valley of her breasts. "Show me," he groaned against her throat. "Show me just how eager you are for me."

He turned her around to face him, but she could not make out anything except the outline of his tall frame and the width of his shoulders illuminated in a thin shaft of moonlight. Sliding her hands down his chest, she reached the buttons of his trousers and undid them, not caring that it was Michael making her feel this wanton. It had to be Michael; she had followed him after all.

And now she realized it had been Michael that night at The Temple of Flora. It should have been Aidan making her burn, she so wanted this to have been with Aidan.

Closing her eyes, she imagined Aidan doing this to her. Pushing aside the guilt, she fantasized that it was really him she was with, and emboldened by the thought, she reached into his trousers, freeing his erection. He was hard, the tip of his phallus was thick and throbbing. He groaned when she swirled her finger along the wet tip of him and the sound made her feel bold. She wanted to please him, to discover what he desired. She wanted to pretend that it was Aidan she was having this effect on.

"Slide your hand down me," he rasped against her neck. "Let me feel your fingers around me."

She did what he asked, sliding her hand up and down, feeling him thicken and lengthen against fingers. With a hissing breath, he reached for her skirts and gathered the chiffon in his hands, raising the fabric until she could feel his hands grazing her thighs.

Gripping him firmer, she cupped the soft sac of skin between his legs at the same time he stroked her sex. She froze at the intimacy of it, but as soon as she felt him part her and his finger stroke the sensitive nub, she moaned and writhed against the wall.

"Spread your legs for me—wide." Not waiting for her to comply, he went to his knees and lifted her leg so that her foot rested on his shoulder.

"What are you doing?" she cried, steadying herself against the wall.

"Tasting you," he said before she felt his hot tongue rake along her folds. "You're so aroused, I want to taste it," he murmured before stroking her with his tongue again. She whimpered in shame and pleasure. She should not be allowing this, and most certainly not here of all places. But how could she stop something that felt this good?

"Hold your skirt," he demanded, shoving fistful of chiffon in her hands. Before she knew his intent, he spread her sex with his fingers and circled her opening with his tongue. "I am so eager to put my cock in here." His voice was full of passion and it made her knees weak. "Would you like that, Emily?

"Yes," she cried feeling her body coil tightly. And then he was circling the nubbin of flesh with his tongue, flicking it so that she was gripping his hair and thrusting her hips in a rhythm he matched with his mouth.

"Come for me," he encouraged.

With a keening cry, she straightened, her body tense, her eyes tightly shut. She didn't think she could bear such pleasure, but then he lowered her leg and stood, bringing his mouth down hard on hers, stifling her cries while his fingers thrust into her, stroking the last of her climax from her body.

"You will remember me tonight?" he asked, his mouth pressing against her brow as the last waves of pleasure coursed through her. She nodded, fearing she had lost all ability to speak. She would never forget that it was Michael who had done this to her, nor would she forget that she had pretended it was Aidan. She was a fallen woman to have done the things she had with one brother while dreaming of the other.

"Tomorrow night, Emily, I will come for you, and I will not deny myself. You belong to me."

"Tell me who has given me so much pleasure," she whispered, needing to hear the words that would draw her from her fevered dreams.

She felt his body stiffen but he did not release her. "I am the Dark Lord and you, Emily, are my muse."

※)(☾☉)(※

Stirring, Aidan stretched then tossed away the blankets covering his legs. Sliding out of bed, he ignored the stinging coldness of the wooden floor and donned his dressing gown. The fire had died, leaving only a handful of glowing embers in the hearth, casting the room in dampness. Outside, he could hear the wind howling through naked tree limbs.

Strolling to the window he gazed out at the black night, watching as a curtain of snow fell steadily from heavy clouds to blanket the ground below.

He did not relish the idea of leaving his warm bed. He had been far too snug and comfortable in it with memories of Emily keeping him warm.

Pushing away from the window, he walked to the hearth, reached for the fireplace poker and stirred the glowing embers, sending an orange spark sizzling up the flue. Tossing two thick logs onto the pile, he waited till the fire caught and flames of heat flickered to life. Shaking off the cold, he reached for a candlestick that sat atop the mantle, lit the wick and made his way to his secretaire.

The small ormolu clock that rested atop the desk ticked quietly on, the rhythm soothing him as he reached for a stack of vellum and dipped the nib of his quill into the inkwell. It was half past four and the earth was asleep. There wasn't a sound to be had, save for the familiar ticking clock, the snap of a log in the fire and the occasional hissing of the candle flame when a draft would breeze past.

Glancing up, he saw a cloud shroud the glittering moon, heard the wind pick up and rattle the shutters outside the window. It was cold and blustery, the atmosphere unsettled, the wind, almost violent. It was the perfect ambiance for writing.

His mind was swimming with prose. Thoughts and desires flooded his brain until he knew that he must leave his bed and scribble them down lest he be plagued by them for the remainder of the night. He had learned over the years that it was best to write while the iron was still hot, while the ideas and images burned in his mind. Waiting till the instrument of his passion had cooled served only to frustrate him.

Tapping the nib against the rim of the silver inkwell, he pondered how a man reputed to be aloof and unfeeling could have become a slave to his passion. For he was a slave to writing.

When he wasn't fantasizing about Emily and his increasing desire for her, he was thinking of writing. Plots and characters burned in his brain and more often than not he found himself gazing out a nearby window, ignorant of all that was going on around him, heedless of voices or conversations save for those running rampant in his brain.

It had always been this way for him—since he was a young boy, alone and isolated at Eton. He had never been able to express himself properly, so his past mistresses and Margaret had informed him. He was closed, cold and unfeeling. Even during his most intimate moments with these women he had held himself back. Never allowing himself to fully feel desire or to express what he was feeling. His lovers always wanted more from him—they needed to hear the words, they had told him. But he was not good with spoken words. But the written word he had mastered.

Something magical happened when he picked up a quill and set it to paper. He ceased to be the Duke of Rutherford and instead became nothing more than a vessel through which the characters in his mind told their story. When he was writing he was someone else—anyone but the scarred and lonely duke.

No one knew of his passion; he had never spoken of it. He had penned several books that were all the rage throughout the ton, but he had written them under a false name, never having shared his success with anyone. To him, writing was the window of the soul. There was far more of him in his writing than anyone would ever know, and he did not want to share that with anyone.

But now Emily knew. His Emily knew his greatest secret—that the man who kissed her so longingly was the scandalous Dark Lord, the man whose erotic fantasies fueled the lustful imaginations of the Beau Monde. Emily was his muse, the passion behind the tale, the woman in each erotic passage.

When he had started such a project he hadn't any idea that his impassioned thoughts would be gobbled up by anyone who could read. He certainly hadn't thought Emily, the woman behind the tale, would take an interest in it. But she had, and that had served his purposes perfectly tonight.

After he had left her in the ballroom, he had been full of impotent rage. Angry with her for not seeing him behind the costume, disgusted with himself for even thinking of playing the part of his brother. When he had stalked away from her, it had been because he feared he'd tear off his mask and show her exactly who held her in his arms. He had so desperately wanted to see her face in the candlelight when she looked upon him. But he had feared her response as much as he longed for it.

Had he torn the mask from his face and allowed her to see the three white jagged lines that ran from the edge of his left brow to the corner of his mouth he would have sealed his fate. He hadn't been ready to show himself—his scarred self—to Emily and see disgust in her face.

That had been the reason he'd told her his secret. When he had felt her tremble against him during her orgasm, when his lips had grazed her smooth skin and sweet neck he had felt the passion in her, knew that she could be made to want him. In the dark alcove, her breasts inches from his hands, his cock pressed up against the soft globes of her bottom, she had wanted him.

His gaze strayed to the glint of iridescent pearls that shone in the candle-light. Picking up the silver netting that had covered Emily's hair, he recalled her whimpers and soft moans. He could still hear the catching of her breath, feel her breasts straining against the bodice of her gown as his hands inched closer to them.

Picking up the quill, he glanced once more at the netting encrusted with pearls and decided that perhaps Emily needed to know just how badly he had wanted to take her in the alcove—how desperately he still wanted her.

Chapter Five

Michael came into the salon shielding his eyes from the bright morning sun. "Tea," he commanded in a gruff, growling voice.

"Under the weather?" Grey drawled, folding his paper and laying it in his lap.

"Damn, but I feel like I've been hit upside the head with a shovel."

Michael took the cup of tea from Jane and walked unsteadily to the settee. Emily studied him from behind the rim of her own cup and watched him flop down on the cushions, one hand holding his cup, the other his head.

"There are eggs and toast on the sideboard," Jane said cheerily. "I can fix you a plate if you'd like. Or we have kippers. Sometimes kippers are the very things to ease an unsettled stomach."

Grey said with a chuckle, "I don't think kippers and eggs go over well when one is suffering the morning effects of too much champagne, my love. Too runny and a bit too slimy to be of benefit." Emily swore Michael turned a ghastly shade of green.

"Bloody hell." Michael winced. "Let us not talk of food."

It was obvious Michael was suffering mightily this morning. Emily had seen her brother hung over from the ill effects of alcohol too many times to miss the symptoms. No, there was no doubting that Michael had gotten terribly foxed last night. The only question that remained was whether he was deep in his cups when he had touched her so intimately in the dark.

Did he recall what they had done? Did he remember what he had told her, that he had claimed he was the infamous Dark Lord? Her brother had always tried to protest that he could never remember anything after a night spent drinking and gambling. Was Michael the same? Had he forgotten their heated embrace?

"More," Michael demanded, holding out his cup to Jane. "Just black."

"Let him get it, Jane," Grey growled, sending a ferocious glare in Michael's direction. "You are no man's servant. It is not your fault he managed to get himself cup shot. It's his own doing, let him see to his own comfort."

"Bloody hell," Michael groaned, waving the cup toward her. "Em, be a darling and get me another cup, will you? I vow I shall cast up my accounts right here if I am forced to get up."

"If you vomit before my wife and Emily, Montgomery," Grey said, "I shall give you a thrashing you will never forget."

"I don't mind," Emily said quietly, rising from her chair. "I shall pour you a cup of tea, Michael."

"What a sweet creature you are, Em," he said, reaching for her hand and kissing her fingers. "You're the sort of woman a man wants to find running his household when he arrives home from Town."

Emily looked down at the man seated before her and could not discern anything familiar about him. His voice, his lips against her skin, even his eyes did not resemble the man he had been last night. There was no delicious tremor snaking down her spine when his lips touched her hand, nor a strange flipping sensation in her stomach when she looked into his pale eyes. There was nothing that rekindled the stark need she had felt for him last night when he'd held her in his arms.

And yet it had been his hands she had burned beneath. His mouth that had brought on the shaking tremors that had rippled through her body. Her visions of Aidan had been nothing but fantasy, Michael's hands touching her had been the reality. But no matter how logical she tried to be, no matter how hard she shoved her dreams aside, she could not stop herself from wishing that it had been Aidan.

"The tea," he reminded her, shoving the cup into her hand and interrupting her musings.

"Oh, yes," she nodded, shaking off the disturbing thoughts.

"How did you find Manwaring's little masquerade?" Michael asked, as he slid further into the cushions so that his pose was at once indolent and insolent.

"Lovely," Jane smiled.

"Highly satisfying," Grey announced.

"And you, Em? What did you think?"

"Interesting," she murmured, stirring the sugar in his tea and walking back toward him.

"Interesting?" Michael asked, sipping the brew.

"Well, everything was a game, was it not? Everyone in costume pretending to be someone they were not."

Michael actually flushed and sipped his tea again. How could this man be the one responsible for filling her body with a rush of desire she never knew was possible? She had lain awake dreaming of him, her body burning for him and yet he'd been drunk when he'd done it. He showed no outward signs of remembering what he had done to her and Emily felt sick at the thought. Perhaps he hadn't even known who it was he was groping in the dark. Perhaps to Michael one female was easily replaced with another. Perhaps it was another man all together.

Aidan... the name snuck into her consciousness. It could not have been him—despite her longing. Aidan never left Jane's house, so he could not have overheard their discussion, and it could not have been him that night at The Temple of Flora. And yet, as she watched Michael, she strived to bring back the heat that had coursed through her veins when he had touched her last night.

In fact, she could not bring herself to believe that her love and desire for Aidan could be so easily swayed by his brother. Just thinking of Aidan made her heart race. And watching Michael made her doubt that he had been the man to awaken her desires.

"My lady," Harding, Grey's butler announced from the doorway. "My young lord is bellowing like a banshee. I believe he requires his breakfast."

"Of course," Jane said, jumping up from her chair.

"I shall come with you," Grey murmured, reaching for Jane's hand. "Let me bring him to you, Jane. I will meet you in our chamber."

Emily watched Grey escort Jane from the room, a feeling of wistful longing twisting her heart. Looking over at the settee, she watched as Michael's head bobbed forward then reared sharply back to rest against the carved wood, a soft snore escaping his lips. Reposed like he was, like a debauched rakehell, Emily knew with certainty that he could not have been the man she had allowed to touch her last night.

Nervous energy trickled along her spine. If it had not been Michael, then who the devil had she been with?

Harding's voice drew her gaze from Michael. "The post has arrived, Miss."

Emily let her gaze slip to Harding's wrinkled hands. One elegant white bloom tied with a blood-red ribbon graced his hands.

"The post?" she asked reaching for the flower and accompanying missive.

"By messenger, madam."

"How beautiful," she whispered, gazing at the lily and its pure white petals.

"And rare," Harding added. "Whoever sent it must have scoured London for it and paid a king's ransom, for calla lilies are not to be found this time of year."

Unable to hide her smile, Emily gazed up at Harding. "I've never seen anything quite as elegant or exotic as this flower."

"Your smile will make him happy," Harding whispered.

"Who sent this?" she asked, reaching for his wrist and stilling him. His dark eyes scoured her face in a very disconcerting way, putting Emily's instincts on alert.

"You do not know?"

"No, I don't."

"I think you do, my lady. You've only to search your heart for the answer."

"Em?" Michael snorted, sitting up and rubbing his eyes. "Oh, wondered if you were still here. Thought I might have a word with you, if I may. It's about last night."

"Search your heart for the answers you seek, my lady," Harding whispered.

"What's he whispering to you?" Michael snarled.

"He's brought me the post, that is all," Emily replied as she watched Harding bow benevolently before her.

"The post? Looks like you're holding some damned flower." Michael rose from the cushions and stood, wavering for the briefest of seconds before walking toward her. "Damn me, Emily, but what rogue is sending you flowers? And a flower with such a meaning?"

"I'm afraid I do not know what you mean."

"That damned lily," he growled, snatching it out of her hand. "It means a forbidden meeting, and this," he muttered, ripping the red satin bow from the stem and snapping the stalk in half in the process, "this ribbon is the color of passion. Who has sent you this?"

"I have no idea," she snapped before snatching the ribbon out of his hand. "But I'm certain it is of no concern of yours."

He reached for her elbow and lifted her from her chair, forcing her to meet his gaze. "Just what happened at Manwaring's masquerade last night, Emily?"

"Why?" she asked innocently. "Don't you remember, Michael?"

His face went white, and Emily knew then that she had her answer. It could not have been Michael she had been with in the alcove. Perhaps he had been her dance partner, but the man who had lit her body afire had not been Michael. Her Dark Lover had been someone else.

With a muffled curse, he dropped her arm and stalked to the window. She didn't wait for him to speak; instead, she lifted her skirts and ran from the room, straight to her bedroom. Slamming the door shut she rested against it and tore open the red wax seal of the missive.

A carriage will be waiting for you at the end of the lane. Come to me at midnight. The Dark Lord.

Swallowing hard, Emily sank to the floor and read the missive again. Here was her chance, an opportunity to experience what she craved. Was she brave enough to reach for it; was she sure enough to accept his offer?

"Who are you," she whispered aloud, "and am I safe with you?"

Chapter Six

The carriage door closed behind her. Settling herself onto the bench, Emily took a deep, steadying breath. She'd done it. She had escaped the house without being discovered. The carriage, its door marker swathed in black crepe, had been waiting for her at precisely midnight.

Jangling of harnesses and the clomping of hooves told her they would soon be on their way, but where they were headed, she hadn't any idea. It was madness, she decided in a rush of panic as the snap of the whip whistled through the air, driving the horses onward. What did she know of this man? Nothing.

Shivering in the cold, she brought her cloak tightly around her and studied the carriage. Was she doing the right thing, or was she being foolish, throwing her reputation to the breeze and all for a taste of illicit pleasure? In truth, was what she was doing more dangerous or illicit than going to The Temple of Flora. What had she known of the men then? Were they just not strangers as well?

She had tried to convince herself it was dangerous and likely would result in nothing more then her reputation lying in tatters before her, but her heart had refused to listen to her brain. Never had her body felt so alive. There was something in the Dark Lord's touch that made her want, no, crave his embrace. She could no more ignore his command to come to him than she could cease breathing.

The carriage rumbled on and Emily forced herself to remain calm, but with every turn of the wheel the carriage brought her closer to her fate, making her wonder over and over again if she was making the right decision. Her heart told her that she must come to this secret meeting and that if she did not, she might not have another opportunity to experience what he was offering. And she so desperately wanted to relive the passion he awoke in her. She had allowed her love for Aidan to keep her passions imprisoned inside her. Aidan did not desire her as she desired him. He would never want her in such a way, he was lost to her, lost in his own misery and couldn't even see her, or the desire she had for him. Her obsession with Aidan was a hopeless pursuit, but her night with the Dark Lord was not.

The carriage swayed to the left and the wheels slowed, coming to a halt seconds later. Emily felt her heart freeze, her blood halted in her veins for what seemed like eternity before she heard the coachman jump from the box and land onto what sounded like gravel.

The door opened, letting in a frigid gust of wind. A gloved hand reached in for her and slowly drew her from her seat. "Your hand trembles. Fear not. You will come to no harm."

Her gaze flew from the gloved hand that encircled her fingers and peered up into a hooded form that shielded the coachman's face. She could not see his features in the dark gloom, nor could she decipher why his voice sounded disturbingly familiar.

With ease he pulled her forward and gently assisted her down the carriage steps. Once outside she shielded her eyes against the blowing snow to see what looked like a crofter's cottage.

"Inside. He waits for you."

She whirled around only to see that the coachman had already climbed up to the box and taken the reins in his hands. Before she could protest, he urged the horses forward and left her.

As if in a dream, she stepped forward, her gaze fixed on a warm glow from the window. It was freezing cold outside, the wind bitter, biting at her cheeks and lips. It would be warm in the cottage. And he would be there.

Without any thought, she reached for the handle, half expecting to find it locked. It turned with ease, allowing the door to creak ever so softly open.

He was in there, waiting for her, perhaps even watching her. Her body felt his presence as she stepped over the threshold, leaving her past behind in the blowing snow and the darkness of night.

∗≈⟨♡⟩≈∗

He watched her through the window, a vision in a white velvet cloak trimmed in ermine. Against the snowy backdrop she appeared as an angel preparing to give herself up to the devil.

She looked up, her green gaze scanning the small cottage that sat at the edge of Grey's extensive grounds. She did not see him through the glass, for he stood in darkness and her eye was drawn to the warm glow of the fire in the room next to him.

She exemplified good and light and he couldn't help but think that he was nothing but a ghost who hid amongst shadows, a voyeur who could do nothing but watch and yearn and dream of possessing such a creature.

The door creaked open and his blood hummed with anticipation, the sort of eagerness that filled one's veins with sexual yearning. His body in tune with hers, he felt her nervousness, could hear the steadily increasing beating of her heart. She was afraid—he sensed it, and found he did not like it. He didn't want Emily to fear him. He wanted her, yes, but he wanted her willingly.

The sound of the cloak sliding from her body slaked along his nerves, stretching them until they were nothing but taut strands. He needed her. His body was crying out for the taste of her skin beneath his lips, her mouth against his. He needed her beneath him, to feel himself slipping inside her body, to release his desire inside her and allow himself the pleasure of falling asleep atop her.

Cracking the door open he watched her standing before the hearth, rubbing her hands before the blazing flames. He allowed his gaze to wander down the length of her body, wishing she had worn one of her lighter-weight gowns so that he could see the outline of her figure. But practical Emily had deprived him of such a pleasure. No doubt she hadn't any idea how arousing it could be to see the curve of a woman's body outlined by flickering flames.

He heard her sigh and he raised his gaze from her rounded bottom in time to see her replace a few loose curls back into the coil atop her head. His gaze slipped down the elegant column of her neck and he couldn't help but feel a sense of satisfaction fill him at the sight of the red ribbon that encircled her throat.

His boot scraped against the wooden floorboard and she whirled around, her eyes wide with surprise and perhaps fear. He wanted to give himself up, to appease her fear, but he stopped, wondering if she would not be more afraid by the sight of him.

He must remember that she did not know his identity. As far as she knew it was the Dark Lord she was meeting. And it was far too early in this game of seduction to admit the truth to her. She was not yet entranced with him. Only when she was a slave to her desires, her desire for him, could he allow her to see him. Only then would he risk his heart and his future by showing her who had awakened her womanly passions.

She stepped away from the hearth and he could not help but hold his breath as she came closer to the room. He could smell her now, sweet roses that reminded him of a warm summer day. He could hear her breathing, rapid and shallow, reminding him of her pants of desire as she came for him and how the sound aroused him.

Bloody hell, he was on fire for her. Never had his cock been this hard, his desire this uncontrollable. He wanted her, with a passion that was near to consuming him.

Stepping into the darkened room, Emily made a slow circle, trying to accustom herself to the darkness. He was here in the room, she felt him, sensed his presence—a sensual, masculine aura that made her blood flow hot and heavy. She heard his breath deep within his chest and she felt desire quicken within her. A reckless yearning gripped her and she was helpless to do anything but give herself over to his invisible force.

"Where are you?" she asked, her voice nothing but a husky whisper.

"Behind you."

She whirled around and felt his large hands clasp her face. His breath was warm against her mouth and she closed her eyes waiting for his kiss. His mouth came down soft against hers and she sighed, letting her body sway into his. He groaned, deepening the kiss, sliding his tongue between her lips, circling her tongue with his as he slanted his mouth over hers while he gently fanned his thumbs along her cheeks.

Moaning, she reached for the ends of his hair and loosened it from its queue. It was soft, the waves spilling through her fingers as she raked her hands through his hair with each drugging motion of his lips. The sound of his groan, their lips crushed against each other, the taste of him on her tongue fueled her desire, made her shed her inhibitions, and she rubbed her bodice, which was unbearably tight against her swelling breasts, along the fine linen of his shirt. His hand shot around to the nape of her neck and she felt his fingers tighten against her flesh, his index finger slipped along the edge of the red satin ribbon, teasing her with his touch. Needing to feel his warm skin beneath her hands, she trailed her finger down his ear and over to his cheek. He pulled away, breaking off their kiss, leaving her protesting and reaching for him.

"So eager, aren't you," he murmured, taking her hands in his and pulling her away from the window. "You are not so innocent are you, Emily? You know how to use your body to make a man weak, to make him burn."

He didn't wait for her answer; instead he placed his hands on her shoulders and turned her away from him. She heard the creaking of a mattress, felt his body slide along hers, felt his knees press against the back of her thighs before he reached for her and sat her atop his lap, her legs dangling on either side of his hard thighs.

"I like you this way, Emily," he said against her neck as he smoothed his finger over her shoulder. "I like to know that you are as eager to experience the delights of passion as I am to show you."

She could only close her eyes and allow her head to hang to the side, letting him nuzzle the hollow beneath her ear and the tender flesh of her neck. His finger traced the satin ribbon and his hand cupped her throat.

"There is darkness in every man, Emily, a place where passions and yearning lurk, a place where an innocent such as yourself should never dare go."

She whimpered, unable to stem the desire rushing through her veins. Was he warning her away from him, from his desires? Was he offering her a chance to run from him?

"Inside of me are dark passions, passions that only you arouse, Emily. I struggle with them. I'm struggling now, trying to subdue the hunger that is threatening to consume me."

"Do you think I am so innocent? You're wrong, I, too have darkness and passion in me. I don't want you to subdue your hunger. I want to share that hunger with you."

His lips skated down her neck to nuzzle at her shoulder and she couldn't help but allow herself to sink further onto his lap. She said nothing when she felt the hard bulge of his arousal beneath her bottom.

"I want to touch you all over. I want your breasts in my hands, your nipples against my tongue, my cock inching inside you."

She sighed, a thrilling whisper that escaped through her parted lips when she felt his erection throb beneath her. Instinctively she brushed her bottom along the hardness, her lips parting in a silent plea for more.

"You like this, don't you?" His hand tightened ever so softly against her throat. But it was not an embrace of cruelty or a show of his strength, instead it was a caress of barely controlled passion. The touch of a lover who was burning with desire. A lover who was burning for her. "You like the seduction of words, the eroticism of being aroused with only my thoughts and desires being uttered in the dark, don't you, Emily? I could make you come for me with only words, do you know that?"

She didn't know anything, save for the fact she desperately needed to feel his touch.

"I thought to seduce you with my hands, with the touch of my lips against your skin, but you're so responsive to my voice. I like that I can make you hot and wet with only words. Tell me, Emily, do you read my column?"

"Yes," she shuddered, feeling his fingers glide along the length of her spine.

"Does it leave you yearning for more?" She nodded and held her breath as he slowly unfastened the tapes of her gown. "Does it arouse you?"

"Very much," she admitted, restlessly moving her bottom on his lap. "But you never tell the whole story—you tease, dangling bits so that your readers are breathless, waiting for your next installment."

His lips grazed her shoulder as he lowered the sleeves of her gown, revealing her shift beneath. "Are you left breathless, Emily?"

He lifted her from his lap and shoved the gown down her hips till it puddled about her knees, then he grasped her by the waist and brought her down on his lap so that her naked sex was atop the smooth silk of his breeches. "Do you want to know what I yearn to write in my column? Shall I tell you and arouse you with my fantasies?"

She nodded feeling her blood heat so hot that she yearned to have him tear the shift from her body. And yet she liked the feeling of the warmth heating her skin and blood. She wanted the words, his heated whispers and dark promises.

"In my dreams, you are mine, mine to command. I touch you wherever I want, whenever I want. You deny me nothing." His finger whispered along her nape, pulling strands of hair free from her coiffure. "You are always naked before me, your breasts, full and large captivate my attention and I cannot help but circle your rosebud nipples with my finger, hardening them until you are panting for more. I would use my tongue to lave them, but then I would be deprived of seeing your face, of watching your body writhe beneath my ministrations. That is how I wanted you that night at The Temple of Flora. You were wet and eager and my cock was straining for release. You wanted my cock inside you, didn't you?" She whimpered, wishing he would do just what he was suggesting.

"How much you like this talk," he whispered. "I can feel you becoming wetter and wetter. It is forbidden and illicit and it calls to your deep desires, does it not? Very well, Emily," his lips brushed the tender skin beneath her ear, and his tongue came out in a short flick before he whispered,. "I will fuck you with words."

She gasped at his crudeness, but at the same time she felt a thrilling sensation snake along her nerves. "Tell me more," she said on a little pant. "I want to hear the words you would write to me in your memoirs."

"I've done things to you in my dreams that you could never know of. I've had you in ways you could never dream of. I've tasted you. I've swallowed your cries of desire and your release of passion. I've watched as you've come for me."

Her breath shuddered once more as she moved her sex restlessly along his hard body, delighting in the soothing, yet painfully arousing feel of the cool silk against her throbbing sex. Her senses were attuned to the feel of him, the smell of him, the deepening of his voice with passion as he told her his secrets. The desire was building, coming to a head as she quickened her strokes, silently pleading with him to touch her. To take her breasts in his hands, to do everything he was telling her he had dreamed of doing.

"In my dreams I've taught you to touch me the way I want. I've laid back upon my bed and envisioned you on your knees, naked and aroused, my cock filling your lovely pink mouth."

Her heart thudded against her breast, her body moving of its own accord with only his words encouraging her. She was so close to something, to an abyss she knew was waiting her.

"That's it, Emily, listen to the words. Feel me, hard and searching beneath your bottom. Imagine me freeing myself and slipping into your heated body. Imagine riding me, commanding me to take you in a way you want."

"Yes,"

"I want to see you on your knees with your perfect bottom before me. I want to watch as I slide into you. I want to hear your moans when you feel me stretching you."

"Oh yes," she cried, digging her nails harder into his legs. He reached for her hips and increased her rhythm until she felt her body coil tightly before she felt herself floating and going limp on his lap.

He reached for her, the first time his hands had really touched her since he began his seduction of words. He wrapped his arms around her and brought her back against his chest while nuzzling her jaw. "What you experienced was only with words—imagine how it will be when I make good on each one of my fantasies."

Tilting her head up, she looked up at his face that was cast in darkness. She could only discern the outline of his hair and shoulders, before the silver moon broke free of the clouds and made its way across the sky. A sliver of light shone in the window, just enough so that she could see a familiar pair of haunting gray eyes peering down at her. Her heart skidded to a stop, and the world seemed to stop spinning. Aidan.

It truly was him. Her deepest fantasy—all her fantasies come true. Elation swept through her and she reached out and skimmed her finger along his jaw, unable to fully understand or believe that she was being loved the man of her dreams.

"Sleep, Emily, and dream the dream of the satiated. We have the entire night before us in which we may pleasure each other."

"Tell me, what pleasure did you experience this night?"

His eyes scoured her face, and Emily had the urge to throw her arms around him and tell him that she knew who he was. That he was not Michael, or the Dark Lord, but Aidan, the man she had loved for a lifetime. But she resisted, knowing that he was concealing his identity for a reason. What reason she would still have to learn, but not tonight. Tonight was for living out dreams and passions. Tomorrow could be for the shedding of secrets.

"Tell me," she whispered, holding his gaze, a gaze that no longer looked haunted.

"I will write it down, my sweet Siren so that everyone shall know of the pleasure you have given me this night."

"But what of your own pleasure?"

"Sleep," he whispered, kissing her brow. "Let me feel you in my arms, your breath against my cheek and your heart against mine. Later I will find my pleasure."

Emily felt her lids flutter closed despite her resolve not to spend these precious hours with Aidan in a state of sleep, She told herself that she would not waste this night sleeping, but as Aidan held her closer to him and she heard the soothing rhythm of his heart beneath her ear she drifted off, locked tightly in his arms.

Chapter Seven

The thin chemise tore easily in his hands and without thought or guilt he ripped it up the center, revealing her pale body in the moonlight. Breasts, round and full rose and fell with deep breaths as she stirred in her sleep.

Hungrily his gaze raked over Emily's voluptuous curves, drinking in everything he had longed to see. There was enough moonlight to illuminate her body and the V between her thighs as she spread them for him. There was just enough shadow to protect his face, to hide his identity from her as he aroused her into wakefulness.

He cupped her breast, stroking her nipple and watching as it puckered beneath his thumb. Already painfully aroused, he felt himself swell further, and to relieve a fraction of the ache in his groin, he brushed his cock along her milky white thigh. None of his suffering was abated however, and he stroked himself along her smooth skin over and over, watching the tantalizing visual of his flesh atop hers.

She stirred and sighed huskily, still slumbering dreamily while he fondled her breasts. His gaze slipped to her face and he watched her lips part when he pressed her breasts together. Damn but he needed to feel those lips on his cock.

Raising himself to his knees, he nudged her thighs wider and kneeled between them, resting his weight on his hands. Pressing forward, he trailed his mouth between her breasts, down her belly where he circled her navel with his tongue. Gooseflesh erupted on her skin, fanning out along her midriff. She stretched then reached for him, clutching his hair in her fingers and he gazed up from her belly and saw her eye lashes begin to flutter, only to reveal her passion glazed eyes.

Tonguing her belly again he listened for her sighs, felt her hips shift on the bed and he lowered his mouth to the curls that were damp. Spreading the soft folds, he raked his tongue up the length of her, waking her with his mouth. She was wet and writhing, her fingers curling in his hair while her hips moved in an intoxicating, erotic rhythm against his tongue that was searching and probing.

"Oh, yes," she sighed rubbing her sex against him. "Please," she said with a keening cry as she tensed and tightened while he drew out her pleasure. But he stopped his ministrations just before she reached ecstasy. He wanted her wild for him, much more so than this. And truth be told, he wanted his pleasure, too.

Sliding along her body, he licked the valley of her breasts and slid his now rampant erection between the full mounds. He showed her how to press her breasts together to increase his pleasure and he groaned, watching his cock slide between her breasts.

"Use your tongue and lick the tip of me."

She did not protest or act afraid. Instead, her pink tongue crept out and licked him slowly, teasingly so that he nudged his cock further into her mouth, and her eyes widened with shock and perhaps wonder.

"How I've dreamt of this. The most intimate of acts a woman can do for a man."

"Show me more," she whispered, meeting his gaze and flicking her tongue along his erection. "Show me what you want."

Needing no more encouragement, he moved away from her and brought her to her knees. Kneeling before her, his erection soaring in the air, he entwined his hand in her hair and motioned her forward so that her mouth was poised over the tip of him.

"Take all of me. I want to watch you on your knees before me."

And then she slipped the tip of him past her lips and put all of him in her mouth. With gentle pressure of his hands in her hair, he guided her into a rhythm that was painstakingly slow and erotic. He told her how to suck him, how to bring the tip of his cock to her lips without letting him slide out of her mouth. He described how to build his passion slowly with tantalizing glimpses of her tongue curling around his shaft and her hand working the length of him as he watched.

She mastered the skill in minutes, and soon he only need groan or fist his fingers in her hair for her to know what he liked.

As she worked her magic on him, he reached for her breasts and filled his hands with them, his fingers becoming more insistent as his desire escalated. Watching her loving him so thoroughly aroused him more than he thought possible. He'd always loved the sensation of a mouth on him and no woman had so eagerly agreed to pleasure him in such a way as Emily had. She was wanton like this and so very adept at fueling his need. Already he was close to coming and wanting to draw it out, he moved away from her, settling himself against the headboard and motioning for her to come to him.

When she crawled on her knees to him, he was already gripping his cock in his hand and stroking himself shamelessly. Damn it all, she was working him up and he needed this release, this climax with her. With a soft purr, she lowered her mouth to his wet tip and he circled her lips with the head of his erection. Her eyelids fluttered closed as he teased her with his cock, and she moaned, as if she were savoring the taste of him.

Slowly her tongue swirled around his shaft until he could not bear it. Pulling out of her mouth he reached for her and brought her legs around his waist. "Lean back on your hands and rest your feet on the bed," he rasped as he parted her thighs and stroked her swollen sex. As she leaned back her sex was exposed, slick and wet and begging for him. Taking his cock in hand he rubbed it against her folds, teasing himself by watching and listening to Emily's escalating pants as he pleasured her.

Her hips were rocking as well as her breasts, meeting him stroke for stroke. It would be so easy to take her like this, to drive into her and watch the whole act. But she was a virgin, and a virgin should not be deflowered in such a way. But the temptation of watching himself take her for the first time was overpowering.

Giving into his desire, he brushed her opening and grinned as she looked up at him through a veil of hair. Teasing her, he traced her slit, watching her passion-glazed eyes widen.

"Please, do it," she sighed, the sound husky and breathless. Nudging her hips forward, she forced the tip of him inside. She was scalding hot and drenched with arousal.

"What would you like me to do, Emily?" he teased, slipping a fraction deeper inside her. She gasped and he watched her toss the hair from her face over her shoulder. He could now see all of her. Full breasts with pink nipples that were pebble hard and lush thighs that were open wide for him. "What would you like?" he asked again, watching as he slid deeper into the curls.

"Take me."

"Only if you watch as I take you." And only then, when he was assured that she watching him inch inside her, did he take her. Not in one swift movement, but in slow, straight strokes. When he was certain that he had aroused her enough, he looked up from their bodies and commanded that she look at him.

Eyes locked, he slid deeply inside, pushing past the barrier that gave little resistance. She gave a little gasp, but then he felt her thighs go tight around him and, guiding him with the inside of her legs, she brought him forward, urging him on.

"Harder? Deeper? Tell me how you want it, Emily."

"I don't know. Just don't stop," she cried.

His strokes were fast, furious, his passion spiraling. He knew he was out of control when he pulled out of her and went to his knees. Reaching for her, he kissed her, his tongue dancing with hers. His fingers slipped down her body until he was nudging them inside her.

"Emily," her name was ripped from his throat and Emily groaned, kissing his throat, wishing she could touch him, but he now had a hold of both her hands.

"I want to take you from behind." Not giving her a chance to understand what he wanted, he turned her away from him and with a hand on her back he pressed against her, lowering her to the silk counterpane. Her bottom was exposed and his hand was tracing and cupping her. And then she felt his erection slide between the cheeks of her bottom as he slipped into her, filling her so that she could only moan.

"Move against me," he commanded, his fingers pressing into her hips. "Move and let me watch your body take me in."

And then she did, feeling him hard and warm behind her. His harsh breaths mixed with the creak of the bed, and all she could think about was how wonderfully thrilling it was to be with Aidan in such a way. She had tasted him, reveled in the way he watched her. He desired her, she knew that now, for he could barely control his strokes. No longer were they smooth and rhythmic, but short irregular stabs that made him groan and grab for her bottom.

He was wild in his passion and she could not regret anything they had done. He had given her passion, and she loved him more than ever.

"Sorry," he hissed suddenly, driving into her one last time. "I'm so sorry, Emily." He collapsed atop her, his weight pressing her into the bed while he kissed her shoulder. "What a brute I was to take you like this, your first time. I really am just a monster, Emily."

Emily smiled secretly. "I don't regret anything. In truth, I am already thinking of the next time."

"Ah, dearest, Emily, so am I."

※~‰(☙❦❧)‰~※

Emily yawned as strolled down the stairs and headed for the breakfast room. She had wasted the morning, slumbering away in sexual exhaustion after returning to Jane's before dawn in the carriage that Aidan had obviously arranged for her.

She had awakened in the cottage to find herself alone in the bed, but the spot where Aidan had lain beside her was still warm and slightly indented from his body. He had not left her alone for long. The knowledge warmed her, although, she would have preferred to have awakened beside him.

Strolling into the breakfast room, Emily found herself grateful that Jane and Grey would be long gone from the table. She would have to eat alone, she mused, not unhappy at the thought. She had much to think of this morning.

A footman opened the door and she breezed inside the breakfast room, happy to find that she was all alone. Gliding over to the sideboard, she poured herself a cup of tea and raised the lid of a silver chafing dish. Inside were curried eggs and bacon set out on a plate for her. Thank heavens for Harding, she thought with a grin, lifting the plate from the silver tray and carrying it to the table. The man was a marvel.

Sitting down, Emily reached for the white napkin, snapped it open and placed it on her lap. Picking up her fork, she bit into the eggs and groaned with appreciation. She was famished this morning. Famished and exhausted.

Tasting more of the eggs, she allowed her mind to wander over the events of last night. She had acted like a common hussy and while she knew she should be mortified by her behavior, she could not summon a suitable amount of regret or shame. She had been with Aidan after all, the man she had loved for years. Who else should she play the wanton for but the man she loved so desperately?

She did love him—utterly and completely. No one made her feel alive like Aidan did. No one had awakened her desires in such a way as he had last night when he whispered his dark words. Good Lord, she had delighted in his heated phrases. She had craved them. And he had taken such exquisite care of her.

She recalled the way his breath whispered through her hair, the way his lips, soft and teasing, grazed her temple. She could almost imagine that Aidan was as much in love with her as she was with him.

While she had delighted in their encounter and falling asleep in his arms, she had been troubled in her sleep. To what purpose was Aidan's seduction? Why was he so determined to keep his identity a secret? Did he think she wouldn't be able to tell the difference between him and Michael? Admittedly at first, she had doubted her instincts, but she now knew that she was correct in her feelings—it was only Aidan that made her feel desire.

Confusion and worry gnawed at her insides, and she shoved her plate away, suddenly bereft of appetite. Did he truly desire her? Did he want her, or was this a case of amusement? Was he bored to tears within these quiet halls? Had he at last decided on a way to relieve himself of the tediousness of staying in a house that was not his own? Or worse, was he amusing himself with her because he wished to irritate Michael?

"There you are," Michael growled before slamming the door shut. "I've been waiting for you to get out of bed all morning."

"Good morning, Michael," she murmured, startled by the barely controlled anger she saw in his expression. She had never seen Michael angry, and certainly never with her before.

"Where were you last night?" he demanded, pulling her up from her chair while his fingers bit into her elbow.

"I have no notion what you're talking about," she replied, trying unsuccessfully to loosen his grasp.

"Don't play the coy tart with me," he hissed, letting his fingers bite into her arm. "I came to your room last night." He brought her chest up hard to his, a look of menace blazing in his eyes. "You weren't where you should have been."

She shook her head, her eyes wide with fear. Had her secret already been discovered? Did Michael know where she had been?

"You weren't in your bed. I searched the damn house and I couldn't find you anywhere."

"Get your hands off me," she spat viscously. 'Who do you think you are coming into my room uninvited?"

"Damn you, tell me. Who have you been with?"

"N... no, one," she stuttered, trying to break his hold.

"Do not lie to me," he roared. "You're not like the others, do not try to act the part now, Emily. I won't let you be like her, I won't " he snapped.

"My lady," Harding announced from the open door. "I trust you found your breakfast."

Her gaze slid from Michael to Harding, whose dark eyes narrowed when he saw how Michael was holding her. "Yes, thank you for your kindness."

"Leave us," Michael gritted out.

Harding ignored him, but continued to hold her gaze steady, as if he were trying to tell her something with his dark, mysterious eyes. "What more could I do to repay your kindness to my little master? Your attention last night was most beneficial, my lady."

"What are you saying?" Michael asked, finally loosening his fingers from about her arm. "What attentions do you speak of?"

"Your nephew, he was unwell. Lady Grey was exhausted with trying to placate him. Lady Beaumont came to the nursery around midnight and soothed both your sister and your nephew. Is that not correct, my lady."

She hated lying, but for some reason Harding thought it prudent to tell a falsehood on her behalf. He would not have made up a fanciful story if he didn't think it was necessary. She had learned many things during her stay with Jane and her husband, and one of those things was never to underestimate Harding's ability to read people's intentions.

"Is this true, Em?" Michael asked, swinging his gaze back to her. "You spent the night in the nursery?"

She nodded and absently rubbed her arm. "Yes."

"Bloody hell," he swore, raking his hand through his hair. "Damn me, Em, you gave me a fright. I thought… well, you know what I thought. That you had run off to meet some rogue."

"Michael, really," she whispered, noticing how they were now completely alone in the room.

"You don't have it in you to do something like that, do you, Em?"

She couldn't help but notice the challenge that gleamed in his eye. It was as if he knew exactly where she had been last night; he was only baiting her, waiting for her to willingly lie to him.

"Come, Em," he tilted up her chin. "Let us speak plainly. We are friends, are we not?"

"Yes," she whispered, absently rubbing her arm. "At least I thought we were."

"Forgive me," he said, brushing his hand along her arm. "I had no right to handle you such as I did."

"Why did you?" she asked, puzzled.

"Because I was afraid that you might have betrayed him, too."

"Michael, of whom are you speaking of?"

"Not yet," he murmured, trailing the back of his hand down her cheek. "It's not time yet, but soon, Emily. Can you wait that long? Will you wait for him?"

"Michael, what is wrong? You're worrying me. It's not like you to speak in riddles."

"Will I be enough, Em, if he won't do what is right?"

She placed a hand over his forehead. "You're not fevered," she said, as she pressed her hand to his cheek. "Did you drink too much last night, Michael?"

A sound from the hall made his eyes dart from her to the door. He stiffened and reached for her. "Follow me," he grumbled, walking to the door.

"Where are you going," she cried. "Truly, Michael, you are not yourself. I don't think you should leave the house."

But he kept walking away from her and Emily followed him, watching as he reached the door and walked out.

"Michael, you are not dressed for such weather," she called, stamping her foot. Blast it, she muttered beneath her breath. She had better follow him. Something was wrong with him and she would never forgive herself if he fell ill.

And once she ascertained that he was feeling fit, she was going to get to the bottom of his perplexing behavior.

Chapter Eight

Trudging through the snow, Emily buried her face against the ermine collar of her cloak. Twisting her fingers tightly together, she sunk them further into her rabbit fur muff.

The air was cold and crisp, making her breath clouds of gray vapor in the bright sunlight. The crunching of snow beneath her boots told her that the temperature was frigid and that she should turn back lest her cheeks become red and chafed in the blustery wind.

But she had not found Michael, and she was worried about him. Their conversation had made little sense and she feared he was confused. Her brother frequently was after his drinking bouts, and she wondered if Michael suffered from the same disorientation the morning after his indulgences.

Lost in her musings, she failed to hear the low voices of men behind her. Had she, she might have been able to lift her skirts and run as fast as her feet would carry her. But so deep in thought was she about Aidan and the strange way Michael was acting that she was unaware of their presence until a firm hand grasped her arm and spun her around. Gypsies.

She watched four men with long curling black hair and beards advance upon her. The one, whose hand ruthlessly gripped her arm, tore her muff from her fingers and tossed it to the ground. "Money," he demanded.

"I... I... I don't have any money. I only came for a walk. I... I can get you—"

He pushed her backward so that she landed on the snow, her skirts raised to her knees. "No, please," she begged, pounding on his chest as he fell atop her, but he was too heavy and the others were reaching for her hands and pulling the cloak from around her neck.

"Pretty," he grinned as he savagely tore the bodice of her gown wide open.

"No, please, don't," she cried out, struggling beneath his weight. "No!" she screamed, pummeling his back with her fists, but the gypsy only laughed at her pathetic attempts.

In the next breath, and with a blood curdling roar, the man was lifted off her, exposing her flesh to the freezing wind. Unable to move, paralyzed with fear, she darted her eyes to the left, just in time to see Aidan atop his horse reach down and grab the man by the dirty collar of his cape. Twisting the tattered wool in his gloved hand, she watched as Aidan tossed the man away from her, swinging him onto the ground, inches away from his stallion's stomping hooves.

"No," the man begged, rolling away from the horse, but Aidan merely pressed his thighs into the horse's flanks, advancing the animal so that it was once again stomping towards the man.

Aidan continued to ruthlessly advance upon the man and she realized by his voice when he spoke that he was in a murderous rage "Your friends might have been successful in fleeing, but you will not be so fortunate."

"Aidan," her voice was quiet, weakened with terror, and she feared that he would not hear her above the howling winds. But he turned in his saddle, his face contorted with rage. His gray eyes blazed the color of metal and Emily covered her mouth with the back of her hand when she saw the hatred in his eyes. The emotion she saw in his expression was the most disturbing she had ever seen.

Turning his gaze from her, he focused on the man who still lay on the ground. "Come near these grounds again, and I will tear you apart, do you understand?" The man nodded, then let out a whimper as the stallion snorted and pranced closer to his head. "Go now, before I change my mind."

The man struggled to his feet before running into the trees, and Aidan swung his horse around. When he came upon her, he jumped from the saddle and knelt to the ground. His eyes looked much different now then they had last night. There was no warmth, no flicker of passion in them, only haunted shadows. "Aidan," she whispered and caught her breath as the wind swirled around them, lifting his hair from his cheek and blowing it away from his face. Her hand, trembling with cold, reached for his cheek.

He pushed it away, refusing to allow her to touch him. If possible, his gaze grew more emotionless as he reached for her, bringing her up against his chest.

"I will take you home," he said gruffly, mounting the stallion with an ease and grace that confounded her.

"Aidan?"

"Do not look, Emily." he growled, before spurring the horse forward.

He told her not to look at him, but Emily could do no such thing. How could she not look into the face of her savior and not wish that he would look down at her and grin that rakish smile she knew he possessed, the one that never failed to send her heart fluttering.

But he refused to meet her gaze and instead kept his attention focused straight ahead, while a muscle in his jaw clenched tightly, telling her that the last place he wanted to be was here, with her in his arms.

※⟨⟨♥⟩⟩※

The door of the mansion flew open and Harding stepped aside, allowing

Aidan to storm through the entrance while Emily trembled uncontrollably in his arms.

"Her room is prepared," Harding murmured, waving him forward. "Mary is even now seeing to her bath."

Emily stirred in his arms and he could not help but look down at her. Her face was a startling shade of white and her lips which had only moments before been a pasty white were now a mottled blue.

Damn it, he thought, gazing down at her pale face, her lids closed and her lips trembling with cold. She'd seen his face and her expression told him all he needed to know. He disgusted her, sickened her. He'd heard her gasp, even above the howling wind. He could still hear that shocked breath and he could not help but replay the sound over and over in his mind. He was nothing but a hideous beast to her. He had been a bloody fool to let himself believe in his dreams.

After placing Emily on the bed, he didn't stay. Instead, he stalked down the stairs, making his way to the study, knowing that his brother would be tucked warmly inside, nursing a snifter of brandy and idling the hours away. Throwing open the door, he was pleased to see that Michael had not changed any of his previous habits.

"Well, well," his brother drawled, placing his glass of brandy on the desk. "If it isn't my brother, the ghost."

"Get up." He stalked towards Michael and hefted him up by his lace cravat.

"What the devil's gotten into you?" Michael drawled, shoving himself away from his hold.

"Why did you let her go?"

"I don't know what you're talking about," his brother muttered, making a show of fixing his cravat.

"Emily, damn you. Why did you let her go outside by herself? She was worried for you, you knew that."

"Emily is a grown woman, Aidan. I'm quite certain she can take a stroll about the property without having to be escorted."

"Haven't you heard, don't you give a damn? She was nearly raped by four men who would have abused her till the breath left her body."

Michael's eyes widened and Aidan felt his anger spiral out of control. "You God damned bastard," Aidan swore, swinging his fist and landing a facer upon Michael's chin with such force that his brother reeled backwards, onto the wingback chair.

Aidan stared at his shaking, ink stained fingers, remembering what he had been doing when he had heard Emily with his brother. He'd been writing to her, pouring out his feelings for her on vellum—and yet she had followed his brother...

"When did you decide to champion her, brother?" Michael taunted, his eyes sparkling as he wiped the trickle of blood that crept out from his split lip.

Looking up from his hands allowing the jealousy he felt all but consume him, he lunged forward, punching Michael once more. "Damn you, you will not destroy her. You will not use her and leave her broken, do you understand me?"

Michael's eyes widened further and Aidan feared that he had given too much away. The bastard would now know that he coveted Emily and Michael would have no compunction about using that information against him.

"Let's just see how much she means to you, brother."

⁂

Moaning, Emily sunk further into the warm water and rested her head against the copper tub. Closing her eyes, she allowed the soothing heat and scented water to wash over her skin, taking away the taint of the gypsy's touch.

"Lean forward and I shall wash your back," Mary instructed.

Emily did as Mary asked, indulging in the pampering her lady's maid was lavishing upon her. Where was Aidan, she wanted to ask. She remembered being held in his arms as he raced his mount back to the house. Remembered the biting breeze against her cheeks and the stinging wind that howled around them. She recalled pressing her body into his warm one, shivering when she felt him tighten his hold around her. She remembered looking up, seeing his expression, cold, implacable, unreadable.

Do not look, Emily. He hadn't wanted her to see the wide jagged scars that ran the length of his cheek. He most certainly hadn't wanted her to touch him. She had seen fear briefly shine in his gray eyes, but only too soon it was replaced with a haunting sadness that made her want to hold him. In that moment when he had lifted her from the snow and brought her tight to his chest, she had never seen a man that was more handsome.

If only he would have allowed her to tell him, to show him that he was wrong, that she was not disgusted by what she had seen. But his pride was pricked and she knew that Aidan had more then his fair share of pride.

The water splashed over her head, only to trickle down her shoulders and Emily sighed, wishing Aidan would come to her so that she could tell him that his scars meant nothing to her, that she still loved him, desired him. But she had the feeling that it would take more then mere words to soothe the ache in Aidan's soul.

"You are shivering again," Mary said. "Come, let us get you into bed." Standing up, she allowed Mary to help her out of the tub. Withstanding Mary's ministrations, Emily stood on shaking legs. "To bed, my lady," Mary ordered and taking her by the hand, she led her to the side of the bed and covered her to her chin with warm blankets. "Now then, drink this."

Emily reached for the mug Mary handed her, noticing the steam that curled in tendrils. "What is it, tea?"

"Magic tea," Mary smiled. "Herbs that will make you sleep and dream only peaceful dreams."

"I'd like that. I vow I feel as though I could sleep a week."

"Then sleep," Mary ordered when Emily at last finished the tea. "Sleep and dream."

Closing her eyes, Emily allowed sleep to take her.

After what felt like an eternity, Emily sat up in bed and looked about the room, disoriented and confused. It was dark outside and someone had lit the candles on the commode. In the hearth a fire blazed, snapping and cracking to life as flame engulfed a log.

Rubbing sleep from her eyes, she looked about the room, realizing that she was very much alone in the chamber. She had a vague, fuzzy memory of Jane and Grey sitting vigil at her bedside. Remembered too, Harding coming into her room and offering her more tea. She even remembered that Jane had brought Michael into her room and he had pressed ardent kisses to her knuckles. "I'm so sorry, Em," he had whispered to her. "I didn't know they were out there. I would never have made you come out if I had known. I only wanted to draw him out, you see," Michael had said, his voice hard and urgent. "I only wanted to make him see that you could be his." She had tried to talk, to ask him questions, but he had shushed her and patted her hand, commanding her to sleep and telling her that he would tell her all later.

But the one person she yearned for hadn't come. Aidan had not come to her bedside and her heart suddenly plummeted to her stomach, thinking that he might never come to her again.

The door creaked open and she looked up, hoping she would see Aidan striding into her room, but it was Mary, carrying a tea tray.

"You are better?" she asked, lowering the tray onto the commode.

"Yes, thank you."

"Here," she said, passing her a package. "Perhaps this will speed your recovery." Emily glanced at the brown package that Mary placed in her hand. "It has just arrived from a messenger," Mary said, as if she could read her thoughts. "I knew you would want to see it. Now," she said, turning to the tray. "I have some supper for you. I shall leave you in peace, if you promise you will eat something."

"I promise."

Mary nodded and bowed before leaving her. When the door closed, Emily pulled the twine that secured the paper and peeled back the wrapping. Her mouth opened on an appreciative gasp as she saw what lay inside. There, nestled in brown paper lay the most exquisite ivory lace robe. Tucked into the gown was a white calla lily secured with a red satin bow and a missive, rolled into a scroll.

She knew who it was from, she needed no signature, only his mark—the lily, to know that Aidan had sent her something. Jumping from the bed, she stood and reached for the folded gown, shaking it so that it opened. Rich, ivory lace stared back her and Emily vowed she had never seen anything as beautiful as the dressing gown. Lace cuffs, three layers thick were edged with pearls. The collar was the same lace flounce as the sleeves, and the front was scalloped and heavily embroidered with gold thread and iridescent pearls.

The robe was at once beautiful and sensual and Emily hastily pulled her plain flannel nightrail over her head and shrugged into the robe. It must have cost him a fortune, she thought as she stood staring at her reflection. No doubt it had come from Madame Chevale's shop. Only Chevale would have such exquisite French lace. Only Chevale could turn her, a plain creature, into a seductive woman with only a bolt of lace and thread. For seductive she was, she admitted, as she studied herself in the looking glass. Her figure was tantalizingly, almost teasingly displayed behind the lace.

Remembering the flower and the scroll, Emily rushed back to the bed and unrolled the missive. It was a new installment of the Dark Lord's tale and her knees buckled when she read the first line.

Tell me, what pleasure have you received tonight... her voice, soft and low, seductive to my ears whispers in the dark and I am left struggling for words, indeed for breath. What pleasures has my darling muse bestowed upon me? The gift of her body sliding along mine. The feel of her bottom, lush and wet grazing along the length of me, teasing me, making me yearn to possess her in a way no man has ever done.

What pleasures, I want to cry as I ravage her lips with mine and reach into her bodice to stroke the breasts I have longed to touch and taste. Only the pleasures that a woman, eager for a man's touch can produce.

A man yearns to see the planes of a woman's face as she writhes in his arms. He burns to hear her whimpered pleas for more, her pants of desires and her cries of release. What more pleasure can a woman bring to a man then to give herself completely to him? To trust him with her virtue and her heart?

That is what pleasure my muse has given me.

Fourth Installment of the Dark Lord's Memoir, The Seduction of the Muse.

Chapter Nine

Turning the key in the lock, Aidan listened for the soft clicking sound before slipping the key free. Striding to the bed, he blew out the candle that sat atop the commode.

The fire had burned low in the hearth and now only glowed with hot coals. The glimmering embers cast a warm orange shadow along the wall and the skin of the woman who lay on the bed before him.

He hadn't been able to deny himself or stay away. The need for the touch a woman had been too strong, too alluring. He craved it, needed it, needed to feel a woman's hands on his body, needed the satisfaction of sheathing his cock inside a wet sheath that he had made ache with need.

But it was not any woman's body he craved, it was Emily's. It was not a hard rut he was looking for but a tender loving, a melding of bodies and hearts and God help him, souls.

And that is what had brought him here. As he stared down at Emily, her body swathed in the lace robe he had commissioned for her, he knew that what he needed tonight was to make love. As his gaze devoured Emily while she lay sleeping, he realized that he wanted—needed—to make love to Emily.

He'd told himself as he'd stalked about his chamber that it was a fool's idea. She despised him, he could still hear her gasp of fear, but he had forced all those thoughts aside and allowed only the memory of her body atop his. Damn him, he could think of nothing other than feeling her wet sex on his cock.

It didn't matter if she was yearning for the Dark Lord. He didn't even care if she believed he was Michael stealing into her room, nothing could dissuade him from his desire. Ever since he had seen that damn gypsy bastard atop her he had been plagued with visions of losing her. Damn, but he couldn't lose her. He didn't think he could live his life without knowing what it was like to feel her spread her sweet thighs for him one more time.

A glowing log cracked, shattering into smaller embers and Emily stirred restlessly, the scalloped edges of the gown parted, teasing him with a glimpse of pale flesh rendered peach by the glowing hearth.

He wanted her, despite his fears, despite not knowing who Emily thought he was. At this moment he didn't give a bloody damn, he only wanted to feel her, to give her pleasure and feel her pleasure him.

Unfastening his breeches, he dropped them to the floor. His cock sprung free, heavy with arousal. Never had anticipation coursed so heavily through him. It was as if he were a virgin again, awaiting his first conquest. He supposed in a way he was, for he was going to make love with Emily tonight, something he had never done before. He was an innocent in the art of love.

Hearing her sigh and watching her mouth part on a soft breath, his body stiffened, and to relieve some of the exquisite ache, he palmed his cock as he studied her and the way she looked in the glow of the fire. How many times had he pleasured himself imagining this? How many nights had he found release with his hand wishing it was her body he was pouring himself into?

Kneeling on the bed, he went to her, almost trembling as he forced himself to go slow and savor every moment. She nuzzled her face into the pillow and he could not help but reach out and slide his finger down her smooth cheek. She was wearing his ribbon again and he felt a possessiveness wash over him that only grew stronger with each passing day.

Lying down so that he faced her, he propped his head in his hand and trailed his finger down her throat to where the lace shielded her body from him. It was an erotic piece of clothing. At once revealing, yet it concealed the places he most desired to see. Her curves were outlined as well as her breasts, hips and thighs, but he could not see her nipples which were only the faintest hint of pink circles beneath the lace design or the dark, triangular thatch between her thighs that beckoned him.

Now painfully aroused, he parted the gown with one finger and allowed himself to look his fill. Breasts, round and full quivered with each of her breaths, already her pink nipples were erect and he could not stop himself from brushing the tip of his finger along them. She moaned and moved restlessly and he watched her breasts sway with the movement.

Grasping his cock, he stroked his length, fearing that if he did not do something to assuage his lust he would spread her thighs and sink into her body.

Needing to feel her, he parted her gown more to reveal her belly and the curls cupped by lush thighs. She was round in all the right places and he would take great delight in learning her, discovering each sensitive spot, ascertaining what made her burn, what would make her wet and willing in his arms. He wanted her clinging and begging him.

He grazed the tip of his cock along her belly, savoring the softness, the wickedness of pleasuring himself while she slept, naked, before him.

"I want you," he whispered in the quiet, unable to stem the words that sprung from the depths of his soul.

"I want you, too," she replied sleepily. He looked up to see her lashes flutter open. She met his gaze and smiled secretly. "Am I dreaming? Have I only wished you here?"

If only he had the strength to ask her if she knew who he was, but he hadn't the courage. He was going to make love to her tonight and he didn't want to do so knowing that she was thinking it was Michael pleasuring her.

"Are you only a dream?" she asked, tracing his mouth with the tip of her finger.

"No," he groaned, reaching for her hand and placing it inside his shirt so that her palm rested against his heart. "I am real. Tell me, darling Emily, do you know who it is who comes to you in the dark?"

"Oh, yes," she smiled, inching closer to him so that her breasts were brushing against his shirt and her lips were impossibly close to his. "I know who you are. I have dreamt for so long that you would come to me."

His stomach twisted cruelly as he forced her words aside. "Sssh, sweet Emily. Let us not talk, but love."

He captured her lips and swept his tongue inside, she mewled softly and brought her hands to his hair, raking her fingers through the length of it and he groaned, needing her hands on him, wishing he could be naked in her arms, feeling those soft fingers stroking his flesh.

"I need you, Em," he whispered against her mouth. "I need to feel you and taste you."

"I need you too," she sighed, grasping his hair as he nuzzled the valley of her breasts. "I want you so much, more then you can ever imagine."

He nuzzled her nipple, listening to her hushed breath, hoping, praying that her words were not intended for Michael. If he was any sort of man, he'd clarify his identity this second, but he could not. He did not want to be faced with the fact that Emily might turn from him. He could not be deprived of the pleasures she was so willingly offering her dark lover.

Flicking his tongue along her nipple, he smiled when he heard her gasp. He released his cock and flattened his palm on her belly. He felt it quiver beneath his hand, felt her tremble as he slipped her nipple between his lips and sucked, slowly building in intensity.

"My God," she cried, tangling her legs with his as she restlessly moved against him.

Her breasts grazed his face, and he could not help but push her onto her back so that he could suck at one nipple and tug at the other. She moaned when he rolled it between his thumb and forefinger and when he tweaked it she gripped his hair and he smiled, knowing that if he slipped his fingers between her thighs he would feel the honey seeping from her body.

Her hands were restless on him now, traversing his shoulders and arms. He felt her fingers pinching his flesh, her nails biting into him through the thin linen of his shirt. Her enthusiasm and heated response encouraged him and he skimmed his fingers down her breasts, past her belly to the damp curls between her thighs.

She whimpered and her eyes went round, and he captured her cry with his mouth, slipping his tongue deep into her mouth as he parted her sex and slid his finger up the slick length of her. He circled her clitoris and she bucked against his hand, moaning into his mouth while she clutched his shirt.

There was no maidenly fear in her, just an exuberance that stole his breath.

At this moment, he didn't give a farthing who she thought he was, he only cared that it was his hands eliciting such a response from her.

"My God," she gasped, tearing her mouth from his as he slid first one, then another finger into her.

"Do you need another to fill you?"

She nodded and reached for him, bringing his mouth down atop hers. He growled low in his throat and plunged a third finger deep within her, swallowing her cries.

"God, but I want you," he whispered, nipping her lips while he continued to finger her tight passage. His thumb circled the throbbing bud at the crest of her curls and he felt her stiffen then arch beneath him.

"Beautiful," he rasped, watching the emotions play across her shadowed face.

Her keening cry echoed along the walls while she stiffened and bucked against him and all the while he drove her on with his fingers till she was panting and writhing and begging for his cock.

"I want to touch you," she gasped reaching for the tails of his shirt. "I want your skin against mine."

His body froze, his mind went blank when he felt the tentative touch of her fingers along his flanks. "No," he commanded, shoving himself away from her. "No, Emily, don't touch me, I cannot bear it."

Emily lay still on the bed, watching as Aidan pushed himself away from her. She would not believe that he didn't want her touch. Letting her gaze skim down his wrinkled shirt, she saw his erection, thick and hard soaring out of a nest of dark curls. He met her gaze through the shadowed moonlight and then he turned his face, refusing to look at her. She had not missed the haunting loneliness that flickered in his gaze and she reached out for his hand, but he snatched it away.

"Em—"

"Ssh," she whispered, realizing at last that he was trying to hide his scars. She recalled that his hand had been burned and cut, the same hand that she had reached for. Remembered too, the burns he'd suffered on his back and recalled the scars on his face as his gaze had met hers that morning. He was afraid of her response and it broke her heart to think that he might think her so shallow.

He swallowed hard and she knew that if she did not do or say something the moment would be over. She could not let it be over, she could not go back, not after he'd taken her so far. She wanted this, wanted it with him.

Her fingers reached out to his thighs and she tentatively stroked the hard muscle. His jaw clenched and she watched his erection swell further and throb, jutting out from the hem of his shirt. Skimming her hand through his dark curls, she captured his erection and smoothed her fingers down the length of him. "Please tell me I can touch you like this." He nodded, and caught her hand in his, curling his fingers around hers, showing her how he liked it.

"I didn't want it this way," he rasped. "I wanted to taste you, to bring you to climax after climax, to have you begging for me to fill you."

"I am begging." She met his gaze. "I want you inside me. I want you to show me what you've dreamed of."

"Emily," he murmured, laying atop her and capturing her breasts in his hands. "I only hope that I can make this right for you. The last time..."

"You will," she smiled, covering his lips with her fingers. "It will be perfect."

As she kneaded his bottom, she spread her legs, showing him that she was submitting to him, in essence she was giving him everything she had left in the world.

"I'll take care of you, Em, I swear it."

"I know it," she sighed, feeling his beautiful fingers part her, teasing the honey from her once again.

"So wet," he groaned, nudging his hardness between her legs. "It's just for me, isn't it, Em?"

"Yes." The impenetrable hardness of him slid into her. She was stretched with him and she had never felt anything more fascinating than knowing that Aidan was inside her, a part of her.

"Em," he mumbled against her throat, driving himself inside her. "Tell me you want me, that it's only me you want inside you. I need to hear the words from your lips."

He believed she didn't know it was him. Somewhere deep inside her she felt his torment, tasted his fear. And yet his fear was not yet strong enough to overcome his insecurities. Allowing her to believe it was anyone other than him thrusting inside her was obviously more palatable then having to confront his appearance, and her response to it.

"Sweet, Emily, give me the words."

He was stroking her so hard, so precise that she could barely even breathe let alone speak. The exquisite sensation was building again and Emily felt herself becoming weightless, floating, waiting for the pleasure to take her.

"Damn it, Emily, I need to know," he growled, his breath was hot against her skin and she felt the perspiration trickle from his forehead onto her cheek. "Sweet Jesus, please tell me that you feel something."

"I love you," she cried, feeling her body splinter. She clutched him tightly, squeezing him to her as he released his seed deep inside her.

She'd said it. At long last Aidan would know how she truly felt. She loved him and never more then right now, when he was still buried deep inside her, his chest heaving. She loved him, and she prayed that one day he would feel the same way for her.

Chapter Ten

The morning sunlight shone through the paned glass. Her cheeks bathed in the warmth, Emily closed her eyes and tilted her face up to bask in more of the sunlight.

Heated memories of Aidan and what they had done together filtered through her mind and she couldn't help but smile as she recalled his second round of lovemaking. He'd been fierce in his passion, all hands and mouth and teeth—and his words—Emily clutched her blanket closer to her chest, the words he had used only added to the need she'd felt in his touch.

"There you are," Jane announced from the door of the salon. "I wondered where you had gone off to."

"I thought only to rest here for a minute," Emily said, opening her eyes and seeing that Jane was dressed for the outdoors. "But then the sun beckoned and the sound of the crackling fire called to me, and I found myself sitting on this lovely window bench, snuggled in this wool blanket."

"Well, after yesterday you need to rest. I only searched you out to inform you that Grey and I are taking the carriage into the village. We will be gone most of the day. If you have need of anything, just inform Harding."

"I will," Emily nodded. "Have fun."

Jane waved and Emily watched the gilded door shut softly behind her friend. Leaning her head back against the paneled wood, she closed her eyes and tilted her face to the sun, sighing when the warmth engulfed her. Breathing softly, her lips parted and she felt herself slide into a deep sleep.

How long she slept she did not know. The sun was still shining, yet it seemed to have moved more west in the sky. The fire had been stirred and another log placed atop the fire basket. Harding's doing, no doubt.

Sitting up, the blanket slid off her shoulders and puddled onto the floor. Bending forward to retrieve it, she started as a hand reached for it. Her head snapped up and she found herself looking into the haunting gray eyes of Aidan.

"Allow me," he said, bending to pick up the blanket. He shook it out and covered her lap with it. His eyes met hers and she noticed the fear shining in them. He wore his hair unbound, the length covering his cheeks and pooling onto his shoulders. Emily wished she could take her fingers and brush back the soft waves. She dearly wanted to see the face—the whole face—of the man who had loved her so completely last night.

He cleared his throat and raked his gaze over her. "How do you feel this morning?"

Was he inquiring about her well-being after the gypsy had traumatized her, or was he wishing to know how she felt after he had so thoroughly ravished her body?

A smile quirked her lips upwards as she recalled just how wonderful she felt. She felt alive and having him so close to her was making her body yearn for the pleasure it knew he could give her.

"You are well?" he asked again, concern, and possibly worry flickered in his gaze.

"I am very well, thank you. In fact, I feel rather fit. I had a wonderful sleep."

"Did you?" he murmured, his gaze dropping to her mouth.

"I did. Such vivid dreams. Such beautiful, beautiful dreams."

He abruptly pulled away from her and stood up, his hands clasped behind his back. He was bathed in shadow but she could see the hard planes of his face etched in the sun's blinding rays.

"I am very glad to hear it." His voice was cold and polite. "Now that I have assured myself that you are well, I shall leave you to your privacy."

"You don't have to go—"

Her protests were drowned out by the sound of the salon door opening and closing. They both looked over and saw Michael. He was dressed in his greatcoat, his riding crop clutched in his gloved hand.

"Where the devil have you been, Emily?" he asked, snapping the crop against the top of his boot. "I've searched this blasted pile of stones for nearly half an hour."

"I have been here most of the morning," she answered sharply, her gaze narrowing as Michael swept his brother a mocking glare.

"Well, come along then. We shall ride into the village."

"I am afraid I am not up to riding today," she murmured, aware of the tension that radiated throughout the room.

"The devil you say," he snapped, stalking toward her and capturing her wrist in his hand. "A bit of fresh air is just what you need. You look pale, Emily. Like a milk-water miss. The ride will restore your color. Come, I insist."

He tugged her, his hand tightening around the delicate bones of her wrist. When she fought to extricate herself from his hold; a hand, the fingers long and elegant and bearing scars, landed atop Michael's black glove.

"The lady said she is not inclined to ride."

Michael stared at Aidan's hand, and she watched his lips curl into a mockery of a smile. "Get your damn monster's hand off of me, brother, or I swear I shall hit it with my crop."

"Michael!" Emily gasped.

"Go ahead," Aidan challenged, "Do your worst to me, but leave Emily alone."

"Alone with you? So that is the way of it, is it? I was interrupting a rendezvous of sorts?"

"Michael, please," she pleaded, noticing the threatening stance that both of them were taking. "Really, I'm not inclined to ride."

Michael's blue gaze slid to hers. "Perhaps you are contemplating another sort of ride entirely, and with my brother."

"Take yourself off, Michael until you can conduct yourself in a manner befitting a gentleman," Aidan growled.

"And you're one to talk, eh, brother?" Michael taunted, shaking off Aidan's grip and freeing her wrist. "You, the phantom who skulks about these halls like some bloody wraith as you watch and spy on everyone."

Emily heard her breath catch, and she looked up to Aidan, wondering how much Michael knew about them.

"Oh, that's right, Emily, didn't you know? My brother prowls about, casting himself in shadow. Why, I have no doubt that he's been spying on you every chance he gets. He's probably seen you in the bath, watched you dress, ha," he grunted, "probably watched you undress, too."

"That is enough—" she snapped, narrowing her eyes. "You've gone beyond the pale, Michael, and I will not have it."

"Go on, tell her brother, tell her what you've been doing. How you have been reduced to nothing but voyeuristic interludes to find your physical release. Imagine having your soft flesh stroked by such a thing?" Michael picked up Aidan's scarred hand and raised it to her face. "Envision this on your flesh, Emily. Picture what the rest of him must look like."

Her face contorted with hatred for the man who would say such hurtful things to his brother. "Stop it this instant," she snapped, "you're being purposefully cruel. Your brother cannot help what has happened to him." She dared a look at Aidan, but his eyes were cold and emotionless.

"Repulsive, isn't it," Michael replied.

"I will not have you saying such despicable things about your brother, Michael. He cannot help what he is."

"And what is that?" Aidan asked coldly, his gaze at last straying to her. "A pitiful excuse for a man who needs a woman to fight his battles? A God damned monster that needs to be pitied?"

"Aidan," she said in a rush, reaching for his arm. "You misunderstand me."

"I hear you quite clearly, madam. I have no need to hide behind your skirts. I have no need for your pity. I am a man, not some weakling who needs you for a nursemaid."

"No, don't leave," she cried when he shook his hand from his arm. "Aidan, please, you don't understand—"

"Don't touch me," he snapped, stepping away from her. "And for God's sake don't look at me like that, like a monster you're longing to save with your sympathy for his misfortune. While I grudgingly admire your forbearance, Emily, I do not require your acceptance. You may think of me what you will, man or monster, duke or ghost, for I no longer care."

"Aidan, please," she cried, trying to run after him, but Michael reached for her and held her to him.

"Sssh," he whispered near her ear. "Let him go. Let him seethe and rail about. It will not take long, Em, for him to come to you."

"You've ruined everything, Michael. Everything!"

Michael looked over his shoulder and slowly smiled as Aidan slammed the door shut. "No, Em, I haven't. I've made everything right. I know that now. That's the first true emotion I've seen from my brother in over a year."

"He thinks I believe that he is a monster. And the way you spoke to him, those cruel, taunting words...." She looked at him as her eyes widened in horror. "You wanted him to think that I felt the same as you. You tried to provoke me because you knew I would come to his defense. You wanted to make me appear as though I was demeaning him with my compassion."

"Emily, there is only one other person on Earth who loves my brother as much as you do." He grinned down at her and brushed away one of her tears. "I love him, Em, and seeing him this way crushes me. He's been so hard to reach. I could no longer stand to see him living as he does. I've known his desires for sometime, Emily. I know where his heart lays. I've known yours, and I could not bear to know that there were two people in the world so perfectly suited for one another separated by fear and pride."

"What are you saying?"

"I'm saying, Em, that I'm drawing him out of his darkness. I'm using the one thing in all the world that would entice him to leave his shadows and step into the light. You, Em," he whispered. "You're his light." A tear trickled down her cheek and he brushed it away with his thumb. "Are you brave enough to follow him into the shadows and allow him the chance to reach for your light?"

"I want nothing more," she said, her voice trembling. "But I don't know how."

"I will help you and when you have healed him with your love, perhaps you will be able to heal the breach between us, because, Emily, I would dearly love to have my brother back."

⁂

I have had her and there could be no woman more sweet or more seductive. My knowledge of her physically is complete, my desire for her unquenchable.

I find myself dreaming of her, even in waking hours, wondering what she is doing, imagining what she is wearing, dreaming of taking it all off and baring her to me. She has made a slave of me, and I have willingly submitted to her.

I must possess her, she must be mine, and yet I sense that no matter how much I burn for her, she shall never feel the same about me. For who could ever love a man such as me? A man who lives amongst shadows and behind his penned words?

No, she will not love me, she will not want me when she learns the true identity of her Dark Lord. The very thought fuels my blood and I cannot bear the idea of not having her by my side. I shall have her but once more. I will take her hard and not care if she resists. I shall show her no mercy, just as she has shown me....

Fifth Installment of the Dark Lord's Memoirs, The Seduction of the Muse.

Emily nibbled on her bottom lip as she stared down at the paper containing the latest excerpt of the Dark Lord's tale. It had been accompanied by a gift, all tied up with a red ribbon and his infamous pure white calla lily.

Glancing at the lace chemise that lay atop her coverlet, Emily picked it up and held it by its thick straps. The lace was fine, exquisite in fact, with an intricate pattern that would reveal more than it would conceal. The color was red. The color favored by harlots, and Emily couldn't help but wonder if Aidan had chosen it because he was partial to the hue, or because he now thought of her as a fallen woman.

As she studied it in the firelight, she knew it would cling to her every curve, that it would mold her breasts and dip scandalously low, more than likely revealing her nipples, and the hem....she tilted her head and studied the rich scallop of lace, the hem would not likely even cover her bottom.

It was a scandalous gift and she had the feeling that Aidan had sent it to her as a way of putting her in her place for what had transpired in the salon yesterday. He was angry, if his absence from the shadowed halls and his lack of nocturnal visits were any indication. The words in his latest installment were all anger too. *I shall show her no mercy, just as she has shown me...*

He was hurting and she couldn't bear to think that she had been the cause of it. Why had she not yelled at him as he walked away, confessing that she knew that he was the Dark Lord and that he was the one to have awakened her to passion? But it had been the look in his eye that had stopped her. Nothing could have penetrated the depth of what she saw shining back at her. There were no words to have saved Aidan from the pain that he had experienced. She'd been shocked by what she had seen, shocked senseless and mute.

I will take her hard and not care if she resists. Her eyes strayed to the paper with Aidan's words. She should probably feel a great amount of fear over that statement, but she did not. It meant that he had every intention of coming to her one last time. She could use that to her advantage. He had used her hard before, and she had begged for every second of it. She would beg again, if only for one more chance to make him understand that it was him she wanted.

Chapter Eleven

Aidan lay stretched on the bed, hands behind his head, staring at the intricate folds of the red silk canopy above him. Damn Emily for tying him in knots, he could strangle her pretty little throat.

Bloody hell, he'd been in a murderous rage ever since that day. He should never have gone to the salon. Never stood towering above her as she slept innocently on the window seat. He damn well should never have made love to her.

His body tightened like a bow and he closed his eyes, forcing away the memories of their sweet lovemaking. He'd never experienced something so enthralling, so utterly consuming as making love with Emily.

If only she hadn't trembled with revulsion.

He had seen it, seen her shoulders tremble as Michael forced her to look at his scarred hand. She had looked at him with such shock, such horror when his darling brother suggested that he was nothing but a horrid monster behind his expensive, fashionable clothes. He'd been enraged by her response to him. Two nights ago she had been so hot in his arms, so wet and willing and she gave him back everything he gave her. Yet he knew that she believed that he had been Michael.

When he started this charade, this seduction of his muse, he knew that it would more than likely end with such results. He had never tried to fool himself into believing that Emily might be able to overlook his disfigurement. He'd been prepared for that. What he had not been prepared for was the gut wrenching agony he felt when she had not been able to hide her reaction.

That hideous, grotesque hand, as his brother had so eloquently put it, had stroked her lovely flesh. It had made her tremble, made gooseflesh erupt along every pore. That hand, with its damaged fingers had made her body hum and sing for him. But Emily didn't know the pleasure that he and his scarred body could give her. She attributed that pleasure to his insolent brother.

Well, she would no longer do that, he vowed viciously. He would make her confront her folly. Ignoring the warnings in his brain, he vaulted from the bed and stalked to the door. He would confront Emily this second, for he had nothing left to lose.

Stalking down the corridor, he heard hushed whispers in the shadowed corner. Stopping, he stepped back, concealing himself from the couple who were feverishly talking.

"Michael, I can't do this," he heard Emily's hushed voice. They were standing at the bottom of the stairs that led to the bedchambers, and Aidan pressed himself further into the alcove behind him. He wanted to know just how intimate she and Michael were.

"You must," his brother growled as he followed Emily up the stairs. "Do you want to be his duchess?"

"Of course, I do. That is all I want," she replied with such vehemence that Aidan felt his breath catch in his chest. Emily a title hunter? He'd never pegged her for such a creature. Margaret had been after his title, but it never occurred to him that Emily cared a whit for his title, or his money for that matter. Furthermore, Michael had claimed that he'd saved him from a similar fate with Margaret. Why now would he be encouraging Emily in the same pursuit as the one he had foiled for Margaret?

"You only need follow my directions, Em. Come to me tonight and I shall tell you what to do. You'll be the Duchess of Rutherford, just as you want, and I will have what I want. Is it agreed?"

Michael leaned forward and pressed a whispered word against her ear. She smiled and looked shyly down at her folded hands. "I will come to you," she said quietly. "But it must be in secret."

"Of course," Michael chuckled. "It is our secret, Em."

And Aidan felt as though his marrow had frozen in his bones.

⚜

Fire engulfed the room and he threw his arms over his face, shielding himself from the heat and brightness of the flames as they licked their way up the walls and the curtains.

He was panting now, running to the door, finding it locked. The wood was much too thick to be heard through, too thick and sturdy to break through. Whirling around he saw the window, the chair sitting beneath it. Coughing, his lungs burning, his eyes tearing with the smoke, he hurtled the chair through the leaded paned glass. The cold autumn wind whooshed into the room causing the flames to roar wildly and spread with alarming speed.

The room was now engulfed with a roaring blaze; so too were the curtains that edged his only means of escape. Peering down at the wet grass below, he tried not to think that he was two stories above it. He tried only to think of survival.

He looked at the window casing, noticing that the glass had not shattered evenly. Instead, long, deep shards hung precariously from the top of the frame, like icicles hanging from a house. He could impale himself on one of them, but he refused to think of that. Attempting to kick away the glass with his boot, he missed, knowing that his mind was growing more poisoned with the smoke and fumes of the fire.

Without any recourse he straddled the part of the window that had been cleared of the glass and struggled to avoid the glistening shards despite his tear-blurred eyes. It was then, without any warning that the wooden rod holding up the luxurious, not to mention heavy, velvet curtains wrenched away from the wall.

He knew, could see what would happen before it did. The rod gave way, taking with it plaster from the wall. He saw the white bits go flying, saw the green velvet engulfed in orange flame come toward him. The wind blew in, licking the flames, sending them shooting out towards him.

And then he felt it, a consuming pain as the curtain panel connected with his silk waistcoat. Fire instantly spread to his shoulders and he arched his back, screaming in agony, pitching face forward in an attempt to avoid further contact with the curtain. The side of his face was horribly mauled by the glass shards as he propelled himself out of the window. Connecting hard with the ground, he cried out—screamed really—with the pain as the flames continued to eat their way through his waistcoat and linen shirt.

Unable to do anything else, he writhed, rolling in the dew covered grass. As he lay on his belly, spent and wondering if he could ever survive such pain, he looked up through the black blanket of night and the cloud of smoke to his brother running toward him.

Aidan! Michael had cried, falling to his knees and seeing if he was still alive. I will save you, brother. I will not allow you to die. And Michael hadn't let him die, even though Aidan had begged for death for months. Michael and Jane—and Emily—had refused to indulge him. They had kept him living, and there had been many times that he had cursed them for doing so.

Stirring restlessly on the bed, Aidan came awake with a groan. He was breathing heavy from the dream and his skin was slick with perspiration despite the cool air of the chamber.

The fire had nearly died, leaving a frostiness to chill the room. He was about to get out of bed when he heard the latch on the door wiggle then click open.

Lying still, he heard Emily's uneven and somewhat harsh breaths slice through the black quiet. Not Emily, his mind shouted, not tonight, not after he'd heard his brother command her to come to him.

He heard the door click quietly shut and he felt his stomach tighten. Soft foot-treads padded across the carpet until he knew that she must be standing beside his bed. With lightening speed he reached for her wrist and drew her down to him. "I think you have the wrong room, madame."

He heard her shocked breath and felt her pulse leap beneath his thumb. Rage threatened his control. She was here in what she assumed was Michael's room, a room where she was going to act the whore for his brother. Damn her, how had he been wrong about Emily? He was so certain, so confident that he had not made the same mistake about Emily as he had about Margaret.

She whimpered when he gripped her wrist tighter and he forced whatever conscience he had aside. She had come to play the whore and he was going to see to it she did just that.

Rising from the bed, he gripped her wrist, forcing her to step back. Her gaze, wide-eyed and frightened, gleamed up at him in the shaft of pale moonlight. Ruthlessly he squelched the niggling voice inside his head, she was here for Michael. He must remember that.

"You've made a huge mistake by coming here tonight, Emily, do you know that?"

"No." She wrenched her wrist free and reached for the collar of the lace robe—the robe he had paid for.

Aidan sucked in his breath when he saw the red chemise that covered her body. Standing before the window, her curves illuminated by moonlight, he felt his cock go rigid. He had never seen anything quite as titillating as the red lace that barely concealed Emily's lush figure.

The bodice fitted tightly against her breasts, the flounced edge dipping so low that most of her breasts were bared. The hem scarcely concealed the shadow of her sex, and Aidan knew that if he turned her around, the curve of her bottom would be bare. His mind supplied the image of his hand tracing that lovely bottom.

"Do you like it?" she asked in her shy little voice that made him want to ravish her. How could she be shy when she had willingly come to a man's room dressed like that?

With lightening speed, he turned her around so that she was facing the wall. He reached for her wrists, holding them above her and Emily gasped as he untied the ribbon around her throat and bound her wrists with it.

"Is this the sort of sport you were thinking of when you came here tonight? Is this what you want?" he panted, pressing his hard body against her back.

She gasped when her breasts grazed the cold wall, but he ignored the sound and pressed her forward. She had never seen him like this, this masterful and dangerous. She was aware of the barely controlled emotion simmering within him.

He clutched her bound fingers in his own hand, while his other hand, warm and soft, stroked the length of her back to where the chemise hung low around her hips. Emily held her breath, sensing the struggle waging deep inside him. He was hurting and no doubt feeling betrayed by what he thought was her aversion to him. She wanted to reach out to him, yet she instinctively knew that he was beyond listening.

"How much I want you like this. Bare-assed and willing," he drawled, sliding his hand down her bottom and cupping her. "I'll wager that I could make you beg for it. God, I want that," he groaned, thrusting his erection against her. "I want to hear you beg me for it."

"I will. If that is what you want, I will beg you."

"You are willing, aren't you, Emily? Willing to do anything to get what you want."

"I am willing to do anything for you."

"For your Dark Lord, Emily? Will you do anything for him? I know how bloody eager you are to please him."

"Just for you," she whispered. She should have said his name, but he gave her no time when he put his knee on the window bench and lifted her leg so that her foot was atop his thigh. Coolness caressed her flesh and she felt his fingers stroke her throbbing sex.

"All for me, is it?" he drawled, trailing his tongue up the length of her spine. "I doubt that, love. You'd do whoever it took to get what you want."

"No," she shook her head and tried to release the satin bond around her wrists, but they would not give way and her attempts only made Aidan reach for her hands and press them against the wall.

"Leave them up," he commanded. "I want you at my mercy. You can be the slave this time, Emily."

"Why?"

He turned her around so that she was looking into his eyes, eyes that were burning with an intensity she had never seen before. Was it all from passion, or was it anger glistening back at her?

"Because you have made a slave of me, Emily. Because this time you shall be my slave. This time you shall learn what it is like to be at the mercy of one person."

Her hands were still raised above her head and the position pushed her breasts forward, making her back arch so that she appeared to be flagrantly offering herself to him. His gaze skimmed the length of her, and she closed her eyes when she felt his fingers encase her throat, then slowly slide down her neck.

She was breathing hard, but not in fear. She was excited, aroused beyond belief. He was dangerous like this and this part of him called to a buried yearning deep inside her. In that second, she desperately wanted to see, to experience everything he was trying so hard to keep from her. She wanted this man—this angry, hurting man. She wanted nothing more than to soothe the ache in his body and his soul.

"Aidan," she moaned when he circled her erect nipple through the lace. His finger stilled and his gaze flickered up to meet hers. "Aidan, please. I burn, I ache."

And then suddenly he ripped her chemise in half, freeing her straining breasts. The lace gave way, exposing her body, and she heard his breath catch.

"Why have you come here?" he groaned, cupping her breasts and stroking her nipples with his thumbs. "Why now? Why me?"

"Because I love you," she cried.

"Me or my title?" he asked, while raising her leg so that the ball of her foot rested against the cushion of the window seat. "Me or my money?"

She tried to talk, but her teeth were chattering and she was starting to tremble with desire. Her body literally throbbed for him. She needed his touch. Needed him.

He went to his knees, his hands stroking the undersides of her breasts before trailing down her belly. His fingers raked through her curls, and she felt his hot breath against her moist skin.

"Why have you come here?" He licked her swollen folds, long and slow he lapped at her and she felt her leg weaken, but he reached for her knee and steadied her, spreading her sex and exposing her to his gaze. "Have you come to play the whore, making me crazed with lust so that your lover can steal into the room and plunge a knife in my back while I'm rutting atop you?"

"No, Aidan," she whimpered, wishing she could run her hands through his hair. "I came to be with you. I will be whatever you want, whatever you desire, if you will only give me the chance."

"So you have come to be my slave," he asked darkly. "Tell me, what of my brother? Will he be the one you imagine doing this with. Will it be his tongue licking you, flicking your flesh until you scream? Will it be him you envision when I have you on your knees, thrusting hard into you? Will you be thinking of becoming the next Duchess of Rutherford while I'm pounding into you?"

"I will think of nothing but the pleasure you'll give me. Oh, God, Aidan, yes," she moaned, thrusting her hips out and rocking back and forth as his tongue greedily licked her. "Oh yes, I'll do anything for this, Aidan."

"Anything?" he asked looking up at her, a slow grin parting his lips. She nodded, and he stood up, reaching for the red satin ribbon that bound her hands. "I will keep you to that, you know. After all, I have a lifetime of fantasies to live out, and in just one short night."

"Aidan," she reached for him, but he grasped her wrist and held her still. Freeing the buttons from his trousers, he slid them over his hips and kicked them aside. Releasing her, he pulled his shirt over his belly and shoulders. Balling the linen in his hand, he threw it atop his trousers, then he reached for her hands before bringing her to his chest and she sucked in her breath feeling his skin against hers for the first time.

"You said you would do anything?" he asked leaning against the wall before tipping her chin up with his fingers. She nodded and swallowed hard wishing she could see his expression, wishing the shadows would illuminate his face and not his body which was looking hard and taut in the silvery moonlight. But this was Aidan. He wouldn't hurt her. She trusted him.

He reached for his erection and stroked it slowly. Her gaze slid to his thick length, watching the way he expertly stroked himself, but he tipped her chin up and forced her gaze to his face. "Make me come with your mouth."

He pressed her down to her knees, his touch not ungentle. She looked up at him and saw that he watched her with his haunting eyes. Still stroking his erect phallus in slow, sensual strokes, he traced her lips with his free hand, his eyes searching her face. "You said you would be anyone," he whispered, "can you be someone who wants me?"

"Yes." She reached out and trailed her fingers down his taut belly.

"Show me," he gritted between his teeth and she looked down to see that he was eagerly pumping his erection. She took him in her mouth and sucked him and he groaned, but he did not loosen his hold; instead he continued to pleasure himself and watch her as she sucked, then licked. "So good. I never dreamed you'd take to this so well, Em. Never have I felt something so damn good." She sucked him harder, faster, matching his rhythm, watching as the muscles of his stomach tensed and bunched. "I'm so close to coming, Em, but not like this."

And then he slid from her mouth and picked her up, carrying her to the bed. Her fingers clutched his shoulders and she felt his puckered skin beneath her fingers. Their gazes met and she felt him stiffen. "I want you, Aidan. I've only ever wanted you."

He placed her on the bed so that she was lying on her back. Tugging on her ankles, he brought her to the edge of the bed and he kneeled down and lowered his mouth to her, licking her with such intensity she felt her orgasm upon her. His tongue was flicking madly along her sex and she felt his finger dip into her wetness and slide along her bottom to the cleft of her cheeks where he circled her slowly, allowing her to accustom herself to the strange sensation. And then one finger entered her slit, another finger, the opening hidden between her cleft. She gasped, shocked at the intrusion, but then he groaned deeply and looked up at her, catching her gaze. "There is now no place where a part of me hasn't been, Emily. I've marked you and you're mine."

She trembled at his words, and knew she was so close to climaxing. He must have known it, because his fingers continued to thrust in and out of her openings while his tongue flicked and laved. She arched her back, the ecstasy rising at a frightening pace. Her fingers clutched the coverlet and her whole body tensed. "That's it," he said darkly. "Let me taste you."

He drank in her arousal, and when she had barely finished arching and squirming, he deprived her of his mouth and moved away from her.

"On your knees, Emily," and he stood back and watched as she did as he ordered. "Lovely," he whispered, trailing his fingers along her bottom. "I can never get enough of you like this."

Slipping his fingers inside her, be pleasured her until she moaned and began to move her hips, then he slid his finger up her cleft and began to circle her. "I have to see all of you. I need to see my finger in this alluring rosebud opening. Beautiful," he said thickly as he sunk one finger within her. She moaned and pushed her bottom out against his hand. "Feel good?" he asked. She nodded her head and looked back at him over her shoulder. Her gaze dropped down to her bottom and she watched as he again slowly sunk his finger inside her. "When you look at me like that it makes me crazed, Emily. It's a look of a wanton and it makes me want to show you everything that a man can do to a woman."

She smiled seductively. "Show me."

His lids hooded his eyes and she saw his sexy grin through the shadows. "Bring your hand to your quim," he commanded. "Let me see you play. Let me see you watching my finger sliding in and out your body."

Her hand slid down her body and with two fingers she circled the sensitive nub of flesh at the crest of her curls. She watched his gaze drop from her bottom, to the shadow between her legs. She thrust her hips back and quickened her strokes, her lips parting on harsh pants.

"Shall I fill you?" he asked, as casually as if he was asking her if she wanted a cup of tea. She nodded and he moved his finger parted her folds before sinking into her sheath.

She moaned, a deep guttural moan and Aidan worked her harder. Damn, but not even the most skilled whore had driven him this mad. Good God, she was making him hot with her sultry looks and her sexy pants. And as he watched her fingers stroke her sex, as he watched his own fingers plunging in and out of her quim, he knew he was riding the crest of a release that was going to be explosive. Nothing made him more frenzied than to know that Emily was willing to play games. Dark, titillating games, he thought, as he heard her ask for another finger.

"Beg me," he commanded.

She looked back at him, her eyes glistening with sensual desire. "Please, Aidan," she gasped as he inserted another finger.

"Have you room for another, Emily?" She moaned and arched her back and he gripped her hip. "Three fingers, Emily, you're a greedy little thing, aren't you? You're already filled with me and yet you want more. But it is not a finger you need, is it? What you need is a cock. My cock."

And then he parted her swollen folds and entered in one thrust. She gasped, but she continued to finger herself. The sight was damn arousing and he stroked her hard, bringing her hips back to him as he stood before the bed. Her breasts swayed back and forth and he reached around and fondled them, more roughly then he ever had before. He captured them between his hands and pressed them together, thinking how he would like to put his cock between them and spurt his release on her alabaster flesh. He swelled even more inside her, and released her breasts, only to watch and feel them sway against his hand. Their gazes met, and he could not resist purposely pinching her nipples and flicking them with his fingers till she was biting her lower lip in pleasure.

"Take me, Aidan." Her lips parted on a moan as she looked over her shoulder at him and he very slowly circled her nipple then flicked it. "I want you. All of you deep inside me."

"Damn you, Emily," he groaned. "Why do you do this to me? You look at me with that look, that look that says you want to be fucked. You say the words I've longed to hear and I want to believe you. I want to believe you want me as much as I want you."

He stroked her harder as if he could make her desire him more with every thrust. He was taking her hard, but she just kept begging for more, making him more reckless, more hungry to possess her.

"Let me touch you, Aidan," she cried as he thrust deep. "Let me see you."

His mind warred with his heart and before he knew what he was about he was sliding out of her body and lighting the taper that sat atop the commode. Her eyes followed him and their gazes locked. He braved her scrutiny for the faintest seconds before he reached for her and lifted her from the bed.

He brought her legs around his waist and pressed her against the wall. "I'm going to take you like I wanted that night at The Temple. Hard against the wall so that you can take all of this inside you." He reached for her hand and wrapped it around his shaft and she felt it pulsating in her palm. "This is what you want, all this, isn't it?"

"Yes," she moaned in a husky whisper. 'All of this hard length I want inside me—all of you—every inch."

"I want to see your breasts bounce with each one of my thrusts. I want to feel them against me. I want to see your face when you come for me."

She pulled his hair away from his face and looked deeply into his eyes. "How long I've waited to see you like this."

He entered her, taking her against the wall, feeling himself sink deeper and deeper into the abyss with every one of her sighs and whimpers.

"Harder, Aidan," she screamed, gripping his shoulders as he pumped into her.

"You want it hard, Emily?" he growled. And he cupped her breast and squeezed. "You want to be taken by me?"

She nodded and wet her lips. "Make me come for you." She met his gaze and he saw such raw passion and emotion flicker in her eyes. "Fill me. I want to know what it is like to come with you everywhere inside me."

"Beg me to fill you, to fill your body with my flesh."

"Yes," she screamed. He slipped his finger inside the tight opening between her bottom, and plunged his tongue deep within her mouth. She was now filled with him.

She clutched wildly onto one of his shoulders, and she moaned and tensed, riding him hard, riding him as if she had been a part of the demi-monde for years.

She sucked his tongue in an erotic rhythm that made him think of the way she sucked his cock and thrust up harder into her and rocked his pelvis against hers so that her swollen clitoris was being rubbed his movements. Suddenly she tensed, her eyes flew open he and felt the surge of her arousal engulf his shaft.

"Aidan" she cried, tearing her mouth from his. But he clutched the back of her head and slipped his tongue back into her mouth, wanting to be totally inside her when she succumbed to her desire. A desire he had created within her.

"I would do anything for you," he groaned unable to stop himself from coming in long, hot spurts. "I would be anything for you, if I could."

Chapter Twelve

"Aidan?"

Her voice was soft, lethal, like a silent blade sheathing itself into his heart. He could not turn around and see her lying in his bed, naked and vulnerable. He did not want to think of what had just happened.

The covers rustled beneath her body and he swallowed hard as he stared out at the black night, trying to focus on anything other than her naked body moving sensuously against the sheets.

Damn him, he should have let her go the minute she came in the room. Whatever had possessed him to light a candle and bare himself to her? She had seen all of him, had braved his face and his body with the strength of a soldier. She had been strong, not even the faintest hint of disgust or displeasure marred her blissful expression, and he began to wonder if Emily was the world's greatest actress.

He had wanted to believe her, wanted so damn much to hope that she truly desired him, but images of her with Michael, the words they had shared kept ringing through his mind. He thought of Margaret, how she had vowed to struggle and bear his lovemaking and think only of her lover as she was suffering beneath him. He wondered if Emily hadn't done the exact same thing. And yet, she had been so damn wild, so hot in his arms. No woman who was merely bearing his attentions would have allowed him to do half the things that she had allowed—nay, begged him to do.

"Aidan," she whispered softly and he felt her face press against his back. Back and forth, she rubbed her cheek along the velvet of his dressing gown. "Take this off," she coaxed, pulling at the collar till the tops of his shoulders were naked to her gaze.

"Haven't you seen enough?" he snarled, then whirled around and away from her searching fingers. "Forgive me if I don't want to be studied like an attraction at a traveling show."

"Aidan, I would never—"

"Do not tell me you wouldn't think such things, Emily," he roared, the anger spurting forth from a well deep inside him. "I know what you think. I've seen your repulsion. Well, you know what?" he snapped, holding up his scarred hand. "These are the fingers you begged to have inside you. Take a good look at this monster hand, Em, because this is what I use to stroke you."

"You foolish man," she snapped, narrowing her eyes and clutching the sheet around her naked breasts that were flushed and swollen from his amorous advances. "You will not succeed in shaming me. I never thought you were a monster. Never. I have loved you since I was fifteen. That love has only deepened over the years. I never stopped loving you, not even when you announced your engagement to Margaret. Although I will confess to trying very hard not to love you after you broke my heart with your engagement. But my love just wouldn't die, Aidan. I loved you even when you thought nothing of me. I loved you when I feared you might die from your injuries and when you decided you needed to become a recluse. I never stopped wanting you, you stupid man. I even wanted you the night at the Temple of Flora. I couldn't stop thinking of you, or wishing it was you touching me. In fact, I pretended it was you."

"What are you saying?"

"I'm saying I love you, Aidan, scars and all. I've known since the night in the cottage that it was you all along seducing me in the night. I knew and still desired you. It is only your pride that won't believe me."

"I heard you with Michael," he hissed. "Don't lie to me, Emily. I heard you say you wanted the title. I heard him tell you that he would get for it for you, all you needed to do was to come to him. Tell me, Emily, did you take a wrong turn or was this part of your plan?"

Her lips trembled and Emily felt the tears begin to sting behind her eyelids. He was so far above her reach, not even her love could save him, could erase this darkness in him. She had been so wrong about him, about love and passion. Her feelings, her love was all in vain.

"I was wrong," she whispered, tucking the sheet tighter around her body and heading for the door. "You are a monster." His face paled and his expression grew murderous and she looked away from him. "Inside you're ugly, Aidan. You've grown cold and mistrustful and I think I've made the biggest mistake of my life loving you for as long as I have."

He followed her, reaching over her shoulder and slamming the door shut. "You leaving this room will be your biggest mistake, Emily."

And then, feeling helpless, she pressed her forehead against the door and began to weep. She was not inclined to weep at the drop of a hat, but she was reeling from the memories of their fevered loving, from the fierce emotions that welled up within her.

"Emily," he said, his voice a gruff whisper. "You're not crying, are you? Tears won't work on me, you know."

"Well, what does?" she shrieked, turning and confronting him with her frustrations. "What works for you?"

He stepped back and leaned against the door, helpless as he watched the tears flow down her cheeks. He didn't know what to say to her to ease the pain, and he didn't know why he wanted to make it any easier on her in the first place.

"Aidan?" she asked, then stepped forward, letting the sheet slide down her body. "What works for you?" she whispered.

He swallowed hard, watching as she walked to him, naked and unashamed, her hands reaching for the collar of his robe, her fingers pulling at the ties of the gown. He watched her, saw her part the robe and slide her hands down his chest and stomach to where his damnable cock was already hard and searching. She would now know what power she wielded over him. All the evidence she needed was there, jutting out between his legs.

"What do I have to do to show you?" she asked. "What do I have to be? The lady?" she asked, kissing his chest and letting the tip of her tongue glide against his nipple. "The whore?" she cupped his scrotum in one hand and wrapped her fingers of her other hand around his shaft.

He closed his eyes and rested his head against the door. "Just touch me, Em. Let me see the desire in your eyes and feel the love in your touch. Make me feel like you did when you made me fall in love with you."

Their gazes met and she traced her finger along his cheek, then kissed him so tenderly he sighed and brought her close to him.

"Tell me again," she whispered tremulously. "I have waited so long to hear the words. In truth, I never thought I would. Please," she said, her voice quivering. "Please."

He licked his lips and looked down at her as she pressed her face into his chest. "I love you. I fell in love with you the night you stayed and nursed me. The night you sponged me and touched me and whispered in my ear and made me want to live. I want that back, Em. I want to feel like that again. I've dreamt of it every night."

"Come to bed, then." Grabbing him by the hand she led him to the bed and pulled him down, kissing him and running her hands along his shoulders and cheek. "So strong," she whispered, tracing the outline of his shoulders and watching as her fingers stroked his scared flesh. She kissed his scarred cheek. "I hate to think of how you suffered, I hate to think of you alone, fearing to be seen. I hate to think of you hiding from me."

"I wanted you to want me," he said huskily, his voice deep with emotion. His hands ran along her side and then up to her breasts where he allowed his fingers to roam beneath the contours of her breasts.

"I wanted you, Aidan, I still want you. Margaret was shallow and fickle, but I'm not. If you would only give me a chance I could prove it to you."

"What I need right now is to know that what you feel is desire, not pity. I don't want your pity."

"I love touching you, Aidan. I will never tire of touching you and looking at you. I've never pitied you, I've only ever loved you."

"Will you ever tire of loving me?"

She looked up and met his eyes. "Never. I will love you forever, and Michael," she murmured against his lips. "He loves you too. It was his plan to enrage you, to make you so angry that you would leave the safety of the shadows and come for me. It is true," she said, seeing how his eyes began to darken.

Aidan drew in a deep breath, and Emily watched the play of emotions flicker in his eyes. "I owe him a great debt then, for it wasn't until he arrived and I saw him courting you that I discovered an anonymous night with you at The Temple would never be enough. I knew then that I would stop at nothing to have you. Even if that meant revealing my true self to you. I've never felt such agony as I did, watching you with my brother, fearing that it was really him you loved—him you thought was coming to you in the dark."

"I always wanted you, Aidan, it was never Michael I desired. And he didn't want to hurt you, you know, but he knew of no other way to bring you out of the shadows. In fact, he asked me to love you and heal you and after I had done so, he wanted me to try to heal the breach between you. He wants his brother back."

"I caught him with Margaret, you know," he said softly. "I came in search for her, trying to tell myself that if I saw her again I would know that it was her that kept vigil beside me, her that had comforted me and kissed me. I thought if I could see her I would know that the love I had felt was for her—but I knew I was only fooling myself. I knew that it was you I loved. And then I saw Michael with her and I knew that the woman who had loved me so deeply the night before could not have been the conniving creature seducing my brother."

"And you have hated Michael for that?"

He looked up at her and smiled very slowly. "No, I never hated him. I hated myself for being blind to Margaret's manipulations. I hated myself for allowing you to get away from me. What a fool I was to have not married you years ago."

"Indeed you were," she grinned, bringing her arms around his neck.

"And I suppose my brother prevailed upon you to do your duty and marry me and beget many heirs thus relieving him of responsibility so that he could resume his rake's life."

She smiled and kissed him. "He did mention something about a charming widow he had met at a country party and how overseeing the duties of your lands and seeing to your large fortune had hindered his pursuits of said widow."

"Then I shall have to get down to the business of procuring my heir and a spare, won't I, so that my poor brother will not have to worry about being a duke." She smiled and squirmed beneath him as he pulled her to him. "Will you give me that, Em, a life of love and a home and family?"

"Yes."

"Then I give you everything I have."

"Your heart and your love?" she asked, peering up at him with her green eyes.

"You've had that for a long time, now, Em and you'll have them forever more, too." Wrapping her arms about his neck she brought his mouth down to hers. His hand slipped between their bodies, her body arched in anticipation of his touch. "I love you, Emily, never forget it."

And then he touched her and as usually occurred when Aidan had his hands on her body, Emily forgot to think, and instead gave herself up to a passion she had only ever found with the man she had loved and thought never to have.

"Aidan," she purred as he slipped inside her. "Won't you tell me more of The Dark Lord's tale?'

"Yes, my love," he whispered. "I shall write down the entire story and read it to you—every naughty bit, while lying in our bed."

"That sounds so very wicked."

"You're my muse, Em. My lover, my love, my beloved. And never have I been so glad to come out from the shadows. You're my light, Em. Don't ever leave me in darkness again."

"Then look at me as you love me, Aidan. I want to see you, the man who loves me. I want to see the face of the man I have always loved."

"Anything you for you, Emily. Anything."

About the Author:

Always a dreamer, Charlotte Featherstone has been in love with the regency era from the tender age of fourteen when she fell hopelessly in love with Mr. Darcy. When she is not indulging in her fantastical illusions of lounging in a corset and boudoir gown while contemplating which invitation for which ball she shall attend, Charlotte can be found surfing the net under the guise of research, chatting with her critique partners about her next 'masterpiece' while conjuring up her next sexy tortured hero.

Occasionally, when she comes back to the twenty first century, Charlotte can be found reading, writing and generally avoiding any duties attributed to 'Domestic Goddesses'.

Charlotte would love to hear from her readers and invites them to visit her at charlottefeatherstone.net *to see where her 'fantasies' will take her next.*

Men you've been dreaming about!

Secrets

Satisfy your desire for more.

eel the wild adventure, fierce passion and the power of love in every *Secrets* Collection story. Red Sage Publishing's romance authors create richly crafted, sexy, sensual, novella-length stories. Each one is just the right length for reading after a long and hectic day.

Each volume in the *Secrets* Collection has four diverse, ultra-sexy, romantic novellas brimming with adventure, passion and love. More adventurous tales for the adventurous reader. The *Secrets* Collection are a glorious mix of romance genre; numerous historical settings, contemporary, paranormal, science fiction and suspense. We are always looking for new adventures.

Reader response to the *Secrets* volumes has been great! Here's just a small sample:

> *"I loved the variety of settings. Four completely wonderful time periods, give you four completely wonderful reads."*

> *"Each story was a page-turning tale I hated to put down."*

> *"I love Secrets! When is the next volume coming out? This one was Hot! Loved the heroes!"*

Secrets have won raves and awards. We could go on, but why don't you find out for yourself—order your set of *Secrets* today! See the back for details.

Secrets, Volume 1

Listen to what reviewers say:

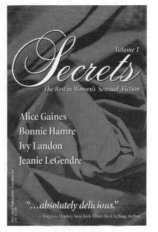

"These stories take you beyond romance into the realm of erotica. I found *Secrets* absolutely delicious."

—Virginia Henley,
New York Times Best Selling Author

"*Secrets* is a collection of novellas for the daring, adventurous woman who's not afraid to give her fantasies free reign."

— Kathe Robin, *Romantic Times* Magazine

"...In fact, the men featured in all the stories are terrific, they all want to please and pleasure their women. If you like erotic romance you will love *Secrets*."

—*Romantic Readers* Review

In *Secrets, Volume 1* you'll find:

A Lady's Quest by Bonnie Hamre

Widowed Lady Antonia Blair-Sutworth searches for a lover to save her from the handsome Duke of Sutherland. The "auditions" may be shocking but utterly tantalizing.

The Spinner's Dream by Alice Gaines

A seductive fantasy that leaves every woman wishing for her own private love slave, desperate and running for his life.

The Proposal by Ivy Landon

This tale is a walk on the wild side of love. *The Proposal* will taunt you, tease you, and shock you. A contemporary erotica for the adventurous woman.

The Gift by Jeanie LeGendre

Immerse yourself in this historic tale of exotic seduction, bondage and a concubine's surrender to the Sultan's desire. Can Alessandra live the life and give the gift the Sultan demands of her?

Secrets, Volume 2

Listen to what reviewers say:

"*Secrets* offers four novellas of sensual delight; each beautifully written with intense feeling and dedication to character development. For those seeking stories with heightened intimacy, look no further."

—Kathee Card, *Romancing the Web*

"Such a welcome diversity in styles and genres. Rich characterization in sensual tales. An exciting read that's sure to titillate the senses."

—Cheryl Ann Porter

"*Secrets 2* left me breathless. Sensual satisfaction guaranteed...times four!"

—Virginia Henley, *New York Times* Best Selling Author

In *Secrets, Volume 2* you'll find:

Surrogate Lover by Doreen DeSalvo

Adrian Ross is a surrogate sex therapist who has all the answers and control. He thought he'd seen and done it all, but he'd never met Sarah.

Snowbound by Bonnie Hamre

A delicious, sensuous regency tale. The marriage-shy Earl of Howden is teased and tortured by his own desires and finds there is a woman who can equal his overpowering sensuality.

Roarke's Prisoner by Angela Knight

Elise, a starship captain, remembers the eager animal submission she'd known before at her captor's hands and refuses to become his toy again. However, she has no idea of the delights he's planned for her this time.

Savage Garden by Susan Paul

Raine's been captured by a mysterious and dangerous revolutionary leader in Mexico. At first her only concern is survival, but she quickly finds lush erotic nights in her captor's arms.

Winner of the Fallot Literary Award for Fiction!

Secrets, Volume 3

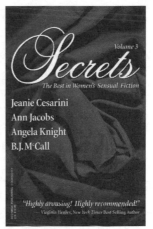

Listen to what reviewers say:

"*Secrets, Volume 3*, leaves the reader breathless. A delicious confection of sensuous treats awaits the reader on each turn of the page!"
—Kathee Card, *Romancing the Web*

"From the FBI to Police Dectective to Vampires to a Medieval Warlord home from the Crusade—*Secrets 3* is simply the best!"
—Susan Paul, award winning author

"An unabashed celebration of sex. Highly arousing! Highly recommended!"
—Virginia Henley, *New York Times* Best Selling Author

In *Secrets, Volume 3* you'll find:

The Spy Who Loved Me by Jeanie Cesarini

Undercover FBI agent Paige Ellison's sexual appetites rise to new levels when she works with leading man Christopher Sharp, the cunning agent who uses all his training to capture her body and heart.

The Barbarian by Ann Jacobs

Lady Brianna vows not to surrender to the barbaric Giles, Earl of Harrow. He must use sexual arts learned in the infidels' harem to conquer his bride. A word of caution—this is not for the faint of heart.

Blood and Kisses by Angela Knight

A vampire assassin is after Beryl St. Cloud. Her only hope lies with Decker, another vampire and ex-mercenary. Broke, she offers herself as payment for his services. Will his seductive powers take her very soul?

Love Undercover by B.J. McCall

Amanda Forbes is the bait in a strip joint sting operation. While she performs, fellow detective "Cowboy" Cooper gets to watch. Though he excites her, she must fight the temptation to surrender to the passion.

Winner of the 1997 Under the Covers Readers Favorite Award

Secrets, Volume 4

Listen to what reviewers say:

"Provocative...seductive...a must read!"

—*Romantic Times* Magazine

"These are the kind of stories that romance readers that 'want a little more' have been looking for all their lives...."

—*Affaire de Coeur* Magazine

"*Secrets, Volume 4*, has something to satisfy every erotic fantasy... simply sexational!"

—Virginia Henley, *New York Times* Best Selling Author

In *Secrets, Volume 4* you'll find:

An Act of Love by Jeanie Cesarini

Shelby Moran's past left her terrified of sex. International film star Jason Gage must gently coach the young starlet in the ways of love. He wants more than an act—he wants Shelby to feel true passion in his arms.

Enslaved by Desirée Lindsey

Lord Nicholas Summer's air of danger, dark passions, and irresistible charm have brought Lady Crystal's long-hidden desires to the surface. Will he be able to give her the one thing she desires before it's too late?

The Bodyguard by Betsy Morgan and Susan Paul

Kaki York is a bodyguard, but watching the wild, erotic romps of her client's sexual conquests on the security cameras is getting to her—and her partner, the ruggedly handsome James Kulick. Can she resist his insistent desire to have her?

The Love Slave by Emma Holly

A woman's ultimate fantasy. For one year, Princess Lily will be attended to by three delicious men of her choice. While she delights in playing with the first two, it's the reluctant Grae, with his powerful chest, black eyes and hair, that stirs her desires.

Secrets, Volume 5

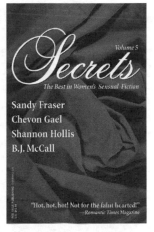

Listen to what reviewers say:

"Hot, hot, hot! Not for the faint-hearted!"
—*Romantic Times* Magazine

"As you make your way through the stories, you will find yourself becoming hotter and hotter. *Secrets* just keeps getting better and better."
—*Affaire de Coeur* Magazine

"*Secrets 5* is a collage of lucious sensuality. Any woman who reads *Secrets* is in for an awakening!"
— Virginia Henley, *New York Times* Best Selling Author

In *Secrets, Volume 5* you'll find:

Beneath Two Moons by Sandy Fraser
Ready for a very wild romp? Step into the future and find Conor, rough and masculine like frontiermen of old, on the prowl for a new conquest. In his sights, Dr. Eva Kelsey. She got away once before, but this time Conor makes sure she begs for more.

Insatiable by Chevon Gael
Marcus Remington photographs beautiful models for a living, but it's Ashlyn Fraser, a young corporate exec having some glamour shots done, who has stolen his heart. It's up to Marcus to help her discover her inner sexual self.

Strictly Business by Shannon Hollis
Elizabeth Forrester knows it's tough enough for a woman to make it to the top in the corporate world. Garrett Hill, the most beautiful man in Silicon Valley, has to come along to stir up her wildest fantasies. Dare she give in to both their desires?

Alias Smith and Jones by B.J. McCall
Meredith Collins finds herself stranded overnight at the airport. A handsome stranger by the name of Smith offers her sanctuaty for the evening and she finds those mesmerizing, green-flecked eyes hard to resist. Are they to be just two ships passing in the night?

Secrets, Volume 6

Listen to what reviewers say:

"Red Sage was the first and remains the leader of Women's Erotic Romance Fiction Collections!"

— *Romantic Times* Magazine

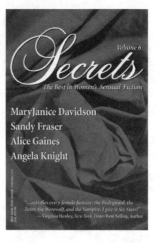

"*Secrets, Volume 6*, is the best of *Secrets* yet. ...four of the most erotic stories in one volume than this reader has yet to see anywhere else. ...These stories are full of erotica at its best and you'll definitely want to keep it handy for lots of re-reading!"

— *Affaire de Coeur* Magazine

"*Secrets 6* satisfies every female fantasy: the Bodyguard, the Tutor, the Werewolf, and the Vampire. I give it Six Stars!"

— Virginia Henley, *New York Times* Best Selling Author

In *Secrets, Volume 6* you'll find:

Flint's Fuse by Sandy Fraser

Dana Madison's father has her "kidnapped" for her own safety. Flint, the tall, dark and dangerous mercenary, is hired for the job. But just which one is the prisoner—Dana will try *anything* to get away.

Love's Prisoner by MaryJanice Davidson

Trapped in an elevator, Jeannie Lawrence experienced unwilling rapture at Michael Windham's hands. She never expected the devilishly handsome man to show back up in her life—or turn out to be a werewolf!

The Education of Miss Felicity Wells by Alice Gaines

Felicity Wells wants to be sure she'll satisfy her soon-to-be husband but she needs a teacher. Dr. Marcus Slade, an experienced lover, agrees to take her on as a student, but can he stop short of taking her completely?

A Candidate for the Kiss by Angela Knight

Working on a story, reporter Dana Ivory stumbles onto a more amazing one—a sexy, secret agent who happens to be a vampire. She wants her story but Gabriel Archer wants more from her than just sex and blood.

Secrets, Volume 7

Listen to what reviewers say:

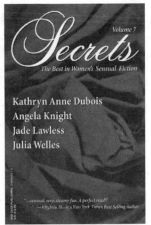

"Get out your asbestos gloves — *Secrets Volume 7* is...extremely hot, true erotic romance...passionate and titillating. There's nothing quite like baring your secrets!"

—*Romantic Times* Magazine

"...sensual, sexy, steamy fun. A perfect read!"

—Virginia Henley,
New York Times Best Selling Author

"Intensely provocative and disarmingly romantic, *Secrets*, *Volume 7*, is a romance reader's paradise that will take you beyond your wildest dreams!"

— Ballston Book House Review

In *Secrets, Volume 7* you'll find:

Amelia's Innocence by Julia Welles

Amelia didn't know her father bet her in a card game with Captain Quentin Hawke, so honor demands a compromise—three days of erotic foreplay, leaving her virginity and future intact.

The Woman of His Dreams by Jade Lawless

From the day artist Gray Avonaco moves in next door, Joanna Morgan is plagued by provocative dreams. But what she believes is unrequited lust, Gray sees as another chance to be with the woman he loves. He must persuade her that even death can't stop true love.

Surrender by Kathryn Anne Dubois

Free-spirited Lady Johanna wants no part of the binding strictures society imposes with her marriage to the powerful Duke. She doesn't know the dark Duke wants sensual adventure, and sexual satisfaction.

Kissing the Hunter by Angela Knight

Navy Seal Logan McLean hunts the vampires who murdered his wife. Virginia Hart is a sexy vampire searching for her lost soul-mate only to find him in a man determined to kill her. She must convince him all vampires aren't created equally.

**Winner of the Venus Book Club
Best Book of the Year**

Secrets, Volume 8

Listen to what reviewers say:

"*Secrets, Volume 8*, is an amazing compilation of sexy stories covering a wide range of subjects, all designed to titillate the senses. …you'll find something for everybody in this latest version of *Secrets*."

—*Affaire de Coeur* Magazine

"*Secrets Volume 8*, is simply sensational!"

—Virginia Henley, *New York Times* Best Selling Author

"These delectable stories will have you turning the pages long into the night. Passionate, provocative and perfect for setting the mood…."

—*Escape to Romance* Reviews

In *Secrets, Volume 8* you'll find:

Taming Kate by Jeanie Cesarini

Kathryn Roman inherits a legal brothel. Little does this city girl know the town of Love, Nevada wants her to be their new madam so they've charged Trey Holliday, one very dominant cowboy, with taming her.

Jared's Wolf by MaryJanice Davidson

Jared Rocke will do anything to avenge his sister's death, but ends up attracted to Moira Wolfbauer, the she-wolf sworn to protect her pack. Joining forces to stop a killer, they learn love defies all boundaries.

My Champion, My Lover by Alice Gaines

Celeste Broder is a woman committed for having a sexy appetite. Mayor Robert Albright may be her champion—if she can convince him her freedom will mean a chance to indulge their appetites together.

Kiss or Kill by Liz Maverick

In this post-apocalyptic world, Camille Kazinsky's military career rides on her ability to make a choice—whether the robo called Meat should live or die. Meat's future depends on proving he's human enough to live, man enough…to makes her feel like a woman.

Winner of the Venus Book Club
Best Book of the Year

Secrets, Volume 9

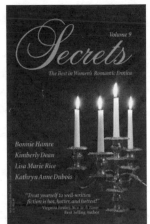

Listen to what reviewers say:

"Everyone should expect only the most erotic stories in a *Secrets* book. ...if you like your stories full of hot sexual scenes, then this is for you!"
> —Donna Doyle Romance Reviews

"*SECRETS 9*...is sinfully delicious, highly arousing, and hotter than hot as the pages practically burn up as you turn them."
> —Suzanne Coleburn, Reader To Reader Reviews/Belles & Beaux of Romance

"Treat yourself to well-written fictionthat's hot, hotter, and hottest!"
> —Virginia Henley, *New York Times* Best Selling Author

In *Secrets, Volume 9* you'll find:

Wild For You by Kathryn Anne Dubois

When college intern, Georgie, gets captured by a Congo wildman, she discovers this specimen of male virility has never seen a woman. The research possibilities are endless!

Wanted by Kimberly Dean

FBI Special Agent Jeff Reno wants Danielle Carver. There's her body, brains—and that charge of treason on her head. Dani goes on the run, but the sexy Fed is hot on her trail.

Secluded by Lisa Marie Rice

Nicholas Lee's wealth and power came with a price—his enemies will kill anyone he loves. When Isabelle steals his heart, Nicholas secludes her in his palace for a lifetime of desire in only a few days.

Flights of Fantasy by Bonnie Hamre

Chloe taught others to see the realities of life but she's never shared the intimate world of her sensual yearnings. Given the chance, will she be woman enough to fulfill her most secret erotic fantasy?

Secrets, Volume 10

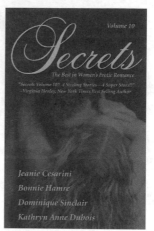

Listen to what reviewers say:

"*Secrets Volume 10*, an erotic dance through medieval castles, sultan's palaces, the English countryside and expensive hotel suites, explodes with passion-filled pages."

—*Romantic Times BOOKclub*

"Having read the previous nine volumes, this one fulfills the expectations of what is expected in a *Secrets* book: romance and eroticism at its best!!"

—*Fallen Angel Reviews*

"All are hot steamy romances so if you enjoy erotica romance, you are sure to enjoy *Secrets, Volume 10*. All this reviewer can say is WOW!!"

—*The Best Reviews*

In *Secrets, Volume 10* you'll find:

Private Eyes by Dominique Sinclair

When a mystery man captivates P.I. Nicolla Black during a stakeout, she discovers her no-seduction rule bending under the pressure of long denied passion. She agrees to the seduction, but he demands her total surrender.

The Ruination of Lady Jane by Bonnie Hamre

To avoid her upcoming marriage, Lady Jane Ponsonby-Maitland flees into the arms of Havyn Attercliffe. She begs him to ruin her rather than turn her over to her odious fiancé.

Code Name: Kiss by Jeanie Cesarini

Agent Lily Justiss is on a mission to defend her country against terrorists that requires giving up her virginity as a sex slave. As her master takes her body, desire for her commanding officer Seth Blackthorn fuels her mind.

The Sacrifice by Kathryn Anne Dubois

Lady Anastasia Bedovier is days from taking her vows as a Nun. Before she denies her sensuality forever, she wants to experience pleasure. Count Maxwell is the perfect man to initiate her into erotic delight.

Secrets, Volume 11

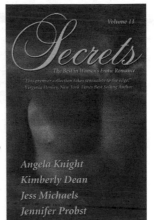

Listen to what reviewers say:

"*Secrets Volume 11* delivers once again with storylines that include erotic masquerades, ancient curses, modern-day betrayal and a prince charming looking for a kiss." **4 Stars**

—*Romantic Times BOOKclub*

"Indulge yourself with this erotic treat and join the thousands of readers who just can't get enough. Be forewarned that *Secrets 11* will whet your appetite for more, but will offer you the ultimate in pleasurable erotic literature."

—*Ballston Book House Review*

"*Secrets 11* quite honestly is my favorite anthology from Red Sage so far."

— *The Best Reviews*

In *Secrets, Volume 11* you'll find:

Masquerade by Jennifer Probst

Hailey Ashton is determined to free herself from her sexual restrictions. Four nights of erotic pleasures without revealing her identity. A chance to explore her secret desires without the fear of unmasking.

Ancient Pleasures by Jess Michaels

Isabella Winslow is obsessed with finding out what caused her late husband's death, but trapped in an Egyptian concubine's tomb with a sexy American raider, succumbing to the mummy's sensual curse takes over.

Manhunt by Kimberly Dean

Framed for murder, Michael Tucker takes Taryn Swanson hostage—the one woman who can clear him. Despite the evidence against him, the attraction between them is strong. Tucker resorts to unconventional, yet effective methods of persuasion to change the sexy ADA's mind.

Wake Me by Angela Knight

Chloe Hart received a sexy painting of a sleeping knight. Radolf of Varik has been trapped for centuries in the painting since, cursed by a witch. His only hope is to visit the dreams of women and make one of them fall in love with him so she can free him with a kiss.

Secrets, Volume 12

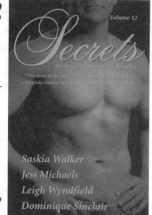

Listen to what reviewers say:

"*Secrets Volume 12*, turns on the heat with a seductive encounter inside a bookstore, a temple of naughty and sensual delight, a galactic inferno that thaws ice, and a lightening storm that lights up the English shoreline. Tales of looking for love in all the right places with a heat rating out the charts." **4½ Stars**

—*Romantic Times BOOKclub*

"I really liked these stories.You want great escapism? Read *Secrets, Volume 12*."

—*Romance Reviews*

In *Secrets, Volume 12* you'll find:

Good Girl Gone Bad by Dominique Sinclair

Reagan's dreams are finally within reach. Setting out to do research for an article, nothing could have prepared her for Luke, or his offer to teach her everything she needs to know about sex. Licentious pleasures, forbidden desires… inspiring the best writing she's ever done.

Aphrodite's Passion by Jess Michaels

When Selena flees Victorian London before her evil stepchildren can institutionalize her for hysteria, Gavin is asked to bring her back home. But when he finds her living on the island of Cyprus, his need to have her begins to block out every other impulse.

White Heat by Leigh Wyndfield

Raine is hiding in an icehouse in the middle of nowhere from one of the scariest men in the universes. Walker escaped from a burning prison. Imagine their surprise when they find out they have the same man to blame for their miseries. Passion, revenge and love are in their future.

Summer Lightning by Saskia Walker

Sculptress Sally is enjoying an idyllic getaway on a secluded cove when she spots a gorgeous man walking naked on the beach. When Julian finds an attractive woman shacked up in his cove, he has to check her out. But what will he do when he finds she's secretly been using him as a model?

Secrets, Volume 13

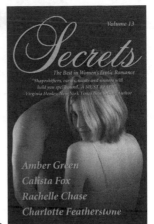

Listen to what reviewers say:

"In *Secrets Volume 13*, the temperature gets turned up a few notches with a mistaken personal ad, shape-shifters destined to love, a hot Regency lord and his lady, as well as a bodyguard protecting his woman. Emotions and flames blaze high in Red Sage's latest foray into the sensual and delightful art of love." **4½ Stars**

—*Romantic Times BOOKclub*

"The sex is still so hot the pages nearly ignite! Read *Secrets, Volume 13!*"

—*Romance Reviews*

In *Secrets, Volume 13* you'll find:

Out of Control by Rachelle Chase

Astrid's world revolves around her business and she's hoping to pick up wealthy Erik Santos as a client. Only he's hoping to pick up something entirely different. Will she give in to the seductive pull of his proposition?

Hawkmoor by Amber Green

Shape-shifters answer to Darien as he acts in the name of the long-missing Lady Hawkmoor, their hereditary ruler. When she unexpectedly surfaces, Darien must deal with a scrappy individual whose wary eyes hold the other half of his soul, but who has the power to destroy his world.

Lessons in Pleasure by Charlotte Featherstone

A wicked bargain has Lily vowing never to yield to the demands of the rake she once loved and lost. Unfortunately, Damian, the Earl of St. Croix, or Saint as he is infamously known, will not take 'no' for an answer.

In the Heat of the Night by Calista Fox

Haunted by a century-old curse, Molina fears she won't live to see her thirtieth birthday. Nick, her former bodyguard, is hired back into service to protect her from the fatal accidents that plague her family. But *In the Heat of the Night*, will his passion and love for her be enough to convince Molina they have a future together?

Secrets, Volume 14

Listen to what reviewers say:

"*Secrets Volume 14* will excite readers with its diverse selection of delectable sexy tales ranging from a fourteenth century love story to a sci-fi rebel who falls for a irresistible research scientist to a trio of determined vampires who battle for the same woman to a virgin sacrifice who falls in love with a beast. A cornucopia of pure delight!" **4½ Stars**

—*Romantic Times BOOKclub*

"This book contains four erotic tales sure to keep readers up long into the night."

—*Romance Junkies*

In *Secrets, Volume 14* you'll find:

Soul Kisses by Angela Knight

Beth's been kidnapped by Joaquin Ramirez, a sadistic vampire. Handsome vampire cousins, Morgan and Garret Axton, come to her rescue. Can she find happiness with two vampires?

Temptation in Time by Alexa Aames

Ariana escaped the Middle Ages after stealing a kiss of magic from sexy sorcerer, Marcus de Grey. When he brings her back, they begin a battle of wills and a sexual odyssey that could spell disaster for them both.

Ailis and the Beast by Jennifer Barlowe

When Ailis agreed to be her village's sacrifice to the mysterious Beast she was prepared to sacrifice her virtue, and possibly her life. But some things aren't what they seem. Ailis and the Beast are about to discover the greatest sacrifice may be the human heart.

Night Heat by Leigh Wynfield

When Rip Bowhite leads a revolt on the prison planet, he ends up struggling to survive against monsters that rule the night. Jemma, the prison's Healer, won't allow herself to be distracted by the instant attraction she feels for Rip. As the stakes are raised and death draws near, love seems doomed in the heat of the night.

Secrets, Volume 15

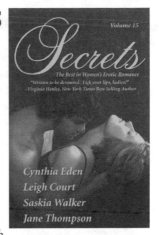

Listen to what reviewers say:

"*Secrets Volume 15* blends humor, tension and steamy romance in its newest collection that sizzles with passion between unlikely pairs—a male chauvinist columnist and a librarian turned erotica author; a handsome werewolf and his resisting mate; an unfulfilled woman and a sexy police officer and a Victorian wife who learns discipline can be fun. Readers will revel in this delicious assortment of thrilling tales." **4 Stars**
—*Romantic Times BOOKclub*

"This book contains four tales by some of today's hottest authors that will tease your senses and intrigue your mind."
—*Romance Junkies*

In *Secrets, Volume 15* you'll find:

Simon Says by Jane Thompson
Simon Campbell is a newspaper columnist who panders to male fantasies. Georgina Kennedy is a respectable librarian. On the surface, these two have nothing in common... but don't judge a book by its cover.

Bite of the Wolf by Cynthia Eden
Gareth Morlet, alpha werewolf, has finally found his mate. All he has to do is convince Trinity to join with him, to give in to the pleasure of a werewolf's mating, and then she will be his... forever.

Falling for Trouble by Saskia Walker
With 48 hours to clear her brother's name, Sonia Harmond finds help from irresistible bad boy, Oliver Eaglestone. When the erotic tension between them hits fever pitch, securing evidence to thwart an international arms dealer isn't the only danger they face.

The Disciplinarian by Leigh Court
Headstrong Clarissa Babcock is sent to the shadowy legend known as The Disciplinarian for instruction in proper wifely obedience. Jared Ashworth uses the tools of seduction to show her how to control a demanding husband, but her beauty, spirit, and uninhibited passion make Jared hunger to keep her—and their darkly erotic nights—all for himself!

Secrets, Volume 16

Listen to what reviewers say:

"Blackmail, games of chance, nude beaches and masquerades pave a path to heart-tugging emotions and fiery love scenes in Red Sage's latest collection." **4.5 Stars**

—*Romantic Times BOOKclub*

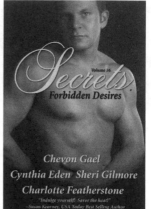

"Red Sage Publishing has brought to the readers an erotic profusion of highly skilled storytellers in their Secrets Vol. 16. ... This is the best Secrets novel to date and this reviewer's favorite."

—*LoveRomances.com*

In *Secrets, Volume 16* you'll find:

Never Enough by Cynthia Eden
For the last three weeks, Abby McGill has been playing with fire. Bad-boy Jake has taught her the true meaning of desire, but she knows she has to end her relationship with him. But Jake isn't about to let the woman he wants walk away from him.

Bunko by Sheri Gilmoore
Tu Tran is forced to decide between Jack, a man, who promises to share every aspect of his life with her, or Dev, the man, who hides behind a mask and only offers night after night of erotic sex. Will she take the gamble of the dice and choose the man, who can see behind her own mask and expose her true desires?

Hide and Seek by Chevon Gael
Kyle DeLaurier ditches his trophy-fiance in favor of a tropical paradise full of tall, tanned, topless females. Private eye, Darcy McLeod, is on the trail of this runaway groom. Together they sizzle while playing Hide and Seek with their true identities.

Seduction of the Muse by Charlotte Featherstone
He's the Dark Lord, the mysterious author who pens the erotic tales of an innocent woman's seduction. She is his muse, the woman he watches from the dark shadows, the woman whose dreams he invades at night.

The Forever Kiss
by Angela Knight

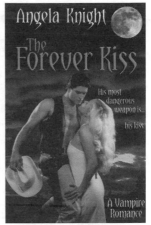

Listen to what reviewers say:

"*The Forever Kiss* flows well with good characters and an interesting plot. ... If you enjoy vampires and a lot of hot sex, you are sure to enjoy *The Forever Kiss*."

—*The Best Reviews*

"Battling vampires, a protective ghost and the ever present battle of good and evil keep excellent pace with the erotic delights in Angela Knight's *The Forever Kiss*—a book that absolutely bites with refreshing paranormal humor." **4½ Stars, Top Pick**

—*Romantic Times BOOKclub*

"I found *The Forever Kiss* to be an exceptionally written, refreshing book. ... I really enjoyed this book by Angela Knight. ... 5 angels!"

—*Fallen Angel Reviews*

"*The Forever Kiss* is the first single title released from Red Sage and if this is any indication of what we can expect, it won't be the last. ... The love scenes are hot enough to give a vampire a sunburn and the fight scenes will have you cheering for the good guys."

—*Really Bad Barb Reviews*

In *The Forever Kiss*:

For years, Valerie Chase has been haunted by dreams of a Texas Ranger she knows only as "Cowboy." As a child, he rescued her from the nightmare vampires who murdered her parents. As an adult, she still dreams of him—but now he's her seductive lover in nights of erotic pleasure.

Yet "Cowboy" is more than a dream—he's the real Cade McKinnon—and a vampire! For years, he's protected Valerie from Edward Ridgemont, the sadistic vampire who turned him. Now, Ridgmont wants Valerie for his own and Cade is the only one who can protect her.

When Val finds herself abducted by her handsome dream man, she's appalled to discover he's one of the vampires she fears. Now, caught in a web of fear and passion, she and Cade must learn to trust each other, even as an immortal monster stalks their every move.

Their only hope of survival is... *The Forever Kiss*.

Romantic Times Best Erotic Novel of the Year

It's not just reviewers raving about *Secrets*. See what readers have to say:

"When are you coming out with a new Volume? I want a new one next month!" via email from a reader.

"I loved the hot, wet sex without vulgar words being used to make it exciting." after *Volume 1*

"I loved the blend of sensuality and sexual intensity—HOT!" after *Volume 2*

"The best thing about *Secrets* is they're hot and brief! The least thing is you do not have enough of them!" after *Volume 3*

"I have been extreamly satisfied with *Secrets*, keep up the good writing." after *Volume 4*

"Stories have plot and characters to support the erotica. They would be good strong stories without the heat." after *Volume 5*

"*Secrets* really knows how to push the envelop better than anyone else." after *Volume 6*

"These are the best sensual stories I have ever read!" after *Volume 7*

"I love, love, love the *Secrets* stories. I now have all of them, please have more books come out each year." after *Volume 8*

"These are the perfect sensual romance stories!" after *Volume 9*

"What I love about *Secrets Volume 10* is how I couldn't put it down!" after *Volume 10*

"All of the *Secrets* volumes are terrific! I have read all of them up to *Secrets Volume 11*. Please keep them coming! I will read every one you make!" after *Volume 11*

Finally, the men you've been dreaming about!

Give the Gift of Spicy Romantic Fiction

Don't want to wait? You can place a retail price ($12.99)
order for any of the *Secrets* volumes from the following:

① **Waldenbooks and Borders Stores**

② **Amazon.com** or **BarnesandNoble.com**

③ **Book Clearinghouse (800-431-1579)**

④ **Romantic Times Magazine** Books by Mail (718-237-1097)

⑤ Special order at other bookstores.
Bookstores: Please contact Baker & Taylor Distributors, Ingram
Book Distributor, or Red Sage Publishing for bookstore sales.

Order by title or ISBN #:

Vol. 1: 0-9648942-0-3	**Vol. 7:** 0-9648942-7-0	**Vol. 13:** 0-9754516-3-4
ISBN #13 978-0-9648942-0-4	ISBN #13 978-0-9648942-7-3	ISBN #13 978-0-9754516-3-2
Vol. 2: 0-9648942-1-1	**Vol. 8:** 0-9648942-8-9	**Vol. 14:** 0-9754516-4-2
ISBN #13 978-0-9648942-1-1	ISBN #13 978-0-9648942-9-7	ISBN #13 978-0-9754516-4-9
Vol. 3: 0-9648942-2-X	**Vol. 9:** 0-9648942-9-7	**Vol. 15:** 0-9754516-5-0
ISBN #13 978-0-9648942-2-8	ISBN #13 978-0-9648942-9-7	ISBN #13 978-0-9754516-5-6
Vol. 4: 0-9648942-4-6	**Vol. 10:** 0-9754516-0-X	Vol. 16: 0-9754516-6-9
ISBN #13 978-0-9648942-4-2	ISBN #13 978-0-9754516-0-1	ISBN #13 978-0-9754516-6-3
Vol. 5: 0-9648942-5-4	**Vol. 11:** 0-9754516-1-8	
ISBN #13 978-0-9648942-5-9	ISBN #13 978-0-9754516-1-8	
Vol. 6: 0-9648942-6-2	**Vol. 12:** 0-9754516-2-6	
ISBN #13 978-0-9648942-6-6	ISBN #13 978-0-9754516-2-5	

The Forever Kiss: 0-9648942-3-8 • ISBN #13 978-0-9648942-3-5 ($14.00)

Red Sage Publishing Mail Order Form:

(Orders shipped in two to three days of receipt.)

	Quantity	Mail Order Price	Total
Secrets Volume 1 *(Retail $12.99)*	_____	$ 9.99	_____
Secrets Volume 2 *(Retail $12.99)*	_____	$ 9.99	_____
Secrets Volume 3 *(Retail $12.99)*	_____	$ 9.99	_____
Secrets Volume 4 *(Retail $12.99)*	_____	$ 9.99	_____
Secrets Volume 5 *(Retail $12.99)*	_____	$ 9.99	_____
Secrets Volume 6 *(Retail $12.99)*	_____	$ 9.99	_____
Secrets Volume 7 *(Retail $12.99)*	_____	$ 9.99	_____
Secrets Volume 8 *(Retail $12.99)*	_____	$ 9.99	_____
Secrets Volume 9 *(Retail $12.99)*	_____	$ 9.99	_____
Secrets Volume 10 *(Retail $12.99)*	_____	$ 9.99	_____
Secrets Volume 11 *(Retail $12.99)*	_____	$ 9.99	_____
Secrets Volume 12 *(Retail $12.99)*	_____	$ 9.99	_____
Secrets Volume 13 *(Retail $12.99)*	_____	$ 9.99	_____
Secrets Volume 14 *(Retail $12.99)*	_____	$ 9.99	_____
Secrets Volume 15 *(Retail $12.99)*	_____	$ 9.99	_____
Secrets Volume 16 *(Retail $12.99)*	_____	$ 9.99	_____
The Forever Kiss (Retail $14.00)	_____	$11.00	_____

Shipping & handling (in the U.S.)

US Priority Mail:
1–2 books .... $ 5.50
3–5 books $11.50
6–9 books $14.50
10–17 books $19.00

UPS insured:
1–4 books $16.00
5–9 books $25.00
10–17 books $29.00

_____

SUBTOTAL _____

Florida 6% sales tax (if delivered in FL) _____

TOTAL AMOUNT ENCLOSED _____

Your personal information is kept private and not shared with anyone.

Name: (please print) _____

Address: (no P.O. Boxes) _____

City/State/Zip: _____

Phone or email: (only regarding order if necessary) _____

Please make check payable to **Red Sage Publishing**. Check must be drawn on a U.S. bank in U.S. dollars. Mail your check and order form to:

Red Sage Publishing, Inc.   Department S16   P.O. Box 4844   Seminole, FL 33775

Or use the order form on our website: **www.redsagepub.com**